NANCY VARIAN BE[...] fantasy novels as wel[...] the DRAGONLANCE w[...] [...]side it. Among Nancy's novels are *Stormblade* and *The Panther's Hoard*. Recent work includes "A Cry in the Night" (with Greg LaBarbera) in Bruce Covill's *Book of Ghosts 2*. Nancy lives with her husband, architect Bruce A. Berberick, in Charlotte, North Carolina.

In his years designing games for TSR, WILLIAM W. CONNORS has written extensively for the RAVENLOFT campaign setting and has recently completed *Domains of Dread*, the RAVENLOFT second edition campaign setting. This fan of old-time radio shows and major league baseball was the primary designer for the DRAGONLANCE: Fifth Age game and has also published short stories in FORGOTTEN REALMS and RAVENLOFT anthologies.

SUE WEINLEIN COOK worked as the editorial assistant in TSR's book department and as a game editor for five years. After moving to Seattle, she became the brand manager for the DRAGONLANCE line and looks forward to many further adventures in the world of Krynn. Sue is married to game designer Monte Cook and collects dragons.

"Restoration" is JEFF CROOK's first published work of fiction, but he has written several AD&D game adventures for *Dungeon* ADVENTURES MAGAZINE. He is working toward a bachelor's degree in English at the University of Memphis.

JEFF GRUBB is an author and game designer. He is the author of *Lord Toede* and numerous gnome stories in the DRAGONLANCE setting, is the co-author with Kate Novak of the *Finder's Stone* trilogy in the FORGOTTEN REALMS setting, and is the author of *The Brothers' War*, in the world of MAGIC: THE GATHERING. He wishes to say that he enjoys spinning tales in Krynn, the Realms, and Dominaria equally well, but's a heckuva commute at rush hour.

RICHARD A. KNAAK's novels, including the New York Times bestseller *The Legend of Huma* and his Dragonrealm series, have sold well over a million copies. His short fiction has appeared in eight other DRAGONLANCE anthologies. Among his most recent novels are *Land of the Minotaurs*, the modern fantasy *Dutchman*, and *The Horse King*. His works have been published in many languages. His web site can be found at http.llwww.sff.netlpeopleknaak.

ROBYN McGREW lives in the desert near Las Vegas. She entered the professional writing field in 1992. Her short works include "Proper Balance" in *Sword and Sorceress* X and "Messenger's Plight" in *New Amazons*.

ROGER E. MOORE, a game designer and editor for Wizards of the Coast, wishes to thank Margaret Weis for her encouragement in his writing career. "After I read *Tower of Midnight Dreams*, which was Margaret's famous Dungeons & Dragons Cartoon Show book about Bobby the Barbarian and Uni the Unicorn, I though, heck, if they'll print this, they'll probably publish anything—even stuff by me!" And he was right. Roger is currently working on new game materials for the GREYHAWK campaign.

DOUGLAS NILES has been involved in the DRAGONLANCE line since its inception, with titles including *Fistandantilus Reborn*, *The Dragons*, *The Kagonesti*, *Emperor of Ansalon*, *The Kinslayer War*, *Flint the King* (with Mary Kirchoff), and the forthcoming *The Last Thane*. Recently he has created the Watershed trilogy, an epic series published by Ace Fantasy. In total, he has authored more than two dozen novels, including *Darkwalker on Moonshae*, the first book in TSR's FORGOTTEN REALMS series. Niles is also known for his many game designs, including numerous role-playing products for Dungeons and Dragons, and award-winning board games based on several of Tom Clancy's best-selling novels.

NICK O'DONOHOE has written many stories in the DRAGONLANCE world. He is also the author of the Crossroads series, including *Magic and the Healing*, *Under the Healing Sign*, and *The Healing of Crossroads*. He warns readers not to become clerics to avoid social unrest or anything else.

JANET PACK has had stories printed in TSR's anthologies *Dragons of Krynn*, *Dragons at War*, and *Dragons of Chaos*. She has also composed music for the DRAGONLANCE sourcebooks *Leaves from the Inn of the Last Home* and *The History of Dragonlance*. Janet's stories are also included in *Testament of the Dragon*, *Fantastic Alice*, *CatFantastic IV*, and *Wizard Fantastic*. Janet lives in Williams Bay, Wisconsin.

"Voices" is black belt and coffee achiever KEVIN T. STEIN'S fourth short story for the DRAGONLANCE setting. Author of *Brothers Majere*, Kevin is currently working on a near-future thriller with Margaret Weis and Don Perrin.

PAUL B. THOMPSON is the author or co-author of eight novels, five short stories, and over three dozen magazine articles. In addition to his seven DRAGONLANCE collaborations with Tonya Carter Cook (most recently, *The Dargonesti* in 1995), he also works as an editor and staff writer for *ParaScope*, an internet news service found at http:llwww.parascope.coml. Married to Elizabeth Wyrick, Paul lives in Chapel Hill, North Carolina.

Laddie, Sasha, Nicolai Mouselayer, Shiva the Destroyer, and Motley Tatters live in a barn in Wisconsin with their two humans, MARGARET WEIS and DON PERRIN. The dogs guard the house, the cats catch the mice, and Weis and Perrin earn their keep by writing the third Mag Force 7 book, *Hung Out*, to be published by ROC, and developing the new Sovereign Stone book and RPG line, based on a world created by noted artist Larry Elmore, published by Del Rey and Archangel Games respectively.

DragonLance® Saga

THE DAWNING OF A NEW AGE
Jean Rabe

THE DAY OF THE TEMPEST
Jean Rabe

THE EVE OF THE MAELSTROM
Jean Rabe

RELICS AND OMENS
TALES OF THE FIFTH AGE
Edited by Margaret Weis and Tracy
Hickman

DragonLance Saga

Relics & Omens

Tales of the Fifth Age

Edited by
Margaret Weis
and Tracy Hickman

RELICS & OMENS
TALES OF THE FIFTH AGE

©1998 TSR, Inc.
All Rights Reserved

Distributed to the book trade in the United States by Random House, Inc., and in Canada by Random House of Canada Ltd.
Distributed to the hobby, toy, and comic trade in the United States and Canada by regional distributors.
Distributed worldwide by Wizards of the Coast, Inc., and regional distributors.

Cover art by Jeff Easley.

First Printing: April, 1998
Printed in the United States of America.
Library of Congress Catalog Card Number: 97-62367

9 8 7 6 5 4 3 2 1

8386XXX1501

ISBN: 0-7869-1169-7

U.S., CANADA,	EUROPEAN HEADQUARTERS
ASIA, PACIFIC, & LATIN AMERICA	Wizards of the Coast, Belgium
Wizards of the Coast, Inc.	P.B. 34
P.O. Box 707	2300 Turnhout
Renton, WA 98057-0707	Belgium
+1-206-624-0933	+32-14-44-30-44

Visit our website at **www.tsr.com**

TABLE OF CONTENTS

Introduction 1

Icefall 3
    Douglas Niles

Legacy 15
    Nancy Varian Berberick

Sword of Tears 49
    Richard Knaak

The Cost 78
    Robyn McGrew

A Most Peculiar Artifact 94
    Janet Pack

Voices 115
    Kevin T. Stein

The Notorious Booke of Starres 137
    Nick O'Donohoe

Scavengers 164
    Jean Rabe

Homecoming 179
    William W. Connors and Sue Weinlein Cook

The Restoration 190
    Jeff Crook

Relics 210
    Jeff Grubb

The Summoners 230
    Paul B. Thompson

Island of Night 259
    Roger E. Moore

Demons of the Mind 312
    Margaret Weis and Don Perrin

INTRODUCTION

The Fifth Age—a time of drastic change for the inhabitants of Krynn. Apparently once more they have been abandoned by the gods. Monstrous dragons have appeared out of nowhere to devour their hapless brethren and lay claim to the land. But it is in the darkness that hope's light burns all the more brightly.

This collection of stories brings back some favorite anthology authors and introduces some new ones. Some favorite characters return as well.

In the lighter vein, Roger Moore tells a gnome story (we warned you!) about a Knight of Takhisis stranded on what he believes to be an uninhabited tropical island, only to find that the island is a lot more inhabited than he could have wished!

Jeff Grubb writes of a peddler peddling tall tales and phony artifacts in a story that proves the old axiom, "Let the buyer beware."

Nick O'Donohoe relates the entertaining misadventures of a stargazer who makes the mistake of attempting to prove to the people of his village that the world of Krynn is round.

Janet Pack is back with another of her delightful kender tales, this time about a kender coerced by an evil wizard into revealing the location of a valuable magical artifact.

Kevin Stein's kender are in hot pursuit of goblins who have stolen a fellow kender's magical cat.

Margaret Weis and Don Perrin tell the story of how Caramon uses his own form of magic to help a maimed veteran of the Chaos War recover his self-respect.

On a more serious note, Doug Niles relates the tale of a centaur, who makes a devastating discovery while tracking an ice bear.

Nancy Berberick tells the haunting tale of a woman who mourns the loss of her magic, only to learn where true magic may be found.

Jean Rabe's sea elves come across a magical artifact that might prove to be their doom.

Sue Cook and Bill Conners tell the tale of the first knight ever to do battle with one of the monstrous dragons.

Jeff Crook's mage, studying the library at Tarsis, makes a terrible discovery in an ancient tome.

Richard Knaak tells the story of a cleric who encounters a magical sword that, in the beginning, seems to act for good.

Robyn McGrew tells how a knight of Solamnia sets out to find food for his starving people. He finds the food and also its guardian—a Knight of Takhisis, who doesn't know the war has ended!

Paul Thompson gives us a tale about the arrival in a village beset by wickedness of a stranger, who is determined to bring about change—at any cost.

We hope you enjoy sojourning in the Fifth Age!

Margaret Weis
Tracy Hickman

Icefall
Douglas Niles

I began my hunt impelled by memories of hungry faces and haunted eyes, four long months had passed since the tribe had eaten anything more than dry roots and hard barley bread. Game had been scarce during the summer, and with an early autumn promising harsh weather to come, the current spell of dry, clear days seemed likely to be my last chance to take some meat before icy winter laid claim to the Plains of Dust.

Revealing my path only to Darr, my mare, I made my preparations quickly and departed from the clan before dawn stirred the Red Wand tribe.

Starting across the plain at full speed, I relished the tears on my cheeks—tears drawn by the wind of a headlong run. My hooves pounded a drumbeat of joy as the miles sped past in a blurry collage of unchanging landscape, tufts of brown grass, and countless identical patches of dusty sand, broken by a few clumps of bushes heavy with autumn berries. Across the dry flatland, I recognized the spoor of small animals, saw the distinctive paintbrush flower of medicinal painroot, smelled the late ripeness of chives and marjoram. I wasn't discouraged by the absence of big game, for it was a given that this close to the tribal encampment the frolicking colts and fillies would long since have driven away any game worthy of my steel-headed arrows.

Though propelled by the clan's dire need for food, I nevertheless relished the freedom of solitude and cherished my release from the fetters of everyday concerns. Once in a while it was good to be alone, to stalk wily game, and simply to run. Now I was prepared to spend as many days as needed to find the spoor of elk, deer, or buffalo.

Before noon on that first morning, I crossed the trail of a small antelope, but I didn't even break stride. My long legs maintained their cadence, a gallop that steadily gobbled the miles. My thoughts gradually focused into a single ambition: I would bring back enough meat to host a splendid feast, a grand festival for all the Red Wand tribe.

I relished the open ground, the vast plains that were home to my clan. To the south, I barely perceived a white line, as much imagined as seen, a place that demarked the meeting of land and sky. That was Icewall Glacier, and from here to there, and as far as I could see to east and west and north as well, there was no clan, no creature, no people who could challenge the mastery held by the centaurs of the Red Wand.

Though this day was cloudless and bright, already I could feel the chill in the steady breeze out of the south. My first drink of the morning, when I kicked through a thin veneer of ice on a water hole, was a clear enough sign. Darr had bidden me all the success the gods might grant, and the sight of her swollen abdomen provided me with additional impetus, for come spring, I would be responsible for feeding another mouth.

After many hours of steady westward travel, I reached the deep, steep-sided ravine that formed one border of our clanhome and was one of very few obstacles across the breadth of the plain. Halting at the lip of the plunging drop, I looked to the right and left, seeking one of the several paths down into the gully. Though no easy descent presented itself, I wasn't particularly concerned. The bottom of the ravine was narrow, but relatively clear of rubble.

I stomped my hooves, tucking my chin to send my

auburn mane cascading around my right shoulder. I held my left arm high, with the powerful longbow already strung with a heavy sinew of braided beargut clenched at the ready. A quiver was slung low across my shoulder, easily accessible below my belly, while a bundle of spare arrows was strapped to the panniers across my withers.

Trotting beside the precipice, I growled almost silently, suddenly impatient. This was one of the few places where a centaur's great size and speed was of no advantage indeed, any human child could scramble down the sloping, rubble-patched incline. Yet if I was to step off the edge, I might tumble all the way to the bottom, no doubt breaking a leg, or worse, in the fall. Instead, I paced along the winding crest, seeking one of the places where I could make a descent with relatively secure footing.

The afternoon was well advanced when I finally spotted a place where a long ridge angled down to the gully floor. The route dropped at a gradual angle and was wide enough even for a centaur's broad hooves. I took one more look across the plains, as flat and featureless as ever, and when I saw the glacier, realized that I had traveled far toward the south. Now the vast shelf of ice seemed thicker, loomed higher against the horizon.

I started down the ridge, feeling the loose dirt and gravel break into a gentle landslide. Half stepping, half plunging downward, I had no trouble maintaining my balance on the natural ramp, finally stiffening my forelegs and skidding on my rump right down to the bottom.

The route at the base of the gully made for easy travel, and I settled into a steady trot, enjoying the sway and curve of the serpentine path. The walls above leaned away to each side, and I kept my eyes on the western face, looking for a route back up to the plains.

That's probably why it took me so long to notice

the tracks. When I finally lowered my eyes, the impressions seemed to leap out at me, bigger than the marks of my own hooves, etched plainly in the flat dust on the lee side of a boulder. Bear tracks, for certain, and they were an unnatural discovery.

The only bears in my experience were the massive and dangerous carnivores dwelling on and around the glacier, to the south of here. Dropping to my knees, I leaned forward and sniffed at the paw print, immediately catching a gamey stench tainted with acidic urine. The spoor was perhaps a day old. I also detected a hint of fish in the bear's scent, and this seemed to confirm that it was an ice bear, for those great predators grew fat off the salmon and seals that thrived along the icy coast of the Southern Courrain Ocean.

Few animals are more powerful or dangerous than a full-grown ice bear. This creature had been padding along to the north, the same direction as I was heading, following the floor of the deep, steep-sided ravine. From the size of the tracks, this huge predator, well removed from its native terrain, was apparently continuing away from the glacier, into the trackless Plains of Dust.

At first it was just curiosity that caused me to follow the trail, and for the rest of the afternoon I loped along at a pretty good speed. The paw prints were faint, but clearly not more than a day old. Even so, I knew the creature was a safe distance in front of me.

Late afternoon shadowed the gully when I drew up short, startled by the sight of the great paw prints gouged into the side of the ravine. The bear had exerted a great deal of effort to scramble upward, emerging from the concealment of the cut to start across to the plains.

Now the creature was on the same side of the ravine as my tribe's encampment.

That realization brought a new sense of urgency, for I could see now that the bear was a deadly threat to the Red Wand centaurs if it remained anywhere on the Plains of Dust. If it could acclimate itself to the somewhat milder temperatures, it might be tempted to stay and prey on the easy creatures of the plain.

The ravine wall was too steep for me to follow the bear's upward progress; once more I would have to find a more negotiable route. Quickly spurring forward, I cantered along the floor of the winding draw, noticing that the cut in the landscape curled west here, veering off its northward bearing. The creature had chosen this spot to climb out, almost as if compelled away from its natural range.

It seemed like a very long time before I finally found a solid shelf of rock that would provide a decent egress. I scrambled upward, bursting onto the plains with an arrow nocked in my bow, as I half expected the ice bear to be waiting for me. I turned my eyes to the right and left, feeling a small measure of disappointment when the mighty carnivore was nowhere in sight.

Returning eastward at a gallop, I backtracked along the rim of the ravine. The ground sped by in a blur. The sun was sinking lower, my shadow spilling across the flat ground before me, when I finally returned to the broken ground where the bear had climbed upward.

I saw the prints, bigger even than a centaur stallion's hooves, heading straight into the plains, and immediately noticed another set of tracks, human sandal prints, that also followed the trail away from the ravine. A plainsman, probably a hunter, had obviously come upon signs of the bear and was thus preceding me by only a short distance. Despite the fact that the bear was a dangerous threat and not the finest sustenance, I felt a flash of proprietary jealousy over another hunter seeking my quarry. We centaurs generally tolerated the humans of the plains, but in this instance, the hunt had become personal. The ice bear intrigued me, and I was determined to be the one to bring it down.

When I care to, I can travel much faster than either humans or bears, and I doubled my speed, scanning the horizon. The wind out of the south was gaining strength, and I felt its icy chill against my back. A haze of white clouds came suddenly into being, eclipsing the afternoon sun. The vaporous barrier quickly grew heavy, darkening to mask the entire sky behind a blanket of glowering gray. Perhaps because I was already disturbed by the strange behavior of my dangerous prey, the weather seemed alarming, like a sentient force of deadly nature.

But I was determined to continue, for I was convinced that the ice bear had become a terrible menace to my own herd. Soon I felt stinging prickles against my skin as sparkling ice crystals swept across the plain in the building gale. Momentarily I wished for a cloak. Like all centaurs, I normally disdained the use of clothing as an unnecessary encumbrance, but this weird early season storm was preternaturally cold. Huffing noisily, I shivered, thinking longingly of Darr. With such thoughts, I was glad I had left our single, shared fur with my mare. She was a splendid female, fast and spirited, and I loved her mightily. It would please me greatly to kill this bear and to bring her another fur as a trophy.

I wondered about the human. Like me, he was still dogging the bear's tracks. No doubt he, too, was bothered by this sudden storm. I stopped for a moment, snorting as I turned and stared to the south. The air there was a haze of murky white, and the ice particles—too tiny, too brittle, to be called snow—whipped against my face. I could soon see little beyond the immediate swirl of the storm. Icewall Glacier was far away now, yet at the same time I had the odd sense that it was closer than possible.

At that very instant, I had the uncanny sensation that I was being observed. It was as though the great storm had eyes, that it stared down from the heights of a bright and colorless sky. A vision of a monstrous head, of limbs vast, fanlike and encompassing, came upon me so suddenly, so powerfully that I felt as though frozen with fear.

With an effort of will, I pulled my eyes away, rearing high, growling, tossing my head. Turning once more to the north, I broke into a run.

It was only a short time later, as daylight faded to pale dusk, that I spotted a cloaked figure huddled against the wind and sleet, plodding northward ahead of me. I recognized the feathered spear of a nearby tribe of plainsmen and hailed my fellow hunter as I drew closer.

"Ah, centaur," he said, shivering. "I see you, too, have found the trail of this unusual beast."

The man was a hook-nosed, swarthy hunter, tall even for his lanky people, though his head barely came to the level of my chest.

"I have followed it all this last day, until now." I was prepared to claim right of first discovery, and my hands remained clenched around my weapon.

From his agreeable nod, I immediately realized that he was about to abandon his pursuit, and his words confirmed this. "Take the beast, then, and good luck to you. For myself, I had half made up my mind to turn back. I feel a strong need to get back to my woman and my lodge. There's wickedness in this storm that cautions me against venturing far abroad on the plains."

"I must make this bear my business ere I return to my own tribe. Such a beast must be slain before it ravages the plains. . . ."

"Bold hunter," the man said, bowing his head. "The storm exacts a toll upon me, I admit. It is some boding of ill."

I snorted, discomfited by his words more than I cared to admit. "It takes more than a gust of wind and a mount of snow to stop me," I vowed.

If he took offense at my boast, the man did not show it. "Then may the gods favor your arrows and your tribe," he said, with another nod of his head.

We parted, soon losing sight of each other in the white gale, and my unease faded as the pursuit became more intense and immediate. Regardless of the human's words of caution, I knew that I had come too far to quit.

I slowed to a walk, reduced to squinting at the ground merely to spot the occasional track in the enclosing dusk. The bear's prints were well spaced, showing that it still moved at a good clip. Finally I halted as daylight fled and left me helpless to proceed. Fortunately the icy precipitation had temporarily abated, and though the wind remained cold, I knew the ice bear would also rest. I would surely catch up with him by midday.

I forced myself to sleep watchfully on my feet, my human torso reclining easily across my equine back. The posture allowed me to doze lightly while remaining alert to any possible disturbance. Several times during the night I started awake, but it was simply nerves—groundhogs in one instance, and the wail of the wind another time. Nothing worthy of alarm, and so I nodded off, anxiously awaiting the first signs of dawn.

Moving again at half-light, I pondered the actions of this bear. The mighty carnivores stayed almost exclusively around the fringes of the vast glacier, a hundred miles or more to the south of this bleak tundra. There seals and salmon thrived along the chill, glacial coast of the ocean, and the temperature rarely surpassed the freezing point. Furthermore, the frost-limned Icewall Glacier and its attendant snowfields provided the white-furred predators with a concealment nearly as effective as a spell of invisibility. Though occasionally an ice bear ventured onto the southern plains, never had I known of one to wander this far from its native range.

Now, as the morning progressed, I perceived that the bear held its course like a compass bearing, straight north across the flat and featureless plains. The day was bright, but the sun's rays seemed pale and feeble against the increasingly chilly air. By now the animal had even moved beyond the area where it might prove a threat to the Red Wand tribe, but still I had no thought of quitting the chase.

Armed with my bow, I could take the brute, and I found myself coveting the huge hide, the fur that would be lush and thick and warm during the coming winter. And the meat would be sufficient for a great communal feast. A wealth of grease, prized by centaur smiths and tanners, would be valuable to all.

Truly this ice bear would be a prize.

Its tracks were still visible in a line of crushed grass across the dry tufts of tundra. Yet by mid-morning, sleet and snow once again appeared, and I realized that within a few hours, the icy stuff could bury the creature's tracks.

Picking up my pace, I loped along the trail, propelled by a growing sense of urgency. I adjusted my quiver across my belly, ensuring that I could reach and draw an arrow in a split second. My eyes peered this way and that, trying to penetrate the thickening veil of the snowstorm.

Again I felt the menace in the chaotic snowfall. There was a peculiarity to this storm that boded ill. Did the ice bear, too, sense the power of the storm? Was it fleeing not only me but also the peril of ice and frost?

The wintery onslaught raged, with crying wind and sharp, stinging snow. Before long the plains were dotted by shallow drifts. The tracks of the bear frequently vanished under the white blanket, but I managed to find my way and push forward. Some snowdrifts reached almost to my knees, but my powerful legs kicked easily through these barriers.

By now my mane and beard were coated with frost. My breath came in clouds of steam, and my bare skin was already pale with frostbite. I tried to flex my sturdy fingers and found with dismay that they were almost numb.

All the while the wind howled relentlessly, lashing my mane. Now it occurred to me that I had been twisted around to end up downwind of my quarry. The bear might possibly catch my scent.

I squinted, trying to see through the white fury of the storm. Plowing onward miserably, I felt increasingly bewildered by this sinister weather. Somewhere out there lurked the ice bear, but I had no way of knowing whether the animal was continuing its purposeful flight or even now was circling back to corner its dogged pursuer.

Then a white mass erupted from my left side, visible only as a flash of movement at the periphery of my vision. I whirled, and the ice bear made a terrible cracking noise. Massive jaws gaped to reveal a pink tongue between black lips and long, yellowed teeth, while horrible claws stretched toward me, eager to rend centaur flesh.

My bow was already drawn, but I shot clumsily, then drew back a second missile. The first managed to graze the bear's chest, while the next shaft plunged through white pelt, heavy sinew, and gristly flesh, burying itself to the feathers in the animal's throat.

Undaunted, the bear pounced again. Casting my bow aside, I reared and drove twin hooves, shaggy fetlocks trailing like battle pennants, into the animal's bloodied chest. The bear's claws raked my forelegs, and I was driven backward from the force of the blows. Trying to ignore the shocking pain, I drew my last weapons: twin daggers, blades long enough to be called short swords in the grip of a human.

Arms extended, I thrust myself forward, my powerful rear hooves churning as they sought purchase on the ice-slicked ground. Clods of dirt flew, and then I found footing. Although staggered by its wounds, the bear nonetheless met me with all the strength of a hurtling charge.

Stabbing one keen blade into each side of the ice bear's neck, I gasped as long fangs ripped through the tough sinew of my chest. Crying out in pain, I heard my ribs crack, felt hot fire burning in my chest. My mind reeled and merciful oblivion beckoned, tempting, but my powerful hands held their grip and the steel blades drove deep into my enemy's shoulders.

Desperately I reared back and plunged the keen-edged weapons again, until finally the creature slumped, and I knew that one of the knives had found the throbbing jugular.

With a groan, I stumbled backward, allowing the suddenly limp bear to fall onto the frozen ground. I gingerly probed the bite wound in my left shoulder, drawing tears with the sudden, jolting pain. I was badly weakened, lurching sideways unsteadily, unbalanced to the point of dizziness. I raised my head and tried to look south, into the storm, seeing nothing but whiteness.

It was at that moment that I sensed a great shadow passing overhead, enfolding the plains and the world in a monstrous blizzard. Almost instantaneously the great form was gone, though the cold was worse, and now the storm was everywhere, surrounding me.

I thought fleetingly of skinning my prize but realized how fruitless that would be.

Clearly the bear had understood better than I. It was fleeing the source—no, the *master*—of this storm. In my headlong pursuit, I had joined him as its victim.

Why hadn't I recognized the truth sooner? I might have spared the bear, who was only trying to escape and survive. I might have spared myself from the white serpentine monster that controlled the snow and ice and wind. Now the storm was conquering the plains, and the centaur herd, if it was not already doomed would have to move fast, to migrate northward in a desperate quest for renewal.

I took one faltering step into the maw of the storm, only to feel the pain in my chest as my broken rib twisted inside of me, slicing into lung and muscle. With a groan, I sank to my knees, shaking my shaggy head, grimly determined to rise once more to my feet.

My strength failed at last in the cold, the ice, the terrible storm. I thought of Darr as I slumped to the ground, resting my tortured brow against the still-warm flank of my vanquished foe.

Legacy

Nancy Varian Berberick

I woke in the small hour before dawn, my head aching as though I'd drunk too much wine, my eyes dry and burning, just as if I'd wept out all my tears. Neither was the case, but still I felt that way. I'd been in the dream again, the magic-haunted dream in which all I longed for beckoned me with whispered words I couldn't understand, with bright clear lights I could see but not touch.

My head throbbed, I dared not open my eyes for fear that even the faintest light of stars would increase the pain. Memory of a sound lingered as I lay quiet in my bed, trying to reckon what had wakened me. Breath still, I waited, and so I heard it again: a quiet tap at the window near my bed.

It was too early for light, so I couldn't see who stood there, but I knew him by his shape, broad in the shoulders, not so tall as I, the fall of his beard thick on his chest. Here was the hill dwarf, Slean Brae, standing among the skeletal remains of summer's herb garden beneath my window, tapping again at the glass to wake me. Outside, stars hung in the sky, faintly gleaming. It was early even for Slean to be abroad, and he was ever the first of us to be up and about. His was the forge fire to rouse, and he loved the early, peaceful hours. Slean's life wasn't so quiet as it had been before I came to live in the little stone house at the edge of his woodlot. He took his peace where he could find it.

Slean tapped again, and I got slowly out of bed. My limbs felt like lead, and I could hardly pick up my feet, so weary was I from the dreaming night. My head still pounded as I wrapped up in the thick woolen blanket from the bed. Shivering in the unlighted hour, I went through to the front room, my workroom, where everything smelled of the herbs I had my hands into every day. Even my Brown Book, filled up with notes and recipes for my potions and teas and salves, smelled that way, as though the very spirit of herbs I wrote about came to live on the pages.

I opened the door to Slean and turned quickly away from the cold rushing in behind him. The hearth fire still slept, banked and the embers breathing only a little. I kindled a twist of rushes at those embers and lighted the oil lamp on my worktable, and in the yellow glow I saw Slean glance at me, close and keen. I needed no mirror to show me my face as he saw it. I found that in his eyes.

Ah, the girl, he was thinking, all white and drawn as if ghosts have been at her. . . .

That well he knew me, to know what I'd been dreaming. That well I knew him, to know what he was thinking. The knowing, his and mine, rubbed raw this morning.

"What?" I said, sharp-edged and wanting to hurry past that look so filled up with old questions.

"It's been calling you again, hasn't it, Leial?"

Calling me again, a magic most people didn't even believe in. I nodded, and had no more than that to give. Still, hope kindled in Slean's eyes, warmed by his faith in me. It was always hope and faith with him. That never changed.

"And?" he said gently.

My head throbbed, pain made my eyes tear up. It shamed me to give him the answer I always gave. "And I couldn't answer."

It shamed me, yes, it did. How else but ashamed

should I feel as one who is shown what she needs
and cannot manage to take it?

Slean saw that, and he let the matter go as he had so
many times before. "They need you at the cooper's,"
he said. "Will you come?"

He never doubted my answer, still he asked
respectfully, as people in Cour always do. They
cherished their young herb woman and accorded
me the same respect they once gave to a real healer,
one of the old kind who used to heal with magic got
for a prayer.

There was none of that anymore, though, magic
got for a prayer. There wasn't even anyone to pray to
for whatever it was you wanted, needed, craved.
Gods had walked away from Krynn, and those old
days were gone, as Slean, who'd once lived them and
now lived on the other side of them, well knew. As I,
who was born too late for them, well knew.

Shivering still, squeezing my eyes shut against the
headache's hammer, I said, "Slean, what's wrong at
the Cooper's? The little girl?" I'd treated Yahn
Cooper's youngest daughter for fever a few days
ago. I hoped he hadn't come looking for me because
she'd worsened.

"Not the little one, not this time. Yahn said his
oldest boy hurt his hand last night stacking wood.
They thought it was all right then, but now they
think it might be broken." He jerked a thumb at my
worktable and asked whether he should pack up
my simples.

I told him he should, and I went to get dressed.
From my bedroom, I called to ask whether he could
tell me more about the Cooper's boy and his possibly
broken hand. He said there wasn't much to tell, only
that the fingers were all swollen and purple, and the
boy couldn't move them. Broken hand, all right, I
thought, pulling on my boots. Out in my workroom
again, I caught the thick cloak Slean tossed to me,
happy to heed his warning that frost had come down

in the night. Snug and warming, I snatched up the pouch Slean had prepared and didn't bother to check to see what he'd put in it. He was good at packing this bag of mine. Six years with me as his near neighbor had trained him to that.

"Go, and don't waste time looking back, " he said, urging me out the door. "I'll be here when you return and you can tell me how it all turns out."

"Go, and don't waste time looking back." It's just an expression, a thing you say to people when you want them to hurry, like "don't spare the horses." I did look back, though, when I reached the bend in the road to the village. I saw that Slean had stirred the banked fire in my front room. The light of it was like a candle in the window of a house where people live who hope you'll come home soon.

* * * * *

Cour sits snug in a long valley, protected from hard weather by high hills, watered by the Wing Swift, the little river not nearly so grand as its name. The widest part of the river lay a half mile outside the village proper, and there Slean had his stone house and his forge, for as much water went into forging as did steel and fire. There I lived, too, in the little house up the hill from his, at the edge of his woodlot. I paid him no rent, but he said I did, in kind, providing salves for the "forge bites," as he called the cuts and burns that plague a smith always. I could have paid in steel coin. I made a decent enough living as Cour's herb woman, but he wouldn't have it.

"I make enough coin myself in these new days," he'd say to any offer of mine. "The clumsiest armorer in the land could find himself rich." Then he'd smile and wink, not something many people ever saw. "Me, I'm not so clumsy, so don't you worry about how I like to have my rent paid to me."

He wasn't clumsy at all, not Slean Brae. The elves

across the border in Qualinesti respected him as a craftsman for the tough, functional armor he sold them. The lords among those folk commissioned him covertly now and then for a suit of gold-gleaming ceremonial armor; they called him an artist. These compliments Slean treasured, but quietly. Close and gruff as any hill dwarf you'll meet, Slean he was a shy man, though most did not know it. He'd grown up in the foothills of the Kharolis Mountains and fled from there in the years after the gods walked out of Krynn to leave so much of our world in the thrall of cruel dragons. There are free lands, though, and Cour lies in one of them. Slean had lived thirty years in Cour, where people see what they expect to see. In Slean, they saw a brusque and quiet hill dwarf, and I don't think anyone understood about his shyness but me. I knew it the first hour I'd met him, on a hard winter's day six years before, when my mule pulled up lame on the road outside his forge. I was a gangly girl in those days, an itinerant herb woman on the road to Solace and stranded in Cour, held by a lame mule and winter falling. "We need a healer here," he'd said, his eyes catching only small glimpses of me, then looking shyly away. I'd warned him I was no healer, only an herb woman, but he'd only smiled and said Cour needed me.

It was only later that I told him what had driven me out of my home village and onto the road. He didn't care about that. "You are what you are," he'd said. "And you did the best you could do. From all this you will learn."

That was Slean, talking like an old man, and not so old at all as long-lived dwarves reckon things.

I warmed, walking, and soon the sound of the river lapping, the wind rippling, made me feel better than I had on waking. A pair of late geese flew over the water, headed south together, wing and wing. The geese, the river, the wind, these are things I like about Cour. Another thing I like is the people. It isn't easy living in the aftermath of gods, but the people in Cour manage. Oh, some will tell you they miss the feeling that gods are abroad in the world. Others long for the way the sky used to look in the days before the gods left Krynn, the patterns of the stars, constellations people had named Gilean's Book or Paladine's Platinum Dragon or Hiddukel's Scales. Slean was one of those. He missed the old constellations the way I missed the vanished magic.

You might wonder how it is that I missed a thing I'd never known, a magic that leaked out of the world before I was born. I might answer thus: It's not true that I never knew the magic, though I was born a full eleven years after it went away. I know about the magic. In dreams, I heard it whispering to me, saw it like pure light dancing before me, calling me. Trouble is, I was never able to answer.

"But you will," Slean said one cold afternoon when I'd come down the hill to get warm in his forge. "Only you must keep trying."

I asked how he knew so much about this magic, and I asked with a bitter edge in my voice.

He didn't care about my mood, and he smiled a little to show it. "Because it wouldn't be calling to you otherwise."

That advice from a hill dwarf, a tribe of dwarfs no different than any other of their kindred in their dislike and distrust of magic.

Slean shrugged when I said that, and he told that in the before-times people used to speak of the art of magic. "And I reckon that one art is the same as another, the creation calling to the artist, trying to find a way into the world." He said this magic calling me was different than the old kind, granted to all those who yearned and studied and prayed for it. "I listen to what people say, that magic can be found anywhere, everywhere. Its power and strength is in the life-force of all things, they say, and it's in the earth itself, in the sky."

We were quiet then, me watching his fire and him working with a file to smooth a rough spot on the ornate helm he was crafting. Soon, though, he spoke again, and he said, "I believe this is true, Leial, because I was there when the world changed. I heard some of the things that people were saying: The gods didn't leave Krynn bereft. There's another kind of magic to be had. You have to trust that it's there for you."

It might be, but for all that magic called to me, I hadn't been able to answer it. All I had were dreams that haunted and taunted and turned always to nightmares of failure and shame. Hard to trust that.

* * * * *

Yahn Cooper and his wife Willa had a big house on the high street where the wealthy craftsmen live, with enough room there for all their three girls and two boys. The rich smell of breakfast cooking, eggs and ham and bread, drifted out from the house when Willa opened the door. My stomach growled over its own emptiness, and it must have been audible. Willa's greeting was to promise me a meal in good time.

"Only, please, come and look at my boy Kern now. He's hurting."

So he was, and I saw it as soon as I entered the bedroom where the boys slept. Only Kern was there now, his brother having been set about the morning chores. Across the hall, the girls slept, one of them the fevered child I'd earlier treated. I'd see her, too, before my morning was done.

I found Kern with his father, the two sitting on the edge of his cot. Yahn had his arm around the boy's shoulders. Kern cradled his left hand in his right, trying for courage and finding what he needed.

"Woodpile toppled on him," his father said. "Half the lot, and we thought sure the boy was smashed and broken. When we pulled him out, though, all the hurt we found was the hand, and that didn't look so bad last night."

Willa made a sound to let me know she hadn't shared that opinion last night.

"It's all right," I said. "I'm here now, and Kern will be fine."

They eased then, their sighs coming almost in union. Willa began to bustle and talk about breakfast and how it would be burning if she didn't get back to it, and would I stay when I was finished with Kern, and she said more after that, though it was said in the front room, from which came the sound of dishes clattering.

"Now," I said to Kern, his father still hovering, "we have some work to do, you and I."

He nodded but said nothing as I sat to examine his hand. The skin showed blackish purple, swelling from the pressure of fluid building within. Wide-eyed in his pain, Kern breathed hard through his mouth.

Slean said of me that I have a healer's heart. I do, too. My heart aches to see anyone in pain and longs to help the weak and the wounded. I'd been that way always, born to the work, and so you see why I longed for the magic. I wondered always what I would have asked of magic, if magic I had? There at Kern's bedside, I'd have asked for a gentler hand, I who was known around Cour as having the gentlest of hands. I would have asked that my work with those poor broken bones in Kern's hand would cause no pain. I had no magic, though, and so the setting of Kern's broken bones wouldn't be painless.

Kern knew that, as I did, but, eyes yet wide, he nodded to me and he said, "Do what you can, please. I'll manage."

I'd always liked that boy, and now liking turned to admiration. Finger by finger, his three broken bones had to be set, and that hurt, I knew it. I'd broken a few in my time, one way or another. He withstood that manfully, and even the harder pain of binding the whole hand. The binding I made so thick and tight I used almost all the bandages Slean had packed.

"Now I'll tell you," I said, "you've done so well I'm going to leave the instructions to care for this hurt with you, because I know I can trust you to do what's needed. The important thing—the only important thing—is this: You mustn't take this binding off unless I say so. It's holding all those little broken bones in your hand still, and that will help them knit and heal. It's going to hurt." I reached into my bag and put a small cloth sack of powder into his good hand. "This is white willow bark, and it helps with pain. I'll give your mother something more to help you sleep. Take the willow bark—only two pinches—when the pain is bad. All right?"

He nodded and managed a smile.

I saw him settle back on his cot and thanked him for his patience. "Now," I said, looking up at Yahn, "how's your little girl? Has the fever cooled?"

"It cools and it heats up again."

"Fever at night, but she's better in the day?"

He nodded, and I told him that sounded about right. "It's what happens when the healing is starting. Let me have a look at her, as long as I'm here."

Yahn and Willa had named their youngest girl Azure, for her eyes were the clear blue of mountain lakes. Those pretty blue eyes shone up at me now, and Azure's sweet smile as she struggled to sit up and greet me.

One rush light glowed on the little table near the child's cot, and I remembered that this little one had a fear of darkness. By the rush's glow, I saw her bundled up in blankets so that only her little face showed, white and thin. It was but a matter of moments to examine the child. A wriggler when she was well, she seemed happier now to cooperate. I found little to fret me and told her parents so.

"I think she'll do fine. Keep her warm—" I tugged at the blankets and smiled at the child—"and be sure she drinks plenty of water. That's the most important thing to keep the fever cooling. I'll come by again in the morning, and I'd be surprised if she isn't very much better."

The little girl smiled, her father nodded and tucked her in more closely, and from the kitchen, Willa called to say she had breakfast for me if I'd care to have some.

I did care to, having missed my own, and we sat for a comfortable time in Willa's big front room while I ate, trading gossip, talking about the good yield the farmers had gotten this year, and all the other things near neighbors discuss. It wasn't until I made ready to leave that Willa sighed and said that she so longed for the old days, "The days my mother used to know, when the healer could come and pray and find the magic and the strength to touch away the pain of a child."

"Was it that easy?" I asked, but only to be polite. My head began to throb with the old pain of dreams in which it was never easy to touch magic, in which ever I failed to do so. Just dreams, you'd say, just that. But those dreams, sometimes nightmares, were more. I knew it, even if Slean had never said it—those dreams were magic calling to me. I had never been able to answer.

Willa, wistful and unaware, assured me it was as easy as that to find magic. "In the old days," she sighed.

When magic could be had for a prayer.

I closed my eyes and found in the darkness small dancing lights to remind me of those in my dreams. Not long after that, I took my leave and went away back up the river road, feeling the old shame. Why, when the magic called to me, could I not answer?

* * * * *

Slean looked like a demon, backlit against the fire of his forge, dark hair and beard edged with red light. Sweat gleamed like fire running all down his arms. Though I seldom failed to scold him for standing sweating in the cold air blowing in through the wide doors, I said nothing this morning. He asked after Kern, and after the little girl, and when he'd heard my short answers, he looked at me long, gauging the depth of my mood. That reckoned, and likely reckoned rightly, he let me be with my silence. Neither did he so much as glance at me as I took a seat on the old three-legged stool he kept in the forge room just for me. He left me to my mood.

Maybe you think it's strange that I took my headache to a ringing forge, but here is something stranger to consider: The pain began to ease moments after I sat down near the hot, high fire. That headache didn't have to do with noise, and the easing of it had all to do with being in company with Slean. Things he knew about me no one else ever did—my fears, my hopes, the sad and sorry truth of failures past and present. These things he accepted, and that acceptance of his was a balm for the wounds.

I sat a long while beside the fire, watching Slean work, hammer and patience and sweat, over the shaping of a broad breastplate of handsome blue steel. He took great pride in making the kind of armor that showed not the least mark of the hammer's hard kiss, and you saw it in his face how well he loved what he created.

The song of hammer iron didn't stay with me long. It slipped away into the background of my thoughts as I gazed into the leaping fire. The warmth bathed me, wrapping me round. Little by little I eased, and the tightness of muscles gave way to comfortable drowsiness. I remembered how hard it had been to wake this morning, regretted the empty dream that had stolen my night's sleep and replaced it with waking guilt. Eyes still on the fire, I didn't see Slean put a stone cup of water nearby for me. I heard him, though, soft breathing and heavy step, and I smelled the sweat on him and the tang of the steel he worked with.

Thirsty before the fire, I meant to reach for the cup of water, but I didn't. I almost moved my hand, then held. My gaze dropped from the flames to their ember bed, the red light there rolling as the embers breathed. My field of sight began to narrow, shrinking in on itself, leaving only darkness at the wide edges. I breathed deeply once, aware of the heat flowing into my lungs. I don't remember the outgoing breath.

Light came to the dark borders of my vision. I shivered, but not from cold. I shivered because something touched me, running along my skin and lifting up the fine hair on my arms, just as when you smell a storm's first lightning. Pure and clear, rippling as though it were laughing, light danced at the edge of my sight. The dream whispered words I must somehow answer.

I cried out with my very heart, with no words and all my feeling, but the whispering grew ever more faint. I reached out for the dancing lights; my fingers tingled when they came close to that clear shining.

Someone shouted, the sound coming from far away. Torn, I wanted to turn to see who'd made that terrified sound, and I wanted to touch the light. I reached, I reached, and the cry sounded again. Turning, I looked up to see Slean grab me by the arms, his eyes dark and frightened, his face white above his black beard. Fear surged through me. I thought, he's hurt, even as I realized it was the look on him made me think so, no mark of cut or burn.

And then I was on my feet, felt the rough wood of the forge's wide shed door against my back, found myself standing outside, breathing deeply of the cool autumn air. I'd have fallen right down if Slean hadn't been there to hold me steady.

"What—what happened?" I asked, my voice shaking, tears rolling down my cheeks. Why did I weep? I looked down at my left hand, and saw the skin of my fingers reddening, white blisters swelling on the tips. To see that was to feel it, and the pain of fire burn roared through my hand all at once.

Still white in the face, he said I'd been trying to grasp the fire in his forge. "And you got too close before I knew what you were about. Now, stay here. I'll be back with something for your hand."

He went back into the forge, but he needn't have worried about me. I stayed, couldn't have gone anywhere if I'd wanted to. All the strength seemed gone from me, and some of the will. I was there, leaning against the door. when he came back. With my own salve, he tended my burnt fingers, and then he wrapped them in clean cloth. Last, Slean wiped my tears with a sooty finger, smiling sheepishly to apologize for the smudges I'd have to wash away.

"Listen," he said, excitement running in his voice. "The magic came calling, Leial. I saw it on you, in your face, in your eyes, right before you went reaching for the fire. The magic came calling after you, here in the waking world."

"And I couldn't answer," I said bitterly. "I lost it again."

"Yes," he said. "You did. But, girl, this magic isn't going to lose you. It knows what all arts know."

The creation calls to the artist, trying to find a way into the world.

I looked down at my bandaged fingers, the pain there throbbing through my whole hand now. In memory, I felt all I'd felt in the fire trance—the approach of magic, the reaching for it, and the lorn sound of my own voice crying as the magic left me.

The creation, the magic, calls to the artist, trying to find a way into the world.

A way into me. "But, Slean, what way can I find to let the magic know how I would welcome it if even the cry of my heart is the wrong answer?"

"Trust," Slean said. "Just that: trust."

"Trust what?"

"Yourself. You'll find the answer, and you'll know it as soon as you do."

Where did all his faith in me come from? I asked him, and he just smiled. "I know you. That's enough. Now, go on up the hill and have yourself a good sleep."

Like a balm, his faith in me, his acceptance of me. Sometimes I thought he was the greater healer. I took his advice, and I slept the day around, into the night and out the other side. No dream came to me of longing and magic and light. It was the best sleep I'd had in a long time.

At the end of the next day, Willa, sent one of her children to tell me Azure's fever was worsening.

* * * * *

I knelt by Azure's bedside, and the first thing I noticed was her eyes. They were not so blue now; rather, they were the muddy color of illness and pain. The child's cheek burned to the touch, and it was almost translucent, showing veins in thin lines just under the skin. I leaned closer and saw that a rash spattered her chin with red flecks, like paint flung from a brush.

Not so bad, I thought, likely caused by the woolen blanket rubbing it or by the skin drying out during fever.

I folded back the neck of the girl's nightshirt, and quickly I pulled back. I didn't mean to. I never did that, no matter what sign of sickness or terrible injury I saw. This time, though, I couldn't help it. My comfortable reassurance of only a moment ago drained to dregs, tasting like sudden bile in my mouth. The rash had begun a relentless march down the child's neck. It seemed to me that I could see it advance even as I stood there. A pricking chill crept along my arms. I'd seen a rash like this before, and I knew what it heralded. I had to swallow, to loosen my fear-dried throat, and then again before I could speak.

Willa knew at once, only to see me, that something was wrong. She drew breath for the questions, the fretting, the fear. I stilled her.

"Willa, how long has she had this rash?"

"Since last I checked on her, right around noon." She looked at me anxiously, her plump and pretty face full of his fear. "Did I do wrong not sending for you right then?"

Outside the house, her other children called to each other at their chores. The song of their voices fell flat in here, all the life leeched out once the sound crossed the threshold. I wanted to look away from Willa, but I didn't. She deserved the truth, yet how could I tell her it didn't matter that she'd not called me sooner? How could I say that if she'd called me at sight of the first little red mark she'd still have called too late?

I knew this rash. It was the first and last stage of a fatal and unnamed illness. Azure's fever was never going to cool. It would burn the child alive from within, and the rash would cover her till all her little body seemed like one big welt. I knew this disease, I knew it. I'd failed to cure it too many times not to recognize the old enemy now.

"Willa," I said, trying for gentleness and hearing my failure in the flatness of my voice. "Willa, this is no simple fever and rash. I don't know a name for the sickness, but I do know this: Don't let your other children come in here. The sickness moves."

She paled, white as her daughter now. "What— what are you saying? Will all the children come down with it?"

The question chilled me, all at once, as though the blood in me was freezing. In my ears, I heard a sound like thunder far off in the sky, the drumbeat of terror.

"I don't know," I said. "But it's best to be careful. Keep Azure to herself, and let me know if things worsen."

I spoke with a lying confidence. What else could I do? I could tell no truth that wouldn't panic her, or anyone she spoke with about it.

Eight years ago half a village had died of this red sickness, and that had been my home village. A cruel killer, the disease had not taken me among all those it had claimed, but it did take my father, and soon after my mother. I was young then, just eighteen, and not so skilled at herb work as I'd later become. After long weeks of trying, after too many deaths, I'd found an herbal concoction that helped only a few, and then only if the sickness was caught early. For the most part, people died. I could not daunt this killer. It had simply shown me to my failures and then sent me into exile. After that deadly failure came all the unanswered dreams of magic calling, and I never told anyone the story of the deaths or the dreams until I told it to Slean six years ago, when I decided to end my traveling and stay in Cour.

Azure sobbed in her fever. Her pale, thin limbs twitched as though in nightmare. It ached me to see that, and I felt as though my heart were breaking with the truth of her fate. She would die.

All the room smelled of sickness, sour and hopeless. For something to occupy my hands and hide the sudden shaking, I rubbed a few leaves of dried sage over the rush light to cleanse the air, then took out some salve from my leather sack, telling Yahn Cooper it would soothe his daughter's rash. It was all I could do, but when Yahn took my hand in his and begged to know if there were other things to try I promised him I would go and study on it.

I don't know what hurt more, his eager thanks or my certain understanding that I had no text to study, and only my experience of failure to show me how things would end for Azure, the little girl with the lake-blue eyes.

What would I have asked of magic, if magic I had? I'd have asked for an army of spells to ward off this enemy, this red sickness. There and then I closed my eyes, not looking for magic, only to close out the sight of the suffering child. I saw the light eager and dancing. My heart leapt, racing as I listened for the whispering, for the call I must answer, and soft it came, words I couldn't understand, asking me something, or telling me something.

Trust, Slean had said, I must trust myself to know how to answer that wisp's voice.

I stood listening for the answer to a question I couldn't hear, stood so for long barren moments, until at last Willa touched my arm. I came to myself at once, empty of what I so needed. Empty of magic's answer.

I was gone from Yahn Cooper's house only just before my bitter tears fell. If there were hope for the little girl, it would not lay in any magic I might find, for I could find none at all.

* * * * *

Stars came out one by one in the dark sky over the Wing Swift River. I stood on the high hill, the one opposite the village, watching the little glittering lights. Looking for what? I don't know now, I didn't know then. Time, maybe, looking for time I didn't have. Looking for a quiet place to think of solutions that did not exist. The red sickness had come to Cour. My old enemy had found me.

Maybe you think I stood there mourning the magic I couldn't ever seem to reach, the magic that couldn't ever seem to reach me. Well, I didn't. All that I'd left behind me, like baggage on the roadside, as I walked from the Cooper's house out to my little house at the edge of Slean's woodlot. I didn't imagine I was done with it, the guilt of all my failures. I knew it would come back to me, and soon, like and hungry wolf snapping at my heels. For now, though, for now there was no time. My old enemy had found me, and it camped in a big house down on the high street, contemplating murder.

Wind blew cool, autumn wind smelling of winter. Down in the valley, lights shone in the windows of houses, like golden reflections of the stars. Behind me, a footfall on the rocky ground. Slean came walking. I didn't turn to see him, or speak to greet him, and he said nothing to me. In his hand, he had a jug, and he sat with his back to the village, uncorking the jug as he made himself comfortable. When at last I looked down at him, he held it up to offer me a drink.

I tasted it and smiled in spite of myself. I'd been expecting the bite of spirits or the tang of wine. What I'd got was a hot tea of herbs sweetened with honey. I nodded to thank him, and he to acknowledge the thanks.

"I heard it from a boy in the village," he said, "that Yahn Cooper's little girl isn't coming out of her sickness."

I nodded. My mouth dried up again just at the thought of Azure and the red sickness, that old enemy of mine lurking near to claim her.

"Leial, can you help her?"

I told him I had nothing but an old, not-so-reliable remedy to try. "And some more skill than I had when I first used it."

He cocked his head in silent question. The answer I gave was a plain one, short and not embroidered with anything to make the picture of plague and death less ugly than it is. He didn't need much more than that, for he knew all the story of what had sent me out of my home village and onto the road of the itinerant herb woman, selling skill and potions to make her way.

We were a long time quiet, and then he said, "I have always felt like a man out of his time."

Something about those words chilled me, deep inside where the wind and cold doesn't reach. I turned away from Cour then, and I went and sat beside him. Shivering, I tucked my hands into my cloak. "What do you mean, 'a man out of his time'?"

Slean kept his eyes on the stars, that field of silver in the sky.

"Look," he said, pointing to a cluster of bright lights right overhead. "What do you see?"

I looked and told him I saw stars.

The answer didn't satisfy him. "Look again."

I huddled deeper into my cloak and turned my face up to the sky. Still I saw only stars. "What am I looking for?"

"More than what you see." He touched my shoulder and pointed east to a cluster of stars much brighter than the others. "What does that look like?"

"Stars, Slean. It looks like stars."

He laughed then, a big booming sound that seemed to bound off the rocks behind us. For all that, though, I didn't mistake it for a happy sound. "Once there was a constellation there that bore the name of a goddess. Mishakal, her name was, and she was the goddess of healing. It was a pretty thing, made of five stars and we used to imagine that if you connected them—" he drew a shape in the air, like a figure eight—"you'd see the symbol of eternity."

I knew it. Healers in the time before the world changed used to have the sigil on their spellbooks. Even today you'll find those of us skilled in herb lore with that star sign on our lore books.

Slean pointed to another quarter of the sky. "And there was a silver dragon to signify Paladine. Right opposite was another dragon, and that was the Queen of Darkness. You knew all their stories when you looked at those shapes, and you could reckon by them, Leial. You could reckon time by their rising and setting. You could reckon the seasons by their position in the sky. In the Kharolis Mountains, in summer, Paladine's dragon hung right over the valley where I used to live. In winter, you'd find it perched on top of the mountains to the west. If you knew your sky seasons, you could even reckon your way home if you were lost."

I glanced at him then, closely in the starlight, and with unexpected suddenness, my throat closed up and tears pricked behind my eyes.

"The sky tells me nothing anymore," he said. "No one knows the names of these stars. I don't think anyone has pictured out the patterns they make now and named them. As long as I might live, I don't think I'll ever know if they do."

I covered his hand with mine, and it was so cold I was moved to chafe it between my own two. He smiled at that gesture from what he'd always called my healer's heart.

"Listen to me, Leial, this is true: I am a man out of his time. Born before this age, and not sure at all why I got to live through the times of change. But you—" he moved his hand, and now it was he holding my hand in his"—you, Leial, are a woman of your time. You were born after the gods walked away from Krynn. You are meant to be here, now, in this time and this place. Ah, don't waste that, girl. Don't give up on the magic you are meant to bring into this place, right now, in this time."

Me, all I could do was shake my head. "I have no time now, Slean, to learn what I've never been able to learn before. If there are gods yet to hear, they know how much I want that magic I always hear and can't manage to answer. However it is, though, things have changed. I've told you what the red sickness is like, and you can imagine what it will do here in Cour. But, Slean, I don't have to imagine. I know what it will do, and I know how fast it will do it. I have to spend all the little time I have working with the remedy I know once helped, sometimes, if it was given soon enough."

He said nothing, and I slipped my hand from his. In the absence of his voice, I went away down the hill. There was yet time to work tonight, and I would waste none of it trying to find what I could not have.

* * * * *

I worked through the night with an ear always cocked, listening for footfalls on the path, for word that matters had worsened at the Cooper's house. By morning no one had come, and the only sounds I heard were the usual sounds of the waking day, the wind in the trees, geese over the river, and the ring and clamor of Slean's anvil. That forge song was all I heard of him. Still, all the way up the hill from the river and his forge, I felt him near. I knew he was thinking about me.

I spent the morning with my Brown Book, searching for the entry that would tell me the herbs I had used eight years before. My notes were thin, only the names of two herbs commonly used to treat fever and one more called rage-wort. Beside that name, I had carefully noted: "Best to use the live herb."

I let the book fall closed. Rage-wort, sometimes known as star-weed or, here in Cour, as heart-bind, was a springtime herb grown commonly in gardens and sometimes found in the forest as late as summer. It might be that I could find some yet, in some sunny place on the warm side of a hill. In a year such as this had been, with cool nights and generous rain, many plants caught a second wind after summer and grew one more time before winter.

I looked out the window to see the sun. Not enough time remained in the day for hunting through the woods. That must be left to tomorrow. Meanwhile I had plenty of heart-bind, dry and hanging over my worktable. You use a live herb for the oils in the leaves and the juice of the fleshy stems. The juice would have long dried away from my harvested herbs, but some oil always remains on the leaves. I hoped it would be enough, and set to work, using my skills to make a tisane.

Outside, the day grew old, and the sun slipped slowly down the sky. Slean's forge was quiet, and a ribbon of comfortable gray smoke drifted up from the chimney of his house. He'd done his work for the day, as I hoped I'd done mine.

* * * * *

Willa met me at the door, her hands all wrung with worry. "She's no better, Leial. Our little Azure is none better at all, and it seems to me that she sinks every hour. She hasn't slept the night or at all today."

The mother knows the child, and I didn't think Willa was wrong in saying that her daughter seemed worse. The rash covered her to the belly now, and showed angry red on her arms. I put another pot of salve on the bedside table and gave the little bucket of tea to Willa with instruction to heat it, but only to warm.

"Will it help? Do you think it will help?"

So many times I'd heard that question! So many times I'd seen the pinched and frightened look on the faces of those whose children, husbands, wives, suffered under the hard hand of this red sickness. I answered Willa carefully, not wanting to raise hope, not wanting to dash it.

"It has been known to."

It had been known to. I myself had seen it work, sometimes, when taken in good time.

Good time, however, must have been sometime before three days. Yahn Cooper's little daughter died in the night. I heard it the next day that Willa hadn't yet stopped crying, and that of all the wailing she'd done, only this remained: A cry to vanished gods and a curse upon them for robbing away the magic that might have saved her little daughter.

She should have cursed me for failing to find what most she needed.

* * * * *

I stood in the dooryard of my little house, looking down on the road to Cour. Knots of people passed by, walking to the meadow north of the village. The sky hung low and gray, and the people all went cloaked against the chill, damp wind blowing off the water. They gathered for the burial of the little blue-eyed girl who'd died in my care. No one, not even Yahn Cooper, forbade me to join them. It was I who forbade. I felt like a stranger there again, as I had when first I came to Cour. Worse, I felt the little girl's death heavy in my hands.

Huddled against the wind, I watched the people go by. It's custom here in this part of Abanasinia to bury the dead at once, be it summer or not. Yahn Cooper had broken with custom; for the sake of his wife, half mad in her grief, he'd let his daughter lie a night in the front room. I wished he hadn't, though; I wished he'd buried her straightaway. It's what is best to do when disease like this red sickness struck. I'd tried to dissuade him, but he hadn't heard.

"You've done all you could," he'd said flatly, the way you speak when you're aching to lay blame and know there's no proper place for it. "Let us do what we must."

I felt myself dismissed then, and so I went away.

Up in the gray, hanging sky, a hawk screamed over the tops of the trees, a struggling rabbit in her talons. Slean and I looked up at the same time, but I looked away first. Tears pricked behind my eyes, the first since I'd heard the news of Azure's death. I pushed them back. I didn't feel I had the right to weep for that death.

"It is as much your right to be there today as anyone's," said a voice, Slean come up from the forge.

He came to stand beside me, and I asked him coolly why he was here. "Shouldn't you be with Yahn and his family now? Everyone else is."

He shook his head. "Not everyone is."

I laughed, a short bitter sound. "Not me."

"Or me. Or Yahn Cooper's middle daughter."

Cold crept along my spine. "What do you mean?"

"Too sick to go, and they're saying it's the same thing that took the little girl."

My hand began to shake; the sound of my heart beating was thunder in my ears. "It's begun, Slean. What will I do? It's begun."

He said nothing, and so I must go on as though he had.

"They trusted me, Slean, and it was the same kind of trust they gave to their old healer." The man who'd lived in the time of magic. Wind in my face stung tears from my eyes. But only wind, nothing more. I could afford nothing more, or I'd fall to weeping, and the tears I'd have shed would have been for myself. "I helped them with all my heart, Slean."

He nodded.

"And in the end, that wasn't enough."

What was I looking for, having said that? Comfort? Understanding? Yes, certainly understanding. I wasn't looking for agreement, but that's what he gave.

"You're right," he said, low and sorry. "In the end, it wasn't enough."

And all my help and small remedies would fail against this red sickness, this old foe of mine. Not enough, never enough.

We stood there for a long time, me shivering, him still as stone as we watched people pass by on the road, walking out to the meadow where Azure would be buried. How many more of these who yet lived would follow her into death?

Sudden wind came strong, and Slean said, "You gave up the magic."

The words stung, and that sting burned deep.

"I—Slean, I can't answer it. I tried. I've tried all these years." I told him it made no sense now to chase after what wouldn't be found. What did make sense was to go and seek the herb I needed, the live heart-bind in the forest. "If I can get it to the girl in time . . ."

He waited for more, yet I had so little more to say about maybes and hopes.

"Is that what you need, then, this weed called heart-bind?"

"It's all I have, and I don't even have it yet."

His eyes told me he thought I had more than a rumor of a remedy, but he didn't persist. Instead, he said, "I know where some's been seen to grow, but only in summer. Might be, though, you'll find that second growth you're looking for now. It's been known to happen."

"Will you show me?"

He nodded to say that he would, but such a look of sorrow sat on him that I could not rejoice.

* * * * *

We didn't go quietly through the autumn woods; we were not wordless under the windy sky. I'd thought Slean was so disappointed in me, in my failure, my decision to try no more for the magic, that he'd have nothing to say. I was wrong. He had plenty to say, about all things but magic and healing. He talked about the work he was doing, how that fine blue steel breastplate was getting to look like one of his better pieces. He was proud of that work. I heard it in his voice. He talked about the gossip he'd lately heard in the tavern at Cour, and there was a lot of that. A shy man, yes, he was, and what time he spent in the tavern he spent solitary. You hear a lot of gossip that way, for the quiet man in the tavern is nearly invisible. When he ran out of gossip, he began to talk about the weather, or the season, at least.

"It's my favorite season, autumn." Acorns dropped all around us, sounding like rain on the canopy of leaves. Slean reached and caught one in midair. "You hear people all the time saying how it's the end of things, the onset of the dead time."

I told him I'd always thought so, and couldn't imagine how else you'd think about the falling season when all around you everything is busy at the task of withering.

Slean shook his head, amused by my answer. "It isn't about death, this season. It's about all the possibilities of spring." He tossed the acorn ahead, and it fell onto soft, springy moss, then rolled into a hollow place between two large stones. "There. Now it's a new tree soon to spring. That," he said, winking, "is autumn."

I didn't have anything to say to that. All my mind was on the search for live heart-bind. He seemed to know that, for he nodded and told me not to fret myself, that we'd find the heart-bind nearby. So he said, but it wasn't, not in the first glade he took me to, and not in the second. Still, he assured me we'd find it, for he'd seen it growing in more than one place.

"It's here for you, girl. Trust me, it is."

And so it was. We'd not walked but two hours past the second glade when the ground began to drop steeply down. The path Slean found for us soon vanished, leaving only rising stone walls and a narrow passage through a glen so deep the sky was only a slip of blue when I looked up.

"There," Slean said, pointing up the west wall. "See it? That patch of green hanging over the ledge right above?"

I saw a clutch of heart-bind growing bright green and shining in the sunlight. My stomach turned to think of that height, and my hands went suddenly cold and clammy. The ledge he spoke of was hardly that, only a jutting of stone that didn't seem wide enough to stand on.

"How will I ever get it?" I whispered.

Slean laughed. "No way I can think of unless you

want to grow wings. Girl, you're as green as the heart-bind itself. Give me your pouch. I'll go and fetch it."

I looked up at the dizzying height, down again to the stony floor of the glen. "How? We have no rope."

He snorted. "I've lived a tame life lately, I'll grant it, but I played on worse grounds than this when I was half-grown and witless with it. Don't you worry about me."

He hung my pouch round his neck to keep his hands free, then prowled around the foot of the wall, searching for a way up. In short time he found it, and he began the climb to the heart-bind. I watched with breath held as he reached for handholds and trusted footholds that seemed like nothing but cracks in the stone. Sunlight shone on him, the same shaft illuminating the heart-bind above. I'd never seen his face the way it was then, bright with eagerness for the dare and the danger. This was who he was a long time ago, before all the world changed around him, when the stars in his sky made shapes like gods to tell him old tales and show him the way home.

I grew cold standing there, deep in the shade of the glen, watching Slean go up the rocky wall, hand by hand covering the distance to the heart-bind. Shivering, I wrapped my arms around myself, never taking my eyes off my friend. I don't know how long that climb seemed to him, but to me, it seemed to last an hour.

Not that, though, not really, for the sun had not moved from the heart-bind in all the while Slean climbed. When at last he gained the ledge, he stood squarely on it and called down to me, words I couldn't make out. He spread out his hands wide. That I understood. He'd found the heart-bind, and there was plenty of it.

"Leave the roots!" I shouted, and he must have heard, or at least understood my concern that the plant be properly harvested. He leaned far over the ledge to show me a fistful of leafy stems. My breath stopped to see him do that, and I only exhaled when he pulled back. The sound of his laughter drifting down to me was meant to reassure, I knew it, but I didn't feel comforted. I wouldn't till he stood foot to ground beside me again.

The pouch stuffed full, Slean hung it back round his neck and started the long climb down. I stopped breathing again, and the pulse beating in my neck grew harder and stronger, and in my mind, I ran over and over all the cautions I'd have called out if I wasn't afraid the sound of my voice would distract him.

Careful, be careful, careful, be careful, oh, Slean, please be careful. . . .

High up in the narrow sky, a hawk went soaring on the currents. I caught sight of her out of the corner of my eye and thought suddenly of the hawk I'd seen over the road to Cour, the one with the rabbit struggling and dying in her talons. Quickly I looked back to Slean, struck by sudden fear. He wasn't a third of the way down, and I clenched my hands together, sure it was taking far longer to get down than it had to climb up.

One step down he took, then another. He reached for a handhold and got a good enough grip to stretch out for the foothold he needed. The hawk screamed, a high sound to pierce the silence. Slean looked up, then quickly back. It was that looking back, that sudden jerk of his head made me scream "Slean!" even as his foot betrayed him, slipping on the stone.

He fell, grasping for the last hold, and not a cry did he make.

All the wailing, all the wailing, was mine.

* * * * *

Oh, I wished for gentler hands! I wished to be able to touch Slean in the discovery of his injuries and not bring pain. Oh, I wished. My wish went ungranted.

I thought his neck was broken. It wasn't. I thought

surely his back was broken. It wasn't. I turned him gently, face to the sky, and the sound he made, a long and low groaning, tore my heart. Bones were broken—his left arm, his right leg—but worse than that had happened. I heard it when he tried to speak, the terrible bubbling in his lungs. A splintered rib, or more than one, had punctured his lungs.

"Oh, Slean," I whispered, already knowing that if I'd had all the stock of the herb woman's trade right here on the stone floor of the glen, I'd not have been able to help him. "Oh, my friend, my dear friend . . ."

High in the sky, the hawk shrieked again. Who would look now? Not me, nor Slean with his eyes on me, his dark eyes so strangely bright. He moved his lips to speak. I thought it was my name his lips shaped, but no word came for me to hear, nothing for me to answer. Tears rolled ceaselessly down my cheeks as there in the stony glen I wept.

What would I ask of magic, if magic I had? I'd ask, I'd beg, I'd plead for Slean's life.

I took his right hand in mine, and cold as it was I chafed it to bring warmth. He smiled a little. Healer's heart, that smile said, ah, the healer's heart. He closed his hand around mine, and I shut my eyes, eager for the dark where magic had always come calling, pleading for the power, the strength to save Slean's life.

Came the whisper, soft as spring's first breeze, and my heart rose, hoping. Came the lights dancing, calling me, calling. Not in the cry of my heart had this magic found its answer. Not in any word I'd ever thought to speak. What, then, would it want to hear? I didn't know any better now than I had all the times before, and in the failure, I had but begging words to use.

Please. Oh, please. Please, he's dying. Oh, please.

Even as I begged, the whisper stilled, the lights went dancing away.

Slean's grip on my hand loosened a little. My eyes flew open to see a small bubble of blood rising at the corner of his mouth. It burst with his breath. He closed his eyes slowly, wearily.

I cried, "No!" and he tried for another breath. I wanted to comfort him, to lift him and hold him in my arms, but I dared not, for the pain of being moved would surely kill him right then. His lips moved again. I leaned down close to hear what he might say. I heard only the bubbling of blood in his lungs. There was no magic for me, none for Slean who had always believed I'd find it when at last I knew how to answer its call.

The creation calls to the artist, trying to find a way into the world. But what good does it do to call to an artist who cannot speak the answer? All my failures fell upon me, heavy as stones, and this last the worst, the heaviest of them all. Slean would die here, and he'd die as much of my failure as of the blood seeping into this lungs to drown him.

"Oh, Slean, I'm sorry. I'm so sorry. . . ."

And then he managed to speak some words. He said, "No, not sorry. Leial, oh, girl, don't be sorry." He had to stop to gasp a breath. "Don't give up. Don't . . . You will find the way to answer . . ." A great shudder wracked him, and he cried out, the first sound of pain he'd allowed. I cried out with him. I couldn't help it. Our voices were one now, bound together as our hearts had been in friendship. His eyes grew dim as he found one last breath.

"Trust me."

"Trust me," he said, just those two small words. I kissed him, my friend, but I don't think he knew it. Somewhere between his last words and that kiss, Slean Brae died.

* * * * *

I spent the night in the glen, alone in the failing light of day, hauling stones to make a cairn for Slean. The floor of the glen made fertile ground for my work, and for that I was grateful, for I couldn't carry him home, and I wouldn't leave him there naked to scavengers. He must sleep decently covered and safe. I wept as I worked, and I learned that it is true, you can weep out all your tears, yet still the choking grief remains.

I have known grief before. I have tended the deathbeds of my mother and father; I have seen people die who trusted me to help them live. I have grieved over my failures, and I have grieved for a cruel magic that lay in the world all around me, calling to be born but refusing to be. Never had I mourned as I did for the hill dwarf, Slean Brae. I knew it, building that cairn, that it might be I'd have friends down the years, a husband, some children, but never would I have anyone to love me as Slean had, in honest friendship, in trust and acceptance of all that I am. To so many people, that kind of friendship never comes. We who have had it know it will never come twice.

By the time the stars showed over the rim of the glen, I'd done my work. I built a fire close to the cairn and sat there to watch the night away. Alone, clutching the pouch filled with the heart-bind Slean died for, I watched the moon rise and the stars wheeling. I heard the night birds calling, the wind sighing down the throat of the glen. All the while, I thought of nothing, I felt nothing. I was as empty as that sighing wind, drained of hope and fear, of care and certainty. Slean's death made a hole in me, a gaping tear through which all that fills the heart went draining out.

The numbness of grief was a strange state to be in, as though I'd been bereft of all my five senses. In that way, I passed the night of Slean's death.

* * * * *

I heard the hawk just at dawn when the light is gray and no shadows fall. The traitor hawk, I thought bitterly, though I had no notion whether this and the one of the day before were the same. I looked up, because you do, you always do when you hear that wild, high screaming. Wings wide, the hawk sailed over the glen, circling lower, drifting down between the stony walls. With terrible suddenness, she dropped straight down like a stone and rose up again, a small, dark animal in her talons. The creature wriggled, struggling for its life. Maybe that struggle upset the hawk's balance, or maybe the hawk never had a good grip on her prey from the start. However it was, the talons snapped open, and breakfast fell out of the hungry hawk's grip.

Numbly I looked away. When I knew the creature was down, I went to see what had escaped hawk death only to find stone death. It wasn't anything big, a young stoat, and I was thinking about eating it myself, cooking it over the cairn fire. I'd had no food since the day before, and now a long walk home to Cour, with certain grief to bring and uncertain help against the red sickness.

I picked up the little stoat, gently because it yet lived, though barely. I moved my hands to wring its neck, to help it out of its pain and send it quickly along the road the hawk had set it upon. As I did, the stoat opened its eyes. Wide and dark those eyes, filled up with dumb animal pain. It never whimpered or made any other sound. It only looked at me. In the moment our eyes met, I felt something touch me, as though I'd been tapped on the shoulder. I looked around, I actually did, though I knew I was the only one standing in the glen. Me alone, hollow as the wind in the sky.

Stark as the whispering voice of unborn magic, come yet again to haunt and harry. I turned from it, that voice calling. I had nothing of hope left to feed it, no trust, no faith. I had only emptiness.

Then, all in an instant, I felt myself filling. Filling—yes, that's the only word for it. Something came to fill me with light, brightness racing into me, through me, and I tell you I had no time to think about this, or words to use in the thinking, but it felt as if what ran in me came at me from the ground, from the sky, from the broken body of the dying stoat in my hands. It came roaring, and it came laughing. It came singing, but I can't begin to shape for you the words of its song. I dropped to my knees, didn't feel the stone biting, and willed all that ran in me to flow into the dying stoat. It wasn't me doing that willing, I knew that. It was me making way for the will of the magic, me acting as a channel for the healing power, the same way the banks of the Wing Swift are a channel for her running water.

In my hands, the stoat twitched, then breathed. Even as I thought, Yes, it might live, the little creature leapt from my hands and went scampering away.

I'd healed, with magic—at last I had healed. The answer to the call the magic sounded was a simple one, yet not so simple to find. It was no cry from the heart, no plea from the soul. The answer was silence, the silence of the empty place where magic can enter in.

* * * * *

Sunlight fell into the glen, the full rosy gold of the early hours spilling down the sky to cloak Slean's cairn gently.

"I found the magic," I said. Ah, to Slean, to him." I answered it fair, and I wouldn't have found it at all if it hadn't been for you." Tears stung my eyes. How hard it was to learn that answer! The pain of the learning would be with me all my days. "It's a legacy, that magic, and there won't be a person in Cour who doesn't know it's a legacy from you."

I plucked a stone from the cairn, stood holding it in my two hands until the sun's light lost its rose and changed all to gold. All around me was silence, and I let the silence stay unbroken until at last I said, "I will miss you, Slean Brae. I will miss you forever."

He knew that, though; it didn't need saying. In some land of the dead beyond this changed world, he who always knew my thoughts knew how much I would miss him.

And so I didn't linger. In the clear morning light, I left there and went out to the woods all filled up with the sad, sweet scent of autumn, and took Slean's legacy home to Cour.

Sword of Tears

Richard A. Knaak

While pulling his weary body over yet another out-cropping, Hermetes found himself nose to nose with a grinning face. Not exactly grinning . . . and not exactly a face. A skull stared back at him, one hollow eye seeming to condemn the bearded, graying man for its condition. Then Hermetes noticed the other pieces of the skeleton, including a hand and broken rib cage.

A minotaur, he estimated, one that had died no more than five years ago. He judged that the minotaur had slipped from higher up and fallen to his death, not the most honorable passing for one of his kind. To stumble and be left as food for scavengers.

The bearded man climbed farther up, searching for a place to catch his breath before he concerned himself with the implications of the skeleton. A broad, flat rock, probably the same rock upon which the minotaur had originally dashed himself into so many pieces, seemed the best spot. Hermetes started toward it . . . and tripped over something protruding from the ground.

It took Hermetes a moment to recognize a sword. Only a portion of the hilt remained uncovered by dirt and rock, and even that wore a thick layer of grime.

With a small pack of supplies, the bearded traveler had come to the jagged hills and mountains far to the north of the city of Kerman to find not a minotaur's skeleton but a missing part of himself. No mountains, no ravines, had existed in this area of northeast Ansalon until the recent horrific war. Tall, lanky Hermetes had just taken up the mantle of a cleric of Mishakal when this war had erupted over the continent.

As his brethren had done, Hermetes had gone out into the world in the name of his patron goddess and utilized the gifts she had granted him to aid the wounded, heal the sick, and try to push back the dark forces trying to destroy Krynn. He had witnessed the suffering of knights and peasants alike, watched helplessly as elves, humans, dwarves, and even kender died for no good reason. The Chaos War, as it was called, had lasted but months, and yet it had shaped Hermetes's world as much as the Cataclysm had no doubt shaped that of his ancestors.

Then, when the world needed them most, Mishakal, Paladine, Gilean, and even the nefarious Takhisis had vanished.

Hermetes absently tugged at the sword, slowly freeing it from its burial. The gods' abandonment of Krynn had been soul-shattering to the young cleric of Mishakal, barely finished with his training. All his beliefs had been based on the truth of his goddess and her work . . . and yet she had abandoned Krynn along with the others.

The sword proved long and light. Although most clerics were not permitted to use edged weapons, Hermetes had grown up in his father's smithy, and he recognized the excellent craftsmanship despite the ravages of war and time. The blade had been scorched black, but the hilt was brilliantly bejeweled, with one massive green stone that glowed in the sunlight. A bell protected the wielder's hand. The blade's edge was unmarred and still sharp.

Hermetes found himself admiring the sword. It had been forged for battle and even now, if wielded, it looked likely to wreak havoc. Whereas the gods . . . the gods had fled.

With a sigh, Hermetes put the sword aside. Since that war, his beliefs had not only been shattered, they had been scattered to the wind. He had tried preaching the creed of Mishakal, but few had listened. Why bother with a goddess who no longer seemed to care?

Only the way of the warrior seemed to appeal to people nowadays. They did not respect a man of peace, but a man of power. They wanted a knight, a champion, a hero. Without meaning to, he murmured aloud the words one bitter old man had said to him after the war: " 'There is no truth now but the sword and the hand that wields it.' "

The sun began to slip away. Hermetes had hoped this pilgrimage to the mountains would give him some clarity of purpose, but as far as he was concerned, his quest had already failed. He would find a place to spend the night, then return in the morning to Kerman. As with much of his life these past two decades, this journey had proven a folly.

A glitter of emerald caught his eye.

The sword again. Despite the waning light, the stone in the hilt glowed. Hermetes reached for the sword, but as his fingers brushed the hilt, the gem burned brighter, as if responding to his touch. The former cleric yanked his fingers back, but when the glow faded, he reached to touch the sword again.

Once more the green stone gleamed. This time Hermetes steeled himself, seizing the hilt. He had no difficulty wielding the long sword. In fact, despite the many years since he had grasped a sword, Hermetes realized the memory of all the maneuvers his father had taught him was still fresh. He felt a rush of confidence; if a minotaur or a bandit dared to challenge him, Hermetes would defeat him in combat. He had nothing to fear from any adversary. Armed with this weapon, he could cut down anyone who stood in his path.

Hermetes dropped the sword, startled by the sudden vehemence of his emotions.

For several moments, he stared at the weapon, uncertain whether to touch it again or race away as fast as he could. The sense of power had both shocked and thrilled Hermetes. He had never been fascinated by power, but when he held the sword just now, he had felt as if power was the answer to all of Ansalon's misery.

And then he heard the voice, ever so faint and within his own head, calling *Master* . . .

At first Hermetes looked around, seeking some newcomer, but then his gaze returned to the relic. The green stone glowed stronger now. The sword in his hand had shifted its angle, the hilt nestling perfectly in his grip.

Master . . . wielder . . . I am yours to be used. . . .

Hermetes knew about magical artifacts, the most legendary of them being the Dragonlances of Huma. As a cleric of Mishakal, he had beheld a few sacred relics blessed by his mistress. Yet now, so many years after magic had vanished from Krynn, to be addressed by an artifact amazed him.

"Who—what are you?" His words echoed in the mountains, taunting him for asking such an outlandish question.

Yet the sword answered. *Master . . . I am the Sword of Tears . . . I have the power to right the wrongs you have witnessed.*

"How did you come to be here?"

Hold me . . . hold me closer . . . the better to hear me. . . .

Hermetes hesitated before holding the sword closer and preparing himself for the worst.

There is nothing to fear, my master. . . . The voice had grown stronger. *I am yours to wield, yours to command.*

Its obeisance eased his apprehension and admittedly pleased him. It had been far too long since Hermetes had been in command of anything. Wielding the sword brought back feelings of the once-mighty power of Mishakal.

I am the sword of champions, the voice continued. *I was once wielded by Huma of the Lance, and with me he slew the grandsire of all dark dragons, Wyrmfather. I have been wielded by humans, minotaurs, elves, ogres, dwarves, even gods. By my hand, the minotaurs' greatest champion, he whose mortal remains lie before you, cut down the servants of Chaos, though he himself was lost.*

Hermetes's gaze shifted to the staring skull. "That was long ago."

Since that time, I have lain buried here, awaiting a worthy soul.

"Me?"

This world has become harsh, the sword said, echoing Hermetes's own gloomy thoughts. *The gods have abandoned us. The time is ripe for strong warriors, strong arms to return Ansalon to the proper path. Peace and justice must be backed by strength. That is the way you think, too, is it not, Master?*

It was. Terrible as it had always been for him to acknowledge such sentiments, the sword understood him. The time of clerics had passed. Preaching peace, friendship, and cooperation was not enough anymore. What the world needed now were leaders who could back their pious words with forceful deeds.

With a relic such as this one, Hermetes might force people to listen to his words. He had come here seeking answers within himself, but it was possible that he had found much, much more. "What do you suggest, sword?"

I will strengthen your arm, strengthen your will. I will serve as your sentinel and guide you during crisis. Ask of me what you will in your thoughts, and I will advise the best choice.

The sun had all but disappeared behind the mountains, but the glow emanating from the hilt of the sword was brighter than ever now and illuminated Hermetes's face.

I shall ever light your path for you, Master.

He didn't think to ask why it called itself the Sword of Tears. All that mattered was his prayers . . . no, that was the wrong term, for that implied that Mishakal might still be present to hear him. His wishes had been answered.

With two hands, the graying, bearded man raised the sword reveling in the green glow. At last Hermetes might lead his children back into the light of hope. "Tomorrow . . . tomorrow I will show Kerman the path!"

Yes, Master, the sword responded dutifully.

* * * * *

Kerman had become a filthy place. After the war, most of those who could had abandoned it for better climes. Those that remained had lived under the yoke of the Knights of Takhisis for more than ten years, until the ebony warriors, too, had found no more use for the once-mighty city. After their departure, governing of the crumbling metropolis had fallen to a series of undistinguished, inept, or vicious leaders. These days it was questionable who, if anybody, ruled the pale shadow that remained of Kerman.

Hermetes watched in disgust as two disreputable men who chanced to bump into each other spouted foul words and threats. *Small wonder my words of peace had no effect. All of these folk understand now is strength!*

Hermetes stroked his short beard, which he had trimmed upon his return, then readied himself. He wore a robe of brilliant white, not because he had once subscribed to the cause of Mishakal, but because it was the only garment he owned that might fit the momentousness of the occasion.

"I will show them the true path," he whispered, not at all recognizing the fanatical edge to his own voice.

They will be yours, Master. You have simply to show them the power. . . .

The sword's words made sense. Should Hermetes raise the magical weapon and shout out to the crowd? They might think him a madman. Perhaps the sword could help. "Do you . . . do you have a suggestion?"

You must find one who is in need, the artifact responded unhesitatingly. *Let me guide you. . . .*

Not certain what his strange companion had in mind, Hermetes nonetheless followed the instructions. The Sword of Tears led him down a short distance to an even more dismal section of the once proud city, where filth filled the streets and the people seemed apathetic.

"They have lost all hope," he murmured.

But you will find it for them again. Here . . . this one will do, Master. . . .

The blade directed him toward a young woman seated in the entrance of a building once magnificent but at some point burned out from within. She rocked back and forth, her face scarred by disease, her left arm a misformed limb twisted at an awkward angle. Beneath the dirt and the jagged scars, Hermetes noticed traces of thwarted beauty. The healer in him wanted to take her in his arms and pray to a goddess who no longer existed.

You can do it. . . . Touch her throat with the tip of the sword. I will do the rest. . . .

Hermetes glanced around. He had already been noticed by nervous onlookers; no one could fail to see his elaborate sword.

The young woman noticed him at the very last moment, but before she could get away, the sword thrust forward. The artifact moved with such speed and precision that he felt certain it would decapitate her. However, the tip did not so much as even pierce her skin.

Around him, Hermetes heard people gasp,

scream, or call out. Someone shouted a name that the former cleric could not make out but assumed to be that of the sword's victim. Hermetes, too, grew nervous as a sick knot formed in his stomach. He tried to pull the enchanted weapon away, but it would not budge.

Not yet. You want to help her. You want to cure her of her troubles. . . .

He started to ask the blade what that meant, then saw the change that had overtaken the young woman. The scars shrank until they ceased to be visible, and the arm, so malformed, grew and straightened. Her expression, frozen in fear, slowly melted into one of wonderment. With the aura still surrounding her, she began to flex her arm, wiggle her fingers. Her hands fluttered to her face.

It is done. Now you will receive your due, Master. . . .

Hermetes did not hear the blade at first, so weak did he feel. As he looked around, the graying, bearded man saw that he was surrounded by a growing throng. Hermetes tried to raise the Sword of Tears in order to defend himself, but it refused to obey.

They do not come to attack. They come to worship.

The artifact perhaps exaggerated. The ragged crowd paused a respectful distance from Hermetes, eyes darting from the sword to the young woman to the one who had seemingly cured her. Among the throng, he saw others who were maimed or ill and in a moment of inspiration he reached out to the nearest, a young boy no more than ten, and summoned him forward. The boy, clearly lame, shuffled nervously toward the robed figure.

Once more the blade rose. The emerald aura flowed over the boy, who, after an initial cry, had begun to giggle. Hermetes watched with as much astonishment as the crowd as the boy's twisted leg straightened.

At last the aura faded, and with a squeal of delight, the boy bounded back into the crowd to an older man and woman. A cheer rose. Hermetes looked around for another unfortunate to cure.

Time . . . You will need time, the sword interjected. *You cannot cure them all at once. First they must understand that you are their new leader as well. You are the one who will show them their future. . . .*

Again the artifact made sense. First Hermetes needed to talk to people, let them know that Kerman would thrive under his guidance. He raised the sword high, which captured the attention of all.

"You will listen to me! You will hear my words! I am Hermetes! Some of you may know me; most do not . . . not yet! I have come to lead you back from the darkness! I have come to restore Kerman to its former glory! The gods may have left us, but we can rebuild our future without them!"

Some cheered, a few muttered.

They must be shown more of the power you wield. . . .

The Sword of Tears carved an arc in front of the people. The tip of the blade grazed the earth, emerald sparks flickering briefly to life. The enchanted sword took Hermetes's breath away and impressed the onlookers.

Where the blade had carved a line in the ground, small, wriggling forms burst from the crevice. Green shoots sprouted, then grew swiftly into young stalks that rose until they reached the former cleric's waist. Vinelike limbs sprouted, twisting around one another.

The miracle was not yet complete. Small flowers appeared on the limbs, and from the flowers burst succulent fruit, as orange as the sunset or as crimson as deep wine.

Tell them you will feed them, cause the rain to nurture their crops, give them all the gods have denied them, if they will but obey your commands, Master. . . .

A heady feeling swept over Hermetes. He repeated

the sword's promises. More cheers arose, yet still some faces were filled with mistrust.

Let the word be spread. Tell them to inform all who their new savior is. . . .

Again he repeated the words, and within seconds, people were running everywhere, eager to tell. Others remained, though, clearly enraptured by the miracles. Hermetes slowly walked through the crowd, reaching out with his free hand to touch a face here, graze fingertips there. His pleasure was dampened only by the great hunger and thirst he felt, and so he plucked one of the orange fruits, ate it, then greedily devoured a crimson one.

His act stirred others, and soon nearly everyone was tasting the fruit. They were the sweetest treats Hermetes had ever tasted.

You are satiated for now. You must show yourself to others. . . .

Slowly Hermetes began to leave the area. Word had already spread, and so new people were added to those already flocking around him. His retinue grew with each step. With magic so rare these past two decades, the coming of a spellcaster could but amaze all who heard or saw. Hermetes flashed his best smile, showing them that he cared for all people. The emerald aura now surrounded him, adding to the excitement of his presence.

The throng continued to grow, and so Hermetes turned and headed toward a nearby open area. His choice was a wise one; newcomers flocked toward him from the opposite direction, so many they almost seemed an army.

Then he saw three men at the front of the throng and paused.

Of the three, two seemed the most worrisome. Hermetes had seen their type before in Kerman; they resembled the brutes who had raped the city in the past while calling themselves leaders. The largest of the pair proudly bore a scar that ran from his mangled nose down to his jaw. His black, bushy hair made him more ogrelike than human, and such a heritage would not have surprised Hermetes.

His companion, on the other hand, more resembled a serpent, thin yet sinewy. Narrow eyes concealed an animal cunning that warned Hermetes of the danger of turning his back to the man.

The third newcomer seemed different from the others, hardly even the sort to associate with them. A balding, crook-nosed man with the mark of a warrior, he studied Hermetes with eyes that analyzed every move. This one had been a commander, perhaps of some force that had fought in the war.

Behind them followed several who appeared to be cohorts of the trio. Without realizing it, Hermetes tightened his grip on the enchanted weapon. Although he recalled much of what his father had taught him as a boy, Hermetes doubted that he had the skill to defend himself against three such savage, intimidating foes.

"I'm Kras," the bushy-haired one grunted. "You must be the so-called mage. This is my city, and I don't like troublemakers."

The serpentine man next to Kras lowered his hand to a wicked dagger on his belt.

I am with you, Master. You have no need to fear. He is a vermin, not worthy of you, a mere beast that thinks himself a man. . . .

Emboldened, the former cleric took a step forward, all the while leveling his gaze at Kras. "I am Hermetes, and I have come to lead my people back into the light. I invite you to join me in this crusade, you and all with you."

Kras bellowed harshly, offending the former cleric's ears. "That's rich! That's mad! I know you, Hermetes Half-Wit! A cleric without a goddess! A fool without power!"

"These people have seen what I can do. Do you need to see also?"

The amusement vanished from Kras's face. "I don't need to see conjurer's tricks!" He drew his sword, a sleek, lengthy blade that once no doubt had been wielded by someone of higher birth than Kras. "This is the power that rules these days! No gods, no goddesses, no mages, and no clerics!"

Cheers rose from behind Kras. The third man, the warrior type, remained calm, simply watching the brute face off against Hermetes. Kras's other companion continued to toy with his sheathed dagger.

"There is no need for violence," Hermetes insisted.

Kras laughed again. "Some leader! You think that even with your conjurer's tricks people would rather follow a cowardly man?"

He must be fought, Master. Look, already there are those who would question your abilities. You yourself said that this is a time requiring great fortitude . . . that the way of peace you once preached . . . peace without force . . . no longer works.

Had he said all that? Even thought it? Hermetes no longer knew for certain. The graying, bearded man had to face this threat if he hoped to lead people to the light.

"You're quiet, cleric." Kras pointed his sword at Hermetes. "A quiet coward."

The Sword of Tears rose to confront the other man's blade. "Come then, Master Kras," Hermetes said. "If the sword is what you worship, then the sword is how we will decide this issue."

No sooner had he spoken when Kras charged. Startled, Hermetes tried to back up, but the enchanted weapon would not let him, instead pulling him forward to meet his opponent's attack with equal ferocity.

Kras appeared stunned by the severity of the counterattack. The Sword of Tears moved with such grace that Hermetes knew everyone there recognized him as an accomplished master. It deftly parried each move by the larger man. The crowd cheered, more and more supporting Hermetes. Kras at last seemed to realize that he stood no chance against this astonishing weapon and backed away. The crowd, though, would not let him pass, determined to see a grand finish.

Now the Sword of Tears darted through his guard, slashing across Kras's face. That proved too much for the scoundrel. Leaping out of reach, Kras tossed his weapon to the ground and raised his hands.

"I yield!"

With much hidden relief, Hermetes pulled back the enchanted blade . . . or at least tried to do so.

With a peculiar wail, the Sword of Tears buried itself in Kras's chest.

A hush fell over the crowd. Hermetes gasped as he watched his adversary pale, shiver, then slump to the ground. The sword removed itself and dropped to the former cleric's side.

It had to be done, Master, or he would have haunted your back, undermined your authority. . . .

"But . . . but he had surrendered," Hermetes muttered.

Look to your left.

Acting without thought, Hermetes obeyed. The sword rose again, moving swiftly in that direction. Hermetes tried to shout, but no sound escaped his lips. Wailing yet again, the Sword of Tears cut a crimson edge across the throat of Kras's thin, snakelike compatriot. Dagger still sheathed, the second man gurgled and fell.

A collective gasp swept over the crowd. The third man stepped away from Hermetes and raised his hands in supplication. However, the anger in his eyes said much.

"There was no need for that," he dared to shout at Hermetes. "Kras surrendered. Nemarik hadn't even tried to attack you."

"I did not want to kill them," Hermetes returned, not at all certain how to explain himself. No one would believe that the sword itself had slaughtered the pair, not its wielder.

He must die also, the enchanted sword insisted, its voice more seductive than ever. *He will rally dissent if he lives. . . .*

The blade slowly rose.

"No!" Hermetes forced the sword down.

The emerald gleam all but faded. The blade did not move again.

Shaken, Hermetes tried to gather his thoughts. As little as he had cared for violence, he understood the sword's motivation for dispatching the two men. Kras had been a monster, the other man his friend and ally. Both were enemies to anyone once sworn to Mishakal.

Perhaps this third man might be deadlier than the other two.

Hermetes shook his head to clear it, then looked at the remaining fighter . . . only to find him no longer in sight. Hermetes belatedly realized the man had melted into the crowd. In fact, several of those he had thought among Kras's following had abandoned the area.

Unaccustomed anger surged through the former cleric. He had been made to look a fool by the escaped stranger. He pointed his sword at a man who had stood near Kras and his companion. "You! Who was that man?"

His target, a shriveled woman, clutched her shawl."He calls hisself Lord Draytor, he does, mas—master! He weren't no friend of Kras; he just worked with him. . . ."

"I want him!" Hermetes surveyed the throng. "Bring him to me!" He raised the Sword of Tears high, and a wind howled around him. Hermetes smiled at the effect this gesture had on the people. They immediately scattered in every direction.

Suddenly weary, he dropped his arm. The wind died instantly, and Hermetes stood alone. He felt hungry again.

What now, Master?

"I do not intend to kill him, sword. I will reason with him, or if that does not work, I will exile him. I am here to uplift Kerman, to give it hope again, not to begin a reign of bloodshed."

But you ought to defend yourself, Master. You must defend yourself when beasts like Kras threaten you. . . .

"I know. That could not be avoided." After a moment of consideration, Hermetes added, "His companion, too. He was about to draw that dagger when I turned, wasn't he?"

Most assuredly, Master. I noted his hand closing upon it just before you struck. . . .

"Then I would be foolish to regret his death. These are times that demand terrible sacrifice." Still, it troubled Hermetes that he felt so little sympathy for the men who had died. Of course, they probably never had any sympathy for those they had crushed under their bootheels.

He noticed then that he had begun to weave back and forth. Hermetes had never felt so weary in his life. He desired nothing more than to go to sleep. If he closed his eyes, then surely matters would be clearer when he woke.

You should lead them, the Sword of Tears declared with sudden fervor. *You should direct their hunt, track down those who would oppose you. . . .*

"I cannot. I must rest, at least for a few hours. I need rest . . . and more food."

Later . . .

"Now." The sword wisely did not continue the debate. Hermetes looked around, caught sight of an elderly man cautiously watching him from a doorway. "You! Is this your home?" When the man nodded fearfully, Hermetes smiled kindly. "You have nothing to fear of me. I simply desire a place to rest for a time. Will you help me?"

The man swallowed. "Yes, Lord Hermetes! My home is yours! Everything I have is yours!"

Hermetes shook his head, both saddened and amused that he evoked such fear in this elderly soul. "I simply need rest and a little food if you have it, good sir. I will make it up to you."

"What I have is yours! Marta!" An old woman, clearly his wife, stepped out of the darkness. "The great mage wishes to eat and sleep in our home!"

"Come in, great mage! Please!"

Hermetes clearly frightened her, too. He resigned himself to their apprehension, thinking that as he became known for his good deeds, people everywhere in Kerman would shed their fear. Sword in hand, the former cleric marched into the couple's home. Once he had slept deeply, he could begin to nurture that trust, starting first with his hosts. He would even show kindness to Kras's surviving comrades, a firm kindness that would prove both his strength and his humanity.

Yes, everything would be better once he had rested.

* * * * *

Hermetes's dreams were an unsettling mix of violence and serenity. He saw the Kerman that once was and the Kerman that ever would be, a glorious revitalization that would prove a beacon to the rest of struggling Ansalon. Yet he also saw battles and war, horrific yet necessary because too many stubbornly refused to accept the light. They had grown accustomed to being half-beasts. Hermetes saw himself enveloped by bloodshed, the one-time healer become the most savage warrior of all.

At last the dreams became too much for Hermetes, and he struggled to awaken. The sounds of battle and riot did not lessen, though, and when the last vestiges of sleep gave way and he found himself once again on the weathered mat supplied to him by his poor hosts, the shouting and the clash of weapons continued to resound from outside.

He did not have to look far for the Sword of Tears; even in sleep, the artifact had remained fixed in his grip. Hermetes quickly rose and hurried to the door. His elderly hosts stood just inside, peering out fearfully.

"What is it? What is happening?"

They gave a start, evidently as fearful of him as of the outside chaos. The man found his voice first. "They're fighting, great mage! They're fighting!"

"Who?" Hermetes pushed past them.

Chaos. Men and women with staffs, pitchforks, axes, and any number of other implements that could be wielded as weapons, fought against people who well might have been their neighbors. Hermetes could not tell which were enemies and which allies, so thoroughly entangled were the factions.

"Who are they? Why are they fighting?"

"They captured the foreign-born lord for you, great mage, but he claims many followers. He worked with Kras, but in another season he would've killed or found himself in Kras's place." The man swallowed hard. "His people, they didn't take to his being arrested, so they've come and freed him. Your side is trying to get him back!"

"Mine?" Hermetes stared at the melee, incredulous. "Mine?" He watched as a woman struck in the head by a staff collapsed and disappeared under the trampling feet. Another man fell with a knife in his stomach. People were dying left and right.

"This is not what I wanted," the stunned Hermetes whispered. "They should not be killing one another!"

They are cattle . . . mindless, the Sword of Tears interrupted, breaking a long silence. *They have not learned their lesson. You must teach them . . . punish them. They will continue this madness until you show them the error of their ways. . . .*

"The fools!" Fury and frustration combining, Hermetes charged out into the street. Few noticed him, so swept up were they in the fighting. The dead and wounded littered the streets, and more than one building had either been damaged or set ablaze. At this point, there appeared no rhyme or reason to either side. As they had done for the past twenty years, Hermetes's fellow human beings had rushed to embrace wanton violence. He doubted many of them knew the original cause of this bloody debacle.

That man . . . he will kill that woman. You must strike before he can!

"Eh?" Reacting to the artifact's warning, Hermetes raised the sword. The Sword of Tears gave a wail, and a moment later the man cried out and fell, his chest splashed with scarlet. The woman he had been about to strike screamed and ran off.

There . . . those two will be run through. . . .

Hermetes swung the enchanted weapon. He cut down one attacker, a second, and wounded a third without caring whose side they were on. It did not even matter; they all acted with the same disregard for life. His fury mounted. Better to start with a clean slate than try to turn these half-beasts into people.

"Stop!" he cried. "Stop this insanity!"

They will not listen. They will never listen until you make them see what becomes of those who do not. . . . You must show them that there is only one choice. . . .

"One choice . . ." Hermetes whispered.

Raise me high and let them know your fury at their base actions. . . .

Hermetes thrust the sword into the air. Once more it wailed. The fierce wind returned, followed by the same thunder.

"Hear me! You will stop this monstrous behavior now!"

People screamed, yet some fought on. Hermetes cried out again, but he could not be heard above the wind and the thunder.

All they understand is violence. . . . They can only learn by the same, Master. . . .

Taught by violence. Yes, Hermetes saw that at last. Beasts only understood the way of the beast.

Use me. Wield me. . . .

Roaring, the former cleric brought down his darkened blade and charged into the thick.

Emerald lightning struck one person, then another. Hermetes did not hesitate. Again and again he unleashed the Sword of Tears.

"Animals, all of you! Animals!"

A young man barely into adulthood made the foolish mistake of raising a staff in defense as he neared. Wailing, the Sword of Tears cut through the staff as if it were nothing but smoke before burying half the length of its blade into the lad's chest. Hermetes turned away before his victim even hit the ground.

More and more broke from the battle, made aware of his deadly presence. Still others had yet to learn. Hermetes snarled, gripping his weapon tighter. Monsters such as these would never be missed once Kerman was back on the path to the future.

Someone stumbled in front of him.

Strike! Strike!

He did so without even glancing at his prospective victim. The wail of the sword all but drowned out the woman's scream. Hermetes stepped over the body.

Behind you! Behind you!

Whirling, Hermetes barely pivoted in time for the artifact to act. The Sword of Tears parried the killing thrust, the attacker's blade slicing past his ear. Moving more out of surprise than fear, Hermetes stumbled back.

"Fiend! Bloodthirsty demon!" Sword bared, a familiar figure confronted the former cleric. The foreign-born Draytor. Kras's friend and, in Hermetes's eyes, the origin of all this madness.

"What sort of creature from the Abyss are you, cleric? What sort of monster of Chaos have you become?"

His words bit deeply into Hermetes. He felt the Sword of Tears tremble in his hand, felt its desire to bury itself in Draytor's throat. "Me? You call me a monster? I would free Kerman, free Ansalon, of all tyrants such as you and Kras! How many have suffered under your hand here? How many have you forsaken in your homeland, for that matter? Did they finally oust you and cause you to flee here seeking weaker prey?"

"Damn you!" Draytor lunged, then quickly withdrew. "I'll not let you talk so! I fought against Chaos in the war, the same monstrous force that destroyed my homeland and many of my people! I joined with Kras because I had no choice, no place to go back to!"

Strike him dead. Cut him down.

"And as for tyrants, even that fool Kras was an innocent compared to your foul self, kind and gentle cleric!" Draytor indicated the devastation around them. "Offer holy gifts with one hand, upheaval and death with the other! Not since the war have I seen terror in so many eyes!"

He talks simply to distract you, Master. Cut him down. . . .

"You speak nothing but lies. The only tyrant here was your friend Kras! I want only to bring hope to my flock, to lead them to the light of a new and shining Krynn!"

"To the light?" Draytor spat in Hermetes's direction. "To death, more like! Look around you, cleric! There're as many slain here by your hand, from your commands, as all others combined! You destroyed friend and foe alike, man, woman, and youth! You've done more in one day to ruin Kerman than a hundred such as Kras could've accomplished in a year!"

"No!" Despite his certainty that Draytor couldn't be a man of honor, his words still stung Hermetes.

Lop his lying head from his body. Still his cursed tongue

forever, urged the sword. *End his lies. . . .*

"I—" Hermetes hesitated, although he did not know why. Draytor meant nothing to him. Nothing.

Draytor gestured. "Look at what you wrought, demon! Look! At your very feet lies one of your trophies, one of the ultimate symbols of your goodness! What menace did she present? What sin did she commit?"

Strike! The Sword of Tears started to rise, but Hermetes fought it down. He had to look. He would deal with Draytor after he had satisfied his curiosity. Nothing the lying foreigner had to show him could change his mind.

The still form of a young woman lay on the ground. Vaguely Hermetes recalled striking her down. He had assumed she was about to attack him. No weapon lay nearby, however. There seemed something familiar about the woman. Hermetes stepped closer.

He will strike while your back is turned! Turn and deal with him, fool! Kill him before he kills you!

A part of him sought to obey, but another part, buried deeper yet somehow stronger, forced him to study this victim of his ferocity. He could only see a side of her face. Slowly the grim-faced Hermetes reached down and turned the woman over.

Pale in death, her face did not at first register. Only when he noticed the recently healed scars, the arm once malformed, did Hermetes recognize his victim. It was the same young woman he had cured with the sword . . . who now would never be able to enjoy the miracle she had been granted.

"Mishakal, no . . ."

He heard footsteps behind him, but despite the sword's attempt to make him turn, Hermetes refused to remove his gaze from the lifeless body. With one touch of the enchanted blade, he had been able to grant a better life; with a second, he had stolen that life.

"This is your future, Lord Hermetes? This is what you'll bring to Kerman?" A heavy object struck the ground next to Hermetes. Draytor's sword. "I know I can't defeat you. I've seen your power. I've nowhere else to go; you might as well kill me now. I'll not live to watch another sample of your butchery."

Now! Now is your chance! Strike him down. Let me feed upon him. . . .

With a force so sudden it took Hermetes by surprise, the Sword of Tears drew him up and tried to make him swing at the unarmed Draytor. At the last moment, Hermetes jerked, causing the wailing blade to miss. Draytor fell back, looking both startled and confused.

The other man stumbled about in what looked like some bizarre dance. "I will not let you!" The artifact twisted and turned, and Hermetes wondered how much longer he could fight it. At the same time, he felt a creeping urge to give in to the sword's murderous instincts.

He will kill you if you do not strike first. He must die! He must feed me. . . .

"Get back from me!" the former cleric shouted at Draytor. "Stay clear!"

You cannot allow him to live, Master. He will haunt you. . . . You must guard your back. . . . Better to be rid of them all now . . .

"I should have left you in the mountains! You are no miraculous gift from the gods, no answer to my woes! You are a demon come to feed on my vanity and despair!"

We are one. . . . You are nothing without me. Without me you can do nothing to save Kerman or Ansalon. . . .

Again the sword whirled him about, facing Draytor.

"No!" Hermetes steeled his will. He wished he could return to the mountains and bury the Sword of Tears so deep that no one would ever again fall victim to its wiles.

Hermetes's world turned upside down. Draytor and everything else melted into a swirling miasma. The former cleric screamed, and the Sword of Tears wailed. Hermetes crashed against a rocky surface, losing consciousness.

* * * * *

When Hermetes opened his weary eyes, all he could make out at first was the sky above. A chill wind cut through his thin cloak, causing the graying, bearded man to shiver. He shook his head to clear his mind, realizing at last where he must be. The mountains.

Thinking of the Sword of Tears, Hermetes stared at his empty hands. What had happened to the enchanted blade? He looked around frantically, almost fearing that he had left it in Kerman. An emerald glitter caught his attention at last. The Sword of Tears lay two or three yards away, near the edge of a deep drop. It lay there, apparently drained, inches from oblivion.

Hermetes made no move toward the artifact. Would it again seize control of him if he came too close? For that matter, why had it brought him back to the mountains when all that it desired lay in Kerman?

Or had he, after all, proven his virtue by returning it to this place?

I can do it, Hermetes decided. It will be weak now. I was the one with power, not it. I can destroy the sword. No one else will ever have to fear its evil again.

Gathering his wits, Hermetes approached the Sword of Tears. All he had to do was kick it over the precipice.

Emerald light flickered within the stone in the hilt.

Master . . . The artifact's voice was barely intelligible, so soft, so weak had it become. Master . . .

"I know now, monster! I know what you did, and I realize what I am. You have enslaved me to perform your miracles and your deeds of evil."

Not true. I had no power of my own, the Sword of

Tears replied. *I feed off my user, as you must realize by now. When the war of gods commenced, I was taken in hand and used to fight the Chaos. When the war was over, I did whatever was asked of me. Good or evil? I care little for such distinctions among mortals. Strength and power are my only destiny. When I was abandoned here. I lay, barely existing, until one came who could feed me . . . or whom I could feed. For a brief time, Master, that was you. . . .*

"I am but human!"

Human, yes, but more than that. I can feel it . . . the strength within you . . . drawing from the world around you. . . . My power grows as you use it . . . a power that could awaken Krynn and change this world forever. . . .

Hermetes could not prevent his mind from drifting. With such potential as the artifact described, he could indeed accomplish miracles. First he ought to make amends in Kerman, prove to them that what had happened was not his fault. . . .

The Sword of Tears suddenly rose and spun about. Before Hermetes could react, the hilt struck him flat in the hand. To Hermetes's horror, his fingers betrayed him, folding around the handle as if caressing a long-lost love.

And that power, that magic, will I command for you, my master . . . my puppet. . . .

Gone were all facades; the relic mocked the fool who had discovered it.

"No! No!" The horrified Hermetes tried to peel his fingers free, but his grip was traitorous. He could hear the sword laughing, enjoying his panic. "You had no power but mine!" he screamed.

You forget, Master, that I have fed . . . not as deeply as I might desire . . . but I have fed on those slain in the city . . . and the more I feed, the greater my power . . . the better to manipulate as I desire. . . .

"I will not be your tool, demon!" Hermetes tried to inch toward the edge, but his feet refused to move.

No more defiance, Hermetes Half-Wit. Defiance doesn't

*work. Ask the minotaur who found me but four years
before you. . . .*

"The minotaur . . ." So the hapless minotaur also
had found the sword . . . and had saved himself by
the only means possible. "He would not be
conquered by you."

*I was weaker then, and he proved to be too obstinate and
much too honorable. But you . . . although you are not a
warrior such as the minotaur . . . your background in magic
will give me so much more. . . .*

Hermetes could feel the sword invading his mind,
taking over his very thoughts. He had come so close
to succumbing to its monstrous ways before, he
could never stop the artifact now. He saw men,
women, and children cut down by his hand as he
dutifully followed the artifact's dictates.

"Mishakal, no . . ."

The Sword of Tears brought his arm up so that the
glowing stone nearly blinded him.

The gods are gone, Hermetes. I am your god now. . . .

"I will not be your puppet!" With a herculean
effort, Hermetes jerked the sword away, smashing
both his hand and the blade against an outcropping.
He cried out from the pain but didn't stop battering
his bloody hand against the rock.

*You will never be free of me, Hermetes. Your life is
mine now. Submit to me. . . . You will come to enjoy my
gifts. . . .*

"Never . . ." Revulsion spread through him.
"Never . . ."

You cannot resist me. There is no hope. . . .

"Never!" he repeated, tears beginning to flow.
Hermetes would have flung himself over the
precipice, but still his feet would not budge.

The wind turned into a howling beast. Dark
clouds swept over the heavens.

*Serve me and you will live well, Hermetes. With power
comes reward. . . .*

The former cleric pushed one foot forward.

"I will not be your slave, Sword of Tears!"

You have no choice. . . .

"I do! I must!" As he spoke, Hermetes felt his legs buckle. He fell to one knee. The tenets of his early training included inner focus, drawing strength from the belief in Mishakal. Was that what had managed to bring him back to the mountains?

"I will not be your puppet, sword!" he cried, focusing his willpower. "I will be your nemesis!"

As he spoke, thunder roared and the wind howled. The malevolent blade no longer taunted him, but he could feel its silent assault on his mind, his soul. Hermetes could only hope that he had enough good inside him to summon the strength for one last chance.

Hermetes, once cleric of Mishakal, thrust the Sword of Tears high into the air. The clouds above were black and the thunder so loud it nearly deafened him.

Hermetes! the artifact screamed. *Master!*

As the jagged, golden bolt coursed down toward Hermetes, he heard the Sword of Tears wail again. . . .

* * * * *

"Amazing . . ."

"I don't think we can go any farther on horseback, Lord Draytor."

"I doubt that it matters." Lord Draytor, still awestruck, reined his mount to a halt. All he could do was stare at the numbing sight that had led him to this place but a week after the riots and fighting that had nearly destroyed Kerman. In that week, Draytor had become uncontested lord of the surviving sectors of the city.

"The bolt must've sheared off a good third of the mountain face" the man next to him muttered.

The lightning bolt had sliced through hundreds of tons of rock as easily as his own knife might have trimmed flesh from the haunch of a deer. The explosion and ensuing avalanche had been heard for miles around, taking the fight out of all the factions of Kerman, especially that following the madman Hermetes. With the cleric vanished, Lord Draytor had ascended to power by proclamation. He had done his best to further the peace process by offering to seek the former cleric out . . . if he still lived. A hunch brought him here, to the mountainside. Seeing what had happened in this place, Draytor had his doubts.

Two men had volunteered to scout the upper regions returned at last, looking extremely exhausted. Draytor waited until they had caught their breaths and sipped some water before questioning them.

"You found nothing?"

One of the men held up a piece of charred cloth that might have once been the same color as Hermetes's robe. "Barely spotted this as we were coming down. Nothing else, sir."

"How did it look up there?"

The other man understood the true meaning of Draytor's question. "The whole side of the mountain is scorched! Nothing could have survived."

Lord Draytor surveyed the landscape, so changed now. He felt as if he had journeyed into some nightmare region of the gods. Nothing could be alive here, not even a crazed cleric.

"If the old one survived, he'd have come back to Kerman by now," the first man said.

"You're probably right." The weary Draytor decided Hermetes must be dead after all. Why had the former cleric come to this place, only to destroy himself? Had it simply been a mistake, a spell gone awry? "We'll probably never know," Draytor whispered to himself.

He didn't need to see any more. The handful of men with him, chosen from both sides involved in the battle, would attest to the vastness laid waste and the unlikelihood of survivors.

"Mount up. It's time we returned." As his

companions obeyed, Draytor again stared at the blasted landscape. To have such power at one's command and not wield it properly. He would have expected a former cleric to better understand the responsibilities. Had it been he who had commanded such abilities, matters would have taken a better turn. Draytor knew he could command armies, rule kingdoms; his success with ruling his ancestral lands proved it.

The others ready, Draytor turned his horse away from the site. As he did, however, he thought he heard someone call him. The veteran commander turned in his saddle and peered off into the distance.

"Something wrong, Lord Draytor?"

No one else had heard anything. Still . . . "No, nothing."

As they rode off, he could not shake the voice from his mind. Something about its beguiling tone.

So much to do, came the unbidden thought. *An iron hand may be needed at times.*

"Yes, it may," he muttered. Draytor gave the mountain one last glance. He could see things clearly now. Perhaps he had been trapped in the confines of a city for too long. Riding up here to the mountains had been a welcome respite.

"Is something the matter, sir?" someone up ahead called back.

Draytor realized he had been lagging behind. "Nothing!"

As he urged his mount forward, the new ruler of Kerman decided he would return here on the morrow . . . alone. For all the devastation, the seasoned warrior found the region inviting. Here in the solitude of the mountains, he knew he would be able to think more clearly and define his thoughts for the future of Kerman.

Now leading, Lord Draytor rode off toward Kerman brimming with sudden confidence. Yes, first thing tomorrow he would make his way back here.

Draytor would find a place to camp, then inspect again the area of Hermetes's disappearance.

Perhaps . . . perhaps he would even find the glittering sword the mage had wielded. Draytor felt hopeful. Better that a sword as well crafted as that one should be wielded by a true warrior and a proven leader. The more he thought about it, the more he became certain he must have that bejeweled blade. It would not be so difficult for him to find, if only he was willing to search a little.

The Cost

Robyn McGrew

Dariot found the encampment of the Knights of Takhisis just outside of town. He approached it cautiously, noting with grim disapproval the death lily emblazoned on the front of the black command pavilion. The two knights who guarded the entrance watched him with wary expressions as he approached.

"Stand and declare yourself," called one of the guards.

Advancing two steps more. Dariot stood just out of striking range of the knights. The man who challenged him looked at least five years junior to the Solamnic Knight and was his opposite in almost every way. The guard was a stocky blond with pale gray eyes, in contrast to Dariot's own dark eyes and almost black hair.

He looked around the camp they were establishing, which was neat and orderly and contained probably close to two hundred knights and their brutish foot soldiers. The muscles in Dariot's stomach clenched and knotted. He was one. Unhappily, he was the only one. Assuming a confident air he did not feel, he looked at his opposite. "You will take word to your commander that Dariot Torson, Knight of the Sword, would speak with him."

The Dark Knight gestured to the other guard without taking his eyes off Dariot. The second knight disappeared through the curtained door of the pavilion.

A moment later, a grizzled knight about Dariot's age emerged from the structure. Cloud-gray eyes focused on Dariot. In a quick sweep, the commander took note of the sword scars on Dariot's arms and the subtlety altered musculature of a trained warrior.

"I am Knight Commander Reginald Asterlain. What can I do for you, Sir Knight?"

The bunched muscles in Dariot's shoulders eased somewhat at the respect in the man's tone. "I have come to negotiate."

An eyebrow raised to the commander's short-cropped hair. "The hamlet is ours already. You are only one knight and cannot hope to defend it against all of us."

"I will if I must," Dariot replied. "However, I propose something more reasonable."

The right side of the commander's lips lifted slightly. "And that is . . . ?"

"A Combat of Honor."

"To the death?" asked the commander, interested.

Keeping his voice to a deadly calm, Dariot matched the commander's smile. "If need be. I do not take any life—even that of my enemy—willingly."

Reginald nodded. "Terms, then. Will you give your word not to resist our taking the provisions we need should you be defeated?"

"I cannot speak for the townspeople, but if I live, I will not resist you. Conversely, should I win the contest, you will leave Prada and its people untouched. Are we agreed?"

The army was not starving. They were simply stockpiling food for themselves and their horses in anticipation of a prolonged battle, fearing that supply lines might be cut. Had the army been desperate—as desperate as the people of Prada after a summer of drought—they would have never agreed to the duel, no matter how chivalrous.

"We will consider this a test between our two gods. I agree to your terms." Reginald turned to the blond knight. "Sir Merek, you always want the chance to prove your loyalty to Queen Takhisis. This would seem a good opportunity."

"Yes, sir," the young knight replied. "Thank you, sir."

By Sir Reginald's command, a circle was scribed into the yellowed grass off the side of the road. The Knights of Takhisis stood honor guard around its perimeter.

Both knights entered. Both saluted the commander, then each knight saluted the other.

"For Takhisis!" cried Sir Merek.

"For Paladine," said Sir Dariot. The combat began.

Merek tested Dariot's defense with an obvious thrust, which he easily sidestepped. Dariot returned the compliment with a slice at the Dark Knight's ribs. Merek turned, hoping to cause Dariot to overreach himself. Dariot compensated, converting to a short stab at Merek's arm. The Dark Knight moved, but not enough. The bright silver blade ripped into the top of his right hand. Golden light played around the tip of the holy sword, blessed by Paladine, protesting contact with a person dedicated to the Queen of Darkness. The smell of burning flesh filled the air. Merek jerked his hand back, a raw red scar crossing from thumb to wrist. The young knight clenched his jaw in an effort to control the pain and retreated a step. Dariot pressed his advantage with an underhand slice.

The swords met in a shower of sparks and a crack of thunder. The Dark Knight's sword was sacred to Takhisis. Black energy crashed against golden, the shock knocking both knights off-balance. Merek recovered first and attacked with vigor. Dariot raised his blade in defense. Again the swords met, and again Dariot felt the flash of energy course through him like a lightning strike. He felt stunned, dazed. He used the last of his energy to thrust at Merek. The younger man barely parried the thrust. The meeting of blessed swords, each sacred to an opposing god, caused lightning to flare. The air sizzled between them.

Dariot slumped to the ground. His mind burned with the effort to stay conscious. The blurry face of Sir Reginald entered his retreating frame of vision. "You fought bravely, Sir Knight. Not well enough to win, but neither did Sir Merek earn a clear victory. I therefore grant a third of the crop to your people. I will leave it to you how to make it last."

Dariot tried to rise, to fight on, but blackness closed in around him and he knew nothing more.

* * * * *

The harvest winds struck Dariot in the face like a cold slap, making his skin burn. At his feet, in her new grave, Elosia gave mute testimony to his failure. Two moons after the Combat of Honor, this gentle old woman had become the first victim of the food shortage. He waited in respectful silence as Sister Lissa pronounced the final benediction. "May Paladine guide you and keep you in his ways and grant you eternal rest."

Dariot brushed the grave dirt from his palms and knees before extending a hand to the aging Cleric of Paladine. Sister Lissa wrapped her withered arms around his sinewy one. Neither spoke as he helped the thin, silver-haired elder up the incline to the road.

She retained her grip on his arm and looked at him, concern narrowing her pale blue eyes. "Dariot, you must not blame yourself for Elosia's death. A full squad of knights could not have stopped the Dark Queen's army from taking what they wanted. You did the best you could and nearly died for it."

He shook his head in disagreement but said nothing. His failure had become a point of contention between them. He had failed and Elosia had died. He would make it up to her by saving the others.

Lissa tightened her grip on his arm. "I know that look. What are you planning?"

They had entered the small village of thatch-roofed homes before he answered. "I have been thinking. The knights did not carry their stores with them. They marched light and rapidly. The knights must have left their food stores stashed somewhere near here. They'll be back for them. I plan to find them before they return."

"By yourself?" She was appalled. "But there will be guards . . . "

"I will not be my myself." he answered. "Paladine is with me."

In the dark of the night, working silently, Dariot considered the leather armor resting on his neatly made bed. He had worn the armor the day he had fought the Dark Knight and not since. He felt unworthy of it. He pulled it on and laced up the sides, taking care to polish the rose and kingfisher on the breastplate.

Heavy on the pillow lay Dariot's blessed sword, still tainted with the invisible bloodstains of those he had been forced to kill. His grief over ending the lives of those so young had nearly cost him his soul. He had almost renounced the knighthood, foreswore the Oath and denied the Measure. His knight commander had persuaded him to undertake a holy quest to try to regain his faith. Dariot had traveled to the village of Prada, where he met Sister Lissa. She had helped him regain faith in his god and himself, which was probably what his commander had in mind. Now he would repay her for that help.

He looked around his small cell and made sure all was neat and tidy. Just in case. A puff of breath extinguished the single candle, plunging the room into darkness. When his eyes adjusted, he slipped out the door.

* * * * *

Merek woke in the darkness of the predawn, gasping in fear. The whole of his body awash with sweat, his mind burned with images: a squad of knights under the command of his cousin Tedren, the ambush costing all save Merek and Tedren their lives, his cousin's arrest, trial, and execution. Then his own interrogation before the knight commander, followed by a Knight of the Thorn waving some foul, sulfurous smoke before him. Images of the world slipping away from him and facing his Queen.

Most intently he remembered the searing agony of her anger and how he had sworn again his undying loyalty. She had accepted his pledge, but he knew that he walked a narrow path. He had thought to prove his worthiness to her in the upcoming campaign, but the meddling Solamnic knight had put a stop to that. His commander had left him behind to "recover" from his injuries, which were minor. Merek knew the real reason he had been left out when the others marched to glory. He had failed to defeat Sir Dariot in the Combat of Honor. Sir Reginald didn't trust Merek anymore. Sir Reginald considered Merek lacking in faith and in Her Majesty's favor.

His sleep destroyed, Merek swung his legs over the side of his makeshift cot and fumbled for the flint on the crate next to him. Finding it, he lit the stump of a candle. The solitary flame revealed little of the cave's vast interior. On the crate rested meticulously folded leather breeches and a steel-studded black leather jerkin to match. Merek pulled on his breeches and knee-high boots, retrieved the jerkin, and tossed it over his arm. He picked up his sword belt and smoothed the covers, then walked into the dark of the night.

* * * * *

In the gray of the predawn light, Dariot walked the hillside above the village. Leaf-bare trees, silent guardians, stood in a circle around the granite stone he used for an altar. Oak leaves already turned gold padded a ground made moist from the first snowfall. The leaves surrounded the altar like a worn hearth rug. When he entered the circle, his presence stilled the voice of a lone sparrow. Dariot unsheathed his sword and set it on the altar. Kneeling, he sank to the cold ground.

"Lord Paladine, Master, please turn again your face to me. I know I failed you." Dariot's jaw clenched at the shame of the memory of his defeat. Tears formed, making his eyes and nose burn. He swallowed the tears and forced himself to continue. "Lord, please . . . do not chastise the people for my weakness. Be with me as I search for the food the knights of the Dark Queen took from us. Show me where to look. Guide me, lord. Break your silence of these last two moons, I beg you!"

Dariot raised his head, searching the sky for some sign to show that Paladine had heard and would answer his prayer. The former constellation of the platinum dragon was gone. A tiny flicker of light flashed from the hills on the other side of the ravine, hills where there were many caves. Caves capable of storing food. Hoping he had not imagined it, Dariot watched for a long time but saw nothing.

Nothing. Just the outline of the rocky expanse silhouetted in the rising sun. Could this be a test of his faith as sister Lissa had suggested? If so, he would not fail it. Bowing his head, Dariot gripped the pommel of his sword until it cut into his hand. "Thank You, lord! I will not fail you again."

* * * * *

Despite the cool fall breeze, a sheen of sweat glistened on Merek's bare chest as he finished the last of his daily sword drills. This morning's workout had done much to restore him. He reveled in the freshness of the air that filled his lungs as he fell into the deep breathing pattern of exercise. He enjoyed watching the way the rising sun glinted off his blade. The burn in his muscles indicated that he had pushed himself right to the edge. Perhaps today his mistress would deign to speak with him again. Pine needles cracked and scattered as he thrust his sword into the ground. Merek knelt before it. "Great Queen, I await your pleasure. Grant me once more the guidance of the Vision and the knowledge that I do your will. Allow me the opportunity to prove my loyalty to you."

No response. No sound but the murmuring of the wind in the trees.

"Mistress, grant me the opportunity to redeem myself!" He remained kneeling before his blessed blade and waited for an answer, as he had waited every day and had for many weeks now. Originally three knights had been ordered to guard the stores. Sir Jankin had left two weeks ago, when the great blackness blotted out the stars, shaking the world to its foundations. Sir Jonathon had departed when the new moon appeared in the sky, along with a red star. Merek had chosen to remain. His commander would have no reason to doubt his loyalty this time. He would guard the supplies until he received new orders.

* * * * *

As the gold of the sunrise faded, Dariot made his way up the side of the ravine and found the remnants of a hastily cut road. The tramping of many feet had packed its surface to a rock hardness. A dusting of leaves and scattered pine cones now covered much of it. On the road's rough-hewn sides, tree roots thrust through into daylight, as if still searching for the nourishing soil that had once fed them. Wagon tracks made shallow grooves in the ground. He recalled the supply wagons rolling out of the village, carrying their food stores. He must be near the cache. They would have hidden the supplies up in the hills somewhere and then traveled on, leaving men to guard them. That would have been two moons ago—one cycle of the red moon and one of the solitary white. But he did not know how to judge time by this single new moon that now shone in the night sky.

The road led upward to the ridge. The flash he had seen came from the top of the ridge above him. Perhaps a reflection off armor or a sword. He would have to be doubly cautious if he wanted to accomplish his mission. Turning his face to the rising sun, Dariot wiped the sweat from his brow and began the steep walk up the road, crunching pine cones beneath his feet. Halfway to the top, the road widened into a clearing which led to the wide mouth of a cave. Before the entrance of the cave was an orderly stack of small sticks and an empty fire pit. Dariot tensed. He had not expected to find the encampment out in the open. The knights must be certain of their ability to protect it. He raised his estimation of how many guards to expect.

Dariot followed the edge of the road, using the scant cover of hanging roots and trees growing sideways. He kept a close lookout for guards but saw and heard no one. The mouth of the cave appeared to be unguarded. A trap? Perhaps they had seen him coming. Drawing his sword, he edged forward, whispering a prayer. "Holy Paladine, favor my quest and grant me victory."

He reached the entrance of the cave. Still nothing, no one. He moved closer, tried to see within. Darkness greeted him. Boldly Dariot entered the cave and placed his back against the wall.

No defender came to engage him.

Doubt pulled at the edge of Dariot's mind. Maybe the knights had not left the supplies here after all. Still, somebody had at one time used this cave for shelter. If so, that person might have left something behind Dariot could use to help the villagers. Keeping his sword at the ready, he advanced farther into the cave.

The air was warmer inside and smelled of moist dirt. Seeing nothing with his first inspection, he closed his eyes to help them adjust to the darkness. From somewhere in the darkness before him, he could hear the sound of running water—an underground stream. Opening his eyes, he looked about. The cave ran deep. The rising sun provided dim but adequate light, now that his eyes had adjusted. Dariot looked to the right first.

Sinking to his knees, he bowed his head in contrition. "Oh, my lord, how could I have doubted you?" he breathed.

The cave stretched into the darkness, splitting into two tunnels. The close tunnel held rows of filled grain sacks, barrels of salted meat, and other foodstuffs. In the tunnel beyond were stored leather straps, staves, and weapons. To his left, the cave opened into a makeshift living area, complete with sleeping area, three cots, and a table. He had indeed found one of the knight's supply stores.

"Thank you, lord. You have chosen to aid your people through those who oppressed them."

Dariot rose and crossed to inspect the nearest grain sack. It sat upright, with the ties loosed, a metal cup next to it. Only half of its original contents remained. He could carry this sack back with him now. Tomorrow he would recruit the strongest of his neighbors to transport enough grain and provisions to last until they could build storage for the balance of the supplies. He knelt, resting his sword across his knee to secure the ties on the bag.

The distinct sound of steel against leather sounded from behind him. Dariot froze in midmovement.

"Step away from the grain."

The baritone voice, although young, had a keen and commanding manner, a manner Dariot recognized. He stood and turned to face Sir Merek. The Dark Knight stood with sword at the ready. He was dressed in simple black leathers, with a death lily worked into the tunic breast. He looked younger than Dariot had remembered.

"My people are starving. Stand aside!" Dariot ordered.

Merek moved his sword from the guard to the ready position and stood his ground. "Do not press me. You will not survive the battle this time."

Dariot advanced, still clutching the half-empty grain sack and leading with his upraised sword. Merek dropped his shoulders and relaxed into a forward stance. Dariot feigned a cut at the Dark Knight's left shoulder. Merek deflected Dariot's sword to the outside. Metal rang against metal, echoing into the dark recesses of the cave. A slice followed hard on the first testing strike. Merek met the slice with a cut of his own. The two holy swords met. Sparks and filings showered the air. Dariot braced himself for the shock, expecting the flash of energy that was the wrath of the two opposing gods.

The sparks fell to the floor and winked out.

Startled, Merek stared at his sword. Dariot took the advantage to thrust and circle in a disarming maneuver. The Dark Knight moved to sidestep the strike, but the defense came too late. Black blade rasped against silver. Merek's sword slid down Dariot's blade and plunged into the sack. Grain fell like rain to the cave floor. Furious at the waste of the precious grain, Dariot pushed the Dark Knight's sword away from the sack.

Realizing what he had done, Dariot looked at his hand. Other than a cut from the blade on his fingers, his hand was whole, healthy. He had touched the cursed blade and had not paid a price for it. Why?

Dariot placed the grain sack on the cave floor. He knew the answer. He had lost his lord's blessing. He dropped to one knee, ready to face honorable death. Lifting his head, Dariot saw Merek kneel opposite him.

Merek's jaw clenched as if he fought himself for

control. "There is only one explanation for such a thing to happen."

"Yes, Sir Knight," said Dariot, "It means I have lost my lord's blessing."

Merek's pale eyes narrowed. "You are mistaken, Sir Dariot. It is I who have strayed."

Dariot considered the other knight's statement. "Sir Knight, since we both believe ourselves at fault, there is only one honorable solution."

"I agree."

They both stood and retreated a step, bringing their swords to the upright position in salute. "To the death," Dariot stated.

"To the death," Merek agreed.

Their swords shifted to the ready position, and their fight began once more. Merek skipped the testing strikes this time and went for an aggressive straight-armed thrust aimed at Dariot's heart. The Knight of Paladine turned sideways and deflected inward, following up with a hilt strike to the younger man's exposed jaw. He pulled back and retreated to a defensive stance. Merek swung with a horizontal slice. The middle, semi-sharp part of the blade cut into Dariot's leather jerkin, grazing the skin along his left ribs. Both men stepped back, assessing their damage.

Merek worked his jaw and wiped the blood from his mouth. Dariot used his free left hand to check the damage to his armor and to shift his shirt so it wouldn't stick to the wound. He nodded his respect for the younger man's skill. Few knights could have returned an effective blow in such circumstances. Merek returned the salute, rubbing the right side of his jaw, where the skin was darkening.

The fight resumed. The cave resounded with the harsh metallic clang of swords scraping and crashing together. Dariot tagged the younger knight repeatedly, leaving a trail of crimson cuts and a few solid slices along the man's unprotected upper arms. But fatigue pulled at Dariot's sword arm. He had not fought in true battle in a long time, and he felt the neglect.

Merek was bleeding from the many wounds. He also slowed in his responses. It was now only a matter of time before one of them would make a fatal mistake. The Dark Knight, seeing a slight opening in Dariot's defense, thrust at the older man's unprotected side. Dariot tried to sidestep the attack but could not move fast enough. Merek's blade dug deep into Dariot's sword hand. Dariot ignored the burning pain and used the closing distance to his advantage, slicing at Merek's eyes. Merek pulled back, but not far enough. Blood flowed from the fresh cut above the younger knight's right eyebrow.

Dariot shifted his sword to his left hand and consigned his soul to Paladine. He could not hope to continue. His opponent wiped at his eyes, clearing the blood away. Merek lurched forward, clumsy with fatigue. He swung his sword and nearly dropped it. Weakened from the loss of blood and length of the fight, Dariot fell to his knees. Merek collapsed, lay panting for air. Neither could continue the battle.

"What does this mean?" The Dark Knight's voice was barely a whisper.

"Perhaps the rumors are true," Dariot said after a moment's thought.

"What rumors?" Merek struggled to a sitting position. "I've heard nothing."

"The rumors that the gods—all the gods—were defeated. That they have gone."

Merek considered this. "That would explain the moons. The white is moving strangely, and the red has vanished."

The thought stunned both of them into silence. The cave's dark walls closed about them.

How can I live without my Queen? Merek wondered in despair.

How can I live without my lord to guide and

guard me? Dariot asked himself in sorrow. How could my people? The thought of his people and how this would affect them checked Dariot's fears. He could not think only of himself. His people had suffered much already from the Dark Knights and the subsequent deprivation.

At length, Dariot rose wearily to his feet. Every muscle ached, his wounds stung. He twitched his jerkin into place and walked to the cave's mouth. The sun had climbed halfway to its zenith. Even the sun itself looked strange and different.

Merek joined him. Both men stood gazing at the road that led down the hillside. "Perhaps—" He hesitated. "Perhaps we should rest and resume the battle?"

"What's the point?" Dariot asked bluntly.

"Well, then, where do we go from here?" Merek demanded.

"We go forward, simply because we cannot go back," Dariot replied. "For me, that means taking care of the people of Prada. Their lives have never been easy, but now with—" his jaw spasmed, but he forced himself to continue "—now, with the gods out of reach, my people will have to learn to depend on themselves and each other. I suppose that will be true everywhere. People will have to band together to survive."

Merek's breathing grew rapid. He shook his head. "I have been a knight in service to my Queen since I was fifteen," he said.

Dariot glanced at the younger man. Even though he had really just met Merek, he had already developed a respect for him. He could guess at the turmoil inside the Dark Knight. Attached to a town and its cleric, Dariot still had a purpose in life. What did Merek have? As a Knight of Takhisis, his purpose had been to serve of the dark goddess through the army. Now, with the Queen gone, the young man had no place to go. Dariot started to put a sympathetic hand on the younger man's shoulder but stopped himself. Merek would not welcome an open show of compassion. If Dariot wanted to help him, he must appeal to the knight's sense of honor. It was a battle of a different sort he waged now—a battle for a man's soul. For surely men still had souls, though the gods might not be there to judge them.

Choosing his words carefully, Dariot launched his first attack. "Sir Merek, I need your help."

"Take as much as you need," Merek said bitterly. He waved a hand toward the dark recesses of the cave.

"That is not what I meant. I mean I need your help."

The knight turned his gaze from the sun and fixed it on Dariot, who shifted under its intensity.

"In what way?" Merek demanded harshly.

"I need you to advise me about the best way to guide my people." Dariot could manage on his own, but Merek needed a place to call home, and a second point of view could not hurt. The knight's training could come in handy, particularly if the people needed to defend themselves against whatever new foes might come to this new world.

A slight lifting of the corners of Merek's lips betrayed his hope. "Do you think your people would accept me? I will not deny who I am."

"I would not expect it of you. We could tell them that an agreement has been reached between us."

Merek's expression hardened. "I will not lie."

"You won't need to. As I see it, the supplies in the cave are now yours. You earned them by remaining at your post. It is up to you to decide what to do with them. As you know, there can be no honor in abundance while others go hungry. Will you agree with me on this and come to Prada?"

"What about the cleric?" Merek asked. "She will not accept me."

"You underestimate her. Sister Lissa will understand."

Merek stood silent for some time, then said softly, "You are correct when you say we cannot go back to the past. We must make our own future. I will stay with you until the winter snow melts. During that time, I will provide supplies and advice."

"And then?"

"I will decide then what path to take. Will this satisfy your need for an agreement?"

"It will."

"Then let us take the grain to your people."

"Our people," Dariot corrected gently.

Some of the tension eased from Merek's face, and he managed a smile. "Our people."

A Most Peculiar Artifact

Janet Pack

"That's almost my very best map," declaimed kender Tangletoe Thistleknot as Cyrenar of the Black Robes eagerly perused his chart of upper central Ansalon. "The details are very fine, as you see. I'll loan it to you, maybe even for a whole week. I won't charge you very much. Or maybe I'll sell it outright. Most of my maps are for sale."

"No," the mage replied tersely, discarding the parchment to the tavern floor and sipping from a wooden cup of red wine.

"But it's a great map," Tangletoe protested, retrieving the parchment. "I spent months working on it!"

"It doesn't, however, show the things I seek." Cyrenar's gorgeous velvet voice tightened with irritation. "If you have nothing more special than that, you're useless to me. Go away."

The half-dozen other patrons of the Inn on the Way near Sanction looked up at the fractious discussion, then reburied their noses in tankards of the innkeep's famous nut-brown ale. The nearer ones scuttled to the farthest side of their tables, unwilling to be closer to the once-mage from three towns away who, though presently magicless, had a reputation for towering rages during which things got broken and strong emotions whirled out of control like tornadoes. A large, watchful, unsavory-looking man sat drinkless behind Cyrenar, arms crossed over barrel chest, gimlet eyes assessing everyone and everything in the common room.

Cyrenar had arrived at the Inn on the Way near Sanction two evenings ago and announced his need of maps updated since the war. The kender had appeared from nowhere just after noon today and announced his name as Tangletoe Thistleknot. He'd dug out nearly two dozen maps from his myriad pouches and spent an hour extolling their virtues before the mage revealed the reason for his interest.

"Artifacts." Cyrenar's ugly tallow-colored fingers, distorted by lumps at the joints and deeply lined by his nearly fifty years, flexed as if he already caressed the objects he desired. "I need arcane artifacts to give me back the magic I once possessed." His cold green eyes bored into Thistleknot's dark brown ones, telling Tangletoe he was no more than a bug compared to the great man. "Make no mistake; that magic was considerable."

Cyrenar's voice, as silky smooth as his fingers were hideous, curled into the kender's ears. Unfortunately, Thistleknot thought, it left behind a metallic frost. Tangletoe was disinclined to trust the mage.

"I have one more," the kender stated reluctantly. "But it's my very, very best map, probably my best ever map. Made it myself, and it shows artifacts, at least certain ones people have discovered since the end of the war."

Cyrenar's interest sparked in his eyes. "Show me."

"I don't think I want—"

"Show me!" the mage commanded, eyes flashing. His barrel-chested companion shifted ominously.

Sighing, Thistleknot complied, pulling a round, waxed leather map case from his belt and carefully unrolling its contents. Cyrenar stretched greedy fingers toward it. The kender leaned away, just beyond reach.

"See," Thistleknot said softly, holding the complicated multicolored chart just beyond Cyrenar's grasp. "Here's an artifact listed, and here, and here's another. Look at this fine detail. I myself traced most of the trails in this region, many of which are little more than paths through the forest. Some of those are only traveled by deer, you know."

"How do I know these artifacts aren't mere fragments of your imagination?" Cyrenar challenged. "I must trust their authenticity and have absolute accuracy regarding their locations." He lifted his cup, sipped again. Droplets like blood clung to the ends of his gray and white mustache when he set down the wooden vessel. The mage brushed away the wine with a much-practiced gesture of one finger, first on one side, then the other, careful not to sully the meticulously groomed short beard that decorated his sharp, unhandsome features.

"I'm no liar," Tangletoe protested, pouting. "I did lots of research and study before I drew that map." The mage's stonelike gaze made the kender squirm. "Well . . . I did a certain amount of research and study before I made corrections to this part," he admitted, pointing to the region around a town called Hetherweave. "I got a lot of the original information from Amburrtail's map, but she insists hers is very accurate, and I believe her. She's one of the best map makers I know, and I know all the best ones alive. Dead, too. Anyway, everything's there, even down to the good-sized rocks they've placed to line the way into and out of this town here. See?"

"What's this 'Peculiar Artifact' listed here?" Cyrenar's jaundiced fingers trembled a little with eagerness, pointing to the place highlighted in a box alone one of the trails.

The kender peered, thought a moment. "I don't know. I've never been to that particular spot, and I certainly haven't heard much about the artifact there. Except that it's supposed to be really powerful."

"It's not far away either, only a day's travel. I'm amazed I haven't heard about it before." Cyrenar turned disconcerting eyes on the kender, studying Tangletoe closely. "What more should I know about this artifact or the region in which it's located?"

"Well . . ." Thistleknot screwed up his face as if trying to remember, making his features resemble a dried-apple doll's head. "It's hilly there. Lots of stone, so you'll need good digging tools if it's buried, which it probably is, being a 'Peculiar Artifact.' "

"That's obvious," the mage responded impatiently. "We can probably find tools in a nearby town. What else?"

"You'll have to cross a river. It's deep and fast. See—that's what the map says."

"Is there a ford?"

"Yes."

"What else? Tell me something important!" The magicless mage leapt from his chair, sending it crashing to the floor. The huge muscled fist of Cyrenar's henchman bunched the kender's leather vest and lifted. Thistleknot yelped as his feet parted company with the floor, but somehow he kept a grasp on his precious, very, very best map.

"It's guarded," squeaked Tangletoe from midair into the absolute silence that gripped the inn's common room. The door banged softly a moment later as a number of frightened patrons abandoned their drinks and slipped out. "The artifact's guarded!"

"By what? How many? What weapons do they have?" The barrel-chested man shook the kender to punctuate each of the mage's questions. Coins, oddly shaped stones, and other loose items from Thistleknot's pouches fell onto the table and bounced to the floor.

"I don't know, I don't know!" he wailed. "Actually, I've never been there!"

Cyrenar looked closely at his captive and read

truth in his face. "Put him down," he ordered. Curling his lips in derision, the henchman opened his fist.

"Ooof!" The kender hit the floor hard, landing on one hip. Tangletoe immediately scrambled after his belongings, despite his new bruise. Stuffing them back into various pouches, he crawled beneath the inn table to hunt more. "I'm trying to do you a favor, you know. You should be nicer to me." He reemerged with lower lip protruding. "I offer you excellent information for free, and and then you throw me around asking trick questions. What's next?"

"Anything we can get away with," muttered the mage. "Very well." He nodded, reaching a decision, and sat down in the chair his burly assistant had righted for him. "That particular map appears to be exactly what I need. How much?"

"I told you it's my very, very, very best map," stated the kender firmly, taking a step backward, the parchment clutched safely in his fingers. "This one's not for sale."

The mage hissed breath between his teeth. "I thought you wanted to do business," he said softly, eyes flaring.

"Sure. I sell maps," Tangletoe said firmly, pointing to the pile of rejected ones. "But not my very, very, very best one."

"If it's not for sale, then we have no further commerce to transact," the mage said. He set his cup to one side of the table.

Cyrenar lunged, so quickly that Tangletoe had little time to react as the parchment flew from his fingers. The heavily muscled thug clamped his hands around the kender's shoulders.

"No!" Thistleknot protested.

"Your map is mine now," stated the mage, gesturing to his henchman. "Take him out and teach him some respect for his betters." He spread the chart over the polished wood. "You know what

I mean. Beat him up. So he'll never follow us."

With a peculiar smile on his face, the big man dragged Tangletoe out of the inn, down the road a short way, and into a little copse of trees that offered shelter from prying eyes. He drew a wooden club from his belt. The kender tried to twist from his grasp and run away, but the man's arms were long and his reactions fast. Thistleknot curled himself into a tight ball, succumbing to the rain of blows landing on his back, shoulders, and head.

"Now I know what an ant feels like during a hailstorm," he thought blearily, and lost consciousness.

* * * * *

One of Tangletoe's blood-encrusted eyes slitted open some time later. He lay curled on his side, half his face pressed into the sweet, soft grass of late spring, quite relieved at still being alive. He was also quite surprised that nothing hurt. Then he tried straightening his legs and discovered the pain. His legs weren't broken, but they felt like it. The same was true of his shoulders and arms, the kender found while levering himself upright and gingerly exploring his hurts. His head seemed to have escaped most of the blows, and there he suffered only the scalp wound that had sent blood pouring down his face to glue his eyelashes together and paste leafy bits against his cheeks. One hand fumbled among his pouches.

"Not here," he muttered around the sharpness of a broken tooth. Slowly he peered around, mainly out of one eye.

Thistleknot crawled to the stream that ran past the Inn on the Way, dumping himself into the cold water without trying to get even his boots off. He vaguely remembered overhearing some cleric or mage saying something recently about cold water being good for swelling. Since his whole body was bruised except for the tip of his nose and one ear, he was happy to immerse himself and stay there for a long time.

After climbing out and sitting in the sun for a while, he felt better. Not much, but enough to limp to the Inn on the Way to scout for his missing things. Tangletoe slipped into the common room without the innkeep's notice to take a final look-see beneath the table. He rescued an oddly shaped grayish crystal he'd liberated from the mage's pouch earlier that afternoon and, reversing the direction of his crawl, pushed himself to his feet, caught the attention of the inn's owner, and opened his puffy lips to ask a question.

The thin man's jaw dropped, unwrinkling the creases in his face. "You're alive!" he exclaimed.

"Shouldn't I be?" Thistleknot asked politely. "Say, has anyone seen a pouch I lost earlier today? Dark brown leather, about this big, this wide, and with long, braided strings?"

The other humans just stared at him, apparently as amazed as the innkeeper. Someone whispered, "He escaped from Cyrenar and the thug!"

"Well, thanks anyway," Tangletoe said, trying to smile and managing what felt like a grimace. "If you find my pouch, will you hold on to it for me? I'll be back in a couple of days."

"Where are you going?" asked the inn's owner.

"To get my map back, of course!" He waved somewhat stiffly to the innkeep and limped out of the common room into the sunlight, ignoring the startled whispers behind him.

The mage and his henchman had a head start toward Hetherweave. "But they'll never get there because they don't know which trail it's on," Thistleknot thought to himself with a very lopsided smile. "I have a map of every deer trail in this area, even the smallest." He sorted it out from among his others and held it close to his battered eyes. "I remember a shortcut, I think . . . right . . . here. Aha!" He followed an almost invisible branching off to the right and turned onto a sun-dappled track little wider than a deer's hoof. If he was lucky, the short-cut would save hours.

Thistleknot marveled that the longer he walked, the better he felt. The exercise seemed a balm to his joints. Only his left leg continued to twinge each time he put weight on it, and his mouth felt funny where the tooth was broken.

But the kender's body tired before long. He stopped, fished in his pouches for dried fruit, nuts, and sugar-preserved meat. Thistleknot feared that if he lay down for a nap, he probably wouldn't get up for several days. He trudged on in a dreamlike state until a familiar voice startled him from his reverie and brought his aching feet to a grinding halt.

"Pile up pine needles for my bed, but make sure there aren't any bugs or twigs among them!"

The mage and his barrel-chested henchman were just out of sight among the bracken, behind a few small trees. Thistleknot congratulated himself on such an excellent shortcut. He scouted a place from which he could spy on them. Up there, on that broad tree branch that jutted in their direction, he'd have a lovely view and be out of sight.

Thistleknot managed to slowly shinny up the trunk to a broad branch that allowed an overview of his quarry through the bracken and saplings. Panting and sore, he set his back against the tree bole and searched his pouches for more edibles. After nibbling a bit of food and drinking sparingly from his water flask, he settled as comfortably as he could against the bole, intent on observing the duo on the ground. Instead, Tangletoe promptly fell asleep.

A delicate touch against his cheek awoke him, followed by a peculiar short-lived breeze. The kender opened bleary eyes to darkness except for two onyx moons shining steadily into his face. He smiled, allowing his eyes to close again, and worked his shoulders into a marginally more comfortable position. How nice, he thought to himself. The moons came to visit.

"Wha—" Moons couldn't visit. His eyes flew open, looking into the reflective orbs of a huge owl before balance deserted him and he plunged to the ground.

"Ahhhhhhhhhhh . . . ooooffff!"

Light flared, along with a silky, threatening voice. "You again! I thought you were . . ." Cyrenar looked hard at his sidekick, who held the torch aloft and stared at the kender in amazement. "I told you to get rid of him."

"I did," said the big, unsavory-looking man in a quiet but confused voice. "I beat him senseless, then I beat him some more."

"You were determined to follow us," growled Cyrenar. "Why?"

The kender blurted the truth. "You have my very, very, very best map, and maybe one of my pouches."

"Ah, of course. Maps and pouches. How very kenderish. Kill him." The mage gestured briskly with one waxy hand. "And this time be thorough."

The burly thug pulled a long sharp knife from a sheath on his belt.

"If you kill me, you'll never find the deer trail shortcut to the artifact," Tangletoe shrilled through swollen lips. The mage's assistant hesitated.

"You heard me," snapped Cyrenar. "Do it, and do it now."

Thistleknot shook his head. "That would be a big mistake," he insisted. "I know all the shortcuts in this whole region. How do you think I caught up with you? I can get you there faster and by a route that won't alarm the guard. Did I mention the guard?" Thistleknot flinched away from the well-honed steel threatening his throat.

The black-robed mage stared hard at the kender while the henchman watched his master for a signal. The only sounds were the torch spluttering and early-season bugs singing for mates. Cyrenar peered into Tangletoe's face, green eyes flaring.

"I'll help you find the artifact," restated Thistleknot. "I know . . . stuff."

"I won't listen to any more kender drivel!" snapped the mage.

"Then I'll help you get away afterward," the kender persisted. "You might have to elude a posse. I know all the trails, even the smallest, most secret ones the mice and voles travel."

Cyrenar glanced at his henchman, who launched a sudden blow at the kender's face from one side. Tangletoe's head impacted his left shoulder and went numb. It took him a moment to clear his mind. Blood dripped from a split lip.

Silence held between them as the mage thought.

"Very well, kender," said Cyrenar gratingly. "You've saved your miserable life for the moment. But if you don't prove of any use, Fhariss here will separate your head from your shoulders permanently." He turned to Fhariss. "Tie him up. I don't want to worry about him pilfering my pockets while I sleep."

"That's not neces—owww!" Tangletoe protested as the big man produced a stout cord and jerked his sore wrists within its coils, then twisted it about his boots. "That hurts!"

"Lie down and keep quiet," Cyrenar ordered, leading the way back to their campsite. Fhariss dragged the kender along behind. "We'll start at first light."

Thistleknot snuggled as best he could into the fragrant bed of prickly pine needles beneath his green cloak, which Fhariss had thoughtfully tossed over him. He was unhappy with his new aches and pains, but the intricate knots intrigued his mind and agile fingers during the long, cool night. The henchman had tied him well, but the kender slipped his bonds well before the leaves of the tallest trees caught the first light of dawn.

"Hey, I thought we were leaving at first light!" Tangletoe hollered, sitting up. "I'm ready to go."

The mage rolled over, targeted the kender with a withering glance, sighed deeply, and pushed himself to his feet. He shivered in the chilly air, pulled his shoulder-length hair behind his ears with a thong, snapped the pine detritus from his cloak, and wrapped the fabric around his narrow shoulders. Cyrenar turned to Fhariss, who was still scratching his head sleepily. "You disappoint me, Fharris. Bring him along, and try not to let him out of your sight. Let's go."

"Oh, here's your rope back." Thistleknot innocently held out the loops. The thug snatched the rope and fixed it about the kender's raw wrists again, eyeing him with suspicion.

"Come on," growled Cyrenar. "I don't want to waste any more time. This way?"

Tangletoe nodded. "For a little while."

The mage stopped, fixing the kender with a threatening look. "If you try to trick me, it will go very hard for you later. Understand?"

For once in his life, Thistleknot only nodded.

They stepped onto the road without breakfast, the humans setting a good pace. The kender found it difficult to keep up, especially when the thug yanked the rope and sent him suddenly careening into trees, thornbushes, or boulders.

* * * * *

Around noon, they came to a halt at the edge of a clearing. Something very undeerlike gleamed in the middle.

It was a full suit of old armor, lovingly repaired and polished. Within it stood a tall, bareheaded young man with a crown of curly brown hair. Pieces of his plate mail clanked softly against one another as he inspected the rings in his coif and buffed its already bright sheen with an oiled rag. His breast-plate prominently displayed a molded rose; his shield, lying among the meadow's early blossoms, bore another. An impressive sword, with a matching dagger, rode his left hip in a battered scabbard. Another dagger, much more ornate, with a ruby gracing its crosspiece, gleamed on the opposite side. Though young, the warrior had a good start on the old-fashioned mustache that declared him a member of the Knights of Solamnia, or scion of a remnant thereof. He leaned against a stout post. That post bore a sign.

" 'Peculiar Artifact,' " Cyrenar read the lettering in amazement. "And there's an arrow pointing down. It's here! This is it!" His forehead crinkled suddenly in a suspicious frown. "What's the best way to approach?"

"Walking right up and asking has always worked for me," said Thistleknot.

"Very well, kender. For once you give sound advice. Let us say I am a traveling scholar searching for legends and knowledge about these artifacts. Fhariss, you're my assistant." He began to remove his black robes, replacing them with a scholar's gown from the cloth bag his henchman carried.

"What am I?" piped up Tangletoe.

"Nothing more than you are, an all-too-obvious kender," Cyrenar snapped. "Keep quiet. You'll live longer."

Cyrenar strode forward, followed by Fhariss and the kender. The mage halted as the tall man leaning on the post turned to him.

"Fair noon." The knight gave the antique greeting as if he used it every day. Brown curls bounced as he nodded pleasantly.

When Thistleknot opened his swollen mouth to answer the knight, Cyrenar hissed, "Don't say a word. I'll do the talking."

Tangletoe clamped his teeth together as Cyrenar turned to the knight. "Good day," the mage said. "I assume you're the guardian of the artifact."

"I am," the knight returned pleasantly. "How may I aid you?"

"I'm a scholar collecting information regarding artifacts," replied the mage. "I've heard you hold one in this very place."

The knight nodded. "And it be one of the more puissant kind, from what I understand and observe. But holding it be an erroneous assumption. Instead, it holds me to duty here."

"What are its properties?"

Thistleknot almost giggled in delight as Cyrenar, wanting very much to appear the wandering scholar, produced a small blank-paged book and a cake of ink and quill in a traveling box. He spat on the ink to moisten it and dipped the end of the quill in the dark stuff, preparing to record pertinent details. Fhariss shot Tangletoe a quelling glance. The kender coughed instead.

"It be a parchment scroll, buried some little way beneath this dust," the knight informed them, pointing downward in immitation of the sign's arrow. "I do not ken to its properties, other than the legend it keeps."

"And what legend is that?" Cyrenar asked.

"That if discovered by the mage with the Name and the Voice, and he be a good mage, that person's powers will double upon pronouncing the words of the scroll. If unearthed by a cruel one, powers increase tenfold after pronouncement. If there be more, I know not."

Tangletoe saw Cyrenar's yellow hands twitch with greed, as if he already held the powerful relic in his hideous fingers. The kender had a difficult time not doing the same himself as a question boiled into his mind.

"I'd like—"

"Quiet!" ordered the mage. He turned again to the knight. "How does the scroll appear? Is it ancient, or more recent?"

"I know not," replied the guardian.

"Exactly what form does it take?" the mage prodded. "Rolled, with beribboned charms? Flat, in some sort of frame?"

"I know not," repeated the knight patiently.

"Who does know? Who's seen it?" Cyrenar asked tersely, losing patience.

"None here." The tall knight shook his head. "Not even the guardian before me admitted to eyeing it."

Standing behind Cyrenar, the kender was in the perfect spot to watch the suddenly bulging veins in the mage's neck subside. He recalled his own question.

"Hey, I'd really like to know if mpff nrqg—" At a gesture from Cyrenar, Fhariss dropped a huge hand over the kender's mouth, obscuring most of Tangletoe's face.

"Are there any records existing of who placed the artifact here?" Cyrenar persisted. "Or what mage laid the spell upon it?"

The knight again regretfully shook his curls. "None of which I am aware."

Cyrenar's green eyes flared. "Then what do you know about it?"

"Did I fail to make myself clear at the outset?" The knight looked chagrined. "If not, I beg your indulgence for having a tongue that often trips itself explaining. After all, my calling is as a warrior, not a wordsmith. Legend has it that the scroll must be unearthed by the right person to become viable. Once read, its powers are spent. No man, nor member of any other race, kens more."

The kender stifled a chuckle at the pure amazement showing on Cyrenar's face.

"Think you," the mage questioned carefully after

a deep breath, "that the artifact is buried in many little pieces?"

"By my sword, no," the knight denied. "That would divide and dissipate its power by the number of remnants. There would be too little for it to achieve beneficent concentration, or so I understand."

"Why are you guarding it?"

The young man straightened. "It is my honor and my duty to ascertain that the right person finds it. And I—" the knight gusted an impressive sigh, which Tangletoe suspected came all the way from his toes "—I am not so much guardian as an explainer, and not a good one, at that. Not once have I drawn steel against an enemy set upon banditry. There have been a few with such intentions, but the artifact be so remote in this place that most resign their determination to find such long before achieving proximity."

"Why do you stay?"

In his turn, the knight stiffened with irritation. "Good Master Scholar, this assignment is my duty and my honor. I will uphold the Oath and the Measure, and the wisdom of Lord Dulthan, who administrates my order, to my last breath." His determined dignity looked most noble on one so young.

Cyrenar bit his lip in concentration, making his beard beneath his mouth bristle. "You say none has seen this artifact. So how did it come to reside here?"

"Oh, certes, Master Scholar. That, at least, is a tale well known to folk about this thorp." The knight's irritation eased, allowing his body to relax a trifle. "'Tis said that a wise cleric called Seroidan had charge of it at the close of the Chaos War. He was beset by a number of opposing factions, all desiring to level the artifact's strength against each other and hence gain precedence over their enemies. Seroidan came from the west and fled into the foothills hereabouts, a region fraught with the tiniest and most twisted of trails, hoping to encourage his pursuers to confusion. During his flight, he contracted a peculiar fever which none, not even himself, could heal. He buried the artifact beneath yon mark a sevenday before he succumbed to the fever's grip and expired. Though many have searched, few have come so far, to the artifact's occult place of repose. Most are wary of its power visiting them wrongly."

"Since I am gathering information on magical artifacts and relics, is it permitted that I stay in this area for a time and glean more details regarding its powers?" asked Cyrenar. "I'll doubtless consult your estimable knowledge again."

"Though I added only a pittance to your own store, little more than hot air. Be thou welcome in the Glade of the Artifact." Smiling pleasantly, the knight returned to examiation of his coif, politely eschewing further inspection of the visitors.

* * * * *

Cyrenar chose a secluded tree beyond earshot of the knight and sat down beneath it. Fhariss creaked onto bent legs nearby, still holding the kender's teather. Tangletoe eased himself onto a soft-looking tuffet of grass. The mage unhooked a skin of wine from his belt, and brought forth bread and cheese from a pouch. Fhariss gnawed a slab of dried meat.

Tangletoe sat quietly, appreciating the delicious scents of the food, which made his stomach roar. He suspected that his silence would drive the mage a little crazy. It did.

"What burning question was it you tried to ask the guardian?" Cyrenar finally muttered after sipping wine and, with a disdainful finger, banishing the droplets that clung to his mustache. He followed the drink with a nibble of brown bread and soft cheese.

"Well, I wouldn't call it a burning question," the

kender replied, wishing for a tankard of ale, with its little bubbles that burst against his upper lip and tickled. "Just the right one."

"And just what question would that be, oh Wise One?"

Thistleknot looked straight at him, all innocence in his brown eyes. "You should have asked about the key."

Cyrenar choked on his wine, spewing its dark beads into his beard. "A key? How did you come up with this illuminating idea?"

"I hear the whole thing's a puzzle." The kender shrugged, then grinned. "I'm really good at knots, locks, and puzzles, you know."

"So . . ." The mage sat back, considering his short companion with a morsel of grudging respect. He stoppered his wine, wrapped the bread and cheese scraps into his pouch, and rose. "Let's try the kender's suggestion." Fhariss, dragging Tangletoe, followed in his footsteps.

They found the knight honing and polishing his sword. "Greetings again," the tall young man hailed as they approached. "I had not thought to see you return so soon."

Cyrenar fished out his little book, ink, and quill. "After mulling over the information you offered previously, I have a few further questions. First, is there anything remarkable about this place that would recommend it as the resting site for an artifact?"

"None of which I know, although you'd best take that up with an historian."

The mage made a note. "Are there rumors or legends as to the size of the artifact?"

"I have heard it be the size of one's palm, but I have also heard it be the size of one's forearm." He smiled. "None surely knows."

Cyrenar nodded, writing. "And—" he paused with what he hoped was deceptive sincerity— "where is the key?"

"Mean you the key to the lock, the key to the fastener, or the key to the maze?"

The mage stared at the knight, flummoxed. He drew a slow breath.

"The key to the fastener, of course," Tangletoe said firmly.

"Shut up, you—"

"Peace, there. Show favor to your small friend, Master Scholar, for he is wise. The key to the fastener be the puzzle itself."

Thistleknot's grin matched the sun. "Thank you! Oh, thank you! May all your children be knights and win big battles!"

Cyrenar turned on Tangletoe, eyes hard with speculation. "This makes sense to you?"

"Sure." He nodded so hard all the braids in his topknot bobbed.

"He who knoweth the key may unearth the scroll," said the knight. With a flourish, he stepped over to the "Peculiar Artifact" sign, yanked it out of the ground, and tossed it aside. "There." He pointed, then stepped back. "The treasure is there."

"I'll keep a good hold on that kender, Fhariss," Cyrenar said, beaming. The mage pointed to the shovel strapped on the henchman's back, and received the rope. Fhariss looked a little sour at having to do all the heavy work.

* * * * *

"Candidly, I be relieved after all this time, and I find my curiosity shivering at the prospect of its sight," the knight sighed, looking over their shoulders. "It will be a boon to apprehend how it appears for certes, instead of retelling mere speculation."

Fhariss found the ground matted with roots of grass and small trees. Grunting mightily, he put his back into each spadeful of dirt. The seventh time he did so, the little iron shovel scraped against stone.

"Find the edges . . . the edges, you dolt!" the mage screamed. "There could be fragile magic warding the artifact!"

Tangletoe couldn't help himself. He assisted by moving loose dirt with his bound hands. A polished black granite box soon lay revealed, longer than it was wide. Fhariss levered it out of the hole.

"Now what?" Cyrenar asked softly, more of himself than anyone else.

"That can I tell you," said the knight. "Say the right word in the right voice over the box, and it will open."

The mage considered a moment, touching the edges of the stone lightly with his ugly fingers. "*Shirak*," he intoned. He recalled having heard another mage say that once.

Nothing.

"Make it more of a question mark," coaxed the kender.

Cyrenar glared at him, then, forcing a polite expression, shifted his gaze to the knight. "Again," said the knight, "your small friend is wise."

"*Shirak?*"

Something clicked. Eyes wide, Cyrenar opened the box.

Within lay a yellowed parchment, rolled and ribboned in red, black, and white. The mage lifted it out reverently and began unfastening the knots.

" 'Be it known to all,' " he read aloud, " 'that whoever finds the Scroll of Tellurius must be a mage of surpassing power and possess a voice unequal in beauty. Otherwise this spell will flare in the wielder's hands. That mage will remain marked forever.' "

Tangletoe, Cyrenar, and the knight held their breath. Nothing happened. Noisily inhaling with relief, the mage read on.

" 'Whosoever finds this scroll and follows the dictums of those of the White Robes, his power shall be doubled immediately and forever.

" 'Whosoever finds this scroll and follows the dictums of those of the Red Robes, good luck shall accompany him immediately and forever.

" 'Whosoever finds this scroll and follows the dictums of those of the Black Robes, his power shall be ten times greater than he has ever known, immediately and forever.

" 'However, whosoever finds this scroll and is in the company of a kender, no matter what the color of his robes, he shall lose his voice forev . . .' "

Cyrenar's mouth worked, but no sound issued forth. His face became mottled red, his eyes wild with anger. After a long moment of startlement, Fharris gave a barking laugh.

"Serves you right," the mage's henchman said, chuckling. He turned to the kender. "Where's the nearest town?"

"Down that trail. It's not far," said Tangletoe. "You can't get lost."

"Thanks." Fhariss started off.

After making a grab for Tangletoe—easily dodged—and strange threatening gestures at the knight—who fingered his sword stoically—Cyrenar ran to catch up. The knight and the kender were left together in the glade next to the hole.

"'Tis over, and we have conquered." The knight turned to Thistleknot. "I am free. You have accomplished a great deed to release me from the onerous task I kept here." He drew the ornate dagger from his belt and presented it ceremoniously to the kender. The knight smiled broadly. "I hail the afternoon we first met and hatched this partnership a ten-day ago. You most certainly have earned your recompense." He picked up the scroll, which Cyrenar had dropped, and finished reading.

" '. . . shall lose his voice forever, and the power of this scroll shall be voided thereafter.' " He frowned, then handed it to Tangletoe. "A most peculiar artifact," he mused.

Tangletoe tucked the scroll into his map case and slipped the dagger into his own belt. He picked up the granite box and tucked it under his arm. "It's been fun, except for the beatings and almost getting killed."

"Certes, you are a most brazen kender. By my troth, I would have waited overlong until one as bored or as devious as you passed by." The knight hefted his shield onto his arm, hooked his coif to his belt, and saluted Thistleknot. "I return to my Lord Dulthan for a new, and I hope more intriguing, assignment. Whither goest thou?"

"I think I'll go—" Thistleknot spun around, then pointed when he stopped—"that way."

"May our paths and our adventures cross again, good Master Kender. Fare thee well." But just to be safe, the knight chose the opposite direction and marched off along a deer trail.

"Good-bye, good-bye!" With a satisfied tune bubbling on his lips, Tangletoe Thistleknot headed into the forest with his new treasure.

A minute later, he reappeared in the glade, his brow uncharacteristically furrowed. "Almost forgot," he muttered, "my very, very best map." He looked down to remind himself in what direction Fharris and Cyrenar had gone and then started off again, just as cheerfully. "Won't they be happy to see me!"

Voices

Kevin T. Stein

"Voices."

"Did you say 'voices'?" Walkagain asked. He and Cleareyes had been sitting on this hill for quite some time, and Walkagain was beginning to feel a curious rumbling in his tummy. This certainly was not the first time Walkagain had heard this sound, but it was definitely the first time he had heard it today.

Cleareyes released his fingers one by one until his hand was open, revealing a purplish pebble he had found. He turned his hand over. The pebble fell to the ground, lost among the countless others. He ran his hand through his reddish brown topknot. He asked, "Do you ever hear . . . voices?"

"Sure! Whenever you speak."

"No, no, no," Cleareyes said. "You know. A voice . . . in your head."

Walkagain's eyes went wide. "You mean you hear a voice inside your head? You are so lucky! What does it say?"

"It says," Cleareyes began, but found he couldn't quite put the voice's words into his own words. "Um . . . well, it mostly talks when I'm about to do something."

"What kind of thing?"

"Oh, you know. The usual things. Running into dark caves, talking to dangerous monsters, pulling the robes of sorcerers . . ."

"Well, what's wrong with all that?" Walkagain asked with rare kender incredulity.

Cleareyes shrugged. "Nothing, I suppose. But this voice . . . lately it's been telling me to stop."

"Do you?"

"Do I what?" Cleareyes asked, confused.

"Stop."

"Would you?"

Walkagain thought about it. "No."

"Me neither," Cleareyes replied. "At least, I don't usually."

Walkagain stared at the ground in thought, digging his toe in an arc into the dirt. When he spoke, he sounded hurt. "How come I've never heard this voice?"

Cleareyes shrugged again. "It started on the way from Kendermore."

"Kendermore!" Walkagain shouted. "Maybe it's the voice of a dead ancestor! I once heard, from my brother Earwig, that sometimes the spirits of our ancestors come back from the dead to tell us some really interesting things!"

Actually Cleareyes thought the voices might be the curse of the great red dragon, Malystryx, who had destroyed Kendermore. He hoped it would go away now that he was in Hylo, his new home. "I don't know what to make of this voice, giving me . . . well, warnings, I guess. Telling me to be— what's that word the humans use?"

"Which word?"

"You know," Cleareyes prompted. "The one that they use. When they're telling us what to do when we're just about to do something brave."

Walkagain slapped his knee. "Oh, that one. 'Caution.' "

"Yeah, that's it!" Cleareyes agreed. "Caution. This voice keeps telling me to be cautious."

"Doesn't sound like a fun voice."

"Oh, it's not," Cleareyes returned with a worried

shake of his head.

"You're making that possum face again," Walkagain said.

Cleareyes arched his back and stretched his arms wide. The warm sun felt good. "Well, possum face or not, I've been thinking about something."

Walkagain brushed some dirt off his silk shirt, then sat down on the ground next to his friend. Whatever was in his pockets rattled loudly. "Let's hear it!"

Cleareyes reached down and picked up a pebble, holding it for his friend to see. "Uh, this is gonna be hard," he began. "I've been thinking about this as we crossed the human lands from Kendermore."

Walkagain nodded encouragingly.

"Now, imagine this pebble represents a person. This person could be anyone, but it's not. It's a hero. It's a legend, like one of the twins, Raistlin or Caramon Majere, or Sturm Brightblade, or Tanis Half-Elven, or—"

"Uncle Tas!" Walkagain cut in with a smile.

"Like Uncle Tas," Cleareyes agreed. "Do you know the difference between a legend and an ordinary person?"

Walkagain thought hard. "One's a legend and one's not?"

"No, no, other than that!"

Walkagain thought harder, but Cleareyes saw his friend was not going to get the answer. He wasn't surprised, since it had taken him some time to come up with the idea himself. He said, "The difference is this: The reason they became legends was because they were part of the fighting among the gods. You couldn't help but become a legend when you're working one way or another for Paladine or Takhisis!"

"Are you trying to say," Walkagain said, slowly forming his thoughts, "that heroes like Caramon and Tanis had no choice?"

"Well, they kind of did and kind of didn't," Cleareyes said. He still wasn't clear in his own thoughts about this particular point. "I've been reading some books I picked up along the way. They're books by these people called philosophers, and they talk about this thing called free will."

"So you're saying you learned something along the way from these books," Walkagain said dubiously.

Cleareyes sighed, running his free hand through his topknot. "What I'm saying is that things aren't the same as they were when these legends lived."

"But we've still got legends!" Walkagain stated emphatically. "I mean, there's still some wizards and healers, and those that can fight."

"But there's more to being a legend than just . . . I don't know, throwing balls of fire or bashing heads. Its got something to do with purpose, I suppose."

Walkagain's dark brown eyes narrowed in concentration, glittering in the fading sunlight. He shook his head slowly from side to side. "So, what were you saying about that pebble, Possum Face?"

Cleareyes ignored his friend's gibe, mostly positive his face wasn't a possum's. "Now you see it," he said, turning his hand over. The pebble fell, lost among the others. "Now you don't."

"It's right there."

"What?"

"Your pebble," Walkagain said, pointing down. "It's right there."

"All I'm saying is that with the gods gone, the age of legends is over. Now everyone is equal, everyone is equally lost in the crowd."

"Yeah, but what about those that can fight?"

Cleareyes waved a dismissive hand. "There's always those that can fight, or build, or talk, or heal. . . ." He let his words drift off, giving himself time to take in the beautiful landscape of his new home. He ran both hands through his long hair slowly.

Walkagain picked up the pebble his friend had dropped and looked at it very closely. "I think that all this you're talking about has to do with that voice in your head. It's certainly one of the weirdest things I've ever heard."

Cleareyes took the pebble from his friend's outstretched hand. Holding it up, he said, "You want to know what this pebble means? It means one person can no longer change the world. It means you really can't rise above your problems. It means . . . all that was the stuff of legends."

"That's so . . . I don't know . . . heavy," Walkagain said, searching for words. After a moment, he snatched the pebble back from Cleareyes, dropping it with great drama into his top vest pocket, above his heart. "It's a swell pebble, anyway."

Cleareyes pulled another possum face.

"Are you hearing the voices now?"

Cleareyes listened carefully. Nothing but birds, and leaves rustling. "Nope."

The sun burnished the sky dark orange, deepening the shadows of the oddly shaped hills. A flying citadel had crashed into the mountain, and the kender aboard it had founded the nation of Hylo just after the Second Dragon War. The citadel peeked out from the treetops, dotting the mountain. Cleareyes stared at the mountains, imagining he could see the vague outline of a castle with its towers and turrets.

An idea slowly rose in his thoughts, but suddenly vanished when he realized they were late. "We'll miss our dinner with Belladonna!"

Cleareyes turned to his friend, slapping dirt and dust off Walkagain's bright, well-made clothes. Walkagain reached up and tweaked his friend's nose.

"You know what Uncle Tas always said about books?" Walkagain asked.

"Actually, no."

"Learning never taught him anything, and books, they were the worst."

Cleareyes laughed, pushing Walkagain toward their destination.

* * * * *

By the light of a comfortable fire, Belladonna had laid out a fine picnic for Cleareyes and Walkagain not far from the crashed citadel. The idea brought about by the sight of the castle remained at the far edge of Cleareyes' thoughts. The sight of Belladonna dressed in deep purple silk, short black boots that reflected the firelight, and a circlet of gold in her auburn top-knot did not help his thinking either. Cleareyes and the woman who now led the kender of Hylo had become quite enamored with each other on the long road from Kendermore. Other than his physical attraction for her, Cleareyes admired and respected her strength of character, strength of purpose. By her own hand, Belladonna had become the ruler of all the kender. Now she had plans for the kender and would never allow them to come to harm again. Cleareyes was sure she would personally fight anything on Krynn to keep her people safe from harm.

"Biscuits!" Walkagain cried out, dropping his hoopak onto the yellow blanket, following quickly after. "My favorite," he added as he spread honey with a silver knife from a small matching server.

"Hi, Billee," Cleareyes whispered, using Belladonna's true first name. He stole a kiss from her cheek, and she smiled briefly. Their burgeoning relationship was not something other kender suspected. They hoped.

When they had met, Belladonna had told Cleareyes her personal life must be secondary to the campaign she desired to wage against the dragon overlords. He understood that for her to appear dedicated to her cause, especially to the Solamnic Knights who lived on Ergoth and the occasional emissary from the Knights of Takhisis, it was best if she be seen as independent and strong in all areas of life. He was more than willing to endure this inconvenience for this woman and the cause they shared.

Walkagain quickly downed the first biscuit and set about to prepare another. "You know, it looks like this knife goes with this little jar," he said, indicating the silver server filled with honey.

"Yes?" Belladonna asked.

Shrugging, Walkagain answered, "Well, it just seeems odd, is all. Don't usually have much that matches."

"It's for occasional guests," she replied. Cleareyes saw Belladonna shift her shoulders slightly. He glanced at her in concern, thinking of the scars made by the fiery breath of Malys the Red. Once he had accidentally seen the extent of her wounds while she was swimming in what she thought was privacy; burns covered the backside of her entire body, from neck to ankle.

"Come on, let's eat!" Cleareyes said with a gesture, shaking his head to clear away the memory.

Belladonna smoothed out the blanket and sat opposite Walkagain, taking a napkin, one that matched the blanket, from a pile in the center. Cleareyes stared back at the mountains hidden by darkness. Krynn's new red star shone directly above where the citadel lay. It was supposed to be a symbol of hope.

He hoped he could get that stupid voice to shut up.

Something slippery darted between Cleareyes' legs and over his left boot. He shrieked in surprise and jumped back, hand on his new dagger.

"There you are!" Belladonna said with a wide smile, holding out her arms. A small cat with fur the silver of new frost jumped into her arms and bumped his nose into her face.

Cleareyes stuffed his hands into his pockets, watching disconsolately as the cat continued to bump his nose into Belladonna's face, sleek body running between her cradling arms.

"Truesilver! Where have you been?" Belladonna scolded, shaking the cat gently.

The cat answered by turning and whipping his thin tail into the side of her head, staring levelly, directly, and apparently jealously at Cleareyes. There was at least one creature who knew of his secret relationship with the kender leader. Fortunately, he was sure the cat wouldn't tell anyone.

"Hey, Truesilver!" Walkagain mumbled around a biscuit. He reached out to pet the cat, but Truesilver jumped down out of Walkagain's reach, prowling curiously around the food, keeping a jealous watch on Cleareyes.

Walkagain swallowed loudly, reaching for some dried sweetfruit. "You never told me where you found such a wonderful cat. Do you suppose he's magic?"

Belladonna also reached for a piece of fruit. Truesilver arched his back to be petted as her hand passed nearby, arched it higher when she ran her hand over his perfect fur. "Magic?" Belladonna returned. "Do you really think it is possible?"

Digging a little farther into his pocket, Cleareyes pulled out a small cloth ball filled with catnip, having made the ball for exactly such an opportunity. He tossed the ball onto the blanket. Truesilver immediately forgot any affection he had for Belladonna and dived after the ball, knocking it farther away. The ball bounced into the silver jar containing the honey, and Truesilver followed after it, digging his nose deep into the honey. He rolled backward in surprise and snuffled as he tried to clear the sticky goo from his nose, pushing his face into the blanket to clean his whiskers.

"Magic?" Cleareyes said, hoping his face shone with innocence. "Well, anything is possible."

The Knights of Takhisis were right: Revenge was sweet.

Despite their rivalry, Cleareyes knew how much

Truesilver meant to Belladonna. The cat had appeared
as if by magic on the road to Hylo, nothing underfoot
one moment, a silver cat there the next. Sometimes it
seemed only the cat could bring a smile back to
Belladonna's face. For that, he liked the cat very
much. Otherwise, Truesilver had made his jealous
feelings very clear, and the feeling was mutual. He
didn't place much hope on their being friends.
Cleareyes went back to staring at the fallen citadel
and the red star.

Belladonna asked, "What are you thinking
about?"

Cleareyes blinked. That idea he had was still too
far away for him to grasp. "I'm not sure," he
responded, looking to face her. "Something about . . .
revenge."

"Re-what?" Walkagain asked, peering up from his
attempt to pet Truesilver again. "I didn't hear you."

"Just as well," Cleareyes muttered to himself. He
took his hands out of his pockets.

"Why don't you sit down and have something to
eat?" Belladonna asked, gesturing at the blanket.

Cleareyes ran a hand through his topknot, unsure
what he wanted. "How have negotiations been with
the knights?"

"The good ones or the bad ones?"

"The bad ones," he answered, glancing at
Walkagain, who went back to picking at the fruit
bowls.

Belladonna reached for Truesilver. The cat backed
away, still cleaning his face. With a sigh, Belladonna
said, "They want to use kender in their plans. They
say they have connections with other knights in
Kendermore. They're supposed to be keeping some
kind of forward post."

"Forward post," Cleareyes offered. He had heard
this term among the knights of both sides. It had
something to do with leaving men in a dangerous
place to gather information or give a warning.

"Speaking of which, any word from those left behind?"

Walkagain fired a fruit pit into the darkness from his hoopak. "Kronn Thistleknot? The hero?"

"No word from him," Belladonna said. With a very human frown, she added, "It's just as well, I suppose. We aren't ready to go into another battle . . . yet. I wonder why there seem to be so many goblins around. Just last week one of our . . . Cleareyes, would you please sit!"

"No, I think I'll—"

"Yeah, sit!" Walkagain swung his hoopak lightly into the back of Cleareye's right leg. With a yell, Cleareyes jerked his leg, accidentally kicking Truesilver in the ribs. The cat screeched and leapt into Belladonna's arms. Truesilver hissed loudly, but not at Cleareyes.

"Truesilver!" Belladonna cried out. Cleareyes turned back in time to see the cat dash off in the direction opposite the bushes.

"Oops," Walkagain said.

"I'll get him," Cleareyes said.

"No, he'll come back," Belladonna replied, still frowning. "He always does."

Walkagain leapt to his feet, hoopak in hand. "I'll help!"

Cleareyes grabbed his friend by the sleeve and shoved him forward in the direction of the woods and the darkness. He muttered, "You bet you will."

Night closed around them very quickly. The voice spoke. *Slow down, Cleareyes. Think about what you're doing. Be cautious.* Cleareyes realized there could be anything in the woods, from huge animals to . . . He told himself when he got back, he would definitely begin training in the use of dangerous human weapons.

But before that, he would turn Belladonna's frown back into a smile if it took all night.

* * * * *

Cleareyes tensed when he thought he saw something silver dart among the bushes, but it was just a
trick of his eyes. The voice kept nagging at him.

"Will you shut up, already?"

"I didn't say anything," Walkagain said.

"Not you!"

"The voice again?"

"Yes, the voice ag— What's that sound?"
Cleareyes asked. He was sure he heard some kind of
reedy, piping sound. It seemed to be coming from
everywhere.

The sound stopped as Walkagain answered. "It's
me! I'm whistling."

Cleareyes winced at the volume. "Walk, don't you
think you'll frighten the cat?" he whispered, hoping
his friend would catch on.

He didn't. "Me? Frighten a cat? Not with this
happy tune!"

Cleareyes ran a hand through his topknot and
looked up. The new red star was hidden by the treetops as the two kender did their best to track that
darn cat. Fortunately the new moon, which had no
other name among the Kendermore survivors
than "New Moon," was full and had risen above the
mountains, lighting the forest with irregular patches
of pale white. Cleareyes guessed they had been out
looking for two hours. He hoped Belladonna had not
decided to wait for them all night, done the smart
thing, gone home.

"Do you think we're very far from Hylo?"
Walkagain asked loudly.

"I don't know. Are we lost?"

"I don't know," Walkagain answered, eyes wide.
"We might be, but we couldn't be that lost, considering we're on an island and if we kept walking in one
direction, we'd reach the water or the mountains, at
the very least, and—"

Cleareyes turned, dagger drawn, as something

large—larger than a cat, certainly—rustled the brush about twenty feet away. He strained his eyes, but he couldn't make anything out. "Walk," he said, whispering more softly, "I don't think we're alone."

"Of course not," Walkagain replied, also whispering. "We're with each other."

A twig cracked behind the two kender, who both turned, weapons ready. A "something," different from the one they had just heard, dashed out of the brush, between their legs, and toward the mountains.

"Truesilver!" Walkagain cried out, dropping his hoopak as he leapt after the cat.

"Blunga!" a number of low, growling voices yelled. Six black shapes, about the size of the kender but squat and lumbering, ran out of the woods. They bowled Cleareyes over and trampled Walkagain into the ground.

"Ugh!" Walkagain muttered, spitting out dirt. He propped himself up on his elbows, brightening. "Hey! that's the first time I've ever been trampled! I don't think I like it much."

Helping his friend up from the ground, Cleareyes kept a sharp eye on the place in the woods where the intruders had run after Truesilver. His dagger was still out. He strained his ears and heard the sound of feet fading into the forest.

The moment Walkagain was on his feet, he moved after the tramplers. "Let's get them!"

Not so fast! the voice said. Cleareyes pulled Walkagain back with one hand. "Wait!"

Cleareyes let his friend go. Walkagain stood, waiting for his friend to move. "What's the matter?"

"Nothing," Cleareyes lied. "I just want to know what we're chasing."

Bending down, he looked at the tracks made by the intruders. There were six of them, all right, and they were wearing boots. "Do you think they're—"

"Goblins? I'd recognize their foul stench anywhere," Walkagain interrupted, rubbing his nose with a dirty hand, darkening his face further.

The two kender heard a loud animal yowl in the distance. Definitely a cat.

"What in the world do they want with Truesilver?" Walkagain asked.

"I don't know, but we'd better find out quick!"

* * * * *

As remarkably skilled as the goblins were at tracking the cat, they weren't very good at covering their own tracks. The kender easily followed the small party of goblins, finally climbing a tall tree and watching from above.

There were six goblins, all dressed in black. One of the goblins, dressed in black but also sprouting fur and feathers and a few twigs from his clothes, was obviously the leader. Their ugly faces were covered by dark hoods with eyeholes.

"What's that one got around his neck?" Walkagain asked, pointing. Glad his friend finally learned to keep his voice to a whisper, Cleareyes looked closely at the leader.

"Looks like a key."

"Wonder if he'd like to trade it for something," Walkagain said.

The leader held his hands up to the sky, turning around slowly and mumbling a goblin chant. Truesilver yowled again, but his screech was muffled. Cleareyes saw the goblins had stuffed the cat into a heavy black sack, from which Truesilver tried unsuccessfully to claw his way out.

"Let's take them!" Walkagain said, putting a piece of fruit he took from his pocket into the hoopak's sling.

Take them all? the voice mocked. *I don't think so.*

"That would be a bad idea," Cleareyes said, forcing the hoopak down with a hand. "We could never take all of them at once."

"Pooh! I myself could take them all at once. I

merely invited you along to be polite."

"Walk!" Cleareyes hissed. "There are too many of
. . ." He let his words trail off.

The goblin leader stopped chanting and picked up
the bag holding the struggling Truesilver, hefting it
over his shoulder and signaling to the others. They
all grunted and nodded. The leader pointed to one of
the goblins in particular, who nodded, grunted, then
sat down hard. He began drawing a clumsy picture
of a dragon in the dirt with a stick. The goblins and
their leader trudged off, mumbling some chant,
carrying the bag with Truesilver in it.

"Now," Cleareyes said.

Walkagain's hoopak snapped loudly, and the fruit
was launched with great force and accuracy. The
goblin's head snapped to the side; he rubbed it, then
fell over.

"All right!" Walkagain hollered, dropping to the
ground. Cleareyes took a little longer climbing
down. The two kender quickly bound the goblin's
hands and feet with rope from Walkagain's pocket,
propping him against the tree.

"How's your goblin?" Cleareyes asked his friend.

"I don't have a goblin," Walkagain answered with
a grin. "Just kidding! I speak it a little."

"Me, too."

The goblin shook its head and tried to move. It
dazedly looked around, finally fixed on the two
kender. The goblin's little red eyes widened, then
narrowed.

"He or she?" Walkagain asked.

Cleareyes shrugged.

The goblin fell over on his side as he struggled
with the bonds. Realizing there was no escape, he
wiggled his body toward the dirt drawing of the
dragon. Walkagain planted his hoopak in the way of
the goblin's progress. The goblin whimpered.

"Hey," Walkagain said, leaning on his hoopak,
preventing the goblin's advance. "Aren't all you

goblins supposed to be, you know, bloodthirsty little doorknobs?"

"Seems like all this one wants to do is draw his dragon. Why don't we let him?"

Walkagain pulled the hoopak up and stepped aside. The goblin let out a squeal of delight and finished drawing the dragon with his toes. He fell over on his side again, as if very tired.

"Uh," Cleareyes began, pulling the spent goblin around to face him. He paused, then said to Walkagain, "What should I ask him?"

"Ask him about Truesilver!"

"Good idea. Okay, goblin, what do you think you're doing with our cat?" Cleareyes ended in his best goblin.

"Ur?" the goblin replied.

"I think you may have asked him about his underwear," Walkagain said.

Cleareyes ignored his friend and pointed his finger in the goblin's face. "You speakee our language?"

Nodding, the goblin grunted, "Me speakee better than you."

"What do you want with our cat?" Cleareyes said, possum-faced again.

The goblin laughed. "Not your cat. Is magic cat. We hear you strong. We belong to ace number one ancient goblin cat-tracker brotherhood!"

"What are you talking about?" Walkagain asked the goblin, fascinated.

"Is magic cat! Only one like it," the goblin reiterated loudly through the hood covering his face. "Goblin shaman will sacrifice cat in high mountain dropped from sky, then dragons die!"

Cleareyes and Walkagain stared at each other a moment, then burst out laughing.

Agitated, he goblin said, "Is truth! Is ancient goblin legend. Shaman sacrifice magic cat to goblin god with special knife, all dragons die. Especially new big ones. This best night to do it, too."

Cleareyes pulled Walkagain aside, hand on his chin. "This . . . guy thinks Truesilver is some kind of magic cat, and their shaman is going to sacrifice Truesilver on the crashed flying citadel, and this will kill all the evil dragons?"

"Seems to be the long and short of it."

Walkagain's face took on a contemplative expression as he rubbed his hand over his smooth chin. "I wouldn't mind seeing that."

"Me neither," Cleareyes said. "But I can't let that goblin shaman kill Truesilver. It would break Belladonna's heart. Let's go."

"What about him?" Walkagain indicated the bound goblin with his hoopak.

Cleareyes stared at the goblin, then cut the rope around the goblin's feet. The goblin managed to stand after a short struggle, facing the two kender.

"Mercy," the goblin said.

Cleareyes shrugged. "Okay." He reached for the goblin's hood, turned it all the way around so the eyeholes faced backward.

"Blind! Me blind!" the goblin howled as the two kender headed off into the night.

* * * * *

Cleareyes and Walkagain easily followed the main body of goblins up the side of the mountain. Both the new moon and the red star had fallen below the level of the peaks, and though the area was only lit by starlight, the noise of the goblin chanting and the yowl of Truesilver were helpful to point the way.

Instead of taking a direct route, as Walkagain had thought best, the two went another way, decided by Cleareyes, or rather, by the voice in Cleareyes' head. They circled around the goblins, a little higher up the slope. Every once in a while, Cleareyes thought he saw something that looked like the stones of a castle wall, but he couldn't be sure.

A fire slowly grew in the darkness from where

Truesilver continued to screech. Walkagain pointed. "I hope they're going to eat now. I'm getting hungry."

"More like they're getting ready for their sacrifice," Cleareyes answered. He peered through the brush toward the fire. Cleareyes saw that the only goblin by the fire was the shaman, the one with all the twigs and fur sticking out of his clothes. The one with Truesilver in the bag. It seemed all the other goblins were drawing in the dirt, probably more bad pictures of dragons. "What'll we do?"

"Let's run and get him!"

"That wouldn't be a good idea," Cleareyes said, cutting off the voice before it could speak. He was definitely getting annoyed with its constant intrusions.

"What do you think, then?"

Cleareyes gauged the situation. The other goblins formed a rough circle around the shaman leader. If they could take out two of them, they could grab Truesilver and run through the hole in the circle. That seemed to be a good plan, and the voice had nothing more to say on the matter. He described his plan to Walkagain, and the two went off.

They approached the closest unsuspecting goblin. Before they reached him, however, they realized that the next closest goblin was about fifty feet away, with a clear line of sight to them. He pointed this out to Walkagain. They scrunched lower to the ground and inched forward.

"Wait!" Cleareyes hissed.

"Why?"

"This won't be much of a surprise attack if there's no actual surprise involved," Cleareyes answered. "We've got to distract him first, bring him out to us."

Walkagain thought a moment. "What about the famous Kender Stone Trick?"

"That thing where you throw a stone and expect someone to go check out the noise?"

Cleareyes returned. "No one's that stupid."

"These are goblins we're talking about."

"Hmm. Good point."

Cleareyes picked up a good-sized stone and was about to throw it when he realized he didn't know in which direction he ought to throw it. He turned to Walkagain in confusion. His companion seemed to understand the problem.

"Well, what's that stupid voice say, Possum Face?"

"Seems like it's only there when I don't need it," Cleareyes answered after listening a moment. "And stop calling me that!" Cleareyes raised his arm and made a quick decision. He threw the rock at his feet, smashing some leaves and twigs.

The goblin didn't move.

"Maybe they can't hear through those hoods," Walkagain offered. He leaned against his hoopak, obviously bored.

Cleareyes picked up the stone and threw it again, and again. On the fifth try, the goblin raised his head from his work. Cleareyes sighed with relief. He had run out of leaves and twigs within immediate throwing reach. The two kender quickly separated, hiding behind some trees.

The goblin didn't think to be cautious, walking boldly from his work, out of the firelight's reach and out of sight of the other. To Cleareyes' amazement, the goblin actually found the stone. He held it up to his ear and shook it. Walkagain's hoopak brained the goblin, sending him sprawling. Cleareyes caught their unconscious victim and silently lowered him to the ground. The voice seemed to like the way things were going, as it was apparently holding its tongue. Or whatever voices inside heads had.

"Now the other one," Cleareyes said, pointing. "Before he notices this one is gone." Walkagain took the stone from the goblin's hand. Cleareyes could see the gears in his friend's mind turning. He said, "You're not thinking of using the Stone Trick again, are you?"

Walkagain shrugged. "Why not? It worked the first time."

Rolling his eyes, Cleareyes pushed his friend forward, careful to keep to the shadows. No voice and no trouble gave him some confidence this second Stone Trick would also work. The two kender took up position behind a nearby pair of trees and tried again.

"My arm's getting tired!" Walkagain complained after the tenth time.

The voice started whispering, but Cleareyes wouldn't let himself hear it. To Walkagain, he asked, "Maybe we should try something else."

"Like what?" his friend answered, glaring at the stone. He seemed to be having a silent discussion with it.

Cleareyes jabbed his friend in the ribs with an elbow. "Like, make a sound like a cat."

"Oh. I get it."

"So go ahead, try it."

"This is your idea. You make a cat sound."

"Me?" Cleareyes replied. "You'd be much better at it than me."

Walkagain wagged his finger. "But this is your plan. You do it."

Cleareyes stood silently for a moment. He didn't want to make the cat sound because the voice kept saying, *If you fail, they'll discover you and you might die*, and he didn't want to think about that. He ran a hand through his topknot and took a deep breath.

"Uh, meow," he said, not too convincingly.

The goblin's hearing was apparently geared to all things catty. He immediately stopped his scribbling and stood straight, peering into the woods.

"Meow," Cleareyes said again, under the encouraging gestures of Walkagain. The goblin glanced over at the shaman, then ahead into the woods. He slowly stalked forward, careful not to step on his dragon picture.

"Meow!" Cleareyes reiterated, more loudly this time. Unfortunately Truesilver must have heard and picked that moment to yowl a reply. The goblin spun toward the sound of the real cat, then back toward the darkness in confusion.

Oops, said the voice.

Before Cleareyes could tell the other kender to do something, Walkagain fired a stone from his hoopak, knocking the goblin flat. Cleareyes' heart raced.

"Now what?" Walkagain asked, triumphant.

Cleareyes pointed toward the goblin shaman. "Quick!"

The kender sprinted from their hiding place, covering the distance easily and with little noise. The shaman was too busy holding the old key up in the air, mumbling goblin under his breath in some part of the ritual of sacrifice, to notice the intruders until they had almost reached him. Cleareyes grabbed the sack holding Truesilver, who howled and howled, and Walkagain cracked the goblin shaman over the head with his hoopak. The shaman pitched forward toward the fire. Walkagain shoved the goblin to the side and snatched the key from the air before it hit the ground.

"Up!" Cleareyes said, pointing up toward an area that looked like a cave as he struggled to keep Truesilver from clawing him through the bag.

The two scrabbled upward to hide. Peering down toward the firelight, they saw the goblin shaman slowly stir from the ground, jump to his feet, and shout for the other goblins. The goblins appeared, and the shaman pointed frantically, away from the cave. They ran off, and the area was quiet again.

"What would Uncle Tas say about that?" Cleareyes said, slapping Walkagain on the shoulder. Walkagain grinned.

"Hey!" Walkagain said. "You don't look so much like a possum anymore!"

Truesilver moaned from the sack, interrupting

Cleareyes' response. He was careful to turn the sack away from himself as he held it open. Truesilver shot out faster than an arrow into the darkness.

"No, wait!" Cleareyes shouted, chasing after the cat.

He stopped himself from pitching over the ledge and landing twenty feet below. He stared at the interior of the citadel, poorly lit from cave-type windows like the one he and Walkagain had entered. Truesilver waited patiently at the edge, staring downward.

"Would you look at that?" Walkagain shouted in Cleareyes' ear.

"Let me see that key," Cleareyes said, clutching a hand to his ear. Walkagain handed over the key. Cleareyes looked at it carefully. It was a long silver key, with some kind of engravings on it, probably what magicians call runes. "I bet this key unlocks something in this castle!"

"Duh."

Cleareyes snatched the key from his friend's quick grasp. "But we'll have to wait. First we've got to take Truesilver back to Belladonna."

At the mention of his name, Truesilver bounded up into Cleareyes' arms, climbing onto the kender's shoulders, continuing to stare down into the citadel with unblinking silver eyes.

"Later?"

"Maybe."

Cat on his shoulder, key in hand, Cleareyes led Walkagain back out to the mountainside. He laughed softly as they reached the outside again.

"What's so funny?" Walkagain asked, a little dejected that they were not going to investigate the keep. And wondering how he was going to get his key back.

"Truesilver," Cleareyes said, chuckling. "If those goblins were right, all we'd have to do to save the world is to sacrifice him tonight."

Walkagain scratched his head. "It would break Belladonna's heart."

Cleareyes laughed loudly. "That's not the point! Truesilver isn't magic."

"You said he might be," said Walkagain, a little resentfully. "I was just wondering."

The cat on his shoulder meowed pleasantly. Cleareyes turned to face the crashed citadel, holding his arms wide, key in hand. "I only said it was possible," Cleareyes said, still laughing.

The voice said nothing.

Turning and poking Walkagain, the kender raced down the mountainside. Walkagain followed on his heels, also laughing and yelling, his eyes fixed on the key and the cat. Just wondering.

The Notorious Booke of Starres

Nick O'Donohoe

I

Above the rooftops and city heat, the observatory tower caught the cool breezes. Arranged near the south window, within easy reach, were a bronze astrolabe, a sextant, a quadrant and plumb line, a golden armillary sphere with twelve ingeniously interlocking circles to show the motions of major heavenly bodies, and a drafting table with pens, silver compasses and calipers, metal curves and rulers. A notched slit in the eastern wall cast a beam that marked the position of sunrise on a timeworn calendar painted around the curve of the west wall.

From the center of the domed roof was suspended a pendulum. The pendulum swung in arcs over a circle on the floor. The circle, divided by arcs into eight segments, told the time of day. Metal tracks in the floor allowed for easy movement of the drafting table and other equipment to the north window.

Once it had been neat, orderly. Now the tracks were covered by stacks of scrolls. Someone had drawn faces inside the sunburst marks on the west wall. The dragonlance that served as axis for the armillary had an apple core speared on it. The window shutters were closed against the noonday heat, but the dust suggested that no one had opened them for months.

A lanky cleric, clutching a fistful of pens, teetered on the stool in front of the drafting table. Leaning backward precariously, one eye shut tight , the other squinting, he flipped the pens one at a time toward an ale stein in a corner of the room. After a particularly artful triple flip, he grunted happily and dashed off ten lines of prose on a piece of foolscap pinned over an unused chart of the heavens. The chart was nearly as stained as the astronomer's fingers.

His assistant, who had been sketching in a large leather-bound journal, looked up. "What is it, Daev?" The feather tip of his quill spun and twitched.

"The last of the book, that's all," Daev replied modestly. "The prologue."

"But don't prologues come first? You wrote the first part last?"

"Of course. It's the only part readers truly care about. Listen, Kael." Daev began reciting, imperiling his balance with every wave of his arm.

"Here, where the wicked gold of sunrise bribes
The wanton night away, and so inscribes
A pen-point fixative for wayward stars
And where, unprophesied, from heaven's cars,
Three moons bless pregnant vessels as they ride,
Sails swollen, laboring on the triple tide,
And where the lonely watchman darkly sees
Comets and planets and catastrophes,

"Let my small book bring peace from troubled skies:
Tides high for travel, light for planting time,
For lovers, moonlight, and for harvest, rime
But not too soon. Grant that my star-blind eyes
See nothing in the night but friendly fires,
And help the sky fix fast our own desires."

Kael blinked, repeated, "The sky fixed fast . . . "

"Fix fast," Daev corrected. "Mustn't pretend the stars don't move."

"Well, whatever. It's wonderful." Kael gazed at him admiringly. "And you can just think that stuff up? Did that just pop into your head this minute?"

"It is pretty good," Daev said, pleased. "I've been thinking about it since I woke up. Since the first rays of pious dawn blessed the tower top—"

"Don't be so modest," Kael protested. "I know you couldn't have been thinking that long. You didn't get up till midmorning. Will the book really do everything you promised?"

"Absolutely. Lovers only promise the moons. I've given the moons and the stars." Daev spun on his stool, swinging his arms. "And if the book succeeds . . ." He shut his eyes blissfully. "Imagine the acclaim! The banquets and the patronage from admiring men and women!"

Kael said shyly, "I admire you." Ignoring Daev's embarrassed cough, Kael added, "And then there's the learning itself."

"Of course, of course. Lore without learning is a sad thing, like unsalted sweat." But Daev was barely listening. "You know, I have always dreamed of being a writer."

Kael's wispy beard trembled. "But you are a writer. You should be writing . . . oh, I don't know. Stories, songs for people . . . maybe a play."

"I've written two plays," Daev said offhandedly. *"The Tragedy of Sturm* and a comedy called *The Kender Kiss*." He rummaged beneath the table, drew forth a sheaf of papers, which he handed to Kael.

Kael read them, then looked up. "Daev, why aren't you writing for a living? I mean for your whole life, not just as a cleric."

Daev sighed. Kael's admiration was sincere but naive. "A writer's life is hard. Plus," he said, more somberly, "it's a very good time to be out of the street and up in a tower."

Kael nodded vigorously, and Daev seemed to hear his own head ring in rhythm; he had been out late last night. Daev realized belatedly that the ringing was not inside his head but outside. The clang of the summons bell mounted above their door. Kael slid *The Tragedy of Sturm* and *The Kender Kiss* inside the journal and sat on it protectively.

Daev opened the door and peered down the spiral stairs. The time-battered bronze bell swung to and fro rhythmically.

Kael said nervously, "Does someone want us?"

Daev gave his assistant's shoulder a soothing pat. He was fond of Kael, and Kael, Daev had noticed more and more, was devoted to him.

"He wants us, we want lunch. Balanced desires, and with luck, a balanced meal. Come on."

They were puffing when they reached the bottom of the staircase.

Daev inclined his head reverently. "Greetings, Most High Tiranus. You do us honor."

"I didn't intend to," the old man snapped. "You should exercise more, Daev. The stairs bother you."

"Better us than you, venerable one. How is your health?" Daev asked lightly. "Does your heart trouble you?"

Tiranus frowned. "You don't care about my health. And as you full well know, my heart will never trouble me."

Daev had nothing to say. It was true.

The old man motioned with one hand; he held his staff in the other. "Come dine with me."

As they stepped outside, Tiranus looked at the sky. "By the way, your book—"

"*The Notorious Booke of Starres*," Daev interrupted. "Nice title, isn't it?"

Tiranus snorted. "It's a title, not a book. Is the book finished?"

"As of this morning, Most High. We will require a team of scribes to copy it before three days are out."

"Does that leave time for you to make new observations?"

"Why would I do that?" Daev began, then caught himself. "Clerics and mages have measured the heavens for centuries, and they've calculated the movements of the moons and of the stars for nearly as long. These are the fruits of our temple's best." He finished with an air of virtue, "It would be disrespectful not to harvest them."

Tiranus sighed loudly. "Meaning you haven't done a lick of work yourself. Another kender-scripted book."

Daev, stung, said, "I prefer to call it well researched. And why should I not rely on the stargazers who came before me?" He struck a pose he had rehearsed for the dying Sturm's lines. "We study the stars so that they may tell us of ourselves. Who knows but that the shape of the heavens might shape our days, our destinies, our heaven-polished world?"

"Ah. Shape." Tiranus thudded the flagstone walkway with his staff. "We will talk more of the shape of heaven." He pointed to the building ahead. "And of the refectory."

Daev inclined his head. "Where, I imagine, we shall dine in contemplation."

Tiranus grimaced. "Not today. My business with you is political; we will go to the Dragon's Thirst."

Kael looked happy, Daev wary.

* * * * *

The tavern was full, the patrons ranging from merchants to gamblers and itinerant singers. A number of the latter waved as they came in. Daev pretended not to notice and halted Kael before he could wave back.

People were standing, though there were several

empty tables near the hearth. Daev saw immediately why the tables were empty; two huge men in helmets and cloaks sat at the best table before the fire. They had their backs to the others, and the only person who came near them was the barmaid, carrying soup and wine.

The barkeep smiled genially at Daev. "Welcome, cleric. The usual?"

"How kind of you to remember, since it's been so long," Daev said, emphasizing the last part of the sentence. "Yes, I'll take a glass of barley water."

The barkeep looked surprised, then gestured to the barmaid, who glided over to their table. She set a glass of barley-flavored water in front of Daev and said in honey-sweet tones, "Welcome, cleric."

Kael looked instantly jealous and resentful. Daev felt as awkward about that as he did about the barmaid's attentions. He glanced sidelong at his superior to see if Tiranus had noticed.

"Soup for three," Tiranus said to the barmaid.

"For four," a dry voice corrected. "And please don't ask if I have money this time; I'm sure one of us does." A wiry dark-haired man with a trim beard sat down in the fourth chair. "You'd think in this company she could show a little faith. Hello, Daev." The dark-haired man smiled at Kael, who smiled back shyly.

"Who is this person?" Tiranus glared at the newcomer.

"I never—" Daev began.

Tiranus glowered. "Don't insult my intelligence."

Daev gave up. "Most High Tiranus, this is the poet—" he glared "—the sarcastic, satiric, annoying poet Hannyl. And a good friend. Hannyl, this is the revered Most High Cleric."

Hannyl stood and bowed. "In the absence of reverence, I hope you will accept my courtesy."

"Thank you. Be seated. Do not interrupt me overmuch, and—" the High Cleric hesitated, then added quietly, "if you will take some advice, moderate your speech a little."

"I wouldn't be much of a poet if I did."

Daev snorted. "You don't, and you're still not much of a poet."

"If you don't mind," Tiranus said acidly, "I did not bring you here to fight about literature." He added, before Hannyl could break in, "And I'm paying for the soup."

The soup, a thin broth, came. Kael and Daev said a quick prayer; Hannyl watched amusedly but waited to eat. Tiranus, leaving his own meal untouched, said to Daev, "This is what I wanted to discuss with you. The shape of the world has long been debated."

Daev saw where this was leading and attempted to head it off. He shrugged. "Who can truly know, Most High? The shape of the world is too modestly cloaked in the folds of heaven—"

Tiranus went on as though Daev hadn't spoken. "Some, namely those of us who worship Paladine, say that Krynn is in the shape of a disk, the Shield of Paladine. Those who serve the Dark Lady say the world is in the shape of a bowl, echoing the bowl of the sky; they divide into those who think that the bowl is inverted and we live at the top and those who think the bowl is right side up and we live at the bottom. Do you address this in your book?"

Daev looked cautiously at Kael, who nodded at him while frowning at the barmaid. "Of course," Daev said self-righteously.

"Good." Tiranus nodded approval. "You know, when I was new to these studies, the refectory that we passed on the way here was just being built."

Daev nodded, thinking to himself, Gods, this man is a teetering, cobweb-smeared relic. The "new" refectory was more than sixty years old, its roof in need of patching.

"At that time, the merchant who owned the palace next to us claimed that we were building on his land," Tiranus continued.

Hannyl sipped his wine. "The merchant lost the dispute, I assume."

Tiranus ignored him. "Our High Cleric, Rydell—later called The Clever—promised to pay for a surveyor to resolve the dispute." Tiranus's dry chuckle degenerated into a wheezing cough. "He walked the surveyor across the property, pointed to where he wanted the boundary line, and said, 'Measure all you want, but get this result.'"

The High Cleric put a hand over Daev's; he was stronger than he looked, and his touch was not affectionate. "Know this: It is a bad time to wander in your faith." He stared gloomily out the window to the cobblestone square outside. "Though some would say it is the safest time to wander, since others rejoice in returning you to piety."

Hannyl grimaced. "The Joyous Faithful Guard." He glanced meaningfully at the two armed, caped figures sitting stolidly on a bench near the fire.

"The same." Tiranus added, "'Generous in seeking, tireless in questioning—'"

"'Certain of redeeming.' I know their creed." Hannyl leaned over and said softly, "High One, are they really what your order wants?"

"With the Distancing"—Tiranus stressed the last word—"of the gods, my order feared chaos. We established a lay order of volunteers, which became a powerful organization. Unfortunately, their leader, Palak, is intrigued by cosmology. It is said he once favored the Dark Lady." Tiranus leaned forward. "He would dearly love to find the rest of us heretical."

Daev felt a sudden chill.

Kael said, "Well, at least they prevented the chaos."

"Sometimes," Tiranus said quietly, "I think chaos would be better."

"I disagree," Daev said. "My faith is unquestioned." He added frankly, "And I would like to keep it that way."

Hannyl chuckled. "We all sing praises to the gods, but the Joyous Guard leads a choir that few join willingly."

Tiranus cocked an ear. "Well, well. Call a dragon and one comes hungry. Here's today's Thankful Choir."

A discordant four-part wail rose from the square outside: " 'Return my soul to Huma's breast—' " The voices, any semblance of harmony tortured out by days of screaming and thirst, were terribly fervent. The two guardsmen by the fire left to watch the show.

Tiranus stared out the window. "Who would have thought they could be heard so well in here?" he said, and, cold-hearted as he was, his voice faltered.

Hannyl said dryly, "Faith carries." They watched without speaking. On the last line, a silver-helmeted man in the dark blue cape of the guard signaled his men. They raised their bows, arrows nocked. The song ended abruptly, as did the choir. A few drops of blood spattered the inn's window.

Hannyl turned away in disgust. "Say what you will, Palak knows how to end a concert."

Daev said quickly and quietly, "Hannyl, I beg you to watch your much-too-honest mouth."

Kael said pleadingly, "Yes, please, Hannyl."

Tiranus said loudly, hoping to cover the comment, "I look forward to reading your book, Daev." He dropped a few coins on the table and made his exit.

The barmaid brought an ale to Daev, who drank half of it immediately and slammed it on the table before the door slammed behind Tiranus.

"Why did he have to bring us here now, while the guard was in the plaza?" Kael wondered.

Hannyl shook his head amusedly. "To make a point, my sweet, innocent friend. And his point is made. Be careful what you put in that book of yours."

Daev drank more ale. His glass slipped in his sweaty hand, bouncing the plate of stew that the barmaid had silently placed before him.

Kael looked up, startled. "Are you upset at his request for us to include the shape of the world?"

"I'm upset because we can't do it," Daev returned irritably. "Look at any of the observations." He gulped more ale. "We have them from a temple in Solanthas, from a temple in Qualinesti, in the same season. We even have one, far older, from Xak Tsaroth. If the world were a disk, or even a sphere, we'd be able to measure the difference in the position of the stars and tell whether the world is slightly or greatly curved." He thumped the table again, this time with his fist. "But we can't, because of the complexity of the gnome-drafted, gully-dwarf-shifted numbers."

"The numbers are simple," said Kael.

Daev and Hannyl said in unison, "What?"

"The numbers," Kael repeated firmly, "are simple." He took another spoonful of soup.

Daev exploded, "For gods' sake, why? We're talking about the ways of heaven."

Kael mumbled around the spoon, "That's exactly why the numbers are simple. I wrote a proof in my journal that makes them so."

Hannyl asked with interest, "Is it plausible?"

"It is certain." Kael's words, seldom witty, were always earnest.

Daev tensed. "And will it embrace the shield of Paladine or the bowl of the Dark Lady?"

After a moment's hesitation, Kael said, "It will reject the bowl forever."

Daev relaxed. "Tiranus will approve. By all means, then, insert it in the book."

Hannyl looked thoughtful. "He might approve. Others might not."

Kael said excitedly, "Will the essay have my name on it?"

Hannyl rolled his eyes.

Daev was shocked. "I include under my name some of the writings of Alennius the Wise. If I'm not publishing his name, isn't it immodest of you to want yours published?"

Kael bowed, stroking his wispy beard. "Yes, it is."

Hannyl said grandly, "Then I'll pay for the last of lunch. Who knows? Perhaps I'm furthering knowledge."

Kael nodded bashfully. Daev finished his stew and went back to fantasizing about banquets and guest lectures.

II

The moment that the first twenty-four copies of the book were completed, Daev wrote twenty-four separate letters of introduction. Each letter floridly and personally dedicated *The Notorious Booke of Starres* to a different knight, lady, merchant, or city father. Daev pleaded for the chance to meet with the esteemed gentlepeople "in the market, after midday" on the same day.

Kael read them uneasily, one by one, at the Dragon's Thirst, where Daev insisted on celebrating. The barkeep was noticeably thinner, his barmaid gone. The patrons were fewer in number as well, except for the Joyful Guard, who had increased. Kael asked, "Why meet them in the marketplace?"

Daev tapped his pen. "Because once I'm seen in public, praised by these fine gentlemen and gentlewomen, other gentlefolk will flock around me. Stop stroking your beard; you're getting crumbs in it."

Hannyl, who had toasted their success several times already, laughed. "He's right. Not about your beard, Kael, about people."

"But what if they don't like the book?"

Daev smiled pityingly. "Did you ever, ever hear of someone disliking a book that was dedicated to him?"

Kael stared, openmouthed. "You're wasted as a cleric. You should have been a bard, or someone who tells stories in the street."

"Or a thief," Hannyl said, smiling. His smile, far more cynical than Daev's, put laughter wrinkles around his dark, quick-moving eyes.

"Or a poet," Daev growled. "I'd be a better one than you." He tossed a roll at Hannyl, who batted it aside. A kender sitting at a nearby table caught the roll and munched on it happily.

"You're sure?" Hannyl finished his latest ale and rose unsteadily to his feet. "I propose a contest." He turned to the kender. "Do you like poetry?"

"Mmmmf?" The kender considered, swallowing. "Not bad poetry, no."

"Good. Then you be the judge between my friend's poetry and mine. Your name, sir?"

"Frenni." The kender looked eagerly at them both, food forgotten. "Is it a fight to the death?"

"Only bad poetry kills people." Hannyl gestured to Daev. "You start."

Daev, amused, thought for a moment. "All right. Just let me think what to do. . . ."

Kael whispered, "Do something from *The Kender Kiss*."

Daev shook his head. "Comedy never wins contests. Ah." He cleared his throat. "This is from a play. After the death of Sturm, one of his company delivers an epilogue:

"Now he is gone where even courage yields
To time, where arms and armaments and shields,
Swords, banners, lances, fame, and heraldry
Drop in surrender to eternity;
Yet he went forward armed in such a grace

As fortifies the soul, and with the mace
Of modesty, broke time's intemperate knife:
He cannot die whose honor was his life."

Hannyl rolled the words in his head as if he were tasting fine wine. "Excellent."

Frenni, clapping, agreed. "Did the kender say that?"

Daev said politely, "No, but he has some nice lines, too."

The kender was only momentarily disappointed. "What else have you written?"

"Come to the square tomorrow and see."

Hannyl, irked, said, "You haven't heard me yet." His smile returned. "And since you did a death song, I'll do one as well. For friends departed." He gestured around the tavern, his eyes hard and bright. "The harvest of holiness. Do you ever miss them, Daev? I do."

Daev said in soft warning, "Hannyl?" He hadn't realized until now that his friend was this drunk.

But Hannyl stepped forward, one hand stretched to the firelight, as he began to recite.

"Sing a song for all the dead,
Songless now, their work debris,
Unrecited and unsaid,
Choked by pain and piety.

"They are gone, but those who stay
Stand accused of faithless crimes:
Kneel off-balance here, and pray
To dubious gods in doubtful times."

He bowed low. "And there you are. Not as pious as your writing, but that's to be expected. . . ."

He broke off, looking at their white faces.

Two members of the Joyous Faithful Guard, their capes pulled back in the tavern warmth, stood behind Hannyl. One of them said sharply, " 'Dubious gods?' Do you doubt their existence, their goodness, their resolve, or something else?"

Hannyl was silent for a moment, then smiled. "Isn't that the best part? 'Dubious.' It could mean so much."

The other guardsman smiled. "Then we have much to ask you."

Daev said hurriedly, "My friend has had too much to drink."

"Your friend?" The first guard swung toward Daev. "And how good a friend is he?"

The other guardsman stopped his companion. "Don't bother, Wirn. You know we're not supposed to redeem a cleric unless we have just cause. And we don't."

Wirn pulled away. "Not yet we don't."

Hannyl put his hand on Wirn's arm. "You heard his poetry; it was . . . different from mine. My words are my own, not shared with anyone." He added quietly, half to himself, "Let me at least die with that much." He made a quick bow to Kael and Daev. "Good night, and congratulations on winning. Be warned, though—it seems I was mistaken about only bad poetry killing people."

Hannyl and his captors moved toward the tavern door, where a large man stood watching. Daev thought numbly, does Palak live in that helmet and cape?

Palak moved aside. The two guardsmen strode out with Hannyl between them, leaving the inn emptier and far more silent.

"I liked your verses better," Frenni said. "You really ought to write for a living."

"You're right," Daev said quietly. "But it's a terribly insecure living, isn't it?" He stared at his ale. "Who can tell the future? Hannyl, with all his gifts, will have nothing tomorrow but a grave. I'll have a cleric's stipend, and an audience."

Hoarse voices rose in desperate song outside. Singing with them, clear-voiced, was Hannyl.

Daev stood suddenly. Kael, with surprising force, grabbed his shoulder and forced him back into his chair. The kender helped pin Daev's arms behind the chair and held on as Daev struggled to free himself. The song ended suddenly, and drops of blood spattered the widow. Daev sagged and slumped forward onto the table.

Frenni said judiciously, "I'd rather sing for bread and ale in taverns."

Kael, watching Daev anxiously, said, "We've tried that tonight. We shouldn't have come here."

Daev stared into the fire, his eyes moist. "We should have done more than come here."

Kael said earnestly, "There was nothing you could have done but die with him."

Daev drank half his ale at a pull, ignoring the tears on his cheeks. "It's not safe here anymore, is it? Someone might speak a heresy at the table, and the Joyous Faithful Guard would come for everyone in the tavern." He glanced around. "But not clerics— 'just yet.' How the guard would love to catch a cleric in a heresy!" He shook his head, shuddering. "When I'm famous, I'll leave this city. I pray the gods let me take a friend with me." He rested his hand over Kael's head. "Would the gods I might have taken two."

III

The sun shone hot, and the canopies in the market flapped in the breeze. In the shade, all manner of wares were laid out—cloth, fruit, fish, poultry, flesh. The men and women behind the counters cried their wares in a singsong cacophony.

Kael sat sketching, waiting for the first of the midday crowd. "How did you get this stand?"

"A fruit merchant lent it to me," Daev said. "I wrote a letter for her to her husband, excusing her recent scandalous behavior. Without going into details, she was most grateful."

Kael, his beard fluttering in the breeze, looked every which way. "I hope someone comes."

"Oh, they will." Daev smiled. "Is this the first essay you've written?"

"No, but it's my first in a book," Kael said eagerly and shyly at the same time. "Have you read it yet?"

"Why?" Daev caught himself. "I mean . . . why do I need to? I'm sure it was brilliant and worthy of inclusion."

"Thank you," Kael said fervently. They watched as a few dozen of the marketing crowd turned toward them. A man with a gold medallion around his neck and another with a conspicuously huge purse strode forward purposefully.

As Daev had predicted, a throng of others crowded behind the wealthy and the important. He accepted their praise modestly and hinted for private readings, dinner and drinks included. Kael, overwhelmed by so many people, edged backward out of the way. He watched the attention Daev was receiving with undisguised pleasure.

A small figure wormed his way through Daev's patrons, held up a copy of *The Notorious Booke of Starres*.

Daev recognized the kender from the Dragon's Thirst. "Where did you get that book?"

"Oh, around," Frenni said vaguely. He cocked his head as someone in the crowd shouted angrily that he'd just been robbed. "Could you inscribe it 'To the Great Frenni'?"

"Why not?" Daev signed the frontispiece with a flourish. "Have you read any of it?"

"A little. I've barely had time," Frenni confessed.

"Tell me, are the essays in here true?"

"Absolutely true," Daev said grandly, leaning on his remaining stack of books lest they disappear into the kender's hands.

"All of them?"

"Of course," Daev answered, faintly annoyed.

"Even this one?" The kender began to read aloud. He had a surprisingly strong, carrying voice for such a little fellow. Those in the crowd gasped. A ripple of astonishment, mixed with fright, spread through the assembled people like gossip or scandal.

Daev stared, upside down, at Kael's essay. Daev recognized the illustration inside the title lettering—a dragon pursued by a comet—as one of Kael's own marvelous sketches. He looked at the large, bold script.

Slowly he registered the upside-down words as he heard the kender reading the essay title aloud. "On the True Motion of Krynn, the Sphere on Which We Live, Through the Void of the Heavens and Around the Sun."

Daev, in a kind of shock, found himself counting the heresies expressed in the title. He had reached four, with the potential for several more, when the first shout of "Blasphemer!" rang out.

He looked up and said sharply, "What? What? Who said that?"

The only answer was a soft murmur, like a low growl, from the crowd.

Kael looked apprehensive. Daev cleared his throat. "The truth of some works is metaphorical, of course; it may be understood best as allegory, possibly even satire."

A stone caught him on the lip, leaving behind a rivulet of blood. Kael said plaintively to the crowd, "But the numbers work—"

Daev tugged Kael by the belt and moved backward, flipping the canvas covering of the booth down over them both. "Run!" Daev said as they fled out the back. They were running between market booths when Kael suddenly skidded to a halt. "My journal."

"Keep going."

"But I left it on the counter."

"It's lost now."

The first of the crowd came pelting after them, stones in hand. Kael said plaintively, "No, it's right back—"

Daev pushed Kael headfirst into a florist's stand. "I'll draw them off! You hide!" He ran down the street as fast as his flopping sandals would permit, shouting hopefully, "He went that way!" and pointing down a side street.

No one was fooled, and the mob grew every minute. Daev dashed down the next side street, then circled back toward the marketplace, hoping to mingle with the tail end of the mob pursuing him. At the entrance to the market, he dashed around a hitched cart, grabbing one of the shafts and spinning it. He leapt over the manure from the draft team, hoping that it would slow the more fastidious pursuers.

The roars behind him ceased suddenly. Daev turned to look.

He crashed into a large man, hugged the man's chest to remain upright, and glanced back at the mob, who would surely catch him now.

The mob had stopped.

A booming voice called out, "Do not trouble this man."

The leaders of the crowd, books in hand, looked suddenly fearful.

The voice added, "And since his work upsets you, leave all copies here." The copies of the book slapped against the cobblestones.

Daev looked up, confused.

Palak, head of the Joyous Faithful Guard, smiled down at him. "You're safe now."

In the silence, Daev heard the soft rustle of robes. Tiranus glided from behind the Joyous Guardsman. The High Cleric smiled coldly at Daev and dropped a final copy of *The Notorious Booke of Starres* on the cobblestones. "Goodbye Daev." he said.

Daev noticed a dark spot on the guardsman's chain mail.

Palak mopped blood from his armor. "As you can see, I was called from my work to find you. And here you are. Running straight to your own salvation. You can't imagine my happiness."

Daev tried to speak, failed, and finally managed a whisper. "You can't conceive mine. If I may ask—"

Palak's eyes glowed. "All your questions will be answered in the night to come. All doubts gone, all fears resolved. It is truly amazing what certainty of wavering spirit comes from the dedicated tutelage of flesh under whips, rods, and blades."

He glanced down at Daev. "Don't weep," he said fondly. "Please don't weep. Not yet."

Daev spent the afternoon gathering up books with a razor at his throat, Guardsman Wirn cautioning him that pulling away or lifting his head would show a lack of humility. As a lesson for his faith—and, Daev suspected, as entertainment for the crowd—the Thankful Choir performed, announcing in vigorous rhythms that the understanding of the stars was not for this world. One of the tenors performed a heartrendingly beautiful solo, set to the text, "The mercy of the gods outshines all ours." Both the tenor's eardrums were bleeding. Daev doubted that the young man heard a word of his own singing.

By late afternoon, Daev's kneecaps were bleeding through his robe and his palms were raw. His throat was cut in two places for the twin impieties of pain and terror. In the center of the market, at a pole normally used for hitching wagons, stood a pile of books. Daev sat back to take the pressure of the stones off his bloody knees and contemplated the stock.

"Now," Palak said genially, "arise of your own will and allow us to fasten your arms to the post."

Daev looked at the crowd, some of whom had already gathered stones. "I hope their aim is true and merciful. Will you cast the first stone?"

"Not at a cleric!" Palak was deeply hurt. "Your office commands respect. You there," he called out. "Drop those. Now." Reluctantly, sorry to lose their sport, the crowd dropped the stones.

The High Cleric came forward, Tiranus carrying a torch. "I assume this means my stipend will not be renewed," Daev said. "So my body is to be burned after my death?" He looked hopeful.

Palak shook his head. "Not exactly. I'm offering you a final chance for penance."

"Breathing in my own books."

"Or you could reject them for as long as possible," Palak said solemnly. "Equally inspiring."

Daev murmured, "Depends on your point of view, doesn't it?"

Too weak to stand, Daev ascended the pyre on his hands and knees, struggling as he slipped against the books. One of the volumes slid under his bloody left palm. He dropped almost full length, wincing as the guardsman's razor once again sliced the flesh of his throat.

The torch approached. The crowd cheered.

"Stop!"

A weeping woman wearing a bride's hooded robe, driving a rickety old farm wagon, appeared at the edge of the crowd. Her sobbing inspired pity, but her swollen belly in a bridal gown inspired laughter.

She pointed a finger at Daev. "Do not burn my bridegroom!"

"Ah, yes," Daev muttered. "I have only been disgraced and tortured. It wouldn't do to forget ridicule."

Palak cried angrily, "Woman, don't interrupt the cleansing of a soul."

"Whose?" The woman thumped her chest, then her belly. "Mine? My child's?" She stretched her arms forward pleadingly. "At least let him marry me, as he promised, before he dies."

The crowd laughed, but there were also noises of sympathy, particularly from the women.

Palak, listening, bit his lip. The woman's robe shifted; she cried out and clutched at her belly. Now even the laughter in the crowd grew sympathetic.

Palak gestured impatiently to Tiranus. "You officiate, cleric. Be brief." A sigh of approval came from the crowd. A marriage and an execution made for a diverting afternoon. A gaggle of young women from the florist's booth appeared as if on cue and hastily distributed batches flowers to the people in the front row: roses, white-eyes, dragonslip, and love-be-true.

Palak escorted Daev to the cart. He climbed carefully into the wagon next to the bride, who teetered on it precariously.

Tiranus grudgingly performed the ceremony in fewer than forty words. At the end, he said peevishly, "You are husband and wife." As Daev leaned forward, the cleric snapped, "No, you may not kiss the bride! You there, give me back that torch. Put him back on the pyre."

The books blazed up. The women from the floral stand piled their flowers on the blaze. The rest of the crowd joined in gleefully. The flowers smothered the fire. Smoke rose from it in choking clouds. Everyone in the plaza coughed and wiped their streaming eyes.

When the air cleared, the flower girls were gone. So was the pregnant bride, and so was the wagon. So, more importantly, was Daev.

The crowd looked around uneasily. No one, from the pettiest thief to the most obdurate heretic, had ever before escaped the Joyous Faithful Guard.

Palak, sensing the crowd's ugly mood, licked his

lips and looked nervous. Hurriedly he knelt, weeping, before the empty post. "We have wronged him!"

Silence fell over the square. Palak continued, "He has been transferred to heaven bodily." He picked up a copy of The Notorious Book of Starres and hurled it aside contemptuously. "This was never his. He was forced to write it."

Palak glared at Tiranus. "How could you falsely accuse one of heaven's blessed? You must answer me, on this and other questions, old man."

For once, Tiranus displayed strong emotion. During the coming night, he would display still more.

* * * * *

A short but rapidly growing distance away, Daev lay bloody and exhausted but happy in the back of a cart. Kael, his beard neatly tucked under a scarf, encouraged the horse to go faster.

"Are you all right?" Kael asked.

"Fine. I trust you realize that this wedding is rendered void by your being a man."

"But it would be binding if I were a woman?"

"Absolutely." Daev added generously, "And since you saved my life, I would forgive your lack of a suitable dowry."

"Thank you," Kael said and shook the reins harder.

Daev laughed suddenly. "I said I'd leave when I was famous, and now I am. Think of it! I'm the only man to escape the Joyous Faithful Guard!"

"Not if we don't keep moving," Kael pointed out and added in a burst of feeling, "I'm so glad I saved you! When my essay got you in trouble, I felt terrible."

Daev joined Kael on the bench. "Don't worry about that," he said generously. "I'm just grateful to you, and proud of you, and amazed that you saved me. Not that you're not brilliant," he added hastily, "but—well, trickery isn't in your nature."

"I've watched you," Kael said. "I've read your writing, and I had extra help."

Kael's pregnant belly disappeared. Frenni popped out from under the robe. "Remember me? I undid your manacles, and my head was the baby."

Daev clapped his hands, ignoring the pain. "The wedding scene from *The Kender Kiss!* I just wanted it to be funny; I can't believe it really worked."

"I wasn't sure the bit with the flowers would work," Kael said. "But it seemed worth a try."

Frenni was delighted. "You wrote a play about me and your lady friend?"

Daev smiled patronizingly. "The play, as always, preceded the action, and Kael isn't a woman."

"Excuse me," the kender said, miffed. "You may be a scholar and a writer, but I'm the one who just spent half the afternoon under her robe."

After a stunned silence, Daev said, "Then you really are . . . ?"

"My true name is Kela." She pulled off the beard, wincing momentarily, and pulled the hood all the way back. She was quite pretty, and her smile, which had always seemed shy but admiring, now seemed more than that.

"And you did all this because you fell in love with me?" Daev asked. "Understandable, but foolish."

"No, no," Kael replied. "I disguised myself to study mathematics and star lore. They say women aren't good at math, and I knew that old fool Tiranus wouldn't let me in the order if he knew I was female." She added, "But I did fall in love with you, and you're right. It was foolish."

Daev turned to Frenni. "And what were you doing down there since we escaped?"

"Reading," Frenni said. "This is really wonderful." He held up a book.

Kela said delightedly, "My journal!"

"It was on the counter with the rest of the books about stars. And there are two plays stuffed in here."

"Thank the gods," Daev said in relief. "May I have the book before it disappears again?"

Frenni handed it over. "I just borrowed it to read it. I didn't think anyone would mind."

"Nobody did," Daev said. "Although it's probably well worth reading." He opened it up . . .

. . . and froze, transfixed. There was a sketch of a fish-shaped device in which people could travel underwater, a diagram of a siege-proof keep and siege engines and towers for attacking others, a wonderful stick-and-pulley mechanism for sewing two shirts at once. There was a device for sailing ships against the wind, and a silk canopy for floating down from cliffs or towers. There was a sketch of embattled flying birds next to a sketch of flying dragons fighting, with detailed notes on the differences. There was a swirling ink-wash rendering of a night battle, swords and all, done in shadows but with every expression and emotion of the fighters clear. On the middle pages, in a two-page spread, was a truly marvelous and detailed sketch of a dove, its chest and belly pinned open and entrails neatly displayed. "Paladine's pa!" he cried, shocked into an expression he hadn't used since he'd left the farm. "You dissected one of the temple doves?"

Kela looked uncomfortable. "More than one, actually. But I didn't waste them, and I quit once I had learned all I could."

Daev flipped through the pages. "And these devices—they aren't like gnome machinery? They'll do what you say?"

"Oh, yes!" Kela nodded.

"Where did all this come from?"

"I get ideas. I write them down or sketch them as they occur to me."

Daev said thoughtfully, "Do you think other things will occur to you?"

"They could."

He passed the book back to her. "You have a

wonderful head. Do your best to keep it on your shoulders. And from now on, before you kill doves or turn the world upside down or do something else enlightening and no doubt worthwhile, ask me."

Kela said apprehensively, "Do you think I might get in trouble again?"

Daev sighed. "I think that your getting in trouble again is only a matter of time."

With surprising practicality for a kender, Frenni asked, "What do we do next? You're going to want a way to earn a living."

Daev and Kela looked at each other. She let the horse slow to a canter. Finally Dave said slowly, "I think I'm finally a writer."

Frenni said excitedly, "We'll put on plays!"

Kela said, "Maybe puppet shows, until we can afford to pay real actors."

Daev shook his head dismissively. "Actors never expect to be paid as promised. Mustn't spoil them." His eyes glowed. "And you can design scenery for the stage. Boats, wagons—"

"Mechanical dragons, gnome machines—"

"Castles, stairways—"

"Thunder, lightning—"

"I'll help build them," Frenni offered eagerly.

Daev looked uneasily at the kender. "We'll use a bare stage for now. I'm sure the words alone will carry the play." He set his jaw. "And I'll write a new one: *The Poet's Farewell*. I only wish I could make it into a book."

"We will," Kela said earnestly. "All we need is to find an audience."

Daev glanced involuntarily over his shoulder at Frenni, who was reading the journal raptly, then at her. "We will," he pointed out, "the moment we publish your essay."

"My essay? Do you think people would care enough to buy it?"

"Well," he said pragmatically, "if it was worth

immolating the author for, it must be worth reading. Would you like to publish it under your own name?"

She was disbelieving but delighted. "You'd give up authorship for me?"

"Please. I insist." He added thoughtfully, brushing a cinder from his robe, "Though I suggest you use the name of Kael. Better for circulation."

He scratched his head. "Which brings up a serious problem. I truly wish to publish it—charging only the most modest of fees, of course—but now we have a shortage of scribes."

But Kela was smiling. "That's not a problem. I have a design for a machine that can copy books. We can make them faster and cheaper than any scribe could."

"Marvelous." Daev thought fondly about the word "cheaper," then stopped abruptly. "Kael—Kela, my dear, is there any chance of this machine causing as much trouble as your other researches? What is this machine, anyway?"

"It's called a printing press," Kela said. "And, no, it shouldn't cause any trouble at all."

Scavengers

Jean Rabe

The pentare's hold was cloaked in shadows, but Telyil's elven eyes parted the darkness and took in dozens of canvas sacks bulging with steel coins.

"A fortune," she whispered.

As the elf moved silently toward the bow, her slender fingers drifted across ivory carvings of exotic animals. A toppled coffer at her feet had loosed rubies and strands of pearls. Diamonds glittered from an opened chest nearby.

"Telyil! Did you find anything?" The anxious voice came from the deck above.

Glancing up, Telyil saw a youthful blue face peering down through the hatch. She shook her head. "Nothing of any value to us, I'm afraid. And you, Rulbir? Did you fare better?"

"In the galley we found the bodies of a dozen men! They must have been trapped when the ship sank. All of them had daggers, some had swords. There was a spear, and I claimed it." He waved the spear. "Only pirates would have had so many weapons!"

That would explain this cargo of pretty baubles, Telyil thought. She pushed off, effortlessly moving through the seawater.

"We recovered a length of rope from the captain's quarters." Rulbir talked as they swam together through the ship's narrow corridors. "It is thin and strong—made from something most fine! There was a shield on the wall. Duqay wants to keep it. Silly of him. It is heavy and will rust."

Within moments, Rulbir and Telyil were on the deck in the company of two other blue-skinned Dimernesti. The salvaged daggers, swords, and shield lay in a net, along with a half-dozen stoppered ceramic pots. There were other various odds and ends: surface tools that the sea elves would find some use for; colorful tunics; and a woolen satchel that, Rulbir explained, contained knives and forks from the galley.

"A good find," Telyil said. "One more to search this day." She pointed toward the northeast, and her companions peered out over the rotting hulks that made up the graveyard at the bottom of the Southern Courrain Ocean. There were nearly two hundred wrecks, and the Dimernesti band had explored almost all of them.

The sea elves believed a dragon was responsible for sinking the ships. Though they had not spotted the beast, they had seen evidence of him—jagged holes in the hulls, a scarcity of fish they used to hunt, and the scorched beds of seaweed they once harvested. The dragon had ruined their territory and turned them into scavengers. The sea elves suspected the dragon used as his lair one of the nearby deep water caves, but none of them were foolish enough to investigate.

"Are you certain we should risk the cog today?"

"Yes, Rulbir," Telyil replied. "But we should hurry."

The Dimernesti never stayed in the graveyard long, fearing the dragon might discover them. They always searched the ships furtively, then returned to their families, safe among the interconnected sea caves beyond the southern edge of the graveyard.

Now the group of elves swam toward the cog, clinging to the shadows cast by the sunken ships. The oldest of the wrecks had settled so deeply into the sand that little of their decks were visible, and what was visible was encrusted with coral and barnacles.

The elves slipped in through a gaping hole. "Duqay, Rulbir, search the cargo hold," Telyil instructed. "Phir and I will take the crew quarters and galley."

Telyil swam toward a hatch and rose to the next level, her eyes taking in ornate brass lanterns, decorative doorknobs, and finely polished wooden walls.

Something heavy had fallen against one door when the ship sank. But Phir was strong and determined, and he was finally able to push the door open wide enough so he and Telyil could squeeze inside.

The room beyond was filled with beds bolted to the floor, sheets floating in the water like ghosts. The bodies of eight sailors, one with badly misshapen arms and legs, bobbed near the ceiling.

"One of the humans lives!" Phir exclaimed.

Impossible, Telyil thought. But as she studied the bloated bodies, covered with sores from exposure to the saltwater, she noticed one that was different, unmarred. The man was moving his legs slowly to keep his head in a space where air was miraculously trapped.

Phir tugged a dagger free from his belt. "I will grant him mercy," he said.

Telyil's hand shot out to stay him.

"But he will drown," Phir protested. "It is a bad way for an air-breather to die. Better he dies quickly at my hand, and with only brief pain."

"No, Phir, not if I—"

"Fruit in the hold!" came Rulbir's voice from the hallway. He poked his head into the room. "Telyil, there is so much of it that . . ." His words trailed off when he spotted the sailor.

"Telyil does not want me to kill him," Phir stated.

"No need," Rulbir countered as he squeezed

inside. "The sea will take him soon enough. But maybe we can talk to him first. Find out something about the dragon that sunk his ship."

"I will talk to him," Telyil said as she swam toward him. She floated next to the sailor and took in his lined face. The man's eyes were hard-looking and distant, and he was babbling to himself softly.

"Grespher. No. Grespher," the man repeated over and over. He met Telyil's gaze and his voice rose. "Nopon. Grespher nopon!" His eyes broke contact, then he resumed his unintelligible mumbling. His facial muscles twitched.

Perhaps he went mad because of what he'd been through, Telyil thought, and he wasn't likely to calm down now that he was face-to-face with a blue woman with pointed ears and silver hair.

Telyil returned to Phir and Rulbir. "I cannot understand him at all. Maybe on the surface it would be different."

"You can't be serious!" Phir spat. "Let him die! There's a dragon somewhere in these waters. The creature might see you. It must be nearby. It sank this ship!"

"We can't just let him die."

"There is much food in the hold," Rulbir cut in. "It will take us at least three trips, perhaps four. Glass containers filled with fruit, meat, surface treats! There is also a fancy red box with a lock that Duqay is trying to open, bolts upon bolts of colorful cloth, and jugs filled with who knows what. Maybe wine! I very much hope so. Let us go home and celebrate this wonderful find! Forget this man, Telyil."

"Rulbir, bring me one of those jugs," she tersely instructed. "Phir, you and the others can start with the goods."

Phir drew his lips into a thin line. "Foolishness," he whispered.

"Yes, it is my foolishness." She offered him a slight smile. "There is a high ridge some distance from here. Above the sea, it resembles the spine of a stone monster. I will take the man there. With luck, he will live and another ship will pass by and rescue him."

They continued to argue, the words heated and angry.

"He will drown long before you reach the surface!" Phir spat, attempting to end the disagreement.

Rulbir returned, holding out a large jug. "Telyil must do what she feels is right."

Telyil emptied the jug, drawing air into it, stoppered it while she tried to explain to the man what she had in mind. He seemed to protest. But she gathered him close and pointed downward, and he grabbed a breath of air before she pulled him under the water.

"You will need this." Rulbir thrust his spear toward her. "In case . . . well, in case . . . of barracudas." He meant the dragon.

She smiled and accepted the weapon, knowing it would be all but useless against a dragon's hide. Then she began swimming, with the sailor in tow, out of the room, down the corridor, into the hull where Duqay was gathering the food containers in a net. She gave the sailor another gulp of air from the jug before swimming out of the gash in the hull.

"There is not much air in this," Telyil said, although she doubted he could understand her. "You will have to conserve it. We have some distance to travel."

He glanced back at the cog. Then he began to swim with her, tugging on her arm when he needed air. The pair kept to the sandy floor. His eyes were wide as he took in the sunken ships. The farther they swam, the weaker his strokes became, and soon Telyil found herself practically carrying him.

"You'll be all right when we reach the surface," she said. "Do not give up. Swim as best you can."

They passed beyond the northern edge of the graveyard, where some of the largest wrecks rested.

He tried to ascend toward the surface, but the elf pulled him back down, kept him following a shelf that angled steeply downward. He was growing weaker with each passing minute, but this was not the place.

Now the floor sloped upward. Telyil moved faster now, for she knew there were only a few breaths left in the jug. Her legs pumped hard as they shot toward the surface.

All of a sudden something slammed into her. It was a brown shark, more than five feet long. Telyil pushed the sailor away and saw that he managed to continue toward the surface. Telyil whirled to face the shark. Its maw filled her vision.

Telyil twisted and held the spear in front of her. The blankly staring creature closed on her from the right, and she darted to the left, bringing the haft of the spear up to thump against his belly. She struck him twice before he moved away. The elf did not use the spear tip on him because she didn't want to risk drawing blood and therefore drawing more sharks.

This time he made a broader circle, giving Telyil a chance to catch her breath. She shot above him, ramming the spear butt down on the top of his head and pushing him away. Then she descended, following him, swatting him a second time. He whipped around, his tail lashing, knocking the spear from her grip.

She clasped her hands together, raised them above her head, and brought them down on his snout with as much strength as she could summon. In the same instant, she moved under him and wrapped her legs about his middle and held on tight. Doggedly she hung on while she pummeled him.

The shark thrashed and thrashed, battering her with its body. Finally she lost hold. To her surprise, the shark dived deep and did not return, eventually disappearing in the shadows along the bottom.

"Looking for something easier to swallow," she murmured to herself.

She glanced up, barely making out the human sailor, still swimming high above her. She swam to catch up with him, although she was tired and aching. Telyil's face broke the surface a few moments after the sailor had emerged. As she took air into her body, the sensation made her dizzy, but her lungs swiftly adapted.

"You are safe now," she said to the man as she approached.

"Dalan," he gasped. "My name is Dalan. And I am far from safe." His lips were blistered and swollen. Raggedly he took in gulps of air.

"Nonsense, Dalan," Telyil said. "We will swim to the ridge. I will help you. There." She pointed with a webbed hand to the north. A jagged line of rocks rose above the water. "A ship will come along. You will be all right. And there you can tell me all about the great dragon that sunk your ship."

"No dragon," he gasped. "Only greed. Far from safe," he repeated. "I am dying." Then softly the words began to tumble from his lips. And Telyil strained to listen.

* * * * *

"Safe!" Dalan hollered across the deck. "Out of range now! Free sailin', mates!"

Sails billowing, the cog cut through the choppy waters of the Southern Courrain, leaving the Bay of Balifor far behind. The sun was setting, the seas a brilliant orange. The wind was strong, ensuring they would make good time.

"When that fat merchant realizes he's been robbed—and who did the robbin'—we'll be too far away for him to catch us!" Dalan gloated.

"Aye, they'll never catch us!" The captain had padded up behind Dalan, slapped the first mate on the back. "Merchant should've known better than to leave his galleon unattended at night, what with pirates around."

The pair chuckled loudly and glanced at the crew, who had already begun to celebrate. The ale flowed freely, and someone was singing a bawdy tune. Amidships, just past the wheel and the grinning helmsman, the bosun had started picking through some of the booty.

Dalan and the captain walked over and eyed the take.

"Plenty of cloth in the hold, too" the bosun said. "Expensive stuff. But we'll have to find the right buyer. Too fancy for most of the southern ports."

"I have confidence in you, Ferdnar," the captain said, leaning over the bosun's shoulder. "You'll find someone who will . . . well, look at this." He bent to pick up a small ornate box, inlaid with silver and brass and held shut by a tiny lock.

The bosun shrugged. "Lady's jewelry, I'd guess. Let's have a look at what's inside." He sat cross-legged on the deck and pulled a thin wire from his belt buckle. "Tricky lock," he muttered. "Small, delicate." Ferdnar cursed as he continued to fumble with the mechanism. "Could break it. No, wait. . . . Got it. There!"

He popped it open, and the captain's hand reached to snatch a fist-sized emerald sphere that rested on a bed of velvet. The captain let out a low whistle.

Dalan stared at the thing. "Gotta be magic, cap'n. Look at the way it glimmers."

It was made of glass, and sparkled merrily. A light seemed to pulse inside it, and bands of green undulated hypnotically across its surface.

"Feels cold," the captain said. "Like snow." He stared at it for several long moments, then passed it to the bosun. "Show it around, but be careful with it. Tell the mates we did well."

The bosun held it gingerly, ran his weathered

fingers across its surface. "Cold," he agreed. "And worth a pretty pile of cold steel."

The captain relieved the helmsman and wrapped his long fingers around the wheel. Dalan followed him, looking over his shoulder at the emerald sphere. He would take his turn inspecting it later on.

"What's this?" The captain glanced at his hand. "In the name of Habakkuk . . ."

Dalan saw it too—a red rash dotting the captain's fingers.

Within the span of a heartbeat, the rash worsened. Now festering boils spread up the captain's arm. Dalan took the wheel and watched his captain rush toward the hatch, no doubt going to the galley to find something to put on the rash. But the bosun stopped him, and the pair appeared to exchange hurried words.

Dalan strained to overhear, the words making him lose all interest in keeping the ship on course. Then he saw the rash on Ferdnar's arms and hands, too.

"Plague," Dalan whispered. "May departed Habakkuk preserve us."

The boils on the captain's arms worsened as he watched, and then the rash spread to his face. The bosun was likewise covered with fresh lesions, and his hands had begun to shake and wither.

"The green sphere," Ferdnar exclaimed, eyes wide.

"Aye," the captain returned. "A cursed thing of magic it is. Below deck with it!" he bellowed to a group of mates who were admiring the sphere, oblivious to the tiny red welts that had begun to appear on their fingers. "Now! Lock it away! Be quick about it!"

When the mates paused, mesmerized, the captain stumbled forward, snatching it in his hands and shoving it in the box. He slammed the lid down and fumbled with the lock. Then he thrust the box at one of the mates. "In the hold!" he gasped. "D'you hear? Get it away from us!"

As the mate disappeared below deck, Dalan swallowed hard and stepped forward. He hadn't touched the sphere, and he didn't want to chance that the magical disease might spread to him. "Sir, maybe we should throw it overboard," he suggested to the captain. "Maybe we—"

The captain whirled on his first mate, his movements clumsy. "The thing's valuable," he said. His lips were cracked, his cheeks bloated. "Can't hurt us if it's locked away. It can't . . ." A pale green foam seeped out of his lips, and he pitched forward.

The bosun joined him a second later.

"No!" Dalan cried. He glanced around the deck, his eyes resting on the mates toward the rear, who hadn't yet had a chance to touch the sphere. They understood and nodded to him. "With me!" he called. Then he bolted down the steps, the others following quickly behind him. The screams of dying men pierced the air above, followed by splashes as some of the doomed men leapt overboard. Then they heard the pounding of feet of other men below deck.

Dalan and a small group barricaded themselves inside the crew quarters, shoved chests against the door to keep those men out who had been exposed to the green sphere.

"Safe," Dalan huffed, leaning against the wall. "We'll wait here for as long as it takes."

"Till they're all dead?" one of the sailors asked.

"Aye," Dalan replied. "Dead or cured, the latter of which ain't likely. Give us time to think. Decide what to do."

A groaning sound cut him off. It was soft at first, then grew, and Dalan watched in terror as the wooden walls bubbled and heaved, resembling nothing so much as the diseased skin of those struck down by the emerald sphere. The very nails of the cracking timbers began to pop out.

The groaning intensified, and the barricaded men looked nervously at each other as the ship shuddered and listed. A crash came from overhead, one of the masts toppling. More screams followed.

"We're doomed," Dalan whispered. "She's taking on water. I can feel it."

"No," one of the mates countered. "We'll make it, sir. We'll be all right, you'll see. We didn't touch the thing. We'll be safe and . . ."

Dalan turned and looked at the man, spotted the first patch of rash on his forearm. Then the first mate closed his eyes and prayed to the departed gods.

* * * * *

"The water must've slowed the disease down. But I know I am dying," Dalan said, his voice almost gone. The skin on his face was dotted with sores, and his fingers were gnarled. A bubble of green foam escaped his mouth as he gasped once more, then was still.

Telyil gasped, remembered that Rulbir said they'd found a box with a small lock and opened it, vaguely recalled mention of something that looked like a pearl inside. She remembered Dalan babbling, "Grespher. No. Grespher." Green sphere.

"No!" She dived. Her limbs ached, but she kicked furiously, surging through a school of startled triggerfish. Hurry! She urged herself. Faster!

Time crawled. Her chest burned, her heart pounded wildly. Her arms felt like stone, heavy and difficult to move. I was a fool to try to save the man, she thought, to abandon the others and bring this man to the surface. And yet, she realized, if she hadn't saved the man, she would not have discovered the horrible secret of the green sphere.

Must hurry, she told herself.

When she feared she couldn't swim another stroke, a broken mast came into view. Hurry!

Three barracuda were prowling at the edge of the graveyard. Telyil angled away from them, knowing she hadn't the strength to fight them.

She passed over the cog, hoping to catch sight of Rulbir and the others, but knowing that they must have headed home hours ago.

Faster! she scolded herself, though she realized she was going slower and slower. Her breath was coming in ragged gasps now.

Then she saw the small entrance of her sea cave home. She slipped inside, looking around for the other scavengers.

"Rulbir! Phir!"

"Dead," came a harsh murmur.

She stared into the darkness and spotted Duqay, leaning against the shield he had retrieved. His bare chest was dotted with the now familiar sores, his eyes swollen shut.

"Dead," Duqay repeated.

"Get out of here!" Telyil managed to say as she pulled herself close to him. "Swim far away! Get away from the green orb and this cave."

Duqay's face contorted. "I can't swim. I can barely move."

She shook his shoulders. "You have to find the strength. Leave. Your presence will kill the others, contaminate them. All the families. Leave!" She pointed him toward the cave mouth and pushed.

Duqay struggled forward, saying something to her so softly she couldn't understand. He groped his way along the wall. Satisfied that he was leaving, she headed deeper into the cave, following a narrow tunnel that led into a series of caverns. The first chamber was empty.

"So tired," she whispered. She hesitated only a moment, allowing herself a deep gulp of seawater.

The next chamber was filled with nearly three dozen sea elves—the entire community. Several of them were tending to two women whose arms were covered with the fast-multiplying sores.

The malady had spread beyond the scavengers.

Telyil swam forward. A dozen of the elves had sores

on their bodies. Getting the sick to leave was madness now. "The healthy ones, then," she whispered to herself. "Leave them!" she shouted, waving her arms. "Leave this cave. It is a plague."

Questions swirled around her, so many she couldn't tell who was talking or what precisely was being asked. She ignored the arguments of a husband who said he couldn't leave his wife. She told them the truth. They were doomed if they delayed.

"Listen to me. Rulbir and Phir died of this plague. You will, too. It spreads quickly. There is no cure. No way to save them. It is a curse. But you might have a chance if you get out now! Take no possessions, no food, nothing that might be tainted. Get out!"

Most of the elves left quickly, fear evident in their eyes. She pushed at the reluctant ones, yelling at them in her weakening voice. "Swim far away! Never return here! Never!"

Within minutes, all of the healty-looking elves save one had left the cave—the man who refused to leave his wife.

"If you stay, you will die with her."

He shook his head. "I will trust to the departed gods," he told Telyil. "There are no marks on my skin. I will tend these people and they will heal. You will see how foolish you were to chase everyone away."

"There are no marks on you—yet," Telyil corrected him. She glanced around the chamber. "Where is the the green orb? The one in the box. It was brought back by the scavengers. . . ."

The man settled next to his wife, draped an arm around her shoulder, and offered her comforting words. "You will not die," he said to her. "Telyil is mad. The others will eventually come back. . ."

"The orb!"

"It is in with the weapons," he said. "We didn't know what it was, so we stored it there."

Telyil scowled at the man and hurried from the

chamber into a narrow alcove. Daggers and spears were carefully arranged on rock shelves, nets hung from outcroppings. The box was there, opened and displayed. Telyil stared at what looked like a huge green pearl. The colors subtly shifted across its surface. It was beautiful.

She reached forward, stopped herself from touching it, felt how cold the water was around it. So cold. Fighting her revulsion, she slammed the lid shut and tucked the box under her arm.

She passed by the husband on her way out of the chamber, noted the first sores collecting on his forehead. "We will be all right, Telyil," he said to her. "You will see."

Telyil stumbled from the cave, leaned against the rocks to keep from collapsing, and gazed out over the graveyard of ships.

"Habakkuk," she whispered. "God of the seas, wherever you are, give me the strength to do this."

She moved slowly through the rotting hulks, pulling herself along as much as swimming. Her limbs protested. Breathing was becoming a task. "So tired," she whispered.

Telyil knew that any passing shark or barracuda could make an easy meal of her. She prayed to Habakkuk and the rest of Krynn's departed gods to make her path safe.

She didn't know how long it took her to reach the northwest part of the graveyard, or how much longer it took her to crawl across an expanse of sloping sand toward a thick coral ridge. The ridge was deep below the surface, too deep for any light to reach it from the sun. It was dotted with caves and devoid of fish and plant life. It was where they believed the dragon lived.

"This . . . largest cave. Must be." She stopped at the entrance, her legs no longer able to move. She glanced down at them; they were covered with sores. Keeping the box under her arm, she reached out and slowly pulled herself inside.

"Dying," she gasped. "Like the others. Must hurry."

Jolts of cold and heat raced up and down her body as she brushed against the bones of large animals— sharks or whales, she suspected. There were smaller bones, from sailors or sea elves, she thought idly.

Far enough, she decided finally. She rested the box on the floor, opened the lid, and stared at the scintillating green orb.

"They say dragons covet treasure." She ran her fingers across the orb's surface and pulled it free of the case. Since she was dying, the orb could no longer hurt her. Then she put the orb on the sand, where she was certain the dragon would see it. "I feel so cold."

Telyil discarded the box outside and sagged against the hull of an old galleon. Her eyes were swollen shut, and she was unable to see the huge shadow that passed over the graveyard and headed toward the thick coral ridge. She struggled in vain to take another breath. "So cold," she whispered as she died.

Homecoming

William W. Connors and Sue Weinlein Cook

"Kellin, aren't we there yet?" rumbled the blue dragon.

It was just Kellin these days. Not Commander Kellin, as it had been during the Summer of Chaos. Not Sir Kellin as it had been during those days of honor and victory, now four years past. Just—

"Kellin!"

The dragon's query came louder than a shout over the rush of the wind and the strokes of the beast's wings against the air. "Where are you taking us?"

"Be patient, Dusk," returned the veteran knight in steady tones. He laid a soothing hand upon the neck of his dragon mount. Then, squinting into the midday sun, he swept his gaze across the desolate terrain of Estwilde. "We're close," he said, more to himself than the dragon.

"Are you sure you don't want to turn around?" asked Dusk hopefully.

"You know I can't go back." Kellin's voice was clipped. "There's nothing left for us there."

The dragon swiveled her head slightly, glancing at her rider out of the corner of one large eye. "The others are still there. We could regroup and lead the squadron again!"

"My foolish girl, there will be no more squadrons." The man clenched his jaw as unwanted memories surfaced: the triumph before the gates of Palanthas, the heady feeling as he flew with his officers over the shining star of Ansalon's civilization.

The dark mass of shadow wights on the horizon. The death cries of his men as the fire dragons claimed them for Chaos. In the wake of the devastating war, few Knights of Takhisis remained alive, and those who did were wise to hide their affiliation. The people of Ansalon were quick to remember the Dark Knights' conquest of the land, but slow to recall their sacrifices in the war against the Father of All and of Nothing.

"But the General ordered us to Neraka," said Dusk.

"Takhisis take the General!" roared a furious Kellin. "Who is she to order us? We captured Palanthas for the Dark Queen—Palanthas!—and yet, where did our victories lead us? Her Dark Majesty abandoned us the moment Chaos challenged her, leaving us to fight her battles alone. Leaving us to die."

"We're not dead" was the dragon's quiet response. "We have a future in Neraka—a new home for all of us who are still alive."

Dusk's words softened Kellin's stony countenance. He patted the cobalt neck. "Neraka is not our home. It is the city of the Dark Queen, and therefore it is empty of honor." He sighed. "I cannot embrace such a home."

The dragon's chuckle took Kellin by surprise. "You find that funny?"

"You may think you've left the knights behind," the dragon said, "but the order lives within you. You'll return to them, and I'll be beside you. There are good days ahead."

The dragon's words were lost on Kellin, who was busy scanning the ground. Suddenly his grip tightened on his mount's neck. "The good days are upon us now, Dusk! Look! There it is! Evermark Keep!"

William W. Connors and Sue Weinlein Cook

Dusk craned her head in the direction her rider pointed. She and Kellin had just rounded a barren peak and come in sight of Ansalon's northern shore. The rough waters of the Turbidus Ocean slammed against the rocky coastline. Into the ancient cliffside was carved a stout fortress, two ruined towers rising from the slate-gray face of the keep. The place looked as though it had been abandoned for a dragon's age.

"Hmf," Dusk exhaled, sounding unimpressed. "You actually lived here once? There's nothing else around for miles."

Kellin merely smiled, drinking in the familiar sight as the refreshing wind breathed across his face. "This is home." Already visions of the two of them living out their days in this, his childhood sanctuary, filled his shining eyes. This is our future, he thought, an island of peace.

Kellin was about to signal Dusk to begin her descent when suddenly, without warning, the blazing noonday sun went black.

He heard Dusk's exclamation and responded to the warning instantly, fighting the feeling that chilled him despite his heavy flight jacket. Kellin pulled sharply on the reins of his powerful blue dragon and ordered her around. Reacting in the space of a heartbeat, Dusk dipped her left wing sharply down and slightly back. At the same time, she sculled air with her right wing and angled her great blue tail to provide a rudder.

Kellin pressed his muscular legs against the dragon's flank and looked upon the future.

"Name of the Abyss!" he murmured.

Man and dragon glimpsed their enemy at the same moment. Barreling out of the sun at him was a monster of nightmare proportions. At first Kellin's mind refused to accept what his eyes told him. No dragon could possibly be that big! This red-scaled horror filled the sky. The deep crimson of its scales set off the ivory white of its teeth, each as long and sharp as a great sword. Its yellow eyes burned with hatred, and the sickly odor of sulfur filled the air around it.

Kellin could feel a great tremor seizing Dusk, then crashing over her. What he felt was dragonfear multiplied tenfold, the instinctive reaction to being in the presence of such a huge, fearsome creature. Horror hung on him like a physical weight. The creature before him could not be real. Shaking with terror, he knew he was wrong as he watched the beast dived at them, wings thrust back, with the dizzy speed of a falling star.

The creature let loose a terrible roar. Kellin stared into a mouth so wide, he thought the beast could swallow his own mount whole. "Wha-" He struggled to find his voice. "What manner of dragon is that?" he cried out to Dusk.

"It is no creature I know!" the blue dragon told her rider, a quiver in her voice. A cold hand gripped the knight's stomach; few sights could unnerve his dragon.

The great crimson form was almost upon them now. Kellin leaned into Dusk's rolling dive, trying to gather his wits. He spoke an order and reversed his pressure on the reins. Instantly Dusk's right wing collapsed along the side of her blue-scaled body, and she gave a single mighty stroke with her left. Wind howled past them in the wake of the plummeting red, filling Kellin's ears.

"We have no quarrel with you, red clanbrother!" Dusk called after the beast in the ancient language of dragons. "Forgo this violence against one of your own!"

In reply, the red spun in midair to face them. "There is no clanmate here," it roared, "only prey!" With a snap of its great jaws, it thrust its great horned head toward them.

"Kellin?" Dusk's impatient query came to him. "Kellin, we can . . . we must get away."

Dusk had always been faster than all the other dragons in the squadron. Kellin knew that a well-executed twist and dive could send them winging their way to safety. Surely to fight such a monster was to die.

But to let such malignant evil go unchallenged . . . ? Kellin fingered his sword pommel, his brow furrowed. Precious seconds spilled away.

Tightening his grip on the reins, Kellin made his decision.

He nudged his mount, signaling a maneuver they had practiced countless times. Obediently, Dusk rolled before the great crimson beast, exposing her belly but bringing up her talons. Kellin kicked his spurs once, crying out a command. The sapphire beast opened her gaping maw, revealing teeth each as long and keen as the warrior's own broadsword.

The giant red was less than twenty yards away and closing fast.

A spider's web of blue-white lightning leapt from Dusk to the other dragon. Kellin snapped his eyes shut, but he was rocked by a brief blaze of light and an accompanying clap of thunder.

The giant red dragon screamed in agony. Traces of blue fire ran along its belly. The smell of seared flesh and dragon's blood found Kellin's nostrils.

"We have drawn first blood!" Dusk rumbled in surprise.

"The battle has just begun!" Kellin murmured in reply. He grabbed for the gleaming lance secured to his saddle. The weapon came free cleanly, and he quickly swung it around.

"True," responded Dusk, "but we have never before faced so massive a wyrm. Let us withdraw now!"

"I can't do that!" But even as he spoke, he realized, with a sinking feeling, that he had underestimated the red. The enormous wyrm was on him again almost before he knew it, its powerful wing flaps deflecting his lance tip before Kellin had managed to brace the weapon properly.

With a loud crack, the lance he had carried since his days at Storm's Keep snapped cleanly in half, then was torn from his grip. His wrist shattered. Pain and anger washed over him.

His best means of fighting the beast, destroyed! A snarl from Dusk warned him.

Dusk twisted to avoid another attack, twisting to elude the raking claws of the massive red dragon. His mount howled as one of the great talons pierced her flank and tore a gaping wound from the base of her neck to the middle of her ribs. Blood flowed freely, and a shower of scales plummeted to the ground below.

Kellin's anger boiled. Such a wound would not go unpunished! Craning his neck, he saw that the speed of the red's dive had carried it far past them. Dusk's maneuver had brought them out from under the attacking wyrm and, with another great stroke of her sapphire wings, the two had escaped from the monster's shadow and into the bright sunlight once more.

His own injury forgotten, Kellin spurred Dusk to greater speed, offering her words of encouragement. But at the same time, a voice he seldom acknowledged—the part of the man that knew fear—whispered that he should abandon all hope. The red was toying with them and would only reward their valor with a scornful death.

As if reading his thoughts, Dusk cried out, "What good does it do for us to die, here and now, Kellin?"

"Sometimes the best choice is to die, my friend." He did not fear dying in battle; years of combat experience had hardened him to the idea. But, by the Abyss, he would find some way to make that monster pay for its accursed arrogance. He gripped his sword handle harder, trying to rally his strength.

"Climb!" Kellin shouted above the winds. "Get

some distance between us!" The knight pounded his mount's neck, leaning forward in the saddle. Dusk growled low in her throat, but, ever loyal, she beat her wings savagely as ordered. Gradually the rolling whitecaps that spread across the Turbidus shoreline began to fall away into the salty haze that hung above the water.

After a few moments, Kellin dared to look over his shoulder. The red had spread its crimson wings wide, catching great masses of air to slow its descent. As the gigantic wyrm pulled out of its dive, the red swiveled its neck up and swept the sky for its prey.

Kellin cursed. The clouds seemed impossibly far away. He took a moment to flex his right hand, but the fingers refused to move, and stabs of pain shot up his arm. He dropped his gaze to examine his broken wrist, scowling. With a few loops and a deftly twisted knot, he tied the reins about his wrist, lashing himself to Dusk.

With his free hand, Kellin drew forth the broadsword that he had been given upon his induction into the knighthood so long ago. It was the last vestige of his regalia, the last reminder of lost faith and lost friends. He pressed the flat of the blade to his lips and offered a word of honor to the memory of his fallen comrades.

"If ever you struck true," he whispered to the weapon, "do so now."

The pursuing dragon roared again, this time close upon his heels. The sound was a tangible force that rolled across Kellin, nearly deafening him despite his padded helmet.

Kellin looked quickly over his shoulder. The red loomed impossible large and drew nearer with every stroke of its great wings. The veteran rider fought down another wave of dragonfear. In less than a minute, he knew, the monster would be near enough to shower them with its fiery breath. Neither of them could survive that.

The red opened its hideous mouth. A predatory gleam burned in the ceature's snakelike eyes as it drew in its breath.

Then suddenly Kellin and Dusk were enveloped in an intangible white gauze.

The warrior let out an unexpected whoop of joy as Dusk shot into the clouds. The blue dragon banked hard to the left, even as a torrent of flame spouted into the whiteness. The cruel fire charred the scales of Dusk's wing tip. The air came alive with a sizzling, spitting sound as fire melted into water vapor. The bitter smoke caught in Kellin's throat, but he fought back his choking and nudged Dusk into a gradual climb.

"There . . . along the coast!" he shouted sickly. His mind whirled. Another glance back showed that the giant red had surged into the veil of vapor after them, its massive wings creating great drafts. The air torrents tore the clouds apart, exposing them to the dragon's ravenous eyes.

All of a sudden a powerful backdraft of mammoth wings hammered the pair with the force of a hurricane. Kellin cried out to his mount, but for all her strength, Dusk was helpless before this gale.

End over end they rolled, Kellin gritting his teeth against the pain as the knotted reins pulled savagely at his broken wrist. Dusk let loose a shriek at the wrenching of her wounded flank. Disoriented and dazed, they began to tumble toward the churning surface of the sea below.

Kellin could see the red swing back to pursue. The former knight was barely conscious. The pain from his shattered wrist clouded his vision with a red haze. Through this agony, he watched the great beast surge toward them. He saw the wyrm bring its talons forward, then sweep its wings back. Absurdly, the image of a hawk swooping down on a tiny sparrow came into his mind. The red's sulfurous smell swept across him. The wicked claws would reach them in seconds.

Dusk issued a growl of frustration. Kellin felt the valiant blue dragon struggle to pull out of her fall. Rage infused the warrior with new strength. With a cry, Kellin brought his sword around. As the keen edge of the magical weapon traced an arc through the smoke-filled air, a shower of sparks trailed, hissing, from the blade.

Just as a gigantic claw began to close about Dusk, the blade cut through the red dragon's scales and pierced the flesh beneath. A rippling wave of fire burst from the weapon. Again Kellin smelled the monster's burning flesh, and he allowed himself a moment of exhausted pride. However, he heard no outcry from the red dragon. Kellin moaned as he realized the creature had never even registered the blow. The sword fell away from his hand, impotent and abandoned.

Dusk turned to face her rider, her eyes slitted with pain and fury. "No more!" With those words, she raised a sharp talon and sheared the reins that bound Kellin to her. A moan of disbelief escaped his lips as the former knight tumbled off the dragon's back and fell.

The passing moments seemed to slow to a crawl. As he plummeted, he remembered seeing the red tighten its grip about the bleeding blue dragon, then savagely crush the life out of his beloved Dusk.

He thought he saw—he couldn't say for certain—tenuous streams of shimmering blue light slowly rise from Dusk's limp body, then move, as if drawn by the red dragon's force of will, to settle around the giant like an aura. After an endless moment, the last of the glow was absorbed into the crimson scales.

Tumbling head over heels through the air, Kellin caught a flash of the red beast twining its neck skyward as it opened its talons and released Dusk, heard its triumphant roar. Was it the pain playing with his mind, Kellin wondered, or the dizzying speed of his fall? But no. All that remained of his blue mount was a desiccated husk, which now spun toward him, the scales peeled away like dry leaves torn from their branches. Flesh streamed away to reveal yellowed bones.

A tear rolled down his cheek as the wind rushed past him. In her last moments, his lifelong friend had despised his foolishness.

The rolling waters of the Turbidus Ocean rushed up to meet him. Kellin had one last glimpse at the jagged coastline, the Khalkist Mountains rising beyond. A land worth fighting for. "Great Queen, protect them," he murmured as the churning waters embraced his broken body.

* * * * *

The sand felt warm and gritty on his bruised face. The great pounding in his head accompanied the throb of his smashed wrist.

Kellin raised his head and fixed his astonished eyes on his sword. Its blade plunged deep into the sandy ground, the weapon stood sentinel like the grave marker of a worthy warrior. The skull of the Dark Knights' crest stared at him defiantly, as if daring him to believe the unimaginable.

"Great Queen . . ." he exhaled, reaching out with a trembling hand to touch the gleaming weapon. Gingerly he pulled it from the sand, then stared at the blade, uncomprehending.

Etched in black on the wet blade were the words, *Protect them.*

Still grasping the sword, Kellin struggled to his feet and angled his head toward the sky. From the position of the sun, it looked as if no time at all had passed since he'd fallen from Dusk's back.

He swallowed hard, guilt-stricken over the memory of his dragon companion, who, thanks to his own lust for a glorious death, had become the first casualty in this strange new war. Cradling his injured wrist, he looked upward and saw the red monster that had killed Dusk.

William W. Connors and Sue Weinlein Cook

Something caught the warrior's eye. A shape appeared in the clouds behind the red—another dragon the size of the red. A glint of emerald in the summer sun told him the newcomer was green.

In the blink of an eye, the green had swept down upon its prey, and Kellin knew it had used the red's distraction with Dusk to maneuver into position. With screams of challenge, the two serpents coiled around each other in ferocious sky battle. For a moment, Kellin felt like shouting encouragement to the emerald wyrm. Then he glanced down at the sword in his hand and knew what he must do.

He must head south, toward Neraka, to warn the knights of this unprecedented monster. He grimaced. The cursed Solamnics, with their stories of great dragons, had been right—dark times lay ahead for every man, elf, and dwarf. As with the war against Chaos, this was an enemy that would call for an alliance between all races, between all knights. He smiled ruefully. Dusk had been right, too, for he must return to the knights.

As the thought sank in, his heart lightened in understanding. Somehow Dusk had known! Cutting him free had been the only way to save him from the wyrm's deadly jaws, the only way to tell the world, to give it a chance. Humbled, Kellin closed his eyes. The honor of his dragon's sacrifice shamed him.

Kellin turned his gaze back to the sky above. The two massive wyrms were locked in battle. Painfully he stood, and painfully he took his first steps. He stumbled, got up, and glanced one last time at the two massive wyrms. They took no notice of the little speck below.

I must tell the world, the Knight of Takhisis told himself as he began his long journey home.

The Restoration

Jeff Crook

Alantine did not care for dwarven music, least of all at this delicate time. In the three years since his arrival in Tarsis to work in the restoration of the Tarsis Library, he had grown used to the sounds of dwarven construction—the tap and ring of stone masons, the deep throaty curses of the laborers, even the braying of the mules used to haul stone quarried outside the city—but this song of the Cataclysm, with each new verse more morose than the preceding one, distracted his mind from the work at hand. He bent closer to the yellowed parchment scroll with its circular stains of pale violet. He concentrated, trying to block out all other sounds.

Most of the writing on the scroll was ruined, but enough remained to hint that it might be a historical document. Certain half-guessed-at names, and notes scrawled in the margin many years after the scroll was originally written, hinted at a date from the Age of Might. A dozen similar scrolls lay near at hand, awaiting Alantine's scrutiny, while the remainder of the desk was littered with scraps and oddments of paper, some as ancient as the scrolls themselves.

Alantine adjusted his robe, preparing himself mentally for the task at hand. His robe was red, a last vestige of his former profession; the robe once marked him as a mage. When the moons of magic vanished from the sky during the War of Chaos, the power upon which mages depended for their spellcraft vanished with them. All that remained of the once-mighty magic of Krynn were a few rare artifacts and items created before Chaos, items like the shiny metallic vial that Alantine now removed from the pouch at his belt. The vial appeared to be crafted of hammered silver, but when he set it on the desk beside the parchment scroll, the light from his single candle shone through it. He noted the level of the crystalline liquid within the vial. Less than half remained, Alantine saw with a sorrowful shake of his head. When empty, another dwindling resource of magic would be lost forever. Therefore, only those documents deemed most promising were chosen for the process Alantine was about to perform.

He removed a soft leather wallet from a secret pocket in his robe. Inside the wallet were three little feathers, all dull gray in color, and each smaller than the smallest finger of his hand. He removed one feather and laid it on the scroll, then returned the wallet to his pocket. Carefully, lest he spill one precious drop, he loosened the lead stopper from the vial, removed the stopper, and shook it above the scroll. A glittering trail, like sparks struck from glowing steel, rained from the stopper. He set the stopper aside.

Holding the vial up to the light of his candle, Alantine dipped the tiny feather into its neck. He watched the feather's silhouette through the silvery glass as it neared the surface of the magical liquid. Slowly he moved it in distances measured by the thicknesses of hairs until the very tip of the feather's quill just broke the surface of the liquid. Even more slowly, he removed the feather until, when it was free from the neck of the vial, he saw a single diamond droplet clinging to its tip. The feather itself had undergone a miraculous change. It was now a brilliant scarlet color and felt soft as silk between his fingers. He lowered the feather to the scroll and breathed on it.

The droplet shimmered, then fell. He watched it

fall as though time had slowed. The droplet struck the page. Ripples of red embers spread slowly from that point; it looked almost like a grass fire on the plains of Abanasinia, seen from a great height at night, as though from the back of a dragon. Where the ember worms burned, they left behind not black ash but clean parchment, containing words and letters and sentences as crisp and black as the day they were penned. The rings of embers slowly burned themselves out, leaving behind a smell of cloves. Alantine pressed a sheet of blotter paper to the scroll, then rolled it up and set it aside. He reached across the desk for the next one.

A shadow within the shadows across from his desk caught his eye. Alantine noticed suddenly that the dwarves had ceased their song, and that the library was dark and silent. He hadn't heard anyone descend the stairs, but then he had been absorbed in his work. Assuming the figure he saw standing quietly beside the stair was one of the library's scholars, he said, "I have just completed the first of the M-eleven scrolls."

Taking the next scroll from the pile and unrolling it on the desk, Alantine continued. "I should be through with these within the hour, if you would like to return for them." He picked up the vial and feather, then looked up at the figure. The person had not moved. "This work is very delicate. Can I help you with something?"

The figure stepped from the shadows, its heavy cowl hiding its face. It wore long black robes, like those of the old order of evil magic. Alantine felt his throat constrict with fear.

This was no scholar! "Who are you?" he asked shakily.

The figure continued to advance silently until it had positioned itself between the desk and the stairs. Alantine gasped. He could see the stairs through the black robes. Icy wind roared down the staircase, coming from the ruined library above, freezing

Alantine and setting him shivering but never stirring the figure's ghostly robes. The candle on the desk dimmed to a weak blue glow. The figure raised its hands to its hood and pushed it back. Strands of snow-white hair spilled out. The candle flickered and died, plunginging the room into darkness. Alantine screamed and dropped the vial.

Red flames leapt from the desk.

* * * * *

Sometimes, when looking around at the ruined inner city of Tarsis and especially at the rising white marble structure of the new library, Eltam missed the quiet order of the halls of his former master in far-away Palanthas. As a young priest, dressed in robes of white to signify his dedication to the great god Paladine, Eltam had served his scholastic apprenticeship in the Library of Palanthas. The ancient halls of that great library were once filled with orderly rows of books, scrolls, and parchment manuscripts, each properly labeled and classified, each cross-referenced, everything in its place. But Tarsis, with its abandoned tumbledown buildings and vine-choked alleys— places so desolate that even the rats seemed to avoid them—depressed him beyond description. As he stood before the entrance to the old library, he gazed off into the distance, where a black storm was rising, sending out its first fingers of gusty wind to stir the dust of the streets. With it came, as if borne by the wind, the sound of loud dwarven music from the direction of their settlement.

Eltam turned back to the library's entrance. On either side of the doorway stood a Knight of Solamnia. The newly-risen wind stirred their long mustaches, but not their reverie; their eyes were far away, perhaps envisioning the glorious battles they were missing while serving in this desolate place. Eltam stepped past them and opened the door to the ruined library.

He had an appointment to meet a young man named Alantine to look over one of the scrolls he'd recently restored. In the dim light that filtered from far below, Eltam began to descend the staircase leading downward to Alantine's study. Suddenly a strong gust of wind ripped past Eltam, tearing at his robes. A scream of terror echoed through the empty hall. The stair was suddenly dark. A flickering red light blazed up from below, making the darkened stairwell look like a large, balefully glowing eye.

"Fire?" Eltam gasped. He felt fear clutch at his heart.

Before he could move, he was rudely shoved aside. "Excuse me, Brother," the knights grunted as they passed. Eltam heard the ringing slither of steel as the knights drew their swords. He fell in behind them, his robes whispering on the stones as the knights clanked and creaked in their oiled armor and stitched leather. As they neared the first sublevel of the library, the red firelight dimmed and was replaced by an ordinary yellow glow, like that of a candle. The knights slowed, and Eltam crowded close behind them.

When they reached the bottom of the stairs, one of the knights called out, "Who goes there?"

A strange and pungent aroma, like cloves, wafted in their faces.

A faint voice answered, "Alantine. It's only Alantine."

Eltam followed the knights into the first great hall of the lower level of the library. A large desk was heaped with tottering towers of manuscripts. At the corner of the desk, a stub of red candle burned in a bronze dish. Behind the desk stood Alantine of Northern Ergoth, a man whom Eltam knew somewhat, having worked with him in the Library. Alantine was disheveled, and sweat gleamed brightly on his dark face.

"What is the problem here?" one of the knights asked.

"It . . . it is n-nothing," Alantine sputtered. "I . . . I

was m-momentarily startled . . . by a large rat."

"A rat!" Eltam exclaimed, suddenly overcome by his concern for the precious books. "Here?"

"And then the wind extinguished my candle," Alantine continued. "Really, it was nothing at all."

"We thought there was a fire," the other knight said.

"A slight . . . accident with a potion. Nothing damaged," Alantine said ruefully. "You can go now."

"But what about the rat!" Eltam protested.

The knights turned and, irritably sheathing their swords, stalked back up the stairs.

"But what about the rat?" Eltam said again. And then he saw that Alantine was quivering with fear.

"There is no rat," Alantine whispered. "Come here and see what has happened."

Eltam clambered around piles of books to stand beside Alantine. The desk was littered with scraps and fragments of parchments, old scrolls, and several ancient books with yellowed leaves spilling from their covers. In the center of the desk was a circular area where all the paper looked as new as the day it was made. Even the brown wood of the desk beneath the papers appeared newly polished. One scroll, lying just at the edge of the circle, was half clean, new parchment, while the other half was crumbling and yellow. Eltam shot Alantine a curious glance.

"I spilled my potion of restoration," Alantine said by way of explanation.

"Oh, no!" Eltam gasped. He had heard of the powers of Alantine's potion, and he knew how precious each drop was to his work. "Was it all lost?"

"Almost," Alantine said. He held the vial up and shook it. "Only a few doses remain."

"This is terrible!" Eltam exclaimed.

"Never mind that," Alantine said, his voice shaking with excitement. "Look what the accident has uncovered!" He held out a small, torn scrap of paper.

Eltam glanced at it, then back at Alantine. The paper was nothing more than a receipt for books. For a moment, Eltam feared the former mage from Northern Ergoth had lost his mind. He looked at the receipt again. Near the bottom, he read,

To be stored on shelf A3, section 242, third library sublevel north.

"I didn't know there was a third underground level to the library," Eltam said.

"Neither did I. Nobody knows about it," Alantine said.

"Oh," Eltam sighed, and then a light of realization spread across his face. "Oh, my!" he exclaimed.

"Exactly, but there's more," Alantine said. "Read here." He pointed to the top of the page.

Eltam read, *I hereby pass into safekeeping the following books, to be held at the Library of Tarsis by Sir Oleade Pnet, Head Librarian, until such a time as I return for them, and under the stipulation that they be lent to no one.* Below this was the signature of the librarian, and below that, scrawled in a thin, whispery script, rather like the spidery lines in cracked porcelain, was a name black with portent, a name that reached across three centuries to evoke fear in those who knew the magnitude of his evil, a name that the merest whisper conjured up, ghostlike, evil itself. A name that slithered from the tongue.

Eltam shuddered as he said it: "Fistandantilus."

"A spellbook of Fistandantilus!" Alantine breathed. "Look, there it is written out: 'One spellbook, night-blue binding.' And to think it was here, beneath our very noses all the time!"

"Where?" Eltam asked.

"On the third level."

"But where is the third level?"

"I don't know." Alantine looked about helplessly. "We have to find it. Think, Eltam, think of the secrets hidden in that spellbook, secrets that even Raistlin Majere may have never discovered. He didn't know about this spellbook, or he would have taken it along with all the others. And now it is ours, ours to find, ours to pry apart."

"Will the spells still work?" Eltam asked dubiously.

"They might! Who knows?" Atlantine was eager. "I have heard rumors that some spellbooks from very powerful mages still keep their magic!"

"What use have either of us for the spellbook of an evil wizard?" Eltam asked, somewhat haughtily.

"None," said Alantine hesitantly. "I guess. But it is of historical value. And we will have the entire third level to explore. What if that section of the library is intact? What new treasures shall you find there? Look at the note! 'Shelf A3, section 242, third library sublevel north.' The third level must be enormous."

"But we don't even know how to find our way down. Where shall we begin?"

"At second library level north, I should think," Alantine answered. "There must be a hidden stair."

Alantine reached behind a tottering stack of books and picked up a travel-worn wooden staff. Eltam looked at the weapon and raised one eyebrow. "Do you think this third level might be dangerous?" he asked.

"Possibly," Alantine answered somewhat vaguely as he rearranged the pouches at his belt. He slid a small dagger from its sheath hidden in the left sleeve of his robe and checked the weapon's point for sharpness. "There's no telling what might have crawled down there in the long ages since the Cataclysm."

"Perhaps we should alert the knights, then," Eltam suggested.

"And share the glory of discovery?" Alantine scoffed.

"Let me at least bring a torch." Eltam removed a torch from a bronze sconce in the wall. He wished he had some better weapon, but for now fire must serve him. He lit it from the candle on the desk; the torch sputtered and burst into life.

Alantine led the way down rows of leaning shelves. They rounded a corner and entered an aisle that took them north. They spent most of the remainder of the night crawling among the stacks and piles of ancient books. Huge shards of masonry had fallen from the roof and crashed through the sturdy oak shelves during the Chaos War, when the Library of Tarsis had been destroyed by fire. Heading north, they climbed over histories of knights forgotten, and histories of knights before Solamnia was even named. They crawled over esoteric sciences thought ancient before the Graystone was forged by the dwarven god Reorx in the depth of time. In order to surmount a pyramid of tomes and broken shelves, they built a stair of geometries describing the portals of time and space. At last they reached the far northern wall of the second level of the great library, and as yet they had seen no hint of a stair, nor any other passage that might lead down.

Exhausted, Alantine leaned against the cold stone wall and sighed. The light of the torch illuminated only a relatively small area around them; the darkness beyond echoed eerily. The torch's flame began to flicker and smoke.

"I wish I had brought two torches," Eltam said. "We'd better get back before this one burns out. I don't want to have to find my way back in the dark."

Alantine ignored him. "It must be here somewhere," he muttered. "It must be."

"It would take years to clear all the books and rubble from this area. It's at least twenty feet deep here," Eltam pointed out. He glanced at his companion. Something seemed different about Alantine. He looked smaller, as though diminished by their failure. The torch began to dim.

Then Eltam felt the pile of books giving beneath his feet, and he suddenly realized his mistake. The rubble and books on which they stood had begun to sink, and they were sinking with it. Like some horrible sand trap built in the desert by a giant ant lion, the books were sucking them down into a hole, a maelstrom of literature that threatened to bury them alive. Eltam clambered up the side, desperately seeking some escape, while below him Alantine cried out in terror. Then, horribly, his cry was cut short. For a moment, all Eltam heard was the muffled grinding of books and his own rasping breath. He struggled to keep the dying torch away from the dry parchment, lest he turn this trap into a pyre as well.

At last the maelstrom stilled. The portly, middle-aged monk managed to clamber out of the sinkhole. Desperately searching, Eltam could find no sign of Alantine. Occasionally a stray tome slithered down the side, but the slope seemed to have stabilized. Eltam called repeatedly for his companion, yet heard no sound.

Slowly Eltam edged away from the hole, inch by inch over the unstable pile of books. The only chance for Alantine's survival was for Eltam to bring the dwarves back to help dig him out. He only hoped Alantine could survive long enough to be rescued. He had almost reached the outer layer of books when the pile began to slip again. He slid a half foot deeper into the hole, stopped, slid another foot. When he stopped sliding, he felt himself balanced at the very edge of disaster. And then the books really broke loose, and he was falling, deeper and deeper, the pages mounting over his knees, over his thighs. In desperation—his last thought for the welfare of the books—he flung the torch away, hoping it would land on bare stone and burn itself out. He watched it fly over the top of the trap as he was steadily sucked below.

The books covered his belly, lapped at his chest; he felt their weight crushing him, their hard corners stabbing his thighs. He didn't pray, because there weren't any gods left to pray to. He just closed his eyes and waited for death in this quicksand of knowledge. The books covered his head.

And then suddenly he was free. He found himself sliding down a chute, loose books pelting after him. The image came to mind that he had just passed through the narrow neck of a giant hourglass filled with books. He laughed, a little hysterically, at the strangeness of his deliverance. The books continued to slide beneath him, and he rode downward on the wave of bound pages. His motion slowed as the books beneath him grew fewer in number, until at last he stopped. He found himself in a stairway of carved stone steps leading down. A queer blue light glowed steadily from below, and a dry, sepulchral air rose up the stairs, as though stirred for the first time in centuries.

Eltam coughed and covered his nose with the sleeve of his robe as he cautiously descended the stairs. At the foot, the stairwell opened out into a small area surrounded on three sides by perfectly parallel rows of shelves vanishing into the shadows. The blue light he had noticed earlier emanated from some point down the aisles directly across from the stair, while to the left stood a desk as massive and solid-looking as a butcher's block. A knight in armor sat at the desk. Eltam realized with a shudder that the knight had been dead for centuries, probably since before the first Cataclysm. His flesh was strangely preserved by the dry air here, his skin as yellow and flaky as old parchment, and his brown-toothed mouth and empty eyes gaped blackly in an eternal yawn . . . or scream. An antique quill stood poised in his shriveled hand; the ink in the bottle beside it had long since turned to dust.

"Alantine!" Eltam yelled, but he regretted his shout before the name had fully escaped his lips.

A hissing noise echoed back from the shelves, like the ghosts of a thousand dead librarians invoking him to silence. Immobile shadows moved all around him. Slowly the shades and wraiths settled and returned to their places. More slowly still did Eltam's heart settle and return to its place. His white robe rippled like a sheet hung out in the wind.

A hissing whisper set his heart racing anew. "Eltam!"

For a moment, he thought the voice was that of the corpse sitting at the desk, but with a suppressed sigh of relief, he saw Alantine emerge from the shadows. The young man's red robe was tattered and filthy, almost black, as though it were stained with old blood. His cheeks were hollow, his eyes sunken. He clutched to his chest a book—the source of the blue light. "Eltam!" he hissed again, pleading. "Help!" His eyes rolled up, and he collapsed to the floor.

Eltam knelt at his companion's side and touched his cheek. Alantine's flesh felt cold and clammy, but he still breathed, albeit shallowly. His hands were frozen around the book—literally frozen. They were white with frost. Eltam chafed Alantine's hands and cheeks, trying to revive him, calling his name. Feeling his neck for a pulse, Eltam found only a slow, sluggish throbbing. He wrestled with the young man's stiffened arms, finally managing to pry his hands free from the book. It slid from his chest to the floor. Eltam pushed the book aside with his foot. Icy pain pierced even the thick leather of his boot; the book's evil magic was palpable.

Free of the book, Alantine began to slowly recover. His flesh warmed, the frost melted from his hands. His eyelids fluttered, and he moaned. He mumbled strange words, words that reminded Eltam of the old spells of magic. Alantine stirred and began to struggle as though against some unseen foe. "Verily, master," he cried. Then he started awake and stared wildly at Eltam.

"Calm down." Eltam said soothingly. "Tell me what happened to you. Where did you find that book?"

"The book?" Alantine gasped. "Did I bring it with me?"

"Yes. Don't you remember?"

"I recall touching it." Alantine sighed and shuddered with remembered horror. The ghastly blue light emanating from the bindings of the book formed shadows over his eyes. "And then the dead began to stir. . . . They touched me with their bones. . . . They tore at me as though they hated me and the book. Eltam! The book is Fistandantalus's spellbook. I believe it was killing me! I couldn't move, I couldn't fight, I couldn't run. . . . I think I fainted. I'm not sure. It seemed more as if I faded from this place into another place, a battlefield, and there were Knights of Solamnia and ogres, and the ogres were fighting in the tents of the knights, and women screamed.

"But then I was on the field, and there were dead bodies everywhere, and one of them was a woman, a young woman in knight's armor, bleeding from many wounds. I tried to help here. I called upon Paladine. Isn't it strange that I called upon him? The wounded woman became a golden hourglass of great value, but the crystal globe at its bottom broke, and all the sand was pouring out on the floor. For some reason, it terrified me that the sand should run out, and I tried desperately to stop it, but there was nothing I could do. I looked around for help, but there was no one there. I was alone on a wide empty plain, and I couldn't see the horizon. The sky and the ground were the same color. But in the distance, there was a rock, and I thought I saw something stuck to it—a black rag. As the last grains of sand funneled through the neck of the hourglass, a shadow fell across me, and looking up, I saw . . . I saw . . ."

"What did you see?" Eltam asked, aghast.

"I saw the ghost of the man who startled me in the library earlier today. Oh, Eltam!" Alantine cried out, clutching at his companion. "It was Fistandantalus. He was real. He wasn't a ghost at all. He told me to take the book, to take it to Palin Majere. I tried to refuse, but he insisted. He has a way of insisting that makes it impossible to resist."

"I think perhaps we should get out of here. These old books . . ." Eltam shuddered. "Nobody knows what forbidden knowledge they contain. Maybe there are things here we aren't supposed to know. Maybe one of those things crept into your dream. Maybe that's why the gods sealed this room."

"What do you mean, 'sealed'?" Alantine asked.

"We must go," Eltam said. "I don't feel right here. Something doesn't want us here."

He helped Alantine rise to his feet; the wounded young man leaned heavily upon him. They began to move toward the stair, but suddenly Alantine stopped. "The book. We have to take the book with us."

"Don't touch it!" Eltam warned, trying to urge his companion forward. "It's deadly. It nearly killed you."

"We can put it in a bag or a pouch. Perhaps in that desk," Alantine said. "I can stand. You go look."

"We should leave it," Eltam said. "The book is obviously evil, and if we try . . ." His words trailed off. His eyes went to the desk. The corpse no longer sat behind it. Instead, the mummified knight stood in front of the desk. Red flames lit his hollow eye sockets. The dead knight moved, and his old bones and parchmentlike skin creaked like an old book being cracked open for the first time in centuries. He pointed one long, clawlike finger at Eltam and moved his mouth in a horrible imitation of speech. Eltam, nearly paralyzed with terror, heard words, a voice like the wind hissing over the Plains of Dust, a voice made hoarse by long disuse and centuries of dry, dusty tomb-like air.

"You must not take the book," the corpse croaked.

"It is my charge. On my honor."

Eltam slowly backed away from the monstrosity, but it remained where it stood, blocking the stairs. "What is it?" Alantine asked fearfully.

"A Knight of Solamnia, I think, doomed to guard this place. But I can't imagine what he did to warrant such a terrible fate!"

"What does he want?"

"He doesn't want us to take the spellbook," Eltam said.

The dead knight's voice grew stronger. He was making a speech long prepared, reciting some history he had spent ages memorizing. At first they could not understand him, but gradually they were able to make out words and parts of sentences.

". . . there I encountered the archmage Fistandantalus, for he was among the court of the Kingpriest. Whereas the Kingpriest was blinded by his own glory, Fistandantalus saw into my heart and knew me for one of his own. It was there he gave into my keeping, among other items, a spellbook. 'Keep it well,' he said to me. 'I do not wish it to remain here. A great and terrible event is about to occur, and I do not want this precious book destroyed. It contains my research into the realms of pure magic. I sought once to escape the necessity of calling upon the moons for magical power. My reasons for desiring a disconnected wellspring of power are secret, but may soon be known to all. As it is, the research failed, but not for any apparent reason. I have concluded that the time is not right, and that the spells, under any other circumstances, would have worked. Someday, perhaps, the time will come. When it does, I will return for my books.' "

Alantine removed his tattered, blackened robe. "We have to take the spellbook, Eltam," he said. "The time he means is now. We'll wrap the book in my robe."

"Here I have remained," the knight continued.

"When Paladine departed from this world, I stirred, feeling the curse lifted from me. Those who had died here stirred as well. But rest is not our lot, for still the geas of Fistandantilus holds us. He gave into my safekeeping the books, until such a time as he returns for them, or sends one of his agents to retrieve them. Among others, one spellbook, night-blue binding." The dead knight paused and pointed at the spellbook lying on the floor at Eltam's feet.

"We have come for the spellbook," Alantine said. "Fistandantilus sent us, just as he said. Eltam," he whispered now. "Tell him we are servants of Fistandantilus."

"I will not!" Eltam cried, turning. "Nor will I even pretend to be a servant of evil. I may not feel the spirit of Paladine in my heart, lending me his strength as he once did. But still I feel something is there, watching over me, surrounding me."

Alantine dropped his robe over the spellbook, covering most of the blue light that emanated from it, casting the chamber into nearly total darkness. The dead knight reached out a hand. "You are not sent by my master. You must not take the book," the corpse hissed. The knight's skeletal hand tried to grab Alantine. Eltam stepped protectively in front of his colleague. The knight lashed out, sending Eltam sprawling.

In desperation, Alantine groped for his dagger. He felt through his robe, hurriedly searching the pockets, but the blade was gone. His hand closed over the vial containing the last few precious drops of his potion of restoration.

The knight towered over Alantine, reaching for his throat with clawlike fingers. "You must not take the book!" he shrieked.

Alantine flung the vial as hard as he could at the corpse's head. Silvery shards exploded in the air; the skull erupted in red flames.

The knight staggered back, hissing, but the hissing

soon became a scream of inhuman pain. Beneath the flames, the shriveled face became flesh; lank, dusty hair turned black and spilled down upon its shoulders. The flames crept down the neck. New blood coursed through throbbing veins, down the chest and across the shoulders. Withered cords became hard muscle. The knight pitched to the floor and lay still. The magical flames burned out. The knight stared blindly at the ceiling; his breast, half in the bloom of youth, half old, dead, mummified flesh, heaved. He sucked in the musty, clove-scented air. The knight moaned.

Eltam crawled to his feet and staggered over to Alantine's side. Blood poured from a huge gash on the monk's brow. "Let's get out of here!" he gasped.

Alantine paused to lift the spellbook and wrap it in his robe. Even through the heavy cloth, he felt its cold numb his flesh and his senses. Fumblingly he swaddled it, covering the last of its queer blue light. Darkness absolute descended upon them as they ran for the stairs.

A heartbeat passed, and they were almost there. Then icy hands grabbed Eltam from behind and flung him across the room. He crashed into a bookshelf. Something struck Alantine across the head; he fell, stunned, dropping the spellbook. A ray of blue light pierced the darkness.

Horrible shapes leapt into being in the light— shades of human spirits, withered men and women with flesh as black as tar and eyes like red coals. Some gloated over Alantine where he lay, half senseless; some floated upon the empty air around Eltam.

The latter clambered to his feet, shaking off waves of nausea. Alantine moaned and thrashed at the shapes coming nearer and nearer.

A huge rage welled up within Eltam. What dreadful fate brought him and young Alantine to this horrible place, to these hopeless straits? Why should they, two simple scholars, die? For the spellbook of an evil man? A spellbook that might return evil magic to the world, without the magic of good to counterbalance it.

Eltam reached into the collar of his robe and drew out the platinum medallion of Paladine upon its chain. He wasn't certain why he still wore it. Its edges were hard, the metal cold; it hung heavy upon its chain and was sometimes a burden when he was especially tired and eyesore from study. Hope? Hope in what?

Eltam felt the cold undead breath of the creatures drawing ever closer. He heard their whispers, their horrible whispers of longing for his warmth, his life. He stared at the medallion. In the olden days, clerics could drive away such creatures with the holy might of Paladine. But Paladine was gone.

"And soon I shall join him, wherever he is," Eltam said aloud.

"Join us. Breathe into us so that we may feel your warmth!" came the whispers from the darkness. Chill fingers brushed his cheek, like wind blowing across glacial snows. He closed his eyes; his lips parted, his hand clasped the hard edges of the medallion.

He heard Alantine scream. Eltam opened his eyes and saw a face, beautiful and pale, yet terrifying, hovering near him. Through the face, he saw creatures swarming over Alantine, cackling with glee. Again Alantine screamed like a man being eaten alive.

"Get back!" Eltam shouted and thrust out his hand. A burning white light exploded from between his fingers, shredding like smoke in the wind the wraith who was stooping to kiss him. The other undead fled like shadows from a newly lit torch.

"Release him!" Eltam ordered.

The dead terrorizing Alantine crept away like cringing jackals, their red eyes burning with hatred.

Only then did Eltam marvel at the light in his hand. He tried to look at it, but it burned his sight.

Has Paladine returned? he wondered. He felt a pain in his other hand. Opening it, he found the platinum medallion, symbol of his former god, biting into his palm. The medallion lay there, cold, powerless. The power he felt surging through his veins came from no god, he suddenly realized. It comes from within me.

"Alantine!" he cried and took a step toward the stairs. An iron rod of pain hammered downward through his hip, sickening him, and black spots burst in his vision. The light from his hand began to fade. He staggered and fell, struggling to remain conscious. Slowly the pain subsided, but it remained buried deep within, waiting. Only the new power he felt, like wine rising to his head, kept the pain at bay.

"Alantine!" he cried once more.

"Eltam?" a voice answered weakly.

Slowly Alantine sat up. In the light from his hand, Eltam saw that the young man was bloodied but still alive. Red wounds tinged with blue scarred his chest and face.

"Run!" Eltam cried.

"What?"

"Get out of here," Eltam told him. "My hip is broken. I can't move. But I'll hold them off until you escape."

Alantine blinked, trying to shade his eyes so he could see. "What is that light?" Alantine asked, awed.

"I'm holding back the darkness!" Eltam said. Even as he spoke, the light began to dim. "You must go. You must escape before my strength fails."

Alantine rose and retrieved the spellbook from where it had fallen.

"Alantine, don't!" Eltam cried. "Leave the spellbook here."

He wrapped it in his cloak and clutched it to his chest. Then he turned and wearily climbed a step.

Alantine looked back, pain and violent emotion

contorting his face. "I must do this, Eltam. I came all this way to bring it back."

"It will kill you," Eltam pleaded with him. "It will destroy everything it touches."

Alantine shook his head and continued to climb the stairs.

"Don't leave me here to die for nothing," Eltam begged.

"Eltam, I . . ." Alantine looked back, guilt-ridden.

Eltam's light grew dimmer. The undead guardians of the library crept in with the expanding shadows, snarling in anticipation. "Alantine!" He groaned.

"You won't die. Don't give up. I'll bring help," Alantine said.

The chamber grew darker. "No!" Eltam said. "Don't come back. Seal this place. Have the dwarves brick up the stairs." The pain from his hip rose in nauseating, throbbing waves. He was looking down a long tunnel, at the end of which was a bright light, and beyond it a young man holding a dark star. "Leave me."

He heard Alantine's footsteps on the stairs. They rose slowly at first, then more quickly, until they were lost at last in the distance. Whispers closed in around Eltam as the circle of his inner light faded and blinked out. He lay back on the stone floor. It felt cold against his shaved head. He had failed. The spellbook had seduced Alantine. Perhaps . . . Palin Majere could yet save him. Ruby eyes and sapphire forms gathered near, burning with hatred.

"Fistandantalus will not be pleased," said a man's voice very near his ear. A dry, dead finger caressed his cheek.

"Fistandantalus is dead!" Eltam said. "He's been dead for over two hundred years." At least the spellbook will not fall into his evil hands.

"No . . . he's alive now," said the voice and laughed.

Relics

Jeff Grubb

---

27 SC

With the passing of the heroes, the incursion of Chaos, and the coming of the great dragons, Ansalon had been irrevocably changed. And yet, at a basic level, most people continued to live as they had always lived. There were lives to rebuild, crops to harvest, meals to cook, and children to raise. As time passed, people began to forget the past or to reshape it in their memories into more pleasing and suitable shapes.

-From the *Chronicles of Nathal*, compiled in 31 SC

The tolling of the bell reached the village long before the wagon did. The sound was a jangling, ear-bursting peal that could not be ignored, that interrupted every thought and impinged on every action in the town. The clamor swelled in intensity as the wagon neared the stockade gates, an incessant herald of the arriving merchant.

Jamie heard it over the rhythmic pumping of the bellows in his father's smith shop. As the other youngsters streamed toward the town's protective wall, Jamie looked to his father. He would not abandon his post without his father's permission, but he was aware that already the others were getting the best spots to watch the newcomer.

The older smith scowled for a moment, then nodded at the boy. In an instant, the youth was gone, bellows in midpump, to join the others at the stockade wall. He squeezed between his friends, Shel and Roger, along the narrow inner ledge, and hung over the side with the other young boys and girls. By that time, the merchant's wagon was almost at the gates, the bell's clanging now immediate and almost painful to the ears.

The clamoring bell was mounted atop a curious cart, slung low in front, with huge, oversized wheels in the rear—large metal monstrosities that seemed to come from another wagon entirely. Indeed, the entire carriage seemed a hybrid of several vehicles merged together, the sole survivor of some sorcerous collision. The wagon's forward half looked like a salvaged boat, the riding board mounted at the dragon-headed prow. The back half, raised above the huge wheels, resembled nothing so much as a small cottage of wood and plaster that had suddenly decided to take up the traveling life. A narrow balcony ran along the left-hand side of the cottage at about shoulder height. Small poles jutted from every prominence and corner of the wagon, from which were hung pennants, tattered but brightly colored. The wagon was pulled by a pair of oxen—huge, lumbering, slow beasts, their harnesses draped with similar tattered pennants. They plodded with a resolute gait that said they were unimpressed by the festive swaths of cloth adorning them.

The bell was perched on the rear, mounted atop a high point of cobbled stone that apparently doubled for a chimney. The bell was connected to the riding board with a thin line, broken and reknotted several times. The wagon's driver yanked on the rope again and again, continuing the clatter until he was right up to the gates. Jamie noticed that almost all the village's young people, as well as some of the older members, were clustered along the stockade wall peering over at the newcomer.

The cart's driver looked as if he were dressed in spare pennants from his cart. His voluminous cloak was a tatterdemalion of differet fabrics, fur stitched into satin, a red silk swatch overlapping a blue cotton lining. The shirt beneath was a solid white linen, and the pants a dependable black leather, stuffed into high boots, but they were overwhelmed by the swirling brilliance of the cloak.

The merchant bore no obvious weapons, and Jamie wondered if this was one of those mythical wizards who haunted the tales his late mother had told before bedtime. He decided against this notion. The old wizards were powerful and deadly, he had heard, and probably would ride on clouds or scaled monsters, as opposed to this travesty of a cart.

The town guard, Roger's father, held up a hand, and the wagon's driver ceased his ringing, but not before forcing one last extended peel that spun the bell over its bracket.

"Who are you?" asked Roger's father, his voice in that deep tone he always used when trying to command respect. "And why do you call all evil down upon us with your incessant clamoring?"

The rag-tattered rainbow of a man, his face weathered and creased, smiled at the guard. "I am a simple peddler, working my stock in trade. I seek to sell my wares within your village, or, failing that, to have your citizens come out to visit my wagon. Either would be suitable, depending on your laws."

Roger's father was unmoved by the options presented. "What do you sell, peddler?"

"A variety of items, both wondrous and sweet," responded the merchant, with the practiced grace of one who has lived through similar, if not identical, conversations. "I have nostrums and novelties from far lands. I carry medicines and salves. I fear no evil, for I bear magical wards and protective amulets. I have candies and sweetmeats for the children—" and with this he nodded at the small heads poked over the wall— "and I carry powerful relics for sale and will tell tales of the great past."

"The past has brought nothing but pain," grumbled Roger's father, "and magic is dead. But you are welcome within our village, and you may endeavor to sell your wares." With that he waved at the gate guards, who swung the stockade doors open.

The wagon lurched forward. As the peddler cleared the gate, he poked his hand into a satchel at his side. He came up with a handful of candy, individually wrapped in brightly colored paper. He scattered the candy in a bright arch to his right, and then another handful to his left. The younger children squealed and dived for the sweets. Jamie himself snagged a piece in the air and quickly unwrapped it. It was a sweet caramel and dissolved on his tongue.

Having purchased the loyalty of the youngest members of the crowd, the peddler guided his wagon through the dirt streets. Roger's father led the way to the open commons at the village's center. A few of the town's sheep baaed in protest at the presence of the lumbering oxen but made sufficient room for the wizened old man and his wagon.

The merchant gave his bell rope a sharp tug, setting off one last jangling peel. Then he rose from his perch and walked around to the left side of the carriage, along the narrow balcony. Those children who had gathered on the right side quickly shifted position, on the off chance that old peddler wanted to pass out more candy.

The balcony was the peddler's stage, keeping him above the gathered crowd. By now many of the townswomen, and those of the townsmen with little else to do, had joined the crowd. The old man smiled at the assemblage, cleared his throat with a theatrical grabbing of his larynx, and began his patter.

"Greetings, good townsfolk," he began, his voice rolling and melodious. "I thank you for taking in this humble traveler, the well-meaning peddler of the past. I am Habakor, the last of Fizban's pupils before the War of the Lance, in these late days reduced to selling balms and sundries, telling tales of history and offering a glimpse of legend. Gather round and let me tell you of all manner of marvels."

The peddler reached into a fold of his cloak and pulled out what looked like a lump of blackened wood set with a translucent, yellowing gem, cracked and fire-scarred.

"This is a fragment of my mentor's own staff," said Habakor, "smashed in his final battle with Chaos all those years ago. Would you like to hear the tale?" He directed the question to a knot of children younger than Jamie, who would rather do anything than their assigned chores.

The younger children gave a hasty assent, and before waiting for the adults to wade in with their opinion, the peddler began to recount the tale.

"My master, Fizban, was a mighty mage, and in the last days of the Age of Dragons, he was sought out to battle the great smoky beast of Chaos." said Habakor. "Fizban was the most powerful of mages of the age, and he was great with wisdom and power. He was aged but unbowed by his years, and magical energies crackled from his hands as he spoke. As his apprentice, a mere lad at the time, I was chosen to accompany him on the quest. I mention this not out of boastfulness but so that you realize that what I say is truth."

As Habakor spoke, he paced the length of his small stage, and all eyes followed him as he recounted the tale of his passage into the Lands of Chaos with his master. His voice was smooth and relentless, speaking as if he had no need to take a breath, each sentence spilling into the next effortlessly and without pause. He told of entering the twisted lands with his master and of the dangers they faced together, each more perilous than the last, until at last they confronted the Chaos beast.

"Dark as the thickest smoke, it was, and it towered above my master and me," said Habakor. "It blocked out the stars, and the moons themselves changed their course to avoid striking it. Fizban turned to me and bade me flee back to the land of the living. I did as he asked, but I looked back once to see Fizban wielding his staff, glowing like the sun itself, battling the blackness of Chaos. There was a blinding flash, then both were gone. I returned to the battlefield and found only the wreckage of his staff where they both once stood. This staff—" the peddler waved the gem-set fragment of wood—"was the last I saw of the mightiest mage of Ansalon. It is said that magic itself died with his passing, and I, for one, believe it, for I have been unable to cast the least spell since his passing."

Jamie inhaled sharply, realizing that he had been holding his breath through the last of the tale. He could imagine the smoky embers of Chaos's domain, the power of the great beast, and the valiant sacrifice of this Fizban, tall and quick-witted, who battled the darkness and defeated it at the cost of his own life.

Jamie's reverie was shattered by a shout from the rear of the crowd. Shel's father, who spent most of his afternoons drinking, laughed loudly and bellowed, "And how much are you selling that trinket for, peddler?"

Habakor's face creased in a deep frown, and he seemed genuinely wounded by the words. "This is my only memento of Fizban's legacy," he said sharply. "I would never part with it, regardless of the price, and I am insulted that anyone would think I would," He paused here and scanned the crowd, as if daring anyone else to challenge his honor. No one responded, and the peddler permitted himself a smile, "Now, if you are intent on purchasing artifacts, I have something in which you might be interested."

The peddler ignored Shel's father's deep chuckle

as he produced a thin blade from beneath his cloak. It was made of fine steel and had a stylized symbol carved into the hilt. It glittered in the afternoon sun. "This is the dagger of Sturm, with which he defeated the female dragon Kitiara in single combat, though at the cost of his own life. Perhaps you would like to hear this story?"

A shout of agreement brought another tale, this one climaxing with the great warrior spilling off the wall of his white citadel, locked in a death grip with a great shape-shifting dragon who was once his lover.

At the tale's conclusion, Old Ben, the innkeep, shouted an offer for the knife. Habakor said the price named was an insult, and Old Ben raised his price by half. Habakor demurred again but finally agreed to part with the knife when Old Ben threw in lodging for the night. The sale was consummated, and Habakor celebrated the sale with another handful of candy to the children clustered alongside the cart.

So the afternoon went. Habakor lectured on a series of herbal balms used by Goldmoon herself to bring her husband Riverwind back from the death's doorway. From the depths of his cart, he presented a great glass sphere, within which, in the days of magic, Raistlin battled with the archlich Fistandantilus. That relic received no offers, but he was more successful with several bottles of a sanguine liquid called Toedesblood, a cure-all supposedly leeched from the living flesh of a great emperor of Flotsam.

There were protective amulets made of dragon scales and charms cut from the tusks of the demonic Thanoi. A frying pan once owned by Tika Majere. Small wooden toys, supposedly first designed by Fizban himself to entertain golden-hued Raistlin as a child, and all manner of rings, once claimed to be magical but now, in these later days, reduced to little more than good-luck charms and keepsakes.

With each new item, there was a story, and with each story, there was a sale, perhaps two. Jamie, Roger, Shel, and the rest of the young people hung on every word, and some parted with their own steel coins for a ring or a bracelet.

Finally, as the sun was kissing the horizon behind him, the peddler called a halt to his sales. He claimed his throat was raw from talk, though he seemed to be just as smooth and melodious as he had been at the start. One last scattering of sweets, and the crowd dispersed, most of the young people excited by the tales, and only a few worried about ignoring their chores for a full afternoon.

* * * * *

Jamie returned to find his father at the forge, as he had left him hours earlier. The older man grunted at the boy and pointed at the bellows. Jamie resumed his position at the forge, working the thick wooden pump handle to keep the coals hot. "Did you have a chance to hear the peddler?" the youth asked at last.

His father shook his head, "There's work to be done," he said gruffly. "No time for foolishness."

"He had amazing things," continued Jamie.

His father looked at him, "You didn't buy anything from him, did you?"

Jamie shook his head, then flushed. He had thought about it, but he didn't feel he could afford any of the wondrous items. Still, the accusation that he might even think about wasting money embarrassed him. His father worked hard and was a prudent man with his money.

Jamie tried another approach. "But he told wonderful tales."

"Lies, you mean," said his father with a deep sigh, shaking his head. "Peddler lies. A sweet tale to sell some gimcrack or what's-it to a foolish crowd. If there is any truth in them, it is buried so deep that it would take ten men with shovels a week to dig it out.

The heroes themselves, if they ever existed, would not recognize themselves. That is the nature of peddler lies."

The father looked at the boy's expression as he spoke, and Jamie's face revealed his disappointment. His father's voice softened just a touch. "When I was your age, Son, before I became the village smith, I met a merchant like that. He had a pair of skulls mounted on his wagon, a large one and a small one. He said the large one was the skull of Fistandantilus the archlich, and the smaller one . . ."

"Was the skull of Fistandantilus as a boy" came a low, laughing voice from the door. Habakor the peddler stood in the doorway, shorn of his tatterdemalion robe, a simple sack over his back. "I've met peddlers like that myself. And if you believe all of them, there are enough pieces of Fizban's staff to build a tower taller than the legendary Mount Nevermind. There are too many rogues and incompetent con men in this business, I'm afraid."

"So you say, peddler," said Jamie's father. "How may we help you this evening?"

"I have business with you, smith," said Habakor, looking at Jamie with one eyebrow raised. "Private business. Profitable business as well. I hope."

Jamie's father gave a small chuckle and waved the boy out the door. His father kept few secrets, but one of them was negotiating with a customer on "private business."

Jamie wanted to remain but would not disobey his father. Of course, the youth circled around to the back of the shop and reentered the forge area quietly from the rear door. Jamie chose a hiding place in the shadows of the back of the shop among a collection of fireplace tongs, pokers, shovels, and other instruments. He wanted to hear what Habakor the peddler wanted with his father.

The two adults, seated across from each other at

the workbench by the forge, were in deep, quiet conversation by the time he returned. Neither noticed him. The peddler laughed and smiled, and his father returned the smile with a deep chuckle of his own.

Jamie recognized his father's chuckle—it was a business chuckle, one used in dealing with warriors and guards. It was a calculated, brief laugh, one that signaled encouragement but not agreement. Jamie could see his father's eyes, and they were as hard as when he dealt with a long-standing debtor.

Habakor the peddler was talking, "As a reasonable man, smith, I think you understand the need for silence on the matter."

"Silence comes at a premium," said Jamie's father. "You've filled my son's head with all manner of wild tales this afternoon."

"Tales you as well heard as a youth," said the peddler, "or versions of them. And they seem to have not harmed you in the least. Young people need such wondrous tales. It gives them hope."

"It gives them ideas," said Jamie's father. "Dangerous ideas in a world much more deadly than it was when I was a boy. Now, where is this black blade you speak of?"

The peddler reached into his satchel.

Jamie almost gasped. The blade Habakor pulled out was twin to the one he had sold to Old Ben that afternoon, a dagger the peddler had sworn was unique. In the light of the hearth, Jamie could see Sturm's symbol carved into the hilt. The peddler handed it hilt first to the smith.

Jamie's father took the dagger, turning it over in his hands. "Solid workmanship. Simple enough design. I suppose it's better that way, eh?"

The peddler gave a mild laugh. "Easier to reproduce, yes. And I can do the engraving myself, so you don't have to finish it here."

"How many?" asked his father. "And when?"

"Your town has been most beneficent," said the peddler. "I will be here for two days. Past that, I find that some customers acquire doubts about my balms and potions, and my tales grow old to their ears. I will need a half-dozen, at least, a full dozen if you can make them fast enough."

Jamie's father grunted, the kind of grunt he used when sizing up a grade of ore or a rival smith's work. "Have to have the boy help me."

The peddler shook his head. "Uh-uh. Do it on your own, slylike. Leave the boy his dreams, smith. I had mine shattered early, and you see where it left me."

"Can get you a half-dozen by tomorrow night, then," said the smith. "And how do you see paying for my services . . . and my silence?"

The peddler leaned back on his seat, "I could pay you in mere steel, petty coins from lost empires and dead kings," he said, pulling another item out of the satchel. "Or I could offer you something of unusual value."

The peddler opened his hand to reveal a stoppered vial made of carved crystal, which caught the reddish light of the forge and scattered it to the far corners of the shop. At the heart of the crystal was a mote of darkness.

"I got this from one of my brother travelers," Habakor said, "who got it from a warrior in the south, who reliably reported having found it among the wreckage of Tarsis. Within this sealed bottle is the spirit of darkness itself, a piece of the great Chaos. Quite the dangerous relic. Quite the conversation piece."

Jamie's father frowned deeply, setting the false blade of Sturm down firmly on the table. Jamie knew that the peddler had stepped over a line. It was one thing for the merchant to casually admit he was defrauding the others in town. It was another for him to try it with his father. Jamie's father was slow to anger, but once angry was capable of rash, sudden actions.

"I don't need your rosewater medicines," snarled the smith, "and I don't like the assumption that I am as gullible as Old Ben and the rest."

"Ho! I would not insult you like that," said the peddler. "For this it truly what I have been told it is. Think . . . you could charge admission or trade it off to some passing warrior or aspiring necromancer. See? The wax seal is authentic, set with the golden sigil of the rulers of Tarsis."

"I would rather have hard currency," said Jamie's father tersely.

"But this is worth twice, three times what I would otherwise pay," insisted the merchant. A pleading tone crept into Habakor's voice, and Jamie realized the peddler was trying to weasel out of paying in coin. His father had already surmised that, and was getting angrier by the second.

"If you don't have the money, peddler," said Jamie's father, "then I have already wasted enough time. I expect you to leave. Now."

"Please, just examine it," The peddler rose from his bench and shoved the vial forward, into the smith's face. "I have been assured by one of the last priests of Mishakal, with her dying breath she told me—"

"Enough!" said Jamie's father sharply, raising his hand to bat away the proffered vial.

The peddler was too close, his grip on the vial too loose, and the smith's blow too solid. The vial tumbled from Habakor's hand and smashed against the side of the fire pit, chipping a white scar into the stone. The vial did remain intact, but the force of the impact cracked the wax seal around its stopper.

There was a tense silence between the two men, the only sound the soft popping of the forge. Then another sound rose in the smithy, a high-pitched ringing. Jamie raised his hands to his ears, but the sound seemed to tunnel into his brain. Jamie's father rose from his bench, a tightness around his eyes.

Both men, and Jamie from his hiding place, peered at the crystal, which now seemed to vibrate and glow of its own accord. The two men looked at each other, Jamie's father raising an eyebrow in curiosity. Jamie's father stepped toward the ringing vial as the peddler stepped back, his face suddenly contorted in fear.

The stopper of the vial shot from the throat of the bottle like a dragon from its den, smashing in a thousand minuscule shards against the stones of the fire pit. Then out of the bottle oozed a thick, oily blackness.

It was the shade of a starless night, without definition. It existed only as a silhouette, a border within which lurked utter darkness. As it spilled out of the bottle, it swelled, until at last it had the size and rough form of a human being. Its head was too large for any human, though, and when it hissed at the men, Jamie could see row upon row of razor-sharp fangs, the only whiteness against the surrounding oblivion.

The peddler let out a strangled cry. Jamie's father cursed and grabbed for the false Sturm knife lying on the table. The shadow creature was faster, however, and lashed out with one sinuous arm. The back-handed blow caught Jamie's father at the side of the head, and the smith was knocked across the room. He disappeared in the shadows, accompanied by a clatter of loose metal and iron tools.

Despite himself, Jamie let out a shout. Both the peddler and the shadow creature swiveled their heads toward him. The shadow creature was only visible by its ivory teeth, which flashed a ragged grin at the boy. The creature hesitated an instant, as if deciding which of the two was the greater threat or the more rewarding meal. Then the beast turned back toward Habakor.

The peddler's face was as white as ash, but his

eyes never left the shadow creature. Blindly he groped for the Sturm dagger, still on the table. His fingers closed around it, and he brought it up, fumbling it as he did so, his eyes wide. Habakor held the dagger in front of him, more as a protective talisman than as a true threat.

The shadow beast made a low, wheezing noise and advanced a step. Habakor responded by stepping daintily backward. Another step forward, another step back. Then the shadow beast stomped its foot, hard. Habakor jumped back and fell over a low bench behind him.

The shadow beast made the same low, wheezing noise, and Jamie realized the creature was laughing.

The peddler cursed and threw the Sturm knife toward the shadow creature. The toss was wobbly, and the blade spun end over end, passing through the creature as if it were made of fog. The knife disappeared into the surrounding darkness.

Jamie was on his feet in an instant, grabbing one of the iron pokers, the closest thing to a weapon at hand. Then Jamie hurtled the workbench and swung the poker at the creature.

This time the cold metal tool ripped patches of darkness out of the beast as it passed through it. The patches drifted to the floor like dead leaves, dissipating as they fell. The attack seemed to have some effect on the shadow beast, however in that the creature let loose a low, guttural howl.

The beast turned and lashed out at Jamie. Jamie dodged backward. The rows of sharp-fanged teeth gnashed once, then twice. Jamie backed up now, keeping the poker in front of him, until he felt the heat of the forge ripple through the back of his shirt.

The darkness beast crouched low, then leapt at the lad. As it leapt, Jamie dropped to one knee. The creature had misjudged Jamie's size and quickness. The shadow creature passed over Jamie's head and landed in the hot coals of the forge.

The beast yelped at the heat, and the edges of its silhouette form began to crackle and burn. It tried to scrabble out of the forge, but succeeded only in igniting more of its shadowy flesh in the process. Jamie shouted and drove the poker through the creature's midsection, pinning it to the hearth. The poker sank through the beast's back with a satisfying thunk, driving it facedown into the coals. The beast thrashed, giving off a sound like a bag of angry cats.

The coals began to glow more hotly, and Jamie looked up to see that the peddler had recovered and was at the bellows, pulling the wooden pump handle down with both hands. The beast squirmed and howled, flailing its arms backward like a man trying to reach an itch at the small of his back. Jamie held tightly on to the poker.

The creature's head then started to pivot painfully, slowly around its neck, purple flames dancing on all sides. There was a snapping noise as it turned its head all the way around. The rows of ivory fangs came into view as the beast slowly, painfully pressed against the forge with its now-ravaged hands, forcing its body up the shaft of Jamie's poker. Its serrated teeth glimmered as it snaked its head forward.

Jamie could not close his eyes as the jaws edged closer, framed in violet flames. He could not let go, for the creature would escape the forge. Nor could he hold on to the poker any longer.

At the last moment the monster was knocked aside by the business end of a fireplace shovel. The creature hissed and squirmed at this fresh attack, but Jamie's father held firm, swatting the creature's head aside each time it lunged at the boy. Jamie tightened his grip and bore the poker down harder, pinioning the shadow beast in place. The entire smithy was lit with purple light.

The entire creature was on fire now, its shadow flesh turning to grayish ash, glowing violet against the coals. The creature's snarls became choked rasps and finally weak, choppy breaths. At last it moved no longer, but for a long time, the peddler kept pumping the bellows and his father kept piling white-hot coals on the beast. Finally Jamie relaxed his grip and withdrew the now-warm poker. Nothing stirred in the coals of the forge.

* * * * *

Jamie gasped, both from the heat and the danger, and rubbed an arm over his sweaty brow. "What was that?" he quietly asked the two older men.

"Chaos minion," said Habakor the peddler, then with a gulp, "or a child of Takhisis. There was a legend of a blackflame creature. Maybe an efreet." He looked at Jamie and his father, then added, "I just don't know. I really don't." The peddler spread his hands wide. "When I bought it, I didn't think it was real. I don't know what to say."

"You'll think of something," muttered the father, righting the toppled benches and table as if nothing had happened. "You still want the dozen blades?"

The peddler opened his mouth, then shut it again. It was a few moments until he spoke. "If it were just the same, I'd prefer to buy your fireplace instruments. All of them. And I'll paid hard coin for them. No barter or trade."

The smith looked at Jamie, then back at the peddler, hefting the small shovel. Jamie gripped the poker tightly.

"No," said Jamie's father. This time, Jamie realized, it was a softer, more thoughtful 'no.'

The peddler righted one of the benches and collapsed upon it. "You don't understand," he said, resting his elbows on his knees, brushing his hair back with both hands. "All the tales I tell are secondhand. I never—" He looked at Jamie, the peddler's mouth tightening for a moment, then he looked away, "I never experienced anything like this. Not personally. I used to believe in such things, but it is a belief that had gone away a long time ago.

"But this . . ." Habakor waved at the smoking firepit. "This is real. This is now. This proves there is some magic left in the world. Magic for ill and perhaps for good. Dangers that can be faced with cold iron and strong hearts. This is something I need to tell people about, to warn them."

Jamie's father shook his head again. "You can tell as many people as you want. But don't ask this smith to sacrifice his hard-earned tools."

"But your tools deserve to be famous!" said the peddler.

"I am happy they are useful," replied the smith, "whether it is as tools or weapons. But here they stay, where I need them."

The peddler was silent for a moment. "If I tell this tale to others, and they come here to see for themselves, what will you do? We could charge a fee, split the money equal-like."

Jamie's father chuckled, then looked at the boy. He said, "Tell the truth about what happened here. About how a peddler came to town with dangerous magic he did not know he had, and how we, the three of us, defeated that magic in this smithy. No tall tales. No evoking of dead heroes. No charges, no selling of fireplace implements, claiming them to be monster-killing weapons. Just tell them what happened." There was steel in his voice.

"Of course," said the peddler. He swallowed hard, glancing at Jamie. He straightened himself on the bench and returned the smith's stare, "I promise," he said, and to Jamie it sounded as if he meant it.

"Do you still want those swords?"

The peddler looked at Jamie again. The boy's gaze made him uncomfortable. He shook his head, "Not as Sturm's original daggers, no. As the workmanship of a brave smith and his son, yes. And

I'll pay in hard coin for them."

Jamie's father smiled, and Jamie saw it was a true smile, not a business smile. "They'll be ready tomorrow."

Jamie was extremely somber, his brows knitted. The smith noticed his son's thoughtful demeanor. "What is it, boy?" he asked. The boy shook his head, as if trying to shake the worries from his head before speaking.

"The crystal vial," said Jamie to the peddler at last. "You said you bought it from a merchant."

Habakor nodded. "Aye, when peddlers meet, we swap gossip and stock. I did pick this up from another of my ilk, not less than two months ago, along with the story he told about it being from Tarsis. I traded him a couple of the Sturm blades for it, and the tale that went with them. I thought little of it at the time."

As the peddler spoke, Jamie looked at his father, who had a hard, worried exression in his eyes. The smith walked over to the forge. He grabbed one of the tools and poked at the coals, making sure that the shadow creature would not rise from the ashes. Then he looked at his son and the merchant.

"And you didn't bother to check as to the authenticity of the vial," said the smith softly. "You didn't bother to open it." His voice was quiet but firm.

"Well, of course not," said Habakor. "I assumed that it was a fraud, like most of the other peddler's lies."

"But it wasn't," said the smith, giving the coals one final stir, then setting his tool back in its holder. He turned and faced the peddler, folding his arms.

"The vial," said Jamie. "Was it the only one the merchant had?"

"Only one?" asked Habakor. "Of course not. No more than I have only one of Sturm's daggers . . ." His voice died out as realization dawned. "Sweet Tika's mercy," he whispered. "There's more of them."

Jamie nodded, and the smith grunted.

"But the others could just be fakes, copies. Maybe I picked up the real one by mistake . . ." said the peddler, but he was already shaking his head. "No. If a peddler had such an item, a real artifact of power, he would not risk copies. But then, he might have gotten them secondhand himself and not known what these vials contain."

"That's doesn't matter," said Jamie's father.

The peddler blinked questioningly at the larger man.

A long silence hovered over the smithy.

Jamie's father held up a meaty hand. "I don't think we have much choice. We were lucky this time. We'll need some planning. Cold iron weapons. And, if need be, a good strong arm to use them."

A horrified look was beginning to spread across the peddler's face.

Jamie looked up at his father. Was he hearing right? But it was the peddler who said, "We?"

Jamie's father allowed himself a smile. "You and I." He put his hand on the lad's shoulder. "You're old enough to manage the shop while I'm gone. You're careful and sure-handed, good traits for a smith."

Jamie looked up at his father. "But I want to go with you." The older man shook his head.

"Not this time," said the smith. "I wanted to go when my father left me to run the smithy. But I stayed and did well by his name. I want you to do the same."

"Maybe . . ." began the peddler, his eyes darting toward the door. "Maybe he could be of some assistance. He certainly played his part today. Whereas I—"

The smith looked hard at the peddler, shook his head. "I want him to stay here. The village needs a smith."

"And a boy needs his father," insisted the peddler softly, but not so softly that the smith would miss his words.

The smith raised his eyes to the peddler, fire in his

eyes. But the fire quickly died, and the smith merely shook his head. The shake became a smile, and the smile became a laugh and a nod. He understood.

* * * * *

In the morning the wagon of the peddler lumbered its way out of the village, heading back the way that it came. It carried two passengers, the smithy and his son. The townsfolk were surprised at first, but adjusted to the new smith named Habakor. Once he sent for some new tools to replace those that left with the previous owner, he proved to be not such a bad smith.

The children grew up, and peddlers continued to come to the village. Some sold things that were useful, but a few sold old relics and told tales of ancient wizards and long-forgotten dragons.

And nobody scoffed at them more than Habakor the smith. He would smile and say that even the heroes who were in these tales would not recognize themselves. And he spoke in the manner of one who would know of such things. For such was the nature of peddler lies.

The Summoners

Paul B. Thompson

The nights were darker now. Without three moons to play upon the inky veil of Krynn's night sky, shadows were longer, the darkness deeper, than ever it had been in the memory of those living.

The traveler stood beneath a live oak. Warm wind stirred the leaves. He gazed from this hilltop to the next, drawn by the blaze of a thousand torches and lamps. The town was called Kerodin. It was not a city, not yet; in just a few years it had grown from a bandits' encampment to a haphazard town of several thousand souls.

No one seemed to sleep in Kerodin. By night, fires glared, and by day, a pall of smoke hung over the sprawl of log houses, enclosed by a wooden stockade. The traveler had been at this spot for two days, observing the frantic daily rhythms of Kerodin and waiting for his comrade Arbelac to enter the town from the north. When enough time had passed for Arbelac to be well placed, he shouldered his bindle and started across the shallow vale to the southern gate.

The valley below Kerodin was littered with ruined farms and sagging shacks, abandoned now for twice twenty years. The traveler walked quickly through the silent remains of former times, when the gods ruled and the moons burned brightly. Not even a dog was left to bark at him as he passed the empty, windowless hovels.

Some grim wit had stuck a horned steer's skull on a post in the path. Beyond it was another post, this one with a horse's head nailed to it. The bleached bone stood out starkly in the dark, and he realized these were macabre guideposts. At intervals, more skulls appeared, and they weren't from animals. It was easy to tell the broad, heavy brow of dwarf's skull from a human's, but a series of smaller, delicate death's-heads troubled him more. Elf? Kender? A human child? He decided he didn't want to know.

The glow of Kerodin's light seeped down the hillside and made his way brighter. The bottom of the hill was scoured clear of trees and brush, even of grass. Rough planks were laid over the muddy earth here and there. The traveler paused and looked back in the direction from which he'd come. This was a killing zone. From the wooden walls of Kerodin, archers and slingers could rain death down on any enemy who tried to charge across this open ground. They weren't complete fools, these townsmen.

A rude gatehouse, ramped with earth on three sides, barred the way. The gate beyond stood open, but a quartet of soldiers stood guard at the gatehouse. Rather, they sat guard, perched on log benches, passing a stone jug back and forth. One of them spotted the traveler.

"Halt!" he shouted hoarsely. He stood with a stagger and ported his halberd. "Who goes there?"

"A weary traveler, seeking shelter from the night."

"Advance and be recognized!"

He stepped forward into the circle of torchlight. Something about his measured movements alerted the other guards. They rose to their feet despite their drunkenness and slowly surrounded him.

"Name?" growled a one-eyed man who wore a corporal's crest on a tarnished Solamnic helmet.

"Hars Falken, of Blöde," said the traveler.

"You're a long way from home, ain'tcha?" said the guard who first challenged him. His breath stank of sour wine. The rest of him was pretty fragrant, too. "What're you doing in these parts?"

"Traveling."

The corporal waved a spearpoint under Falken's chin. "Travelin'? What for?"

"I'm searching for some people who're lost."

"Yeah? Who?"

"The righteous."

There was a pause, the length of one breath inhaled. As one, the four soldiers burst into harsh laughter.

"You're in the wrong place, sonny boy!"

"We don't allow the righteous in this town!"

"Why are ya lookin'? Think they're extinct?"

"You don't know where you are, do ya?" said the corporal. He raised his halberd and leaned on the shaft. "This here's Kerodin, boy. Ain'tcha heard of it? The freest town in the world, where a man can do anything, whatever pleases him." He winked broadly. "If he has gall and the cash to pay for it, that is."

"And you see no error in that?" asked Falken.

"Seems right sensible to me." The corporal leaned forward. "Now, here's the thing: You want into town, you gotta make it worth my while. Understand?"

"You want gold?"

"Gold is always good, but I'll take good steel if you got any, or drinking liquor."

Falken spread his hands. "I am a poor man. I have nothing but a few copper pieces."

The other soldiers snorted and turned away. "You ain't gonna go very far in Kerodin, sonny," said the corporal. He tossed his halberd to a comrade and laid hold of Falken's homespun cloak. Roughly he flipped the wrap back and groped through Falken's clothes for a hidden purse. The traveler simply stood there, hands out, and let himself be rifled.

The corporal's blunt fingers found a hard object at Falken's throat, under his shirt. He worked it out and by torchlight saw it was a sizable pendant, wrought in white metal. The design was unusual, like two arrows meeting vertically, point to point.

"What's this?" the soldier demanded.

"A family heirloom," Falken said dryly.

"Silver, is it?"

"White gold."

One-Eye closed his fist around the pendant and snapped the cord. "It ain't much, but it's been a slow night. You can enter."

Wordlessly Falken rearranged his clothing. The other guards had mauled his bindle, so he took a moment to repack it. By the time he started up the earthen ramp to the open gate, the guards had resumed their slovenly positions.

The corporal held up the pendant, peering at it. "Hey," he called. "What's it mean?"

"It's a symbol. It represents the striving of mortals to reach out to the gods, and the gods responding to their effort," replied Falken.

"Ain'tcha heard? There ain't no more gods!" The men laughed again.

"What was lost may be found."

Inside the stockade, he was immersed in a riot of sensations—smells good and vile, roasting meat, perfume, spilled beer, and the garbage and manure that filled the muddy street. Music from half a dozen sources assaulted in his ears: wailing pipes, the thump of wanton drums. Torches and lamps blazed everywhere, yet the streets still seemed dim. Drunkards with broken voices croaked songs from the shadows. A trio of wastrels, naked to the waist and smeared with mud, ran past Falken, laughing like maniacs. Somewhere a woman screamed.

He had a choice of three streets, and chose the center one, mostly because a plank walkway there offered a chance to get out of the pervasive muck. A jumble of houses rose up on either side, the hoardings on the upper floors almost closing out the starry sky. It was like traversing a deep drainage ditch. Or a sewer pipe.

A shower of liquid—he dared not ask what kind—hit the planking a few steps ahead of him, followed a heartbeat later by a large crockery urn. It shattered, flinging sharp fragments everywhere. Incoherent shouts ensued, a splinter of wood and glass, and two figures, twined together in deadly embrace, hurtled from the heights. They hit the walkway with a crack and lay still.

Falken rushed to them. It was a man and woman, neither clothed. The man's hands were knotted around the woman's neck, and her lifeless hand still clutched a dirk whose business end was buried in the man's ribs. No one seemed to care about the violent tragedy that had just occurred. Those afoot in Kerodin, insensate and insensible, passed by the fallen bodies.

Numbly Falken walked on. The street opened into a large, irregular square, lined with gaudy taverns. A public well stood at one end, and he noted it carefully. The well was a good landmark at which to meet Arbelac later. He drew up the mossy bucket and cupped some cold water to his lips. He applied the next handful to his flushed face.

Amid the shouts and raucous merrymaking around him, a voice filled with genuine terror cried out, "No! No, don't! Someone help me, please!"

There were five men outside a well-lit tavern, hooting at their prize. They ringed in a young girl, no more than sixteen. In turn, they forced upon her rough kisses and even rougher embraces. She gasped again. "By the gods, let me go!"

In an instant, Falken was among them, shoving the men aside. They were drunk and resented the stranger's interrupting their sport. In short order, Falken was kicked and beaten to the ground.

"Finish him off," suggested one of the bullies.

"He's not going anywhere. Let's have the partridge first. . . ."

In the momentary confusion, the girl had crept

away, but she had a long rope tied around her ankle. Her tormentors caught the trailing end of the rope and stopped her with a sharp jerk.

Falken wiped mud from his eyes and looked around. A city guardsman had parked his halberd by the tavern door before going in. That would do.

"Come here, little bird," one roughneck cooed. He hauled on the rope, hand over hand, even as the girl clawed at the planks to resist him. He never got to her. The flat of a halberd axehead connected with his skull, and down he went.

His friends gave a collective howl for blood. Falken held the halberd shaft in front of him like a quarterstaff, fending off their angry, clumsy attacks. After he laid out two men with well-timed blows, the last pair decided the prize wasn't worth the effort and fled. Falken dropped the halberd in the mud.

"Are you all right, girl?"

Wide-eyed, she tried to stand up and run away. Falken planted his boot on the rope.

"Let me go!" she screamed.

"Peace! Be still, will you? I will not harm you." He held out his empty hands and took his foot off the rope. "See?"

She ran anyway. Falken wearily strode after her. The frightened girl kept looking back over her shoulder at him, and during one such glance, she ran right into a hitching post. She pitched into a watering trough.

Falken hauled her out, spitting and trembling. The girl parted her sodden hair with her fingers and pushed it away from her face. When she opened her eyes, Falken was leaning on the trough, holding out a flannel kerchief.

"Wipe your face," he said. She took the cloth gingerly, as if it might bite her. "What's your name, girl?"

"Pais . . . just Pais."

"Pais is an elven name." She did not reply, but looped her wet hair behind her ears. They were long and faintly pointed. Pais was half-elven.

"What did those men want with you?" he asked.

She stared. "Wasn't it obvious?"

"But you're only a child! Where are your parents, your brothers? Why are you alone in such a place as this?"

She gave him back his kerchief. "None of your business," she answered, sniffing.

"I saved you back there, you know." She nodded sullenly. "I ask nothing in return but your story."

Arms folded, Pais said, "My mother and father are dead. I have no family. I was living with a farmer and his wife a few leagues from Kerodin, working in his orchard for my keep. When the apple crop failed, we came to town to sell what we had. . . ." Her voice trailed off. "And the farmer sold me."

"Sold you?"

"Yes, to the keeper of the Axe and Brand Tavern, back there."

"I see."

Falken went back to the square in front of the tavern and recovered his bundle. To his mild surprise, Pais followed him. She cringed when loud, drunken laughter roared out from the tavern doors.

"What shall I do?" she asked faintly.

"Do what you will." He walked away.

She caught up with him before he plunged into the warren of streets entering the north end of the square. "Wait! Take me with you!" she said.

"Time is short. I'm trying to find someone here . . . a friend."

She stopped and stamped her foot. "Takhisis take you, then! Why did you bother to help me if you don't care?"

Falken said, "Because you pleaded for help in the name of the gods."

"You still worship them?"

"I try to do their work."

Pais's brow furrowed. "You're a priest?"

"Some have called me that. I've taken no vows."

"You carry no arms, either." He shrugged. "Will you take me out of this awful place?" Pais said. She reached out, took his hand. Falken's hand was scarred and bore fresh cuts from his fracas with the ruffians. "Please?"

"I give you my protection," Falken said, removing his hand.

He went on, with Pais at his heels. He walked for nearly an hour, circling through the labyrinthine streets with no obvious purpose or destination. Arbelac was a chameleon, adept at disguise and misdirection. He could be anywhere. Well past midnight, Falken paused at the mouth of a short alley. He gestured. "Here I shall spend the night."

"What? Out in the open? Can't we take a room somewhere?"

"I have no money for lodging. This place is drier than most, and with a wall at our backs, no one can creep up behind us and do mischief."

The alley was cobbled, which meant a respite from the ever-present mud. Falken squatted and untied his bindle. Pais heard the chink of metal. Then he drew out a gray woolen blanket. He tied the corners of the bindle back and shoved it in a corner, protecting it with his body and using it as a prop for his head at the same time. Tomorrow he would make himself known in this town.

Pais, whose layered clothes were still damp, shivered on the cold cobblestones beside him. Without a word, he took the blanket off and draped it around her shoulders. In moments, the exhausted girl was asleep, curled up close to him. Falken studied her profile: the elvish ears, the dirty blond hair matted against her skull. Her face was drawn from hunger, but there was a firmness in her jaw that spoke of toughness inside her slender frame.

Partridge, the drunkard called her. A game bird indeed.

* * * * *

Pais was gone when he awoke. The blanket was neatly folded beside him. Oh, well, he thought. At least she didn't steal it.

He was used to sleeping in the open, but the smoky air of Kerodin made him cough. Falken rose and stretched. This would be a busy day.

When he reached the mouth of the alley, Pais appeared suddenly. She was chewing on the stump of a loaf of brown bread, which she offered to Falken.

"Breakfast?"

He took the long loaf, tore it in half, and gave her back the end she'd bitten. "Thank you," he said. "I don't suppose you found anything to drink?"

Her other hand held a large gourd. She sloshed it, demonstrating it was full. "Barley milk."

He sniffed the gourd's neck. The contents were halfway gone to becoming bad beer, but he was thirsty. They walked down the street, passing the gourd back and forth.

Daylight did nothing to enhance Kerodin. Wreaths of smoke hung over the town, and the unpainted log and plank houses had weathered dull gray. As they wound down the street, they had to step over bodies lying in the mud. Some were dead drunk; others were just dead.

"Is it always like this?" he asked.

"I've been here ten nights and nine days," Pais said. "This is a typical morning in Kerodin."

Above, someone dumped a bucket of offal and rotten vegetables into the street. As soon as the mess hit the ground, a trio of children emerged from a doorway and began picking through it for morsels they could stomach. Revolted, Falken grabbed the nearest urchin. The hollow-eyed child curled up into a ball to ward off the blows he thought were coming.

"What're you doing?" Falken said sharply. The other children watched warily but did not stop scavenging.

"S-Sir?" said the boy.

"What are you doing, eating garbage?"

"I'm hungry, sir."

"Where are your parents? Why aren't they feeding you properly?"

"Mama's drunk again, sir. Papa went to the gaming house four nights past and hasn't come back."

He set the child on his feet and gave him what remained of his bread. The other two, seeing their brother's good fortune, rushed over and clamored for bread of their own.

"All right, all right! You'll all get bread!"

"Falken—" Pais began. He silenced her with a stony glance.

He marched ahead, with the girl and children in tow. A few streets over, he found a small square. A few squalid vendors had carts set up, peddling their wares. The baker's cart held short brown loaves, four deep on top.

"Bread," Falken said.

"Of course, excellency. I have the best bread in Kerodin. How many loaves do you require?" the baker replied. She was a stout woman, with a large hairy mole on her cheek.

"As many as they can eat," he declared, sweeping his arm to include the children and Pais. At this, the baker frowned.

"I ain't feedin' no scum of the streets," she said, spitting. "Let's see the color of your money."

He grabbed her by her apron and dragged her across the cart. "If I had steel, I'd give it to you directly!" The baker blanched. Her lips parted to shout. "But as I have none, I presume gold will have to do."

He lifted his left foot and braced it against the cartwheel. The bottom of his heel slid forward, revealing a cavity in the leather. A stack of coins, wrapped in a scrap of lace, nestled in the hole.

"Come here," he commanded. The three boys, none older than eight, lined up and began filling their arms with loaves. At Falken's urging, Pais joined in, too. When they had all they could hold, Falken said, "How much?"

"Uh, sixty . . . sixty-two coppers." He gave her a single gold coin. With trembling hand, the baker returned his change, which he promptly distributed to the children.

"You, boy . . . what is your name?"

"Gadric, excellent sir." He was the oldest and biggest of the three.

"Gadric, you and your brothers will now earn the coppers I gave you. Go throughout Kerodin and tell everyone you meet that I shall be speaking in this square at the hour of noon. I have an important message that every citizen should hear. Tell all the children. Tell the hungry ones, the beaten ones, the sick, and the dying to come here at noon. There will be food for everyone, as far as this gold will go. Can you do that, Gadric?"

Arms and mouth full of bread, he nodded with vigor. Pais said, "Shall I go, too?"

"Yes. Tell everyone you meet."

The boys ran off in different directions, eager to carry out their benefactor's request. Pais lingered behind.

"What is this all about? " she said.

"I will help anyone who wishes to be helped," Falken said. "That's all you need to know."

Something in his voice stirred her. Half afraid, half thrilled, Pais hurried on her way. The strange dark-eyed traveler paced back and forth in the square, hands clasped behind his back. The frightened baker packed up her cart and rolled it away. Her colleagues quickly followed suit. Whatever was about to happen, they didn't want any part of it.

* * * * *

People began to arrive. At first they came in twos and threes, the very poorest of the poor. Bewildered by the vague promise of help and dazzled by the sunlight in the square, the first arrivals huddled in the shadows of the overhanging houses.

After them came the young and less destitute. Some were mothers with drawn faces and a baby on their hip; others were sharp-faced teens who eyed every stranger for a purse they might clip. Swaggering bravos from the taverns and gaming houses came, hands on their sword hilts, giving each other steely stares and posing on lean, muscled legs, like greyhounds straining on a leash. Courtesans and merchants of vice came, in coarse but gaudy clothing. As the square filled, soldiers of the type Falken encountered at the gate arrived. The locals were not intimidated by them, and in the press, the soldiers had to settle for positions on the fringe of the crowd.

Falken had thrust a stave in the ground in the center of the square. He watched the shadow shorten and shorten. When it all but vanished into the base of the stick, he turned and walked to the highest point on the square, a walled well. The crowd parted for him.

"It is now noon of the tenth day of the fifth month of the thirty-third year since the gods left Krynn," Falken began in a strong, clear voice. "In that time, many strange and dangerous events have troubled the land. Dragons are said to hold entire realms in their scaly grip. Knights of both darkness and light battle for supremacy. The old order is overthrown, and here in the remoter provinces, justice and decency have been forgotten."

"Here! Here!" a man shouted. Rude cheers rang out.

"It cost me a family heirloom just to enter this town. In my first hours here, I found a young girl in the hands of five cowards bent on dishonoring her. I found children eating garbage from the dirt because their elders were too besotted to feed, clothe, or wash them."

"Tell us something we don't know," said a woman.

Falken frowned. "Is this the life you want? Can you not claim a better way for yourselves?"

"We like things just fine! Mind your own business, you old woman!"

"Who does he think he is, the Kingpriest?"

"Where's the help you said you're bringing us?" shouted another woman. "I need bread for my children, not speeches!" Supporting shouts for the young mother's challenge echoed through the square.

"Wait!" Falken held up his hands. "There is more at stake here than bread! I'm talking about changing your lives forever! I hold out to you the chance to live every day in peace and comfort!"

"Yeah, and how do we do that?"

"We must return to the old gods. Rebuild the temples, light the sacrificial fires. If we all do this, the gods will return and restore justice to Krynn."

Half the crowd erupted in sarcastic laughter. Clots of mud and rotten fruit began to rain down on Falken. He made no attempt to dodge them. Thrusting out an accusing finger, he thundered, "You have forgotten what virtue is! You think of nothing but your own pleasures! You wallow like pigs in the filth of the streets! Are you unthinking beasts? Can't you see beyond the next cup of wine, or the next roll of the dice?"

The shower of garbage increased. Cries of "No! No! Liar! Kerodin is free, Kerodin is free!" drowned out the minority who favored Falken's ideas. Then a rock was thrown instead of mud. Falken heeled over backward and seemed to fall into the well.

The shouting died. Moments later, Falken stood up again. He'd snagged the windlass rope to avoid plunging twenty feet into the water.

"Heed what I say!" he said. His lower lip was split and bleeding. He wiped the blood away. "Destruction awaits all those who turn their backs on the gods!"

"They turned their backs on us!"

A portly, middle-aged man, draped in a rich purple robe and wearing a ring on each finger, shouldered through the press. His hair, a pile of coal-black ringlets, set off the jeweled circlet perched on his brow. Brawny bodyguards shoved people aside to make room for their master.

"I am Clavis, once a priest of Shinare. I survived the Second Cataclysm. I saw good and virtuous folk annihilated in a flash of fire. Of what benefit was their virtue to them? I starved and wandered for years until I came to Kerodin. Here I learned true wisdom. The happiness of mortal man is pleasure, not empty piety!" The bravos, merchants, and travelers bellowed their agreement. "I am also a lord magistrate of Kerodin, and I order this man's arrest!"

"On what charge?" Falken demanded.

"Inciting a riot, making false claims, and tampering with public order. Take him, men."

The bodyguards drew cudgels and advanced on Falken, but in their haste to lay hands on the malefactor, the guards trod on the feet of some of the young wastrels near the well. The affronted gamblers and roués lashed out with fists, and a melee broke out. The square erupted in a fury of shouting and shoving. Falken stood above the fracas, hands on his hips, disgusted by the whole scene. He was about to shout for order when he spotted a familiar face in the throng. Arbelac, wearing the cap and cloak of a well-to-do traveler, made eye contact with Falken. He touched a finger to the brim of his cap and nodded.

Cornets blared, and the soldiers loitering on the edge of the square formed ranks and drew their swords. The mob shrank from the sight and stroke of real steel. In minutes, forty soldiers had hacked their way to the well, on the way rescuing Lord Clavis. The fat magistrate was spattered with mud and his elaborate coiffure was gone, revealing a bare pink pate.

"Get that son of a whore!" he howled.

The few yards between Lord Clavis and Falken were filled with a small knot of children and poor people. They closed ranks, unwilling to yield yet fearful of the bright steel swords of the city guards. Among the children, Falken saw Gadric and his brothers. Pais stood in the front rank, her arms around the shoulders of two elderly women. Arbelac had worked himself nearer.

"Will you murder us all?" Pais said. The soldiers shrugged and looked to Clavis for orders.

"Of course not," he said unconvincingly. "But I wonder what sort of prophet of virtue stands behind a bulwark of children and old folks for protection."

With a curt nod, Falken warned Arbelac not to interfere, then jumped down from the wall. Pais said, "Don't! He's just baiting you!"

"He's using the right bait," Falken said grimly. He separated the children with gentle tugs. "I'll not buy my freedom with the blood of innocents."

The guards seized him by the arms and forced them behind his back. Thongs pinioned his arms together. The position was so painful Falken could not stand up straight. Shoved, he stumbled forward a few steps until he stood face-to-face with Lord Clavis.

"Were you really a priest?" asked Falken, teeth clenched in pain.

"In another lifetime," Clavis said. "Come. It's time you had a taste of Kerodin justice."

"Your lordship has forgotten something. . . ."

"Oh? What is that?"

"Your hair."

A guard bent down and retrieved it. He and his

fellows stifled giggles at their master's loss of face—
or rather, loss of hair.

Clavis snatched the wig and circlet from the
guard. "I will deal with you later," he hissed. Then he
turned to Falken. "As for you, my friend, you shall
learn a new virtue at the end of a lash!"

They marched Falken away, unresisting. The
crowd dispersed until only five people were left in
the square: Gadric, his brothers, Pais, and Arbelac.
Falken's dark-eyed friend approached the girl and
boys.

"Who are you?" Pais asked. Tears brightened the
corners of her eyes.

"A friend of your friend," Arbelac said.

* * * * *

The soldiers took Hars Falken up the hill to a cluster of buildings more finely made than any others in
town. The stone-faced houses formed a ring that
frowned down on the ruder plank and log houses of
the commoners. Here the wealthy and powerful vice
lords of Kerodin dwelt in vulgar splendor.

A cloth hood, reeking of sweat and dry blood,
was pulled over Falken's head before he entered the
lords' dwellings. He was kicked and pummeled
through one house and back into tʰe open air again.
He could feel the heat of the afternoon sun on the
stiff, black canvas hood. He heard a clank and a
squeal, and a heavy door was opened for him.
Down steps . . . fourteen, fifteen, twenty. The air
grew clammy and dank. A dungeon.

His hands and feet were tied to upright wooden
beams and the hood whisked away. The room was
dim and smoky with burning torches. Falken's eyes
adjusted, and he found himself facing a low table, at
which Lord Clavis was seated. Empty chairs flanked
him on either side.

"Are you judge and jury together?" Falken asked.
"Do you think we're barbarians here?" Clavis

replied. Under the circumstances, Falken decided not to tell Clavis what he thought. "Your trial is set for sunset. The other high magistrates will be here then to decide your fate."

A narrow slit window was set in the stone wall, high above the judges' table. Already the light was golden; in a few hours, it would turn rose, then red. There wasn't much time. . . .

Falken said, "Who will defend me? Will I have counsel?"

"No, but you may speak on your own behalf." Clavis looked at his dusty wig, lying on the table in front of him. "Do not hold out hope. You will be condemned."

"I have no doubt about my fate."

Clavis came around the table and stood nose to nose with Falken. He was a big man, as tall as Falken, though much heavier. "You're truly not afraid to die," he said.

"My destiny is in the hands of the gods," he said. "Not yours."

Clavis snapped his fingers. A masked man appeared on Falken's right, a cat-o'-nine-tails resting in the crook of his beefy arm. "Prepare the prisoner," said Clavis. "I want him properly penitent when the other magistrates arrive." He added mockingly, "If the gods exist, they'll certainly come to rescue you. If not, I shall see you at sundown."

The masked man knew his work. He laid on with his whip until Falken passed out. Cold water was thrown on him, and he revived, only to feel the cat's sting again. This time no amount of water would restore him, and he lapsed into a profound void, his silent fortress against pain.

A dim red glimmer danced before his eyes. He thought of the dull red star that haunted Krynn's skies, a remnant of the cosmic upheaval three decades past. Simple folk spoke of the red star as if it were a god, but Falken knew better. To him, it was an omen, a promise from the true gods that they would return someday. To hasten their return would require sacrifice, sacrifice the color of that star. . . .

The wavering glimmer resolved into a lamp on the judges' table. Falken lifted his head. An aged man in a dirty gray robe was waving a vial under his nose. The pungent smell of asafetida woke him as rudely as a slap in the face. He coughed, and blood flecked the old herbalist's robe.

"He's awake, my lords."

The five chairs were now filled by the rulers of Kerodin. On Falken's far left was a bearded elderly man with burning eyes. He was counting a stack of steel coins and scribbling figures on a scrap of parchment. On his left was the lone woman of the group. Of mature years, the woman had features that implied she had once been quite beautiful, before overindulgence in food and drink had hidden her charms under puffy, sallow flesh.

Clavis occupied the center chair. His wig was clean, combed, and restored to its place atop his broad skull. On his left was a much leaner, younger man, handsome in an angular way, with unruly blond hair and a livid scar across his forehead. The last magistrate was about Falken's age, somberly dressed. In another age, he might have been a cleric or magician. He seemed to deliberately court the shadows at the end of the table, leaving Falken with no clear image of his face.

Clavis cleared his throat. "Hars Falken, of province and providence unknown, you stand accused of fomenting rebellion in the city of Kerodin. How do you plead?" he said, reading from the document in his hands.

Falken licked his swollen lips. "Is that all? I thought there were four or five charges against me."

"We compromised on this one," said the woman. "It's sufficient to cost you your head."

"He has only one head," said the young man, smirking.

"As my wise colleagues Haleia and Vernando say, the case against is simply one of incitement of rebellion. Will you plead?" asked Clavis.

"There's no doubt of my guilt, is there?"

"None."

"Do as you will, then."

"What say you? Urmarr, stop counting your money for a moment and pay attention!"

"Guilty. He's guilty," said Urmarr, who did not stop counting or even look at Falken.

"Haleia?"

She shifted luxuriously in her chair. "Guilty," she purred.

"Vernando?"

"Guilty and unrepentant, I'd say."

"Sarkindon?"

The shadowed judge held out a hand, clad in close-fitting kid gloves. He extended his thumb and turned it downward.

"Guilty," Clavis said for him. "I, too, vote guilty. We, the high magistrates of Kerodin, by unanimous vote, find the accused guilty. The sentence: You shall be taken to a main square of the town tomorrow at dawn, when your head shall be struck from your body by the town headsman."

If it came to that, Falken would submit to the axe for the sake of his cause. Arbelac would see the mission carried out, . . . Still, the smugness of his judges roused him to anger. Falken snatched at his bonds. On his best day, he couldn't have broken them. The effort only made the frame shake. Urmarr, startled by the sudden display of anger, spilled a stack of coins across the table onto the floor. The old man crawled under the table and began picking up the shiny steel disks.

"Get up, you old fool," Haleia said. "Show some dignity."

"Leave him to his money," Falken said. "It will avail him little enough in the future."

They stared at him incredulously, Urmarr from his hands and knees. Clavis burst out laughing.

"He's off again," Vernando said with a sneer. He leaned back in his chair and put his expensively tooled boots on the table. "Are the gods going to smite us? Is that what you mean?"

Falken said nothing. Vernando, Haleia, and Clavis taunted him awhile, but they tired of this sport when Falken stayed dumb. At length, Clavis dissolved the court.

"You are all welcome at my establishment," he announced. "Wine is on me."

"I gave up a pleasurable rendezvous for this business," Vernando complained. "What about that?"

"Oh, all right. Wine and the companion of your choice at my house. Half price."

"Half? You chiseler!"

"Stop whining!" Haleia snapped. She draped a fox stole around her ample shoulders. "If it were my house, I'd charge you double!"

They went out, squabbling in familiar fashion. In passing, Clavis trailed off with a gesture. "Good-bye, Hars Falken."

The dungeon door slammed. Falken thought he was alone, but then a movement caught his eye. The somber-clad judge, Sarkindon, had risen last from his chair and was standing silently under the high window.

"Are you a seer?" he said in a loud whisper. "What do you know of the future? What awaits Kerodin?"

"So you can talk."

"A draconian once got too close with a sharp implement," Sarkindon rasped. "I killed him, but I was left with a slight speech impediment." He faced Falken, who saw by the better light in the center of the room that Sarkindon's neck had been slashed long ago from ear to ear. A long, waxen scar sealed the wound.

"Who are you?" whispered the judge.

"A man seeking enlightenment for the whole world."

"That's not an answer."

"That's all the answer you're getting."

Sarkindon circled him, pausing by Falken's outstretched left arm. "That being so, I think I shall take a trip. Yes, I shall leave tonight. Any suggestions as to where I should go?"

Their eyes locked. "Try north," said Falken.

"East it is. Farewell."

* * * * *

Hars Falken did not sleep that last night, partly because he was tied upright, but mostly because he kept thinking about the coming day. It worked on his imagination with such vigor that sleep was truly an idle dream. He wondered where Arbelac was at that moment, what he was doing.

The slit window was tinged with gray when four soldiers arrived for him. One of them was the one-eyed corporal he'd met when he first entered Kerodin.

"Ha," said the corporal, still reeking of drink. "Looks like you shoulda tried another town!"

"I came to the right place," Falken replied as the soldiers loosened his bonds. "Things just didn't go quite the way I expected."

He could barely stand, but the soldiers let him wash his face and drink a few dippers of fresh water. Then they lashed his wrists together and led him out.

It seemed as if all of Kerodin had turned out for his execution. The sky was threatening, with blue-black clouds boiling over the wooden walls, propelled by a fresh easterly wind. A pair of cornets and a drummer led the procession down the hill to the main square. Every few paces, the horn players let out a few mournful bleats while the drummer kept a steady rhythm for the marching soldiers.

So swift was the course of Kerodinian justice that no platform had been erected for the beheading. Soldiers made a box in the center of the square with their halberds, keeping the quiet crowd back. In the middle of this human corral, a block was set. The headsman stood ready, his arms folded. When Falken saw him, he wondered if someone taught them to stand that way. They all did it. . . .

He saw no sign of Arbelac or any other friendly face.

When Falken entered the square, a great shout went up from the crowd. The drummer missed a beat when he heard it, and the escort detachment eyed the people massed around them. A couple thousand people filled the square, and there were about a hundred soldiers present to keep order.

Thunder cracked, and a cold gust of air swept over the crowd. The mob surged toward Falken, pressing the ring of soldiers inward. The commanding sergeant barked at his men to stand firm. With a clatter of halberds, they pushed the mob back.

He reached the block. The headsman, who wore an expensive, brightly burnished steel visor and helmet, planted a burly hand on Falken's shoulder and forced him to his knees. Falken scanned the faces in the crowd again. He spied Pais, pressed hard against a pair of crossed poleaxes. Arbelac stood behind her, his hand resting on her shoulder. His black eyes were hard as flint. No trace of his thoughts escaped his lean countenance. Gadric and his brothers were at Pais's feet. The boys were weeping, but Falken saw Pais was grim and composed. The poise of elven blood does tell, he thought.

His knees banged against the paving planks. "Lower your head," muttered the executioner. "Do as I say. It's worse for you if you resist."

Falken looked up. "I will not bow my head to any man."

"Suit yourself, fool."

The drummer switched from his dirge to a rapid tattoo. The high magistrates had gathered at the east end of the square, protected by their private bodyguards. They had folding chairs set up for their comfort and hampers of rich food by their side. Clavis was sipping from an enormous silver goblet. Sarkindon was not with them.

The drummer lifted his batons. Up went the ax. Falken stared straight up into the heavens.

A flash as brilliant as the sun, but silent. Was this death?

And then explosion and chaos. Falken was hurled backward. The ax fell on the block, bounced off, and landed by Falken's feet. It was followed by the crumpling body of the headsman. He fell heavily over his own chopping block, and Falken was amazed to see a smoking hole punched through the polished steel helmet.

The crowd burst through the slender line of soldiers and surged forward. Falken staggered to his feet, dazed, until Arbelac and Pais reached him. Arbelac shouted something, but Falken couldn't hear him. A knife appeared in Arbelac's hand. He slit the leather lacings around his wrists. His mouth moved, but Falken still couldn't hear anything but a dense humming.

"What?" he managed to say. Pais took his arm and dragged him into the crowd.

Rain poured down, chased by swaggering peals of thunder. The square was full of fighting, screaming people. The soldiers, hardly crack troops, were submerged in a sea of rage and terror.

Falken, Arbelac, and Pais reached the west side of the square. A soldier slashed at them, but five boys, none older than twelve, threw themselves at his legs and wrested the halberd away from him. With his free hand, he tried to draw his sword, but Arbelac stepped in and wrenched the blade away, cold-cocking the man with his own sword pommel. The humming in

Falken's head had changed to a roar, which he realized was the true sound around him.

"What—what happened?" he shouted in Pais's ear.

"Lightning. Lightning struck the executioner!"

Had the gods preserved him after all? But there was no time to digest this wonder. A fellow with a fancy dueling sword thrust at Pais. Arbelac tossed the soldier's sword to him. Falken pushed her behind him and presented his blade. The soldier's broadsword was a clumsy thing, but Falken used it with evident skill, forcing the bravo back. He tripped over another fallen Kerodinian.

"To the gate . . . hurry!" Falken said.

As they left the square, Falken paused. He watched a dozen townsmen, poor and flush alike, catch Urmarr the moneylender and beat him senseless, not forgetting to search his clothing for every steel coin it contained. Lord Clavis, a mountain of purple velvet in a torrent of homespun, had lost his wig again as he and his bodyguards laid about them with swords and cudgels. A youth ran past them, whooping, waving a gauzy woman's dress over his head. Falken recognized the gown Haleia had worn at his trial the night before.

They ran through the narrow streets in the pelting rain. At an intersection, a score of children appeared in their path. It was Gadric, with his brothers and some friends.

"Take us with you!" they chorused.

"Go on, go on," Falken said, panting. "Stay in front of us and run!"

There would be pursuit. Clavis and his men had fought free of the riot and came hard on their heels. Someone among them had a bow, and arrows whisked by them in the street.

The stockade was ahead, the notched logs streaming water in the rain. The fastest children were almost to the untended gate when the portal suddenly swung shut. Lord Clavis and a dozen armed men filed out of a side street and the gatehouse.

"Surrender now, or see these whelps cut down!" Clavis bellowed. The children clustered around Pais and Falken. Arbelac tried to shield Falken, but was pushed aside.

"Watch yourself," he said quietly. "One of us must get out of town alive."

"That was always my intention," said Arbelac, smiling.

"Well? Will you yield?" called Clavis.

"Would you really kill them all?" asked Falken.

"What do you think, my lad?"

He wiped rain and dirt from his face. "You would. I just wanted to make sure."

Falken ran at him, sword upraised. Arbelac, unarmed, followed. Falken expected the bodyguards to close in and shield their master, but Clavis waved them off. He held a slim saber whose hilt was as jeweled as the rings he wore. He met Falken and checked his rush.

The portly ex-priest was no tyro. His saber flickered uncomfortably close to Falken. Falken parried, but with a twist of his wrist, Clavis brought the curved edge of his weapon up under Falken's defense, nicking his right ear. Pleased with his coup, Clavis smiled.

"Enough," Falken said. He thrust at the bigger man's chest. Clavis backpedaled. His sandals caught in the hem of his soaking velvet gown, and he tripped. Falken bore in, not stopping until half the length of his sword was protruding from the judge's back.

Everything seemed to stand still. Falken recovered and readied himself for an onslaught by vengeful bodyguards. But with their master slain, the guards were unemployed, and they did not feel like crossing swords with a man they'd seen saved from the ax by a stroke of lightning.

Pais and Arbelac pushed aside the log that held the gate shut. With a wave of his sword, Falken urged everyone out.

A hundred paces from Kerodin, Falken threw down his sword. His back was aching from the lashing, and he was stupefied with exhaustion. He wavered, and was about to fall when many hands braced him.

"Easy, excellency," said Gadric. "Let us help."

Pais was under his arm. "Thank you," he said.

"For what?"

"Who turned the people out to see my beheading?"

She helped him step forward. "Not I. It was Arbelac's idea. He was going to fling gold coins into the crowd so they would fight over them. We would have tried to free you in the confusion."

"I saved our coins," Arbelac added, shaking his cloth purse. "The lightning did the job better than money could have. It was a miracle."

"A sign from the gods," Falken said.

The rain had stopped by the time they reached the far hills. The children were buzzing about like flies, delighted to be out in the fresh air and open country. Falken stopped to rest on the same hill from which he'd first observed Kerodin. Pais caught rainwater on a sheaf of ivy leaves and brought it to him.

"Drink," she said.

The water was cool and sweet. He felt he could sit there forever, washed by the breeze, with the half-elven girl crouched at his feet. The children were playing in the ruins of some ancient edifice nearby. Suddenly their happy chatter died.

"Falken," said Pais, gripping his arm.

He opened his eyes. A man in battered, mismatched armor, mounted on a large horse, towered over them. His lance was resting in his stirrup.

"Hail, my lord," said the mounted warrior. "Greetings to you, Captain Arbelac."

The latter tipped his bedraggled, foppish hat.

" 'My lord'?" wondered Pais.

Falken stood. "Well met, soldier. Whose man are you?"

"Colonel Darion's troop of lance, my lord. Scouting for your lordship's main army."

"Army?" Pais repeated, her voice rising. The children drifted in, frightened by the armed rider.

"Don't you know who this is, girl?" asked the lancer.

"Hars Falken, of Blöde."

"General Hars Falken, for your information," Arbelac said.

Falken rose stiffly and put a hand to Pais's cheek. "Don't be afraid," he said. "My army is all around us. You're safer now than you ever have been in your life."

She gazed at the surrounding hills and trees, which gave no sign an army was near. She looked, saw nothing, and shuddered.

* * * * *

An escort of fifty mounted men arrived and took them back to the army's main camp. They were not splendidly trapped knights in bright armor and heraldic figures. Falken's men wore the arms of a dozen nations, patched and painted and generally looking like remnants from an armorer's scrap bin. Arbelac gratefully shed his dandy's cloak for dented breastplate and helmet. Only one item seemed universal in Falken's army—the emblem all the officers wore, which was also repeated on the banner brandished by the lead horseman. It showed a stylized red arrow, point down, meeting an identical black arrow, point up. Gadric asked what the symbol meant.

"That's the emblem of our crusade," Falken said. "We are the Summoners."

"But what does it mean?" asked his brother, Toli.

Arbelac pointed to the horseman's flag. "The red arrow represents the gods, who are above us. The black arrow represents us mortals, who are below. Our goal is to convince the gods to return to Krynn and restore morality and order."

"By force, if necessary," Pais said flatly.

"Yes."

Barely a league from Kerodin, they came upon the main camp of the Summoners, calmly deposed in a large walnut grove. Falken's men made no cookfires, which would have given away their position. Everything was hushed and expectant.

His chieftains gathered around Falken's horse and hailed him with genuine relief.

"Looks as if my lord had a rough time in town," said one gray-bearded warrior.

"I went to gauge the townsfolk, and this is my evidence." He removed his tattered shirt, displaying the welts on his back. An angry rumble rose from the officers. "The Kerodinians will not submit willingly," he said. "Even if they would, I would still raze that evil cesspool to the ground."

"What?" Pais pushed through the assembled warriors. "Where's the justice in that? Many innocent people live within!"

"Who is innocent?" Falken said severely. "The people rioted during my escape, but only to lighten the pockets of their betters! As I far as I am concerned, the only innocents are you and these boys. The rest are condemned."

She clutched at his calf. "Do not do this, my lord."

"Blood is the price of deliverance," Falken replied. "As a healer cuts away the corrupt flesh of gangrene, so shall we excise the wicked. The gods will see our serious purpose then and bestow their bounty on us forevermore." He reined his horse around, pulling free of Pais's grasp. "Let the order be given! The army will break camp. We will surround Kerodin, and no quarter shall be given. Their defenses are modest, and their fighters are corrupt." Soldiers began to run, spreading the general's word.

"Use fire," Arbelac suggested. "Most of the town is wood."

Two days later, Kerodin was a smoldering heap of ashes. The Summoners swept down on the town. Not trained in the patient art of the siege, they threw themselves at the stockade in endless waves. After the furious day-long assault, some soldiers from Kerodin surrendered. They were put aside under guard while makeshift catapults rained blazing tar-soaked bales of hay on the town's rooftops.

Falken rode out to see the prisoners, flanked by Arbelac. Some ninety-eight men-at-arms sat dejectedly in a small hogpen, stripped of armor, their legs hobbled with chains. A hundred archers stood guard over them.

The general rode slowly around the pen, studying the defeated men. "You," he said, reining up. "Come here."

One man stood up and shuffled to the fence. His eye patch was gone, but Falken recognized him as the corporal of the gatehouse guard.

"You have something of mine, I believe." The corporal stared stupidly at the ground. At a gesture from Falken, two of his men seized the corporal and tore open his shirt. The Summoners' pendant still hung from his neck.

Falken leaned down and snapped the string. "What was lost can be found," he said.

The corporal's one eye widened in terror.

"Begin," said Falken. The archers nocked their arrows.

Island of Night

Roger E. Moore

This is a gnome story, though only one gnome knows the tale.

It was hot that morning, damnably hot. Far too hot for late autumn on Ansalon or anywhere else on this now truly godsforsaken world of Krynn. Angren stared out over the side of the rowboat at the sunlit waters of the lagoon as the half-naked brutes hauled on the oars in unison. Angren was barely aware of the surging of the boat or the barbarians' rhythmic song, the coarse words flowing from their tongues like a shaman's chant. All he felt was the thick, burning air, hot and dry as a fired oven. The Chaos War was over, the Dark Queen and the other gods had fled, and this world and its people were abandoned like ragged children whose parents left days ago for a distant tavern. Only the heat stayed, a last curse for the lost.

Angren grimaced and closed his eyes, covering his face with a weary hand. Every muscle in his neck and shoulders was as tight as a knot. I risked my life on a gamble and lost everything, he thought. I saw hundreds of my fellows die to conquer this damned world for the glory of our queen, and at the very moment when we drove off Chaos, she left. And with her went everything I had ever fought for and earned, all of it gone, just like that. Just like that.

He opened his eyes and looked down, opening his empty hands. He imagined that somewhere at this very moment, beyond the stars or wherever the gods of Krynn had gone, the Queen of Darkness was having her nails buffed. A bowl of grapes and a glass of wine waited by her elbow, and someone was singing for her. At this very moment, she might be thinking of her faraway knights and snickering at the memory. Rage rose within him. He closed his eyes again, and his hands trembled. He wondered why she had abandoned them. He never stopped wondering why she had left him.

Angren took a shaky breath of hot air and wiped his brow. He was drenched with sweat and irritable as a viper. His wet black hair clung to his brow and neck. His rune-engraved helmet and black iron mace lay forgotten on the plank seat beside him. The helm and mace had once been magical. His armor had been magical, too, but all magic on the world had fled with the gods. His magnificent black armor, forged and enchanted for him at terrific cost, now had no ability to protect him from heat, cold, rain, and other torments of the weather. It was merely black-painted steel with pretty engraving, patches of rust showing where the paint was chipped. Angren was rusting, too, deep inside where only he could see it. His spells and the spells of all priests had fled with the other magic when the Dark Queen and her cohorts took off two weeks ago. Now he was just a man with black armor and a mace. A man with no magic at all.

Angren shook his head.

One of the barbarians at the oars broke off his chant, eyeing his liege as if about to speak. Angren sensed the man's gaze and looked up, his glare poisonous.

The brute thought better of speaking and applied himself to the oars, looking away as he rejoined the chant of his fellow savages.

Angren looked away. He could not cast spells any-more, but he was a good fighter. If anyone pushed him just a little too far, he would splatter the contents of his victim's head in every direction. His crew feared him more than they respected him. But they all knew that something had changed in him, that his priestly powers were not what they were. He could abuse them only so much before they would turn on him and discover that he had no spells at all. Rumors of the passing of magic were everywhere now, all through the ranks, though no one was eager to test the possibility. Not yet.

As one, the brutes suddenly turned about in their seats to watch the approaching shoreline for enemies. Angren reached for his mace, giving the beach only a glance. He could not bear to put on the scorching hot black helmet in this heat, so he left it. Instead, he turned, frowning, and glanced back at the small black ship anchored in the still lagoon, its dragon's head prow hovering stiffly over the water. The *Ebony Fang*, its barbarian crew, and its black-armored officers were his to command. He was still a knight—but he couldn't bring himself to add the words "of Takhisis." He was a knight with no patron or meaningful goals, much less a single spell.

The boat was about to land. Angren half arose and gripped the side of the rowboat as the shore drew near, then swung his legs over the side and into the shallow water. He steadied himself, then released the boat and waded to shore. The water came up to his knees and soaked his cloth leggings under his black armor. You wouldn't be soaked if your armor had still been magical, said a little voice inside his head. He knew the water would drench him, he'd look like a drowned gully dwarf, but he waded ashore any-way as he had always done. His pride was all he had.

The brutes shipped their oars and leapt out them-selves, hauling the boat onto the sand as they followed in their leader's footsteps. Angren stopped ten feet past the surf. He held his long black mace with careless fingers as he eyed the lush greenery that surrounded them in this sheltered cove. Exotic scents of tropical flowers and rich soil filled the air—a jungle paradise. He judged they were two hundred miles west of Sancrist Island, perhaps more, near the equator in the Sirrion Sea. A horrific gale had blown them off course the night before as they were returning to Storm's Keep with military reports; otherwise, they would never have found this place. A lucky accident. His lips pressed together tightly. He was such a lucky man.

"Jukisho! Jukisho!" one of the brutes shouted.

Angren turned, surprised. All the brutes were looking down at the white beach and pointing.

Footprints, small and barefoot. The beach was covered with them. Angren had not noticed them before now. They had to be fresh, made just that morning. It had not rained during the gale, but the winds had been very strong. Were children here? Or something worse, like kender?

Stirred to action, Angren pulled a red pennant from his belt and waved it violently from side to side over his head, facing the ship in the lagoon.

"Man your stations!" he roared. The brutes and sailors raised the alert. Some ran for the boats, others for the ship's armory to get weapons and supplies. Their shouts drifted over the bright blue water. Another four boats would be ashore in minutes, loaded with savages and youthful, black-armored Knights of Takhisis. Angren considered going to the rowboat and putting on his helmet, in case there was a fight, but he decided not to bother. He cared about nothing with the Dark Queen gone. If there were enemies here, he'd give them a warm welcome.

"Spread out in threes!" he shouted to his own men. The six brutes with him on the shore drew their swords, formed into two squads, then plunged into the overgrowth, following the tracks. Angren strode into the jungle himself, shoving aside thick green leaves and dangling vines from his path.

He was only fifty feet into the overgrowth when he broke through into a clearing and saw the trench. He glanced about, then cautiously stepped closer. The pit was long and narrow, three feet wide and over twenty feet long. The bottom was nine or ten feet down. Sand and soil were piled along its sides, and vines hung down into the pit from the tops of the piles. He thought at first the trench was a latrine. He looked around once more for enemies, but he saw and heard no one except the distant brutes. He stared at the trench for several seconds more before he realized that it might actually be a trap.

If so, the design was fairly clever—and fairly stupid—as traps went. If a victim fell into the pit, he could not climb up the steep sides to escape; the soil would crumble and drop him back into the pit, maybe burying him if he weren't careful. If the bumbler pulled on the vines to climb out . . . Angren eyed the uppermost part of the vines. Each vine was buried in the soil at the top of a long mound of sand and earth. Pulling on a vine would pull the pile of sand down on top of the bumbler's head, burying the unfortunate in a moment. Clever, except that the pit was in plain view. The sand appeared to be freshly unearthed, so the trench must have been dug that very morning. Perhaps his ship's arrival had interrupted someone's efforts to conceal the trap.

But why had the pit been dug? Warring savages from another island, or perhaps shipwrecked minotaurs? It was unlikely minotaurs would be this far west of Sancrist, though the horned ones were master sailors. Minotaurs themselves could have dug the pit, for that matter. Anything was possible, he supposed. Two weeks ago he would not have believed it possible to be minus his gods. Anything was possible.

Alert, wary, Angren walked slowly past the pit into the riot of greenery beyond. He discovered a second trap, laid out precisely like the first, missing all camouflage. Maybe this was a trapmaker's training ground, he reflected. An island for amateur savages. He suspected the answer was something different. If his brutes didn't cut the locals here to pieces upon finding them, maybe he would discover the reason.

A cry went up from the brutes, far to his left. He headed in their direction through the jungle. They'd caught someone, he could tell. He hurried, slowed by the dense growth that blocked his way and the clumsiness of his heavy armor and its wet padding.

Then he heard his brutes laughing. Laughing?

Arriving on the scene, he saw the grinning brutes and their captive. He muttered a curse as he came to a stop, panting from the exertion of trying to run in full armor in the abominable heat. The excitement of a fight went out of him, and he was just tired and angry. No wonder the traps were so precisely but incompetently made.

The diminutive, ragged figure with kicking feet, held aloft by the laughing brutes, was a gnome.

* * * * *

They tied the gnome to a stake on the beach like a dog, a rope bound tight around his waist in back and his callused hands fettered in front. He was searched but had no strange mechanical devices that could blow everyone within bow shot to pieces. That was a relief. The brutes were unfamiliar with gnomes and merely found their three-foot-tall captive amusing. Angren had met a few gnomes personally and hated the whole miserable race.

The little fellow squinted up at Angren as he approached, the sun at the knight's back. The balding gnome was as brown as a nut, and his tangled white beard stuck out in all directions. The dirty clothing had been badly sewn together from scraps. He was in desperate need of a bath; he'd likely not bathed in years. Angren figured him for a castaway, possibly from a shipwreck but just maybe left here by humans who could no longer tolerate his dangerous mechanical toys. The little guy had been here a very long time, that much was certain.

And if the gnome had been here a very long time, the island was no doubt completely covered with pit traps by now. The knight sighed.

"Do you speak?" Angren asked, regarding the gnome with faint curiosity. He could not have anticipated this sort of encounter under any circumstances.

The gnome, still squinting up into the sun, nodded once. Angren deliberately stood very close to the gnome so the small fellow had to crane his neck to look up at the black-armored human's face.

"You can either speak or die," Angren said calmly. He meant it.

The gnome appeared to understand him perfectly, judging from the look of shock on his face. "Sh-sh-" said the gnome, struggling with a word as he pointed with fettered hands to the lagoon behind Angren.

Angren's fingers undid the mace's strap from his belt, and he hefted it experimentally.

"Ship," wheezed the gnome suddenly. "Y-Y-You c-come . . . th-th-that ship?"

Angren swung his mace down lightly and knocked the gnome's arms away. "That is my ship," he confirmed. "Give me your name. Your short name." Angren was mindful of the absurdly long appellations that gnomes regularly gave themselves.

"Huh—Hudge. Hudge," said the gnome, gently rubbing his bruised arm against his thigh.

"Hudge," repeated Angren. "Excellent. Hudge, when you speak to me, you will call me sir, or you will regret it. Do you understand?"

The gnome seemed surprised and confused all at once. His gaze went to the long black mace in Angren's right hand. He seemed to shrink. "Y—Yes, sir," he wheezed anxiously.

Angren nodded. "Excellent, Hudge, excellent. Well, now, I am going to ask you some questions. You must answer truthfully, or again you'll regret it. You seem to understand common speech well enough. How long have you been on this island?"

It was obvious that the gnome was straining for words. This was highly unusual. Most gnomes would talk your ears off in a minute; they never lacked for something to say, though they did lack any useful topics of conversation. Hudge chewed his lower lip as he considered the question, his face tense. "F-F-Fifteen years," he said in a whisper, looking up again. "Sir."

"Very good. Fifteen years is a long time. How did you come to be here? Shipwreck?"

The gnome hesitated, then nodded, his gaze lowering. "Yes, sir," he said. Angren could barely hear him. "It was . . . it . . . accident. Ship . . . crashed, sir." He turned, looking down the beach to the right into the jungle, and pointed again but with his fingers only, his arms down in front of him. "Over there, up the beach."

Angren looked, saw nothing but thick green jungle. "I see," he said, turning back. "Any other survivors, or just you?"

The gnome nodded a bit. "All s-s-s—um, all gnomes survive, sir."

"Then where are the others?" asked Angren patiently.

The gnome's face took on a sad, tired look. "They . . . are all gone." He looked up at Angren, squinting so much that Angren could not see the gnome's eyes.

The gnome did not see Angren's right boot lash out until it was too late. The kick caught him in the stomach and knocked all the wind out of him. The gnome collapsed and rolled on the ground, gasping in agony.

"You forgot to say 'sir,' " said Angren, almost kindly. "You have to remember to say 'sir.' Will you remember that next time?"

The gnome, his face contorted into a mask of pain, uttered something that sounded vaguely like "sir."

"Get up," Angren ordered.

The gnome forced himself to his feet, swaying as he stood hunched over and clutching his stomach. The gnome looked down at Angren's black boots.

"The other gnomes are gone now?" Angren asked in a flat, crisp voice.

The gnome nodded again. "Yes, sir," he wheezed.

"This is like dragging gully dwarves out of the cupboard," said a black-armored man behind Angren. "Just kill the little cockroach and be done with—"

"If I want your opinion," said Angren loudly, without turning around, "I'll beat it out of you." The man behind Angren fell instantly silent. "I'm growing bored," Angren told the gnome. "Talk."

An hour and a few more kicks later, Angren had the gnome's story. Fifteen years ago, the gnome had been some sort of crewman aboard an experimental ship powered by steam engines, voyaging from the gnomes' mountainous island home of Sancrist. Angren had never heard of a steam-powered vessel, but he knew gnomes and was willing to accept the possibility. The ship had wandered far off course and run aground here. The gnomes had repaired their ship and left, leaving one gnome behind by accident. The gnome—Hudge, Angren remembered—had been living in a cave in the hills. The story made sense. Angren doubted that the easily distractible gnomes on the ship ever figured out that they were short one crewman.

Hudge lay gasping and sobbing on the ground, curled into a tight ball. Nothing useful would be extracted from him for now. Angren nudged the gnome with a boot tip, then left him and walked off to where most of his crew had gathered on the beach, near the boats. The gnome was alone on the island. Angren was sure of this. Gnomes were terrible liars. There was still much to learn about how the gnome had managed to survive here, but that could be beaten out of him later. Angren would order a search to find the high cave the gnome said he used for shelter at night, to avoid "them." The identity of "them" was not yet clear, as the gnome had taken too much punishment by then to elaborate precisely. Angren had the idea that "them" might be wild pigs or large crabs. Their presence would not be unwelcome, especially around dinnertime.

The crew made their report. The ship would be fully provisioned by the next morning. Angren made sure his navigator marked down the isle's position on the sea charts. He named it Angren's Island. It wasn't much, but the major real estate on this world had already been spoken for. You did the best you could with what was available.

Angren spotted his first mate. "Kinnor," he called crisply.

"Sir," came the reply from across the camp. It was the knight who had spoken out of turn earlier. He left a conversation with another knight and came over with a salute.

Angren did not return the salute. "Never interrupt me again while I'm working," he said bluntly, "or I will kill you where you stand."

"Yes, sir," said the knight quickly, head bowed.

"Have the men pitch camp tonight on the beach if they wish. We'll explore tomorrow, then head for home."

"Yes, sir," said the knight, and turned to go.

"Oh," said Angren quickly, "be sure to have the men look for traps tomorrow. Pit traps." He looked across the camp at the gnome, still curled into a ball on the white sand. "Our friend's been building lots of them here, and I'd hate to lose anyone to a damned gnome. Carry on."

"As you wish, sir," said the knight. He hurried off and shouted for the men to muster for an announcement. Angren paid no attention. He was immersed in a very odd thought that had just come to him. Almost a dozen identical pit traps had been discovered that afternoon, all undoubtedly built that very morning in the jungle near the lagoon. How could one gnome do all that? How could one gnome even dig a single trench that was over three times his height with vertical sides? Angren was amazed that he had not thought to ask earlier.

He rubbed his shaven chin thoughtfully. It would be a tough night for the little gnome. The brutes would undoubtedly think of a few games to play with him. Tomorrow, however, would be much worse. Angren had lots more questions for him. The gnome should be grateful for the break.

* * * * *

Just before sunset, Angren returned to his cabin aboard the *Ebony Fang* and locked the door. The air was hot and thick; opening the shuttered window did no good, since there was no breeze, so Angren closed and barred it to keep out tropical insects. He stripped naked and climbed into his bunk for an early rest, but he couldn't sleep. He rolled from side to side, sweating atop his wet and filthy sheets. His cabin felt like a coffin, the stifling air pressing down on him like a dozen feet of black soil and rock. It was still better than sleeping on deck or on the beach with the rest of the crew, he decided. He was the commander, for one thing, and he hated to associate with his inferiors. He treasured his privacy, more so now that his magic was gone and his pride needed shelter. His mind ran over the events of the day.

He sat up abruptly in total darkness, sweat running down his face. He had drifted off to sleep, but something had just awakened him. Had someone called out? He strained to hear any sounds at all.

Something was not right. Something had just . . .

The shrill, distant scream pierced the dead air like a bolt. Angren was out of his bunk and on his feet in a second, fumbling in the blackness for his clothing. Another scream rang out, a different one now, thick with terror. Many voices shouted now, far away, probably from the beach. Angren found his damp leggings and struggled with them. He heard more shouts and recognized the voices of his brutes. He didn't understand what they were yelling.

He jerked his wet leggings up, felt for his leg armor, and began to tie the plates on with clumsy fingers. It was impossible to find the leather straps in the dark. He dropped a shin guard and cursed, damning the Dark Queen, swearing he would cut her to pieces if he ever found her in the afterlife. He could have cast a light spell if he'd had his magic now. He could have slept in his armor if it had been magical. He . . .

Something scraped loudly against the cabin wall less than arm's length from him in the darkness. Startled, Angren flinched, caught his foot on something, and fell to the floor. He lay flat, gasping for breath. The scraping noise began again, sounding like claws raking against the wood. Animal claws. He realized after a terrified moment that the sound was not coming from inside his cabin, as he had feared. It was coming from outside his cabin, from the hull of the ship at the waterline. He struggled to his feet.

A man screamed directly above Angren's head. He fell back again, arms instinctively shielding his face and eyes. Boots stamped across the wooden deck above, knocking dust down on him from the ceiling. More confused shouts now, foul curses, and a wild, wailing scream. Angren had heard the roar and shouts and screams of battle many times, but it was nothing like this. The hair stood up on his neck and back. He crouched on his knees and listened, staring

blindly up at the dark. What was that other sound—
a constant baying or yelping from many throats at
once? It was like . . . like baying dogs, but it couldn't
be dogs.

Scratching and scraping noises ran swiftly up the
wall of his cabin again, causing him to turn and stare
fearfully in that direction. The scraping noise was
followed by thumps on the ceiling and scraping,
dragging footsteps that ran over his head. Things
were climbing up the hull of his ship from the
lagoon. More things were climbing his wall now,
climbing over the deck railing and dragging themselves swiftly to kill his screaming men. The low
baying cries multiplied. The ship rocked slowly back
and forth like a giant's cradle.

On hands and knees, Angren felt his way through
the intense darkness to his cabin door. He banged his
head into a chair and knocked it aside. He muttered a
curse, barely able to speak at all with his terror-dried
mouth. He felt the door with an outstretched arm and
reached up for the handle. Don't turn it! a voice cried
out inside his head. He hesitated, then carefully
reached up again as the racket above continued
unabated. The handle turned, but the door did not
come open. The lock. He reached for the key on his
neck chain, then remembered he'd taken the chain off
and left it on the floor by his bunk.

A loud bang sounded directly above him. A body
struck the deck; someone had fallen from the rigging.
In the distance, a man was bawling like a boy, pleading to the gods to save him. Boots—fewer of them
now—stamped across the deck in every direction,
fleeing or fighting the scraping, dragging noises.
Why am I still here in my cabin? Angren asked himself. Nevertheless, he made no move to go back to his
bunk, find the key, and unlock the door. Why am I
still in here? He heard the baying sound rise and fall,
mixed with the dying cries of his crew.

Someone in heavy boots was running down the

corridor toward his cabin. The man was screaming Angren's name. It was the first mate, Kinnor. He was screaming for Angren to save him. Angren could barely tell what Kinnor was saying, but he heard scraping and dragging feet descend the stairs behind Kinnor and move rapidly up the hall behind him with a baying moan. Kinnor shrieked incoherently like a madman, pounding on the door, until the scraping and dragging feet reached him.

Angren clamped his hands over his ears at the demonic shrieks that came next. Plugging his ears didn't help. The screams filled Angren's head and spilled out into the universe.

He tried to move away from the door, but he lost his balance and fell. The floor was wet. The wetness was warm and a bit sticky, and it covered his hands and arms and face and lips and ran into his mouth. Blood. Blood running into his room from under his cabin door. He knew it was blood even though he couldn't see a thing. Little cries came out of his mouth, cries that a frightened baby would make.

A foul odor, nauseating and corrupt like something left dead and rotting for ages, filtered into the room. A low moan, very clear and loud, came from right outside his door. Claws raked down the length of the door once, then began digging swiftly at the doorjamb. The handle rattled and turned; the door thumped and shuddered. Angren heard it perfectly well even with both hands pressed to his ears. He heard it even as he screamed for it to stop, screaming until he was hoarse, but the scraping and raking and digging and moaning and baying at the door went on without stopping as more things came down the hall and gathered there, trying to open the door and reach him. At some point, his mind overloaded with terror, Angren felt very light and faint, and he floated away.

* * * * *

Angren woke up from a terrible nightmare to find himself ashore, standing on the beach. He didn't remember how he came to be here or why he was here. He held his black mace in his right hand. The air smelled like dead, rotting fish. He looked around at the cratered, blood-splattered sand and mopped his face with a chilled, damp hand. He was cold as ice but sweating like a sieve under a pump. He was sweating so much that he thought he would sink if he weren't careful. But he was so cold that his sweat would freeze, and he would turn into an iceberg. He wouldn't sink like his men, who had vanished in the night. Not a soul could be seen. Where had they gone? Whose blood covered the deck of his ship and stained the white sands of this beautiful beach? Perhaps they had gone to find the Dark Queen.

It was curiously easy to think, but it was very hard to remember. Angren could not recall what he had been doing even five minutes earlier. It wasn't important, though, because he had a far more important mission now. He had to tell Storm's Keep about this island and how cold it was. The Dark Queen would be back just in time to hear his report. He would be her favorite, then—Angren, the Dark Queen's confidant.

He eyed the scattered remains of a nearby bonfire, its ashes cluttering the beach. He sniffed the air. It stank horribly, a burned odor worse than charred fish. He knew the stench; it was familiar, but he couldn't remember what it was. For some reason, he thought of the smoky pyre at a funeral service he had once attended for a fellow knight on Storm's Keep. Angren blinked in the bright sunlight. He stared at the remains of the fire pit. Lying in the ashes was a blackened human arm. The fingers were mere nubs. The arm ended at the elbow, where charred bones stuck out.

His stomach heaved and he had to vomit. He clapped a hand over his mouth and staggered back, waving his mace to ward off the nauseating odor. Then he doubled over and retched until he could scarcely breathe.

Gasping for air, he looked up, his head as empty as his gut. He saw the gnome. The ragged, brown-skinned, white-bearded little fellow was watching him from behind the trunk of a distant palm. The gnome had somehow escaped being tied up on the beach, and now he peered at the tall knight with wide blue eyes. Why wasn't he with the rest of the men from the ship looking for Takhisis? This gnome was disobedient.

Angren straightened and cleared his throat. He started to ask the gnome for a password. Instead, he fell forward, face down, on the white sand.

* * * * *

There were moments when he felt he was waking, but he fought it and sank back into oblivion. When he finally did awaken, it was very dark. He was having trouble breathing, and it felt cold. He was cold all over. He shivered and could not stop.

"Drink," said someone by his ear. "Drink this."

He did. It smelled bad but tasted good. The warmth poured into Angren's throat and spread throughout his body. The shivering ended. He licked his lips and was asleep again in a second.

* * * * *

It was dark, but he came fully awake. He turned his head left and right, but saw nothing. He was under a blanket of some kind. It was night. No, that wasn't exactly right—he was indoors. He was back on the ship, he thought, though he suddenly hoped he was not. He shifted and turned, then realized that he was lying on solid rock covered by a bed of dry, crackling leaves, over which was spread a rough material like sailcloth canvas. The air smelled of dampness, dead leaves, and many other things—all foul.

"You awake?" the gnome asked.

Angren didn't answer. He pulled a hand from beneath the blanket and touched rock face. The rock was cool, not wet and not cold as in a deep cavern.

"It was a time and a half bringing you up here," said the gnome. "It's lucky for you that my life quest was improving simple mechanics to make simpler mechanics. Pulley, inclined plane, lever, all that. One of me with one of you equal to three of me in weight. Wasn't easy. You from Solamnia?"

Angren let his hand fall to his chest. He was weaker than he'd thought. "Yes," he said. True in a way, as he had sailed from Palanthas before landing here.

Danger, said a voice inside his head. *You are thinking about the past. This is dangerous. Think of something else immediately.* He knew the voice was correct, but he couldn't say why. He made himself relax and lay back again.

Almost immediately he remembered what he had fought to forget.

He rolled swiftly to get out from beneath the overhang. He tried to get to his feet in the pitch-black chamber, but fell over and crashed heavily into some kind of basketwork, knocking it all over the place. He struggled, half buried under baskets and completely entangled in his blanket. Panic seized him and he shouted.

"Wait! You're wrecking the place!" cried the gnome. "Stop! I'll get you out!"

Angren lay back again, exhausted. He panted and gasped as someone dragged the twisted blanket away from his feet and shoved the baskets aside.

"Where am I? How did I get here?" Angren asked finally.

"Told you," said the gnome, hidden in the darkness. "Dragged you up the cliff face with a couple of pulleys and some rope. Had to cut off your armor. Sorry, and many apologies about that. Too heavy for me, wouldn't fit in the cave, so I left it. It should still be at the bottom of the cliff. They don't bother things like that, and it wouldn't be much good to you here."

That explained where his armor had gone, though Angren had not even missed it yet. He searched his memory. He remembered everything now, or almost everything. He was in great danger, so he made an effort to keep his mind focused on one thing at a time. First things must come first, he told himself over and over. "I meant, how did I get off the ship and into here?"

"Heh, got me there," said the gnome. "Guess you just jumped off. Found you walking 'round the beach, shivering and soaked. Didn't know where you'd come from. For a moment, I was afraid you were one of them, but they don't fall down like you did. Don't bleed, either. Knew you were still alive, so I brought you up."

Angren was filled with questions. But he didn't want to ask them.

"Water," he said instead.

"Oh, certainly. You sound Solamnian a bit, though your accent's not quite right," said the gnome. There was the sound of pottery clacking together, then a thup as a cork came out. "Your vowels are a little long. Here you go. A bit hard to see, maybe."

Angren reached out in the direction of the gnome's voice. It was impossible to see anything, even with his eyes adapted to the darkness. He stretched but felt nothing. "Where are you?" he asked.

"Oh, wrong direction," said the gnome, slightly to his left. Angren swung his arm and bumped into the gnome's hand, splashing cold water over his skin. "There you go," said the gnome as Angren caught the cool cup and brought it to his lips. The water smelled of clay and damp earth—not musty, but it had an underground smell, like a cave. Angren drank it down in one gulp. The water had an earthy flavor, but it was acceptable. And it was very cold. He drank three cups.

At last he set the cup on the ground between the two of them, on what he guessed was dry straw or grass. Then he sagged back against the ground and breathed deeply for a long moment. The gnome was uncharacteristically silent again.

"That's better," Angren said in a quiet voice. Nothing was really better, but his head was clear now. He swallowed and rubbed at his face. He had to ask a question he didn't want to ask. "What were those things?"

"What?"

"Those . . ." Angren couldn't think of the words. He had never seen what had attacked his men and carried them off. "Those . . . night things," he finally said.

"Ah, thought you knew that already," said the gnome. "You said you were a priest of some sort when you were raving a bit there on the beach. They're ghouls."

"Gh—" Angren's mind didn't immediately accept that information, even as the word almost came out of his mouth. But his soul knew the truth. He was not going to see his crew alive again. "Ghouls," he said, forcing the word to be spoken.

"Yes," said the gnome matter-of-factly. "Marine ghouls, you know. There's an old Solamnic term for them—Children of Zeboim, I believe."

"Cursed of Zeboim," corrected Angren automatically. He had heard the term misused before. The truth slowly sank in. Marine ghouls, here, hundreds of them. Ghouls that clawed their prey down and ate it while it was still hot and screaming.

"Yes, you're right. That is the proper term," said the gnome. "They come out at dusk, quite promptly. I believe they must bury themselves in the sand in the shallow waters around the island just before sunrise, hiding from the light and heat, then crawl out once it gets dark."

Angren had trouble swallowing. His mouth was bone dry. "They're around this island?"

"Oh, yes. Hundreds of them. I'm not very good at estimating their numbers at a distance, but I've managed to get an approximate count by making some measurements—studying footprints, estimating crowd densities, that sort of thing. It's not wise to stay outside for too long after dusk, if you get my drift here, but you can get a pretty good—"

"Wait . . . wait a minute." Angren took a deep breath. "Why are they here? Do you know why they're here, the—those things?"

"Why they're here?" the gnome repeated. "Oh, certainly. They're dead."

"Yes, yes, I know they're dead, but why are they—"

"Oh, I've explained it badly. I'm sorry. They were killed here. They were killed here by other ghouls, and every time someone is killed by a ghoul, he turns into a ghoul, too. They reproduce by murder . . . isn't that the strangest thing when you think about it? They're dead, or undead, rather, and they have no other enemies at all except the living, so they just keep growing in number. I think some of them are quite old, really, but I'm no expert on dead things. They all look very decayed as far as I can tell, falling apart here and there, but they seem to be fairly tough. They're hard to kill."

Angren lay back and let the facts seep through his consciousness. "I don't understand how they got started here," he said finally. "Why there are ghouls here at all."

The gnome grunted. "That's very odd you would say that, because I've thought about that very thing many times here, listening to them howl as they do at night. How they got started here. I think it was the treasure. I can't be sure about that, but they all head for the treasure first thing after they get out of the water. They try to get to me, too, but that's later, and they can't climb up or down too well here. They try it and fall back."

"Are you talking about a cursed treasure? A cursed treasure here?" Angren asked. It was entirely possible. He had read about Zeboim's habits in the library at Storm's Keep. The sea goddess was not above cursing a hoard of valuables if she had been offended. He had never imagined a curse like this one, however. Sea ghouls were very rare, normally.

"Hmmm," said the gnome. "Cursed. Yes, it would have to be, wouldn't it? Only the curse, if there is one on the treasure, did nothing to me. I wish I had thought about a curse when I found the treasure. I would never have gone near it then. None of us would have. Too late now."

The gnome wasn't being very helpful in answering the dozens of questions Angren needed answered. He kept his temper now, however. This was neither the time nor place to indulge in cruelty. Later, certainly.

"I'm not really up for a long story," said Angren, trying hard to see anything at all in the darkness around him. "Still, I would like to know how you got here, and what this treasure is, and whatever other information you have about this . . . lovely place."

The gnome was silent. Angren heard the wind moaning outside, only it didn't sound like the wind after a moment. It was the same sound he'd heard the night his ship was attacked. The wailing, moaning sound rose and fell. Angren was suddenly very cold.

"Can they get in here . . . wherever this is?" he asked, panicked. "The . . . the night things . . . can they get in here?" He could not stop his voice from trembling.

"Eh? Oh, no, no. Like I said, they can't get in here. It's dark out now, so the island's theirs until dawn.

We've got plenty of time for rest and talk. I was just thinking about how I got here. It's almost funny, because it isn't a very long story, all things told. You know how we gnomes like to run on and on about things, but this isn't that kind of story."

He stopped again and was very quiet. After waiting for what seemed like an eternity, Angren was on the verge of asking for the information more forcefully when the gnome began in a voice that was soft and distant.

"I was in the crew of the *Valiant Aftershock the Ninth*, the steamship. You may have heard of it, but I doubt it. News of the project was of no interest to anyone but us gnomes. Anyway, we had developed a new form of propulsion, using steam as its source but directing the energy into a sort of turbine . . . it's very complicated, and I don't care to go into it. It wasn't my life quest, you see, engineering wasn't. I was into simple mechanics. We could make a steamship go very fast. Extraordinarily fast. It fairly blew our beards off when we stuck our heads out of the portholes. It was actually quite exciting in a way, you see, even when we couldn't turn it off. The engine, we couldn't turn the engine off, that is. Moved us along at a marvelous rate. But we were lost shortly, and after a few days at sea, we ran out of food. We were preparing to eat the leather seats, I recall, when the island came into view, and we managed to steer for her and come in for a hard landing."

Angren followed most of this narrative without trouble. He could imagine what the gnome meant by "hard landing" and did not ask for clarification.

"It was well for us that we landed in the evening," continued the gnome. "I recall seeing the sun going down through a porthole and thinking that at least I knew where west was. We had damage control first, as always, and then we had to draw up lists of thing to do once we left the ship, and—" at this point, the gnome's words came more slowly "—and about the time we were working out those last hundred or so details, we encountered the . . . we became aware of the . . . the ghouls." His last word was barely audible. He paused for breath. "We were very lucky, I think, that we did not open the ship's doors or portholes that evening, so we were still locked inside making up the lists when they came ashore. I think we had everything closed up because we couldn't stand the wind when we were moving so fast earlier. It was funny, I think, how a little thing like that . . ."

Angren said nothing after the gnome's voice faded. He was thinking about his own ship, remembering the claws raking the wood of his door, tearing at the wood of the deck above him and the floor beneath him. They had even torn their way into the cargo hold. The crew had left the hatch covers off the hold to lower sacks of fruit and casks of fresh water into the ship before leaving the island. There was no reason to lock or bar any door. The ghouls had come right in, into every place on the ship where a crewman could be—except Angren's own cabin. He had been very close to meeting the night things himself, but for his door and its single lock and his habit of sleeping alone.

Angren realized he had both hands pressed over his eyes. He rubbed his face as if nothing were wrong. It was foolish to worry what the gnome thought of him, he thought, since the gnome couldn't see him. Then he remembered that gnomes *could* see in the dark. They could see the body heat from living things, leftover heat from old campfires, any sort of heat, and it was very clear to them. He alone of the two could not see without light.

"So," Angren said, beginning to act as if he could see in the dark. He pretended to inspect his fingernails. "So you met them."

"Uh. Oh, yes, we met them." The gnome's voice was unsteady and weak. "We met them, sort of. We didn't leave our ship for two days. The captain went out in the early morning of the third day, when the ghouls were gone, and he collected some fruits and nuts from the forest around us. Our ship had plowed into the trees lining the beach, about a mile from where your ship is, and it had knocked down many of the palms. He threw the fruits back into the ship, the captain did, and we ate with the worst manners I can remember. Pigs, all of us. He was quite a hero to us. He threw lots of fruit back in, and eventually we were able to come out and explore a bit, but we were back in right away in the evening, you can believe that, before the ghouls came back at night. We locked up the ship, and we were safe, though I don't think we ever really believed we were completely safe from them. It had been very exciting up till this point, and now it wasn't exciting at all. We would have given up our souls or maybe our steam engine to be off this island. We were here for quite a while."

The gnome paused, and Angren heard him pour a cup of water for himself and drink. The gnome gave out a shaky breath when he was done.

"You said 'we' were here," said Angren carefully, "but now they're not."

"What?" said the gnome. "Oh, the others from the ship. They're gone now. They left. We were here for one hundred and fifty-nine days exactly, they and I. And then they left."

Angren rolled over on his side, looking in the direction of the gnome's voice. "Why did they go but you stayed?"

He heard the gnome yawn. "It's a story, but we're going to need our sleep." There was a rustling sound, as if the gnome were moving a large, rough canvas around. "We're going to need a lot of sleep before tomorrow. We should talk later. I must be the rudest person, and you'll have to forgive me, but this has been a tiring day for me."

Angren listened in disbelief as he heard the gnome shift around, then sniff and fall silent. This gnome was certainly different from any other he'd ever known. "They left you behind?" Angren asked again.

The gnome cleared his throat. "We have a lot to do tomorrow. Sleep now. We are better off talking in the daytime, when they aren't around. We will have a whole day for talking and finding food. And we can take a look at your ship. It should still be there."

The last comment caught Angren off guard. He rose up on one elbow. "The ship is still in the inlet?"

"Yep," said Hudge sleepily. "We have a little time left with her before the storms or . . . or whatever."

"What do you mean? What do you mean by storms or 'whatever'?"

"We're right in the tropics, of course," said the gnome sleepily. "We get a lot of storms here. Always do, all year long. Other ships came here after my ship left, but they're all wrecked now. No crew is left to tend to them after the ghouls come out, so they get busted up, roll over, and just fall apart. Those ghouls, they help out, too, by tearing away at the boards and such. Maybe a month, that's all we have, and your ship will be all over the place."

Angren's lips parted, but no words came out. This was the worst news of all. He didn't give a damn about the crew, but he needed that ship.

The gnome sniffed, then yawned again. "We'll sort it out tomorrow."

"We need that ship to get off this island," said Angren.

He heard the gnome snort softly. "Tomorrow we'll take a look at it. Let's sleep for now."

There was no more conversation. After many long minutes, Angren lay down on his back and stared up into the most complete darkness he had ever known. He needed that ship. He was getting the hell off this island, no matter what it took. He concentrated so intently on this one thought that he could not sleep for hours. The occasional howls from the ghouls did not help, either. He had to get off this island. He *would* get off this island. He was going to escape, by the gods, and that was all there was to it.

As his thoughts progressed on this topic, he began to think about this treasure the gnome mentioned, this cursed treasure of Zeboim, the sea goddess. Lord Ariakan, the founder of the Knights of Takhisis, also happened to be the son of Zeboim herself. She would look favorably on the knight. Angren might be able to wing a prayer to the old sea witch and have the curse . . .

Angren frowned and shook his head. He had almost forgotten that the gods were gone now. But wouldn't their departure remove the curse from the treasure? All other magic had fled the world, so why not this curse, too? If he could haul that treasure to the ship and get off this island . . . He tried to figure out how to rig the sails by himself to get home. He could set up ropes, maybe, to adjust the sails from the deck. Actually, he would be better off heading straight east for the mainland, Ansalon, unless he could catch a favorable wind. It was risky but worth it.

He finally tried to shake off these troubling thoughts and get some real sleep. He heard the gnome's soft snoring now—nothing particularly bad, certainly, as Angren had heard far worse. Wasn't worth kicking him for it.

Kicking him for it. Angren remembered that he had kicked the gnome. The gnome didn't seem to remember the incident at all, or hadn't let on that he did, being too cowardly. That might work out for the better for now. The gnome—whatever his name was, Angren had already forgotten it—would come in handy for his knowledge and whatever he was able to carry from the treasure cave to the ship, just before Angren left this miserable place. Angren nodded to himself. He had it all figured out now, and he could go to sleep.

He rolled over on his side, curling up. He was exhausted, but he was a light sleeper under any circumstances. In the unlikely event that the gnome awakened before him, he would be on guard, and the gnome would not be able to tie him up or cut his throat. One never knew with allies.

* * * * *

Angren blinked. A faint, gray shroud of light filled the cave, which was smaller than he'd thought. If he stood up, he would bash his head on the ceiling. He looked about for the gnome. The gnome was already awake, stretching his arms, half covered by a dirty white blanket that looked as if it had once been part of a sail.

"Sun's almost up," said the gnome, sitting and scratching himself. Hudge, that was his name. "We'd best get ready to move."

They climbed down a forty-five-foot cliff using a thick rope Hudge had strung through a pulley spiked into the trunk of a tree that grew straight out of the cliffside, six feet over the cave entrance. Angren noted that the pulley was a standard ship's model from a large sailing vessel. Angren wondered what ship had used the pulley, and what had happened to that ship and its crew. He could guess. He stared down from the cave for a long time before he descended, searching the trees and undergrowth far below for signs of movement.

The walk to the beach was nightmarish. Unconcerned, the gnome moved through the thick greenery as if strolling through an overgrown park. Angren's hands trembled. He walked as if in a dream. He was barely able to keep up his courage to follow the gnome and not run back to the cliffside cave. He feared that at any moment a dead hand would reach for him through the huge green leaves and yellow flowers. It would have claws for fingernails, and he would scream long before it touched him, just as his men had screamed.

The gnome pushed through a thick rustling wall

of palm leaves and vines, revealing the white sand of the beach ahead. He walked out into the open, then stood with a hand on his hip, completely relaxed. He picked at his nose, staring across the lagoon.

Angren stepped onto the beach and looked out over the gnome's head.

His ship was still there. The *Ebony Fang* was safe. The wave of relief that washed through him could not be described. His knees grew weak, and his breath came out in a grateful rush. He feared he might faint.

The black ship rode high in the water. The anchor was down, the sails were furled, the port longboat was gone. Angren looked swiftly up and down the beach. The longboat was nowhere in sight. He could still get to the ship and climb up the anchor chain if he had to. A rush of energy flooded through him. He knew how to handle the ship by himself in an emergency. It would be hard, terrifically hard, but he could do it. He could and would do anything to get back to Storm's Keep, anything at all.

The gnome walked off while Angren was in his reverie. The small fellow stopped several dozen yards away, looking at the ship through squinting eyes. The sun was up but not above the treetops. The island seemed fresh and new with the dawn, and strangely quiet.

"See that?" the gnome said, pointing to the ship. "Thought they'd do that first. They may be dead, but they can still think. Hmmm."

Puzzled, Angren walked over to where the gnome stood. He examined his ship, his ride to freedom and sanity. The ship's rudder was gone.

"They got your rudder," said the gnome. He sounded like a farrier looking over a nobleman's finest horse, casually pointing out that the horse was lame and would have to be destroyed. "Bet they were working on that all night, tearing at it. Either they don't know how to use tools anymore now that they're dead, or they can't use them with those claws they grow when they turn into ghouls. Anyway, they do pretty well with those claws alone. They must be powerful strong to do that. They leave quite a mess." The gnome paused, examining the ship a bit more. "Tore off your rear sail, too, the lateen one. Is that the right word, 'lateen'? That little triangular steering sail? Looks like they got that, too."

Dazed, Angren looked up and saw that the gnome was right. The mainsail was still furled high and untouched, as far as could be told, but the lateen hung in pale, thin tatters from the backward-tilted rear mast.

"Oh, no," Angren whispered. He felt as if he had been shot through the heart. He shifted his head back and forth, hoping that simple act would adjust his view of the sail and rudder and suddenly reveal that they were perfectly fine after all. It didn't work.

"Got anything aboard that you need carried off?" the gnome asked. "If we can find that boat of yours—if they haven't wrecked it yet—we can get over to bring—"

"No!" roared Angren. He screamed, his face contorted into a mask from the Abyss. "No! Keep off my ship! You keep off my ship, you gods-cursed, stinking, pus-eating maggots! You keep off my ship! Don't you dare touch it!" He screamed and screamed, and in the red haze of his rage, he waded out into the water of the lagoon up to his knees, screaming foul oaths at the monsters who dared touch his ship. He hated them. He was going to kill them all, because he was a cleric of Takhisis, and she wouldn't stand for this crap. He was going to kill them all, all the ghouls, by the gods, because clerics had the power to destroy undead just by commanding it, and he had that power in spades. He was a Knight of Takhisis, a Skull priest, and he could drop undead in their tracks. This was his ship, and he was going home on her with a load of treasure and leaving this nightmare forever.

Someone was screaming at him. He turned, nearly falling in the shallow water.

The gnome was on the bank, waving his arms madly, eyes white and round. He was screaming, too.

"Get out of the water!" he was screaming.

Angren could hardly hear him through the rage pounding in his ears. He stepped forward.

He stepped on something like a branch under the sand. It moved under his boot.

He knew what it was. In that instant, he knew exactly what it was and what he had just done.

Angren felt a fear so endless and vast that it left every other emotion behind. He leapt, surging forward through the water, trying to lift his feet out of the water entirely and run on the surface, but that was impossible. He felt something stir in the water right behind his feet, brushing his ankle, just inches from him, and he knew what it was and he fought the water in front of him, the water that held him back. His feet came down foaming, striking the sand only long enough to shove him forward out of the water, but it wasn't fast enough. It wasn't fast enough because there was a dead thing behind him. One of his crewmen. He knew without doubt that it was one of his crewmen rising up to show the brave Knight of Takhisis what the next plane of existence was like as one of the Blessed of Zeboim, which was the blasphemous name sailors gave the sea ghouls, the most awfully damned of the damned, and the only hard part about becoming a ghoul was the tearing and eating and pain and screaming, and his legs were almost free of the water now, and he was on the beach and running for the trees, and but for his foot catching something and throwing him madly off balance, falling face first into the sand, he would have been into the jungle and long gone.

He screamed and kicked and clawed at the sand to get to his feet, but there was no one behind him now. No one but the gnome, running after him, arms waving, face ashen. The brown gnome was as pale as the white sand. The gnome stopped short, since Angren was still waving and kicking, but feebly. The dead thing was gone. Angren stopped and fell back on the sand, arms covering his face. His shoulders shook with sobs. He cried and shivered in terror as the gnome stood helplessly by, trembling as well, and ripples spread out from the lagoon as something the size of a man stirred under the water, throwing up clouds of sand for a few moments before it was hidden again and still, and all was quiet as it had been only five minutes before.

* * * * *

"They won't come out of the water in the day-time," said the gnome.

"Shut the hell up!" shouted Angren. He sat on the beach, arms folded over his updrawn knees, staring at his ruined ship. He was okay now, he told himself. He could handle it now. Even if he wasn't a cleric anymore, and even if he had no power left over undead such as ghouls, which were all over the place here, just under the sandy bottom of the lagoon and probably around every shoreline on the island, he could handle it. He'd be damned if he'd lose control again.

Neither said anything for several minutes.

"Hungry?" asked the gnome hesitantly.

Angren didn't answer. The gnome wandered away, returning with a round yellow fruit that he held out to Angren. Angren didn't take it. The gnome left the fruit on the sand beside him.

Angren's stomach was a massive knot. He couldn't think about food now. He was trapped on the island, but he wasn't going to stay trapped. He was leaving, and soon. Very soon. He didn't know how, but he'd be off this island in no time at all. No time at all.

"I'd like to show you around the island," said the gnome.

Angren didn't answer. The gnome went away.

Several hours later the gnome came back. Angren was walking up and down the beach, head down. He stopped, kicked at the sand, toed small hills and ridges, walked on.

"Would you like—"

Angren glared at him.

The gnome stopped, then cautiously went on, "—to see the island?"

Angren stared at the gnome with hatred. Then he rubbed his face and eyes. "Yes," he said at last. "Yes . . . the island." He shivered as if someone had walked over his grave.

The gnome managed to work up a smile. "Excellent," he said. "May as well get around while we still have a few hours of daylight left to us." The gnome turned, finger pointing as if lecturing to a classroom. "You should always head back for the cave when the sun drops below the treetops. That will give you a good hour before dusk. Never forget that." He hesitated, unsure if his words had angered Angren. "It—ah—it has helped me to keep that in mind," he added lamely. "One good hour."

The tour did not last very long. Most of the small island could be seen clearly from the rocks atop the gnome's cliff cave. The cave was set into a large cliff that jutted out from the side of what might have once been a small volcano, now entirely overgrown in dark, brilliant green. The cliff itself was barren, all plant life pulled up and hacked away by the gnome to prevent ghouls from hiding there and surprising him.

After all the locations of the local fruits and lagoons were pointed out, the gnome waved a hand at a low hill about half a mile away. "And that's the treasure cave. That's what I call it. It's not a real cave, just one that someone dug out. We can go see it if you like."

Angren chewed on the inside of his cheek. He felt no sense of excitement at all. "Sure. I like treasure as much as anyone."

They climbed down the side of the dead volcano and walked through the overgrowth along a narrow path that the gnome had hacked out long ago, using a machete he had made from a rusted sword blade. They soon arrived at a low, round entrance. "That's it," said the gnome. "That's what I think they stay around here for, the ghouls. Treasure cave. Must be theirs or something."

Angren looked into the darkness beyond the entrance and swallowed. He knew that sea ghouls could not stay on dry land for very long, or else they would decay rapidly. They needed the sea's moisture and salt to continue in their undying state. As they dried out on land, they decomposed and literally fell apart. So there should be no sea ghouls in the little cave with the treasure.

Angren's face twitched. He stepped forward.

Nothing happened.

He ducked his head and walked, stooped over, into the cave. The cool air stank like dead, rotting fish. He hesitated, listening.

He heard nothing.

He went on.

The ceiling rose from the low entrance. Angren straightened slowly, eyes adjusting to the dark. It was obvious that the cave was artificial, at least in part. It was well reinforced along the walls with timbers, painted over with illegible symbols and letters and runes. As he stepped forward, his foot struck a large pile of small metallic objects. Angren looked down in the dim light. There was just enough light from the entrance to see what the pile was.

He instantly forgot about the timbers and walls and runes and his rage and his terror and the ghouls and his ship and the gnome. He forgot about being the has-been cleric of a runaway goddess on a war-torn world with no magic. He forgot every-thing.

He was standing at the edge of a mountain of coins. Mountain was the right word. It was a staggering hoard, almost seven feet high and maybe fifteen feet long, made up of coins of every sort. Angren had not guessed that there were a tenth as many coins in the world as he stared at now. There were gold coins, silver coins, steel coins, copper coins, bronze coins, round coins, oval coins, square coins, coins with holes in them, coins printed with letters from alphabets long gone from memory. The treasure trove of the world was laid out before him.

Dazed and disbelieving, Angren crouched down and touched the coins. They were cool and hard and made clinking noises. He slowly picked up a handful, and some fell from his fingers in a glittering shower. The coins were real. It wasn't a dream.

He felt faint. He leaned back against a wall for support. Now his vision had adjusted to the darkness, and he could see vessels and cups of precious metals, jeweled helmets and sword hilts, rings and necklaces and bracelets and anklets, amulets and tiaras and even crowns, all half buried beneath the mountain of coins. Diamonds, rubies, emeralds, sapphires, garnets, pearls, and gemstones he'd never seen before gleamed dully in the dim light, clasped in settings of worked gold and enameled steel.

"What?" he rasped, turning. The gnome had said something.

"Can't imagine where this all came from," the gnome repeated, waving a hand at the unspeakable riches. "I have a few theories, but who knows?"

Angren looked back at the treasure mountain. Wealth enough to buy a continent. Half of it could buy Solamnia. It wasn't possible.

"The most reasonable theory, as far as I know," the gnome went on, "is that the ghouls brought it here themselves. I've heard that Zeboim is a jealous goddess, and she might wish her treasure—that is, all the treasures lost at sea on shipwrecks brought together in one place. Only I can't imagine why she would want the treasure on land, because she's a sea goddess, of course. It certainly is peculiar." The gnome picked up a coin and flipped it with his hand. The spinning coin skipped off the treasure pile in two places before hitting a far wall and falling among the others with a dull clink.

Angren reached down and pulled a silver cup from the pile of coins. He turned it in his hands. The cup had once belonged to the seafaring minotaurs, if the engraved portrait of a bull-man in plate armor on the cup's side was any clue.

The gnome stepped outside, then came in again. "We have to go," he said.

"Wait a minute," said Angren. He had no intention of leaving yet. He didn't know how much time had passed and didn't care.

"The ghouls are coming in an hour," the gnome said. "We'd best go now. You don't want to be here when they show up. They all come here every single night."

Angren grimaced, reluctantly stood. He kept the silver cup, but the gnome didn't seem to care. He followed the gnome back to the cave in the cliff, and they ascended as rapidly as possible. Once inside the cave, the gnome lit a small oil lamp, then swiftly set about blocking off the entrance of the cave with a wood and metal door backed by stones. Angren lent a hand. By sundown, they were ready.

Only moments after they sealed off the cave and sat down to wait, Angren heard a strange, low howling noise from far away. His hair stood on end, and he shivered. The gnome did not react and went on preparing a light meal for the two of them, made from fruits gathered a few days earlier. They ate in silence as the scattered baying and howling increased and drew nearer.

Angren forced his thoughts away from the ghouls. He toyed with the silver minotaur cup, then put it aside. Far too much had happened today. He needed time to sort things out. He bit into a ripe purple fruit and chewed slowly. It should be possible to get to the ship with a raft and load all the treasure over a few days. Maybe there was a wheelbarrow or something on the island, some sort of cart. What sort of tools did the gnome have? Angren swallowed and started to ask. Then he thought of the pit trap he'd looked at only two days ago. The carefully dug pit that no gnome could possibly have dug.

"Um," he said, waving at the gnome. He couldn't think of the gnome's name again. "Listen, I wanted to ask you something about a trench I found when I arrived here."

He described the pit only briefly before the gnome suddenly said, "Oh, yes. Forgot about that entirely." The gnome held up his right hand and tugged at a ring on his middle finger. The gnome handed the ring to Angren. "My digging ring," he said. "Don't put it on. I don't want it to dig through the walls just as our undead neighbors are arriving."

Angren took the ring and rolled it between his fingers. "Digging ring," he said.

"Yes. It came from the treasure pile. It allows you to dig pits and trenches in no time at all. The pile is full of magical things like that. Pretty useful, some things are, but most are junk."

The words were on Angren's lips to call the gnome ignorant. Magic was dead.

But the gnome had dug the pit on the morning Angren and his ship arrived.

The pile is full of magical things like that. "Magic," said Angren. His face was blank. "You said the treasure has magic artifacts?"

"What? Oh, the treasure, yes, it certainly does. Weird stuff, some of it."

"But how is that possible?" Angren said in quiet disbelief. "It can't b—"

He stopped there. If the gnome had been here for fifteen years, he could not have known about the flight of the gods, the Chaos War, or anything else. The gnome said magic worked here. He had almost certainly used it two days ago. That wasn't possible at all, but then how . . . ?

"This thing still works?" Angren asked. "The magic hasn't . . . gone out of it or anything?"

"Works fine," said the gnome, eyeing Angren in confusion. "What a strange question. Well, anyway, this reminds me that I should check the traps tomorrow morning first thing. I have to dig more pits again."

"Why?" asked Angren. Slowly and unwillingly, he handed the ring back to the gnome, who took it and put it on again.

"Those are my ghoul traps," said the gnome. "Dig them deep enough, and the ghouls can't get out once they fall in, messing around in the dark like they do. They keep clawing at the walls, pulling on the vines, dragging the dirt and sand down on their heads, and soon they just bury themselves. Never had one get out after that. I get rid of a few every night, except for last night, when I forgot about it. Too excited at having you here." He grimaced. "I'm afraid that, um . . . the crew on your ship . . ." He broke off, unsure of how to phrase his next words. He shrugged after a moment and pretended to drop the matter.

But Angren knew exactly what had not been said: "The crew on your ship added to the horde of ghouls, and they undid all my recent work at killing them."

"Who were they all originally, the ghouls?" he asked.

The gnome snorted and shook his head. "Oh, I couldn't say. I have a theory, one that's unfortunately impossible to test, that the ghouls are all drowned sailors who were raised up by Zeboim. Couldn't say why she did it, but it does make sense. They have every sort of rag on them for clothes, but I can't make out uniforms or emblems or whatever. Impossible to say what they were like to start with. Could even be some elves among them, though I'd guess most were humans. Some I'm sure are minotaurs, or were, judging from their size and those horns."

Angren nodded. He thought about the treasure cave as he listened to the ghouls howl and whine outside, far away. Tomorrow, he thought. I'll get back to the cave tomorrow and get my own magic rings. And if the gnome's taken them all, he'll just have to suffer a bit and hand them over to his guest.

Angren yawned and told the gnome he was going to turn in. The gnome agreed. Angren hadn't slept well the night before, and he craved rest now.

It was interesting, he reflected as he was dropping off to sleep. Not a word from the gnome about being captured and chained to a stake on the beach just two days ago. It was if the whole incident had been forgotten. At least the gnome knew who was boss here. That would become even more apparent very, very soon.

* * * * *

Angren was awakened by the sound of metal banging on metal. *Ghoul* was the first thought in his head. He rolled violently, shielding his face and pulling up his knees.

"Whoa, there! Whoa! It's okay," said the gnome. "Just making some breakfast."

Angren let out his breath and swore explosively. He sat up, careful not to bang his head on the rocky overhang above his rude bed. "Just keep the noise down," he snapped. He sat for a few moments, collecting his thoughts, then cast aside his rough sail-cloth blanket.

Breakfast was brief and without conversation. "Let's get out of here" was all Angren said before they left.

The gnome went off to check his ghoul traps. Angren went immediately to the treasure hoard. The place stank anew of dead fish and drying seaweed, hallmarks of the ghouls' nocturnal visit. He didn't care about them as much now. He was adapting to this mad island quite quickly. He probed and hunted among the coins and precious things in the semidarkness, searching for anything of special interest. New ideas came to him all the time. If this was the only magical treasure left on Krynn, and it all still worked, he would be a king—no, he would be an emperor, a ruler not seen since the Kingpriest of Istar. He would leap to prominence in the Knights' hierarchy, maybe even take charge of it. He would gain rulership over vast territories. He might share a bit of his secret wealth with those under him, forging their loyalty.

But first he had to get off the island. He stopped sorting through the mountain of riches and considered this problem. The gnome was the key. He had to know a way. If he got here, he must know a way off. His fellows had long ago left the island. How did they leave? Angren was an idiot for not asking before. He tore himself away from the treasure and went out in search of the gnome.

"What happened that you were left behind here?"

The gnome jumped, startled. The gnome was in process of digging another pit and had not heard the knight approach. The gnome was in the process of digging another pit. Angren watched the digging ring in operation. Wisps of sand drifted down from the air around the pit where the gnome aimed his right fist. The gnome was half done with another trench already.

Magic really did work here! It was a dream come true!

"Oh!" cried the gnome. "I'm sorry! You startled me. Sorry about that. What happened that . . . ?"

". . . that you were left behind here," said Angren

sharply. "What happened? You said the other gnomes left you here. What did you mean by that?"

"Oh." The gnome was surprised by the question. He seemed to consider an answer, then looked away, embarrassed. "Oh," he repeated, and he took a ragged breath. "Well, um, we got here on our steamship, the *Valiant Aftershock the Ninth*, as I told you, and because we'd hit the beach so fast and run it up on the shore so far, it wasn't possible to haul it back to the sea by ourselves, not without cutting down two or three hundred trees for roller logs, and then we'd need a crane to lift the ship, and rope for the crane, and so forth, and the . . . the ghouls were a bit troublesome, you see, so we wound up getting nothing done at first. We'd been here for a good while before one of the turbo pump engineers found the stickytrees over on the far side of the island. There was a whole grove of them. We called them stickytrees because the sap, you see, was all sticky and gummy, but after you left it out and it dried, it wasn't sticky anymore. It was rather like . . . it was like cloth, almost, flexible and soft, whitish in color, so we tried some experiments with it and found that, though it wasn't good to eat, you could make balls with it. Some of the crew sewed up their clothes into a sort of big, hollow ball, covered the whole thing with stickytree sap, and managed to inflate it with a pump on the ship. When we covered the air hole with more stickytree sap and let it dry, we had a big ball. We had a great time with it—invented some beach games and had regular teams and competitions—and we also—"

"Shut up," Angren interrupted. He stepped close to the gnome and crouched down so that his eyes were level with the gnome's. "Shut up and listen to me. I want to get off the island. I want to get off this island in the worst way possible. I don't want to hear all this garbage about shipwrecked gnomes making big play balls. I want to know how the other gnomes got off the island. I want to know that right now."

The gnome edged back away from him. Angren could tell from the gnome's face that he remembered perfectly what had happened that first day they had met. "Yes, of course. I was getting to that," said the gnome carefully. His face was lined with anxiety. "I really was, honestly . . . sir. As—as I was saying, sir, the others, one day they got to playing with this ball, and one of them knocked it way up high by bouncing it off his head, and that's when someone else got to thinking about balloons, the floating kind that—"

"A hot-air balloon," Angren slapped his knee. "By the gods, yes!" He knew about several experiments conducted with large balloons, the air in them heated by magic to make them rise to great altitudes. Humans toyed with them on occasions. He'd heard stories of a city—he forgot which one, but he thought it was a kender town—that had sent hundreds of colorful balloons aloft on a celebration day. Balloons were nice as curios but were worthless otherwise. But now there should be no reason, if they were large enough, that hot-air balloons couldn't . . .

"Was that how they got off the island?" Angren demanded, grabbing the gnome's thin right arm. "They made a balloon and flew off?"

"Yes . . . yes, it was!" cried the gnome in fear. Words poured out of him as he tried to pull free of the human's strong grip. "Yes, sir, it was! We built a great balloon, a monster, and attached it to Old Number Nine by rope cables. It was a huge thing, a hundred and fifty feet across if an inch, and it took us half a year to build it and the secondary, and we stored them in the cave where I live now. We found a magical torch in the treasure, and we used it to fill the balloon, and it went up just like that!" The gnome ran out of breath and panted. "And then we took off," he added in a tired voice. He swallowed and sighed, slowing down. "I miss them," he said. "I miss them very much. It's been—"

"So why'd they leave you?" Angren asked. He'd already let go of the gnome.

The gnome looked down at the ground, breathing heavily. "It wasn't really their fault, their leaving me. It couldn't be helped. We inflated the balloon for the last time on the one hundred and fifty-ninth day after a lot of tests, and we took off late in the morning, as soon as we could, so we'd have a whole day to see where we were floating off to. The high wind currents in this region all head eastward, being equatorial. The ship's navigator had figured our position to be almost exactly due west of Sancrist by about two hundred and forty-two miles. We'd get home in a week or so just by floating on the wind. We took off, and then things started to go wrong. The anchor cables that held Old Number Nine down, two of them didn't release from the ship at takeoff. The cables dragged after us and snagged in the trees and stopped us cold, right up there in the air. I was closest to one cable, and I ran over to cut it loose, but the cable was too thick and we had left the axes behind. I don't know what came over me then. I didn't think about anything but getting the cable free. I grabbed hold of the cable and climbed down it, hand over hand, with my legs wrapped around it. I climbed down until I reached the tree and then unwrapped the cable until it pulled free. I climbed down the tree trunk, a palm, and then ran to the tree where the other cable was snagged, but the tree snapped off halfway up, and the balloon pulled free with the treetop entangled in the cable behind it like a tail, and away they went. They waved and shouted and tried to throw another line down to me, but we must have grossly underestimated the lifting power of the balloon, for they kept going up, and there I was on the beach, shouting and waving back, and that was that. They were gone. They were all gone."

The gnome fell silent, head hanging low. Then he took a deep breath, let it out, and walked away with slumped shoulders.

Angren let him go. He sat back on his heels and wiped at his mouth. The amount of work it would take to build another balloon was staggering. He was daunted by the very thought of it. And he didn't recall hearing any old stories from Solamnians about a balloon full of gnomes flying back to Sancrist or Ansalon. Maybe they'd crashed into the sea, or else they were still up there, circling the world forever. Stupid gnomes. It figured.

He stood up and stretched. He needed a balloon. His ship was useless without a rudder and with the lateen ripped up. He needed a . . .

Something came to mind, something the gnome had said. He got up and walked around the half-dug pit, following the gnome. He found the gnome behind some trees, wiping his eyes.

"You stored the balloon in your cave," he said.

The gnome nodded. "Yes, sir. It and the secondary."

"The secondary."

The gnome nodded again. "Yes, sir."

"You mean a second balloon."

Another nod.

"Is the secondary one still there?"

"Oh, no. We took it out the day before we—they—left, in case there was an accident with the first balloon and we needed the other instead. When the other balloon was inflated, we hid the secondary so the ghouls wouldn't find it. It's still here."

Angren crouched swiftly and seized the gnome by the shoulders. His grip was tight and painful. "Can it fly?" he shouted in the gnome's face. "Can it? Is the balloon in good shape?"

The gnome gave a frightened nod. His eyes were the size of bird eggs.

Angren shook the gnome violently. "Why in the damned black Abyss didn't you say so?" he screamed. "You've had another balloon here all this time? Why in the Abyss didn't you tell me that?"

The terrified gnome tried to speak but couldn't. Angren shoved him away. The gnome fell on his back. "Another balloon! Here you sit all this time on this lousy island, and you have another balloon but you don't use it! The gods curse your rotten race! You idiots! You people could think your way out of an open bag!" He paused for breath.

"Oh," he said, and suddenly he began to calm down. "Hey," he said. "I'm the idiot. Why am I so upset? The balloon's here and we've got a way to get off this island! Yeah. Gods, but I'm the idiot."

Angren held out his open hand to the gnome, who recoiled in fear.

"Hey, forget what I said." Angren was almost smiling. "I have a bad temper. I get out of hand, but I don't mean it. I can't help it sometimes. Let me help you up, and let's forget about it."

The gnome stared at Angren with an open mouth, then slowly reached up and took Angren's hand. The knight lifted him to his feet with one easy pull. The gnome was a little heavier than Angren had thought, but no more so than a snot-nosed kid. Angren gave the gnome a friendly pat or two on the back. "Okay," he went on. "Let's take a look at that balloon."

Angren followed the gnome's lead. The gnome walked in a hunched-up way, nervously stealing glances back at Angren as they went. They walked for several long minutes before Angren realized they were heading toward the lagoon.

They stepped out of the overgrowth and onto the beach again. The black-hulled *Ebony Fang* still rode high at anchor. The knight noticed that the ghouls had been at work again, deeply scarring the boat's hull and scratching away the paint in many places.

"What are we doing here?" Angren asked, puzzled. "I thought we were going to see the balloon."

Wordlessly the gnome examined the sand on the beach, then, after eyeing the trees, selected a spot twenty yards away. He knelt down and began digging into the sand with his hands. He stopped after a few seconds, and Angren heard him mutter, "What am I thinking?" The gnome stood up, backed away from the spot, then aimed his right fist.

Sand erupted and flew in every direction. Angren thought for a moment that some kind of animal was trying to emerge from the hole until he realized it was the gnome's digging ring at work. Angren drew closer so he could see what was happening.

The digging went on for several minutes. Then came a scraping sound. The gnome relaxed and dropped his arm. He walked to the edge of the ten-foot pit he'd dug. The gnome peered over the edge, then turned to Angren and pointed into the pit. "There it is," he said.

The gnome did not say "sir," but Angren didn't reprimand him. He strode to the edge of the pit and looked down. Wooden boards were visible at the bottom of the pit, like the long-buried floor of an ancient home.

"The secondary balloon is down there, all wrapped up," said the gnome. "The hand pump from Old Number Nine is there, too, which we turned into an inflating fan with a hose we made from the stickytree sap. Two more magical torches are there as well. It's everything we thought we'd need if we had to come back to the island, though now that I think of it, it wouldn't have been easy to get back because the wind wouldn't blow us back here. It goes east, not west, so we'd just keep on going eastward, and we couldn't have come back if we had wanted to. And that was why they couldn't come back for me." The gnome brushed a hand through his filthy white hair.

"Uh-huh," said Angren. He stared down at the boards. "You say the balloon is under there? Is that some kind of cellar?"

"Yes. We had to keep the ghouls away from the balloon, you see. Sir."

"How are we supposed to get the balloon out? It must weigh a ton."

The gnome snorted softly in a goodhearted way. "Oh, that. That's what this is for." He reached into a pocket and pulled out another ring. "This is a telekinesis ring. Found it in the treasure pile long time ago. I was the one who moved the balloons around to help bury them."

Angren held out his hand. The gnome grimaced, realizing he might have made a mistake, but he dropped the ring into Angren's hand. Angren rolled the ring between his fingers, then put it on. He admired it a moment. It was only a plain gold band.

"Telekinesis," he breathed. "I had one of these once, several years ago before the gods left. I used it for all sorts of things at Storm's Keep. Best little freight hauler in the business. Couldn't pick up a ship, of course, but you could do a lot with it." He grinned at the gnome. "Bet you couldn't pick up your Old Number Nine with this, could you?"

The gnome shook his head unhappily. He timidly put out his hand, palm up, to get the ring back.

Angren looked at the gnome, looked down at the ring. He slapped the gnome across the face. The blow staggered the gnome, and he fell backward into the pit with a heavy thump.

Angren aimed his fist, ring out, down into the pit. The gnome rose out of the pit and floated over the sand toward the lagoon. Magic. The word rang in Angren's head. The gnome rolled in the air, vainly trying to get his balance and footing. Angren dropped him a few feet offshore into the shallow water. The gnome flailed in the lagoon, then rose to his feet and quickly staggered out. He fell to his knees, coughing up water. His left cheek was a bright, angry red. Angren could see his finger marks on it.

"I think now we're finally straightened out about things," Angren said pleasantly. "I'll take that other ring." There was a brief struggle between the two. When it ended, Angren put the digging ring on his left hand.

"You know," he told the gnome, who was sprawled on the sand at his feet, "just two or three days ago, I thought the world had come to an end for me. Completely. I used to be a cleric for Takhisis before the gods left Krynn. You didn't hear about that, did you?"

The gnome failed to respond. He lay on the ground, facedown in the sand, hands covering his head.

"Well," Angren went on conversationally, "the gods are gone, so you can call on any one of them, all of them, but they won't respond. Zeboim, if she really was the one who left this treasure behind, is not coming back to claim it. It's mine now, I believe, and . . . and wouldn't you know, I've just figured out how to bring all that treasure down to the beach, get it loaded onto my ship, and get off this island. I might even take you with me." He reached down and pressed a finger into the gnome's back. The gnome flinched at the touch. "If we happen to fly over Sancrist Island, where your little rat race comes from . . . I might even drop you off there." Angren grinned broadly. "Get it? Drop you off?"

No answer. Angren kicked the gnome. The gnome gasped and groaned aloud, clutching his side. "Get up now," Angren ordered. "We've work to do, and not much time to do it. You're going to teach me about this balloon, how it works and everything. Tomorrow we're going to take it out, look it over, and then we're going to attach it to my ship. I can use the ring to pull the ship in to shore to beach her. I think this ring should be able to do that." He eyed his ship in the lagoon. "I may be able to keep the balloon flopped over the masts, so it doesn't hang down low enough for the ghouls to reach it. The day after tomorrow, if all goes well, I'm going to load up the ship with Zeboim's treasure. It shouldn't take long if this ring is like the one I used to own. Then the day after that . . . off we go." He grinned again. His eyes were cold. "I said 'we,' but that could be just 'I' unless you get up and get to work. I'd hate for you to stay here with the likes of my old crew around, especially in their condition."

The gnome groaned and slowly rose to his feet. One hand was pressed to his side, where Angren had kicked him. He never looked up.

"What do you say to that?" Angren said, eyes narrowing.

The gnome nodded once slowly. "Yes, sir," he said softly.

"Excellent." Angren glanced up at the sky, then down into the pit. "I'm going to bury this thing again, but we'll get back to work on it first thing in the morning. It's growing late." He laughed, the first time he'd laughed in weeks. "Can't work when the sun's almost down behind the trees, can we?"

He laughed again. The sound of it echoed across the lagoon and into the trees, where it was already very dark.

* * * * *

In the end, it took six days, not three, to fix up the balloon, hang it from the ship's rigging and masts, tie it down to the deck and railing on bow and stern, then install the inflation fan and magic torches. Moving the treasure was the last thing they did. That took only one day. When the treasure was out in the sunlight, the pile seemed smaller than it had in the darkness of the cave. It didn't gleam as brightly as Argren had expected, either. Perhaps that was a result of old slime or sea salt coating the treasure. Angren frowned and picked up a few coins that had fallen from the great load, which had to be broken down into smaller piles for the telekinesis ring to lift and carry through the air before spilling them into the ship's open cargo hold.

Angren believed the gnome was right about this being treasure stolen from shipwrecks in this part of the sea, if not the world over. Zeboim had probably kept it piled up on land instead of leaving it in the sea because on land it would attract sailors and treasure hunters, the perfect way to increase the might of her ghoul army. It made perfect sense. Zeboim would do that sort of thing.

"Bitch," he said, flipping a coin into the air. He caught it and pocketed it with the other stray coins. He was leaving nothing behind. He had a world to conquer—or buy.

On the seventh day, at dawn, Angren walked the deck aboard his ship. The sun rose from a flaming red sky in the east. It was going to be another scorcher of a day. Angren had carefully reassembled the pieces of his armor into a full suit that morning, then put it on. He had his mace at his side. His helmet was below in his cabin. The balloon inflated swiftly as the magical torches and hand pump poured hot air into it. The only drawback was that the ship smelled terrible, like dead fish. He was never going to get the stink of the sea ghouls out of the wood.

Angren eyed the little gnome, puffing and sweating on the main deck beneath the low mouth of the balloon as he worked the hand pump. It was actually a two-person pump, but the gnome was doing famously by himself. Not that he had any choice in the matter. He must want to leave this island very badly; he was working very hard to get the balloon ready. The gnome said he had even bolted down the hatch covers over the cargo hold. Pity about that. But that was the way of things, wasn't it? One day the gods cast you aside and leave, and there you are, on your own little island of darkness, and no one around to rescue you. You just have to count on yourself in times like that. Angren hummed a few bars from an old marching song the knights sang at Storm's Keep during their drills.

The balloon reached full inflation by midmorning, a monstrous off-white sphere with irregular bulges here and there. The balloon seemed solid and stable enough, however. It was made up of hundreds of long, vertical strips of some rubbery material, sewn together with the gods knew what, maybe gnome shoelaces. It was well over a hundred feet across.

The deciding moment came when the *Ebony Fang* rocked to one side beneath the balloon, all its boards creaking loudly in protest. Thrown off-balance, Angren grabbed at a ratline and held on. Then, with a popping of joints, the black ship lifted free of the lagoon. Water cascaded from the hull into the lagoon. Four thick cables held the black ship down to about ten feet above the water, anchoring it in four directions to shoreline trees. The bow hovered above the sands where the ship had been beached for loading.

Angren looked over the side and nodded. It was time, he decided. He pushed away from the railing and casually walked over to where the gnome stood, peering over the side of the ship on his tiptoes. The gnome was too absorbed in the view to notice Angren's approach.

Angren aimed the telekinesis ring, caught the gnome with it, and dragged the kicking, shouting little fellow—what was his name?—away from the railing. Angren carried him over the side of the ship, then dropped him into the sand from an altitude of a couple of feet.

"You should be grateful I didn't let you go in the deep end of the lagoon," Angren called out as the gnome regained his feet. "I think I have it all down now, how to run this thing by myself. I don't plan to go too high above the sea, but I've got plenty of ballast, just in case I need to climb. You're an amazing teacher. I'm quite in awe. Maybe you can teach a thing or two to my old crew while you're here!" He laughed aloud. He felt better than he ever had in his life.

The gnome stood on the beach, watching Angren with sad, lifeless eyes. He appeared to have expected this.

"I must say, you're taking this well," Angren shouted. "That's good. I hate whiners."

Quickly he busied himself with the cable releases. The ship tilted precariously, almost throwing Angren overboard, before the last cable came free. Then ship and balloon surged upward into the clear, red dawn at rapid speed. Angren looked over the side and cheerfully waved to the gnome. He continued to watch as the gnome shrank below him. The island grew smaller, the gnome vanished in the greenery, and Angren was far, far away from the island of the children of Zeboim. Cursed of Zeboim, he corrected himself, then shrugged and smiled. Who cared now? He had her treasure, the treasure of a goddess. And soon he would be king of the world.

* * * * *

The day was long and hot. Angren spent much of the time in his cabin, but he was too nervous to rest. He came out and inspected his flying ship many times, barely able to believe the events of the last few days even now. Ah, but his luck had definitely changed. He laughed a great deal as the day wore on.

The storm caught him completely by surprise. It whirled out of the west at dusk, a vast tower of boiling clouds rising above a black base of flickering lightning and dense rain. Helpless to do anything about it, he stayed on deck and watched it approach. He finally judged it best to check the cargo holds and head below to his cabin to ride it out.

He made his way across the rocking deck and squatted down by one of the cargo hatches. Odd, he thought. The hatch wasn't bolted at all. The thick latch was shut, but it had been left unbolted—all last night, probably. Angren glanced around and saw that the other hatches were similarly unbolted and shut. Damned stupid, incompetent gnome. He shrugged it off and gripped the bottom of the cover. One . . . two . . . three, he counted silently, then lifted the cover free. He shoved it aside and looked down at his treasure.

He froze for a moment, then threw himself back on the deck. Animal-like whimpers came out of his throat. He snatched at the hatch cover and tried to toss it over the hatchway, but it didn't fit over the opening. It clattered, tilted diagonally, then fell into the hold with a thump.

A low moan like a baying hound went up from inside the cargo hold. The cry was taken up by other inhuman throats—many hundreds of others, all below his feet.

Angren tried to stand, but his legs were rubbery, all soft and weak like dried stickytree sap. He dragged himself away on his hands and pulled himself up on the ship's rigging, unable to take his eyes from the hatchway.

The storm was upon him. The sunlight faded as the top of the sun fell below the horizon and was gone.

A clawed, pale hand shot up and gripped the edge of the open hatch.

* * * * *

Hudge stood alone on the beach. The ship and balloon were now out of sight in the red morning sky. He was too tired and drained to do anything more. All these years of waiting for rescue, or at least companionship, and this was how it went. It was almost too much to bear.

It had to be done, though. He nodded. It had to be done.

He reached up and gently touched his cheek where the knight had slapped him. The knight shouldn't have done that. That had been too much.

Hudge shook his head at the memory.

After a while, he turned and walked away. He paused by a palm tree to reach down and dig with his hands into the sand. When he found the cargo-hatch bolts, he went down to the lagoon and hurled them into the water one by one. Nothing stirred in the shallow waters of the lagoon.

He had taken great pains to measure the cargo capacity of the black ship's hold when the knight wasn't looking. The treasure would take up a lot of room there, but there was still more than enough room for anyone compelled to follow the treasure to climb into the hold at night and go along. Several hundred ghouls could fit into the hold, in fact, but only if someone remembered beforehand to leave the hatches unlocked so they could get in.

That night, after the thunderstorm had passed, Hudge climbed to the top of the small volcano and looked eastward under the infinite stars. Nothing came out of the sea to trouble him. He wondered what had happened to his shipmates on their balloon ship after they left all those years ago. He had long ago forgiven them for not returning. It couldn't be helped. But—and he thought this was the strangest part—he felt his life had gone for the better because he had remained behind. It was lonely at times, but he felt satisfied, too, in a way, even comfortable. He listened to the sea whisper to him from all the island's beaches, felt a warm tropical breeze run over his face beneath the lone, strange moon, and eventually he forgot about his shipmates on Old Number Nine. He even forgot about the bad knight whose name he could no longer recall.

Instead, he began to think about the world of simple mechanics.

Demons of the Mind

Margaret Weis and Don Perrin

Crockery crashed to the floor, plates smashing, mugs cracking, sounding like the last note from the last trump of doom. The noise—coming on a warm, gently quiet, sunny afternoon in midsummer—startled Caramon, who jumped violently and struck his head on an overhanging shelf. Rising ponderously to his feet, he glared over the counter, wincing and rubbing his head.

Tika dashed past, giving Caramon The Look on her way. Caramon always thought of her look as The Look, spelled with capital letters. He had been on the receiving end of The Look very often in his married life. The Look said, plain as speech, "Not a word to me, Caramon! Not a single word!"

Caramon had fought goblins, hobgoblins, draconians, dragons, and the odd assorted thief, rogue, and evil cleric. But he knew better than to challenge The Look.

Caramon loved his wife dearly. If anyone on Krynn had asked him to name the most beautiful and wonderful, the wisest and bravest woman he'd ever known, he would have said Tika Waylan Majere instantly, without a qualm or a second thought.

Gray streaked her red hair now, her face showed the marks of laughter, the tracks of tears. She had fought at his side during a war to bring the gods back to Krynn, she had stood by his side during the war that presumably saw the gods leave Krynn. Caramon and Tika had buried two dearly loved sons during the last war, been present at the funerals of two dearly loved friends. Their love kept them strong, comforted them in their sorrow.

Most important, Caramon credited Tika with saving his life during the terrible time when he had come close to falling a victim to the brain-rotting effects of the potent liquor known as dwarf spirits. She had sent him on a quest to find himself, to find his own strength, his own worth as a person. A world without Tika was a world in which Caramon would not want to live. But when she gave him The Look, he wished a portion of that world might open up and swallow him.

Biting his tongue, he ducked back behind the bar, continued to mop up spilled ale.

"There, Jassar," Tika said, her voice coming to him from the kitchen. "There, girl, don't take on so. It's only a few broken plates and a mug or two."

Caramon groaned. He knew how Tika counted. "A few" meant fifteen or twenty, in all likelihood. Caramon had never known a barmaid to be so clumsy.

He bided his time, said nothing until that night when the inn's doors had closed on the last customer and he and Tika were making ready for bed. Caramon sat on the bed, pulling off his boots. Tika sat before her mirror, which hung on the wall before her. She brushed her hair one hundred strokes as she did every night. Caramon felt safe in bringing up the subject, for her back was to him.

"I know you're fond of her, my dear," Caramon said, "but that Jassar's got to go."

Caramon had not taken the mirror into account. He discovered, too late, that The Look worked equally well by reflection. Bouncing off the mirror, The Look struck him squarely between the eyes.

"She hasn't been with us that long. She needs a

bit of training. The trays are awkward and hard to balance. She was upset about something that happened at home," said Tika, brushing her hair with unusual force so that it actually crackled.

Caramon breathed a sigh. When Tika started handing out excuses, he knew he was safe. The Look had been reflexive, apparently. He had to tread cautiously, however.

"Jassar's been with us for three months now, my dear," Caramon said mildly, careful to make it an observation, not an argument. "She was okay when she started—not great, but okay. But she hasn't gotten any better. In fact, she's gotten worse! The customers are complaining. She mixes up orders, when she remembers to bring the orders at all. She's jumpy as a kender in a prison cell. That's the fifth tray of plates she's dropped this week. I've had to replace them at least once a week, and now the potter grins from ear to ear when he sees me coming. He's planning to build a new house on our business alone! We're losing customers and we're losing money. I'm sorry, Tika, Jassar's a nice girl and all, but we can't afford to keep her."

He prepared to duck, should The Look come his way. But Tika only sighed, set down her brush—after only seventy-nine strokes—and turned to face him. Her face was drawn, softened.

"This is the fourth job she's had in a year. Without her work, she and her husband will starve."

"What's the matter with her husband?" Caramon asked. "Why doesn't he pull his share? Come to think of it, I don't believe I've ever seen him around."

"You would if you went to the Trough," Tika said, her voice low.

"Ah, that's the way of it, is it?" Caramon looked grave. He had spent considerable time at the Trough himself once, back in the dwarf-spirit days.

"He's a cripple. He lost his arm in the war," Tika added by way of explanation.

"Our sons lost more than that," Caramon returned quietly. "They gave their lives. This man's the lucky one"

"He doesn't seem to think so. Anyway, that's why Jassar's mind isn't on her work. She's worried about him. I know how she feels, Caramon. I understand. I know what it was like when you were drinking. At least you didn't . . ." She stopped.

"Didn't what?" Caramon frowned. "He doesn't beat her, does he?"

"He always says he's sorry afterward," Tika said. "Now, Caramon, it's none of our business—"

"Yes, it is!" Caramon stood up, his fist clenched. "I'll give him a taste of his own medicine and see how he likes it! There's no bigger coward than a man who beats a woman."

"Caramon, don't! Please!" Tika crossed over to him, put her hands pleadingly on his chest. "You'll only make things worse for her."

"Well, now," said Caramon, smoothing down his wife's rampant hair, "I won't be rough with him, though I'd like to. But I can at least talk to him. I know what it's like to have your head in a bottle."

"Then Jassar can stay?" Tika asked, nestling against her husband's broad chest.

"She can stay," said Caramon, sighing. "And the potter can have his new house."

* * * * *

The next day, Caramon took off his apron, folded it neatly over the bar, and left the inn. As he walked along the boardwalks—the town of Solace was built in the tops of the giant vallenwood trees, its buildings connected by swinging bridges and boardwalks— people called out greetings, came to shake his hand, engage him in conversation. Children ran to be lifted onto his broad shoulders, cats rubbed around his ankles, dogs jumped up to lick his hands.

A modest man, Caramon was always astonished

at the attention, received it with true pleasure. When he looked into Tika's mirror, he saw a middle-aged, stout (not fat, stout) man, with maybe a chin or two more than was absolutely necessary. He honestly could not understand what people saw in him. What he couldn't see, but which others did, was a face whose customary cheerfulness was tempered by a gravity that opened hearts to him, for he seemed to say, "Whatever your sorrow, I have known it, and yet I can still find joy in every sunrise." Caramon Majere was now one of the best liked, most admired men in Solace.

But that hadn't always been the case. Caramon remembered when he'd been the most detested man—a sodden, blubbering drunk. People had avoided him then, children had fled in terror, dogs sniffed him and trotted off in disgust. He hadn't liked himself then, and so he wasn't surprised that no one else liked him either. He pondered on his own past as he followed his wife's directions to Jassar Lathhauser's dwelling, located in the old, run-down, and mostly abandoned part of Solace.

Few people came here anymore. No respectable citizens, only transients, rogues, squatters, and derelicts. The houses perched sullenly and precariously in the trees, ready to tumble down at the slightest provocation. Caramon had proposed more than once that these unsafe houses be torn down and new homes built in their place. He made a mental note to bring it up again at the next town meeting.

He found the house, which he was relieved to see was actually somewhat sturdier than the others around it, and knocked on the door.

No answer.

Jassar's husband was inside. The smell of dwarf spirits was rank. He was probably sleeping off last night's toot. Caramon banged loudly on the door, then recollected that this would have little effect. He recalled the dwarves who had spent the night hammering in his head after a drinking bash. The man wouldn't be able to hear the knock on the door for the thuds between his ears.

The door wasn't locked, didn't even have a lock on it. Caramon shoved it open. The smell of dwarf spirits and vomit hit him full in the gut. He wrinkled his nose, glanced about the one-room shack. The man lay facedown on the bed, still in his clothes. The sun coming in the window seemed repulsed by the sight, for it glanced off the foot of the bed, didn't come near the head.

Caramon turned on his heel, walked out the door, and headed for the nearest town pump. He filled a bucket with water, ice-cold from the deep well, and brought it back to the house. He flung the water on the slumbering drunk.

The man sat bolt upright, sputtering and gasping with the shock. "You bitch! What do think you're doing?"

Bleary-eyed, he couldn't see who was there. Assuming it was his wife, he swung out with his left fist. He had no right fist. His sleeve hung bare from the shoulder down. "You know better than to wake me. . . ."

"I'm not your wife," said Caramon sternly, his booming voice rattling the cracked windowpanes. "You can take a swing at me and welcome, Gemel Lathhauser. But it's only fair to warn you that I hit back."

The man looked up, startled. Then he scowled. "What's the idea . . . bargin' in here? . . . Get lost. . . ."

"My name's Caramon Majere. Your wife works for me at the inn. I've come to talk to you about her."

"Did she say I hit her? If she did, she's a liar. It's none of your damn business anyway." Gemel lurched to his feet. He was unshaven, unwashed, his clothes much the worse for wear. Yet he must have been a good-looking man once. His body was still strong and well muscled, though he had the pot belly of a drinker. The jawline that was now weak and puffy must have once been firm, decisive. And when he had referred to his wife as a liar, he'd actually had the grace to look ashamed of himself. He obviously didn't like what he'd become any more than she did.

"Your wife loves you," Caramon began.

"She doesn't love me!" Gemel snarled, anger burning away the fog left by the spirits. "She pities me because of this"—he grabbed hold of his empty sleeve, gave it a shake—"and won't leave me alone. I'd be better off without her, but she keeps hanging around."

"You figure if you hit her enough you'll drive her away," Caramon said. "Look, Gemel, I've been where you are. I know what you're going through—"

"No, you don't!" Gemel shouted, with a vehemence that shocked Caramon. "You've got two good arms, blast you! How in the name of the gods who forsook us can you know what I'm feeling! Get out, you bastard!"

Gemel grabbed hold of Caramon's shirt with some wild thought of shoving the big man out the door.

Caramon brushed off the man's trembling hand with ease. "Now, look here," he said, trying to be patient.

"No. You look!" Gemel kicked Caramon in the stomach.

Caramon doubled over, groaning, fell back a step.

"Get out!" Gemel said again, grinding his teeth. "Mind your own damn business."

Caramon sucked in a breath. "You just made this my business," he said and, head down, he charged straight at Gemel.

The two crashed to the floor, shaking the house and causing it to creak ominously. The men punched and jabbed. Though Gemel lacked an arm, he was younger than Caramon and someone somewhere had trained the man for combat.

Caramon was rapidly becoming winded. He drew

back his great fist, thinking to end it with a single punch, when he saw tears streaming down the face of his opponent.

Caramon lowered his fist. "What's the matter?"

"C'mon, hit me, damn it! Hit me!" Gemel collapsed into a heap. He began to sob uncontrollably, violent sobs that tore at him.

Stunned and embarrassed to see a grown man weeping like a child, Caramon didn't know what to do. Reaching out, he patted the man tentatively on the shoulder.

"It's my arm!" Gemel cried, his voice choked. "It aches. It aches constantly, and I can't stop the pain."

"Did I land on it too hard? I'm really sorry," Caramon said, overcome with guilt.

"Not my left arm," Gemel said. He sat upright, wiped his face. "It's my right arm. My sword arm. My hand's clenched around the hilt so tightly, I can't let loose. I can't make the aching stop."

Caramon stared blankly at Gemel. "But you don't have a right arm."

"I can damn well see that," Gemel snapped, glowering. "It still hurts, though. I can feel it! Day and night. I can't let loose of the sword! I can't sleep. I can't work! I'm going to go crazy! I'd chop my arm off if it weren't already gone."

Privately Caramon thought Gemel might already be crazy. He decided it would be best to humor him.

"So you drink to . . . um . . . ease the pain?"

"Hah!" Gemel smiled bitterly. "You'd think that would help, wouldn't you? But it doesn't. I can still feel my arm ache no matter how drunk I get. But at least I can sleep."

"That's not sleep. It's a drunken stupor," said Caramon. "How did you lose your arm?"

"Why should you care?" Gemel returned, sullen. "It happened."

Caramon regarded him thoughtfully for a few moments. "Here, let's get you cleaned up. When was the last time you had a good meal? One you didn't wash down with dwarf spirits."

"I don't know," Gemel said wearily. He stood up and almost fell over. Staggering to a rickety chair, he sat down, covered his eyes with his good hand. "What does it matter to you, anyway? I'm sorry I kicked you, but if I want to drink myself to death, what right have you got to stop me?"

"It's a matter of crockery," said Caramon. "And the potter building a new house."

"Huh?" Gemel stared up at him.

"Never mind," Caramon said. "I'll give the problem some thought. Now, let's get a good breakfast inside you. There's nothing much goes wrong with a man that ham and eggs can't cure. And while you're eating, you can tell me all about the battle. I was a soldier myself once, you know," he added modestly.

* * * * *

"You're right, Caramon," said Tika the next morning. "That Gemel's gone raving mad. How can an arm that isn't there hurt? How can a hand that doesn't exist hold a sword? I'm going to tell Jassar to leave him right this minute. She can live here with us until . . ." Tika paused, stared at her husband. "What are you doing?"

"Just packing up a few things," Caramon said, stuffing a shirt and a change of stockings into a leather bag. "I'm going to take a little trip. He doesn't know it yet, but Gemel's coming with me. We'll ride the horses. They could use the exercise."

"They could? He is? You are?" Tika stared at her husband in astonishment. Perhaps one reason their marriage had been so enduring was that he could still surprise her. "All right, Caramon," she said briskly, hands on her hips. "What have you got planned?"

Caramon paused in the act of rummaging for his

walking boots. "I know what Gemel means about the arm that isn't there hurting him. I felt that way when Raist left to take the black robes. Like part of me had been cut away, and yet that part still ached. You sent me away on a quest to find myself. I think it's time Gemel made the same journey.

"In the meanwhile"—Caramon slowly unfolded a piece of paper he'd had stuffed in his pocket—"take this to John Carpenter. Have him make me a box to these dimensions: three feet in length, two feet wide and one foot high. Cut three holes in the end, two of them six inches in circumference. No lid. The box is open on the top, and I want a wooden divider running down the center.

"Tell him to make the box of used wood from some of the dilapidated shacks, so that it looks really old. Oh, and tell him to carve a Sign of the Eye on it—you know, the symbols the wizards used to use. He should have it ready for me when I get back, say in about three weeks."

Tika walked over, placed her hand on Caramon's broad forehead. "You're not running a fever." She eyed him suspiciously. "*You* haven't been at the Trough, have you?"

"I'm fine and I'm sober," he said, smiling at her. Leaning down, he kissed her. "I'll be back in three weeks. Take good care of Jassar."

"You're not going to tell me, are you?"

Caramon shook his head, looked grave. "You are my wife, Tika, and I love you better than I love life itself but you can't keep a secret to save your soul."

Tika's cheeks flushed, but Caramon was so earnest and so serious that her anger changed to laughter. She admitted, grudgingly, that he might be right.

"The gods go with you, Caramon," she said, kissing him tenderly.

"There aren't any gods, remember?" he said.

"Who says? Fizban? You'd take the word of an old fool who can't remember his name half the time? Be off with you, Caramon Majere. I haven't got all day to stand around and talk nonsense."

Gemel had at first refused to go. He had been adamant in his refusal. Caramon had not argued with him. The big man had simply planted himself in Gemel's house, immovable as Prayer's Eye Peak, stating that he intended to sit there for a month if necessary. In vain, Gemel had argued and threatened and cursed. Caramon had said only two words: "Get dressed." He had refused to even tell Gemel where they were going.

Now they'd been on the road for a week, and Gemel still didn't quite know why he'd come, except it seemed the only way to get this big, galumphing oaf of an innkeeper out of his life. Yeah, so Majere had been a Hero of the Lance. Gemel had heard the bard's stories, the minstrel's songs. He knew all about Caramon Majere—how he'd fought dragons and even the Dark Queen herself. How his brother had been the greatest wizard who had ever lived.

Maybe. Maybe not. Minstrels and bards were singing songs about the Chaos War, too. About the glory and the honor. They never sang about the fear that turns a man into a whimpering child. They never sang about the blood, the death, the pain.

Gemel rode along morosely, gritting his teeth against the aching of his arm, refusing to talk except to hint now and then that they might stop at a tavern and break the journey's monotony. Caramon always refused. They ate what food he'd brought, and when that was gone, they ate what they could catch. The hot sun and activity baked the dwarf spirits out of Gemel. Food began to taste good to him again. Caramon was an excellent cook on the road; his rabbit stew was the best Gemel had ever eaten. By nightfall, Gemel was so tired he fell asleep immediately. But he always woke in the night, woke with a cry, clutching the arm that wasn't there.

On the eighth day, they rode into northern Abanasinia, not far from the coastline, and Gemel realized where they were headed. He came to a stop, glared at Caramon.

"What the hell do you think you're doing? Is this some sort of sick joke?"

"The battle was close by here, wasn't it?" Caramon said, looking around. "The graves were marked with a sword, so you said."

"My sword," said Gemel thickly. Tears wet his eyelashes. He blinked them away, tugged on the reins so violently that the horse whinnied in protest. "I'm leaving."

Caramon reached out, caught hold of the horse's bridle.

"The sword," said Caramon urgently. "The sword that you hold in your right hand. You've got to find that sword."

"You're the one who's crazy," Gemel returned. "What the devil does my sword have to do with anything?"

"You know that my brother was a great wizard," Caramon said.

"Yeah, so what?"

"I learned a good deal from him." Caramon's tone was solemn. He spoke in a hushed whisper. "There's magic at work here, Gemel. I know it. I can feel it. You've been cursed by a Chaos demon. I can lift the curse, Gemel. But I need your sword to do it."

A curse! Gemel considered it. Of course. That would explain everything. But could a Chaos demon really be removed by a fat, middle-aged innkeeper? He regarded Caramon doubtfully.

"Magic doesn't work anymore. I've heard wizards complain that their spellcasting abilities are gone. So even if your brother was some great archmage, what does that matter now?"

"Raistlin traveled to the Abyss," said Caramon. "He was master of the Tower of High Sorcery in Palanthas. He knew a great many magical spells. Now, no one else knows this"—Caramon lowered his voice conspiratorially—"but he taught me some of his spells. I think one of them will help you."

"How? Make me a new arm, a silver arm, perhaps, like that blacksmith the bards are always yammering about?" Gemel sneered.

"No," Caramon said quietly. "But I think the magic will take away your pain."

Gemel gazed at Caramon long and suspiciously, searching the big man's open, genial, and sympathetic face for the least hint of laughter, of guile, of pity.

Caramon returned his gaze steadily.

"C'mon. I'll show where I put the damn sword," Gemel said grudgingly at last.

They found the mass grave where the knights had been hastily buried. The hilt of Gemel's sword—a plain iron sword, not a fancy sword like the Solamnic knights wielded—rose from a barren plain. Though the site was far removed from any village or town, it was swept clean and neat, almost as if some loving hand took care of the grave site by brushing away dead leaves and sticks. In the center of the small burial mound, near where Gemel had thrust his sword, a wild rose bush grew and flourished.

Dismounting from his horse, Gemel walked slowly to the graves. He gazed in wonder at the rose bush, tears stinging his eyes. He laid his hand upon the sword's hilt. . . .

* * * * *

Rain dripped from his sodden hair into Gemel's eyes, momentarily blinding him. He blinked the water away, trying desperately to see and not having much luck. A tree branch scraped across his face. He shoved it aside and pressed forward. Sir Trechard, the battle commander, was somewhere up ahead.

Gemel felt for the message case for the hundredth time, checked to make certain it was securely strapped to his thigh. He had an urgent message from the captain to deliver to the commander, and Gemel didn't have time to waste stumbling about in the rain and the darkness. Since he couldn't see all that well, he used his other senses to try to make out what was happening. He could hear the jingling of chain mail, the cries of men in battle. And there was that strange smell, the peculiar smell that had stung his nostrils for the last fifty paces or so.

He could identify the scent of pine and the smell of wet, decaying vegetation. But there was another odor, one he could not place. Vague childhood memories returned—a scorched tree in his village, a tree blasted apart by lightning. The smell brought back the memory of the dazzling, flaring light, the deafening boom of the thunderclap. Gemel peered ahead through the torrential rain, trying desperately to see something, anything.

Strange, this rain. After months of drought, the worst drought Krynn had seen, this rain should be welcome. But it wasn't. It had an oily feel and an iron taste to it, almost as if the skies rained blood.

"How do those idiots in command expect me to deliver a message if I can't see a damned thing?" he muttered to himself, using the soldier's customary method of routing fear, which was to complain about his superiors. Though he couldn't see a thing, his hearing told him that he was drawing close to the battle.

The fir trees came to an end finally. Gemel looked out onto a windswept plain, and he breathed a relieved sigh. He'd been told to find this very plain. Sir Trechard and his forces were supposed to be around here somewhere. The knight commanded the left wing of the small army that was fighting for its life in the forests far north of Qualinesti, fighting the terrible demons of Chaos.

Gemel could hear the sounds of battle, but he still couldn't see a thing. He waited in the shelter of the forest, hoping to be able to determine what was going on before he walked into the midst of it.

Lightning flashed, illuminated the scene. Gemel saw, but though he saw, he didn't believe. He didn't want to believe.

A group of knights and a small band of spearmen were drawn up on the barren plain. Approaching them were several gigantic monsters the likes of which had never before been seen on Krynn. Perhaps the monsters had emerged from the sea, perhaps they sprang up from the riven ground or were formed of the black clouds that hung low and menacing from the sky. Whatever they were, they came from Chaos—shapeless masses of oozing darkness. Huge tentacles dangled from their bodies. If they had eyes or ears or mouths, these could not be seen, but they knew where to find their prey, for they advanced steadily on the knights.

The knights held their ground.

"Throw!" cried a voice that Gemel recognized as that of Sir Trechard.

A deadly volley of spears hurtled through the rain toward the tentacled monsters. Gemel's heart was cheered, for the spears were well thrown, their aim was true. They must destroy the Chaos spawn.

The monsters made no attempt to duck or avoid the spears. Instead, the hulking creatures began to spin around and around, whirling fast and then faster, spinning now so rapidly that their tentacles blurred with the motion, and Gemel was dizzy from the sight. The spears struck the whipping tentacles, which sliced up the wooden hafts as easily as a knife slices through butter. The broken spears plummeted harmlessly and ineffectually to the ground.

The whirling monsters began to surge forward toward the knights. The wind generated by their spinning hit Gemel a blast that nearly knocked him down; the smell of ozone and sulfur was pungent, gagging.

The spearmen wavered, then, panic-stricken, they turned and fled. The knights in their bright armor remained to hold the line.

"Hold steady, Knights of Solamnia," called Sir Trechard to his remaining men, his voice calm. "We've faced worse than this. Paladine is with us."

Gemel's first thought was to follow the example of the spearmen and run. Then he recalled his message, its urgency. He was not a knight, nor ever hoped to be a knight, but he had taken an oath of fealty and loyalty to his commander. Gemel would not let his comrades down. He would not let himself down by breaking that oath.

Gemel forced himself to move forward, clutching his sword in a deathlike grasp. The hilt was slippery from the strange rain. Gemel gripped the sword tightly, so tightly that his right arm ached with the strain.

The monsters were closing with the knights.

Sir Trechard dashed forward, struck at one of the monsters, thrusting his blade straight into the dark and whirling center. The sword, blessed by Paladine, glowed blue, and the whipping tentacles had no effect on it. The sword struck the heart of the monster. Lightning crackled and the monster blew apart, spattering the knights and Gemel with foul-smelling gore. Nothing daunted, the other monsters whirled on toward their prey.

"They can be killed, men!" Sir Trechard shouted. "Stand fast."

Emboldened by the sight, Gemel reached for the message case. He prepared to make his final dash, when he felt wind on the back of his neck, heard a horrible whip, whip sound coming from behind him. The smell of ozone was intense.

He turned fearfully to see one of the whirling monsters bearing down on him.

Gemel swung his sword wildly at the monster, but his blow was deflected by a spinning tentacle. Another whiplike tendril smacked Gemel in the thigh. The force of the blow flung him backward, tumbling head over heels. He landed heavily on the rain-soaked ground.

Terrified that the monster would come after him, Gemel scrambled to his feet, his sword ready. The whirling monster was intent upon attacking the knights, the greater threat. It paid no more attention to Gemel.

He stood still a moment, weak and shaking, glad for the respite. He couldn't stay here long, however. He had to complete his mission. Taking a step forward, he sucked in a breath as pain flared through his injured leg.

He tried to examine the extent of his injuries but could see nothing for the strange darkness. Every fiber of his clothing was soaked, either with blood or rain. He couldn't tell which.

Sir Trechard was only a few feet away. Gemel lurched toward the commander, every step bringing a gasp of pain to his lips. The knight attacked one of the monsters with his sword, only to have his blow deflected as Gemel's had been.

"Sir Trechard!" Gemel yelled.

Sir Trechard looked over his right shoulder, attempting to find the shouting voice.

Gemel yelled again. "Sir! I have a message from Rac Vandish for you. He requests— Look out, sir!"

The Chaos monster surged forward. Sir Trechard stabbed at it desperately, but the whipping tentacles tore the sword from his grasp, sent it flying. And then it was as if the knight were being struck from all sides by a thousand whips. The tentacles sliced through the knight's metal armor as if it were sheerest silk, laying bare the flesh beneath, stripping away that flesh. The blows flailed the flesh from his bones, his face dissolved in a welter of blood and bone. And still, horribly, Sir Trechard lived, though now his very innards were exposed.

With a bubbling scream of agony, he fell to the ground.

Gemel choked on his own bile. He gripped his sword even harder, the hilt cutting painfully into his hand. Using all his strength, he brought his sword down upon the monster. The blade entered the maelstrom and hit something substantial and, he hoped, vital. Lightning flickered from inside the monster, its whirling motion slowed, but the monster was not yet dead. Gemel's sword was lodged inside it. He tried to let go of the hilt but discovered, to his horror, that he could not.

A bone snapped in his upper arm. Then the monster pulled Gemel's arm from out of his shoulder socket. The arm, still holding the sword, tore loose, spraying him with his own blood.

Gemel sank into a spinning torment of whirling, lightning-tinged darkness.

He woke to find himself inside a tent. Looking through an opening in the top, he saw clouds still covering the sky. The air was hot and smelled of blood and lightning and death. Memory returned, and with it the pain in his right arm. Yet he remembered clearly having seen the arm torn away. Perhaps it hadn't happened! He'd been dreaming. He could feel his arm. His arm hurt. He had not lost his arm after all.

Lying on a blanket on the ground, he looked over to where his right arm should have been.

There was nothing there, nothing except some blood-soaked bandages wrapped around his mangled shoulder. He began to weep.

A soldier entered the tent.

"You're awake. Excellent. How do you feel?"

"How the hell do you think I feel?" Gemel snarled savagely. "My arm is gone!"

"Still, you can count yourself lucky," the soldier answered. "You were the only one we found alive on that plain. It's a good thing we had one of our druid healers with us, or you'd be dead, too. He cauterized your wound, stopped the bleeding, and gave you a potion to ease the pain."

"How long have I been unconscious?" Gemel asked.

"Maybe a day and a half. We're still burying the dead."

"What about—" Gemel swallowed his sudden fear—"what about the Chaos monsters?"

"Destroyed. You and the knights did a good job. The reserves pushed forward and killed the monsters that were left. Hey, what are you doing?"

"Standing up." Gemel grunted. "I've got two good legs at least. Show me where you found me."

"I don't think—"

"Show me!" Gemel yelled.

"It's pretty horrible," the soldier said.

"I know," Gemel said grimly. "I was there."

The soldier eyed him dubiously, then, seeing Gemel standing upright if a little unsteadily, the soldier shrugged and nodded.

"Here's where we found you." The soldier pointed to a spot on the rain-swept plain.

The ground, the straggling grass, the weeds, were all covered with blood, as if the sky had rained blood, not water. Nearby, a group of soldiers, pale-faced and sweating, were digging an enormous pit in which to bury the dead.

To bury what was left of the dead, that is.

There were no recognizable bodies, only parts of bodies—a foot here, a leg there, a trunk somewhere else. Metal armor, cut to ribbons, chain mail scattered about in bits and pieces. The scene was horrible, gruesome. Every so often, one of the soldiers would turn from his task and go off quietly by himself to retch and heave.

Gemel began to shake. The bile surged up in his throat, but he forced it back down. His arm, the arm that wasn't there, ached and burned.

A pile of weapons stood near the bodies, gathered together to be laid to rest with the knights. Among them was his own sword. His was easy to recognize. The knights had carried valuable swords with engraved remarques and roses on the hilts. His was just a sword.

The soldiers placed the body parts in the ditch. Gemel just stood there watching. One-armed, weak, and light-headed, he could do nothing to help. He could give nothing now but his respect and his remorse. If it hadn't been for his distracting the knight, Sir Trechard might not be dead.

The soldiers completed their work quickly, eager to have the horrible job finished, eager to hide the bloody remains beneath mounds of dirt. They held no ceremony, made no speeches about the knights' courage and loyalty. There wasn't time. The war still raged. The soldiers shoveled dirt into the ditch until it was filled.

Gemel retrieved his sword, held it clasped tightly in his left hand. His grip was painful, it hurt him and he let go. His sword fell from his left hand. But his right hand only clasped the blade harder, tighter.

The soldiers finished the grave. There was no stone, no way to mark the place where Solamnic knights had died fighting for a noble cause. Gemel leaned over and picked up his sword again. Carrying his blade awkwardly in his left hand, he walked over to the foot of the grave site.

He jammed the sword, point first, into the soft ground.

Gemel turned and started to walk back. He collapsed before he had taken a step.

* * * * *

"I was the only survivor of that battle," Gemel said. Holding the sword, he jabbed the rusted point again and again into the soft ground. "People say I'm the lucky one." He snorted, glanced over at the grave site. "Their pain is over. They can sleep."

"Yeah, I know," said Caramon quietly. "They told me the same thing after the end of the Chaos War. After a dark knight brought me the torn and bloodied bodies of my sons. After I had to tell their mother that two of her children were dead. After I had to plant the vallenwood on their graves, when I should have been picking flowers for their weddings. It took me a long time before I finally admitted to myself that people were right. Before I quit feeling guilty because I was alive and my sons weren't."

Gemel looked down at the ground, said nothing.

"What were those monsters you fought?" Caramon wisely changed the subject.

"Some sort of Chaos monster. The very gods themselves fled from them, or so they say."

"You didn't flee," Caramon said. "You held your ground. You and the knights."

"Yeah. We held our ground." Gemel was bitter. "And what did they get for it? That bit of ground right there where they're lying. Well, Majere, I have the damned sword. Now what? You going to rub bat guano on it or something?"

"We have to take it back to Solace," said Caramon. "The magic spell my brother taught me will only work back there."

"And Jassar thinks *I'm* crazy," Gemel muttered. He paused a moment longer at the grave site, then turned away. He and Caramon had taken only a few steps when Gemel stopped. "Wait a minute. If I take my sword, there won't be a marker anymore."

"Yes, there is." Caramon pointed to the rose bush, whose red and white blossoms filled the air with fragrance. "That is their marker. Look at it, Gemel. Have you ever seen a rose like it? And where did it come from? Nothing but grass and weeds for miles. Yet here roses bloom, here roses flourish."

"That's true," Gemel said. He gazed out over the

barren, sandy plain covered with tall brown grass and scraggly weeds. And there in the center of the small mound stood the rose bush with its green leaves and white blossoms, each with a drop of red at its heart. "That's true."

"And people say the gods have left us," Caramon said, smiling and shaking his head. "Now let's go back home."

* * * * *

"Caramon!" Tika was scandalized. "What are you doing? That's my best linen bed sheet!"

Caramon looked up, flushed a guilty red. "I'm sorry. I thought it was an old one. I . . . um . . . I need some wizard robes. . . ."

Tika glared at him. "Caramon Majere, this has gone far enough. You couldn't work a magic spell if your life depended on it, and you know it!"

"It's not *my* life we're talking about," Caramon said, holding the sheet up to his chin and attempting to measure it on himself.

"Gemel's, you mean? You're giving that poor man false hopes, Caramon, and I think it's cruel! And now— Oh, for mercy's sake, give that to me!"

Snatching the bed sheet from her husband, Tika spread it out on the bed, eyed it thoughtfully. "Now, if I cut it this way, we'll have room for the sleeves. . . ."

"Thank you, my dear," Caramon said, kissing her cheek.

"I hope you know what you're doing," Tika said darkly.

"I hope I do, too," Caramon muttered, but not until he was sure Tika couldn't hear him.

* * * * *

The next morning, the Inn of the Last Home was not open for business, much to the dismay and shock of the citizens of Solace. Rumors abounded. The younger members of Solace's population risked their necks climbing the great vallenwoods to try to peep into the windows. Since the windows were stained glass, this proved a failure. The inn had remained open through war and plagues. What dread incident had caused it to close this day, no one knew. But everyone in town waited out front to find out.

Only four people were inside the inn—Caramon, dressed in white robes and looking very magnificent; Tika, looking grim and nervous; Jassar, wan and despairing; and Gemel, dubious, doubtful, and hung-over.

"Finding that cursed sword only made him worse, not better," Jassar said tearfully to Tika. "He holds it and stares at it and then flings it to the floor, then picks it up again and hurls it down again. And all the time he complains of the pain!"

"There, there," said Tika, holding Jassar in her arms and soothing her tenderly. "It will be all right. Caramon's a good man. A little daft, maybe, but a good man. That must count for something."

On a table in the middle of the inn sat the magical box. Three feet long, two feet wide, and one foot high, the box looked very impressive and mysterious with its cabalistic symbols carved into the wooden sides. The top of the box was open, revealing two compartments running the length of the box, compartments that were separated by a wooden divider. Two round openings were in the front of the box, one for either compartment. A slit had been cut in the center. Laid over the top of the box was a thin, diaphanous cloth, thin as cobweb, which Tika recognized as one of her very best elf-woven scarves.

"Bring me your sword, Gemel Lathhauser," said Caramon in a suitably impressive-sounding voice.

Gemel came forward, surly and embarrassed. Standing in front of the box, he looked up, his expression so desperate, yet so hopeful, that Caramon was forced to avert his head a moment, rub his eyes, and clear his throat before he could continue.

"Place the sword into the slot here in the front of the box," Caramon ordered.

Gemel's hand shook. He missed the slot the first few times, but then managed to slide the blade into the slit in the front of the box between the two compartments. The blade disappeared.

"Very good." Caramon drew in a deep breath, let it out in a gust. He was prepared. "Now, whatever you do, do not touch the cloth covering the top of the box. It has been enchanted with powerful spells taught to me by my brother, the great archmage, Raistlin Majere. You must follow my directions exactly. If you deviate from them even in the slightest, the spell will fail. Do you understand?"

"He sounds very powerful," whispered Jassar, awed.

Tika only shook her head and rolled her eyes.

Gemel stood straight and stiff-backed. "I understand," he said gruffly.

"Take your place in front of the box."

Gemel breathed deeply. Steeling himself, he walked forward.

"Now close your eyes," Caramon continued. "I will cast the spell upon the box and cloth, and then, when I count three, you will place both your arms, real and phantom, inside the box, up to your elbows."

"Then what?" Gemel was suspicious.

"And then the magic happens. Close your eyes," Caramon ordered testily.

Gemel sighed, shook his head, and closed his eyes.

Caramon began to chant mystical words, words with a spidery feel to them. His voice rose to a crescendo, and he clapped his hands loudly and suddenly, startling all of them, including himself.

Gemel jumped at the sound, but he did not open his eyes.

"The spell is cast. Place your arms in the box,"

Caramon instructed.

Gemel hesitated, then, stepping forward, he put his left arm into the hole on the left side of the box, made as if to put the missing right arm into the hole on the right.

He gasped in astonishment. "I don't believe it! It's incredible! I can feel both my arms in the box!"

"Good," said Caramon, smiling in satisfaction. "Now you may open your eyes."

Gemel opened his eyes, looked into the box, and sucked in an awestruck breath. Jassar and Tika crept forward to see.

"My god!" Jassar whimpered.

Inside the box were Gemel's two arms, left and right, and two hands. Both Gemel's hands were clasped tightly into fists.

"We must be silent," said Caramon, "and let the magic work."

They were all quiet, all awed and amazed. Outside, the breeze freshened, the limbs of the vallenwood swayed, the inn rocked gently, as it was sometimes wont to do. A kettle, balanced precariously on the hearth, fell to the floor with a sharp bang. Tika gasped and clasped her hands over her mouth.

"That is the sign! The magic has worked! Through the power of my brother," Caramon said, "I have given form to your arm within the box." He repeated the magic words, then cried out in stentorian tones. "Chaos demon, I charge you, release your grasp on this man's flesh!"

He looked at Gemel. "Now open both of your fists and relax your arms."

Slowly Gemel released the tightly clenched muscles in his hands. His fingers uncurled, unclasped. His hands relaxed. Both hands relaxed. Gemel stared down at his hands through the cloth.

"Quickly!" Caramon cried. "Pull your arms out of the box! The demon has freed you. I have it under enchantment, but I can't hold it for long!"

Gemel jerked his arm from the box. He stood staring at the place where his right arm had been, dumbfounded.

"I don't believe it! I don't feel my arm anymore! The pain is gone!"

Gemel's knees gave way. With a shuddering sob, he sank down into a chair. Jassar, weeping joyfully, put her arms around him. He reached out with his left arm, took hold of her, held her tightly.

Tika stared at Caramon with wide-eyed wonder. "Caramon?"

"Yes, my dear?" Caramon said, turning to regard her with calm serenity.

"Nothing." Tika looked dazed. She peered trepidly into the box. "Is . . . is the demon really trapped inside there?"

"Right here," Caramon said. He plucked the scarf from the top of the box and tossed it into to the inn's gigantic fireplace. There was a flash of blue flame and the scarf disappeared. Though it had been her very best scarf, Tika never said a word.

"The demon is gone. It can never harm you again." Caramon stated. Removing the sword from the box, he handed it to Gemel. "Keep this to remind you of the brave men who died . . . and those who live."

Gemel reached out, clasped hold of Caramon's hand. "You have saved my sanity and my life. How can ever I repay you?"

"Stay out of the Trough, for one thing," Caramon said sternly. "You owe that to yourself. As for repaying me, there's odd jobs you can do around here."

Gemel smiled ruefully. "Jobs for a man with only one arm?"

"Build up the strength in that arm," Caramon answered, "and there will be work for you aplenty anywhere."

* * * * *

Rumor flashed around Solace that Caramon Majere had performed a magic spell, had caused a one-armed man to grow a new arm. Panic ensued. Some people flocked to the inn, hoping for a miracle of their own, while others took fright and insisted that they would never again set foot inside the accursed place.

Throughout the day, Caramon maintained steadily to one and all that he hadn't done anything out of the ordinary, and since everyone knew that Caramon Majere was incapable of telling a lie and since he went about his business the same as usual and did not pluck any Chaos demons out of the spiced potatoes, people began to think the rumor was just that—a rumor. By dinnertime, everyone in Solace was laughing heartily at the thought of Caramon the wizard.

All except Tika. She had seen the two arms inside the box, she had seen Gemel freed from his pain. She treated her husband with newfound respect all that day—treatment that he thoroughly enjoyed, for where is the married couple, no matter how happy, who don't now and then take each other for granted?

That night, alone in their bedroom, Tika sat down wearily.

"What a day!" She sighed. "I'm glad it's over."

"So am I," said Caramon. He carried with him the magical box, which he placed on Tika's nightstand.

Tika cast the box an uncomfortable glance. "Don't you think you should keep that locked up somewhere safe?"

"Oh, I think it's safe enough," Caramon replied complacently.

Tika, looking doubtful, picked up her hairbrush.

"Where's my mirror?" she demanded suddenly, staring at the blank space on the wall. "It's gone! Caramon, some thief has stolen my mirror!"

"I didn't steal it, my dear," said Caramon slyly.

He reached into the box and pulled out the mirror, which he solemnly handed back to his wife. "As the kender said, 'I only borrowed it.'"

Tika gazed at the mirror, she gazed at the box. Then she threw the hairbrush at him.

The World Needs Heroes!

You've read the adventures of Ansalon's greatest heroes—now it's time to join them!

Unlock the secrets to the Saga's greatest mysteries with the DRAGONLANCE®: FIFTH AGE® dramatic adventure game, a storytelling game that emphasizes creativity, epic drama, and heroism. It's easy to learn and fun to play, whether you want to roleplay characters from your favorite DRAGONLANCE stories or spin new tales all your own. Best of all, the DRAGONLANCE: FIFTH AGE boxed set and supplements offer a treasure trove of engaging source material not found in any novel!

Knights, freedom fighters, mages, and mystics—the heroes you play rise above the ranks of common folk to discover the wonders of magic and defend Ansalon from the dragons that threaten it. Come, hero! Make your mark on this Age of Mortals, and be remembered forever in legend.

Find the DRAGONLANCE: FIFTH AGE game and supplements at your local book, game, or hobby store. To locate the store nearest you, call Customer Service at (206) 624-0933. See our website at **www.tsr.com** for more information.

DRAGONS OF
SUMMER FLAME

MARGARET WEIS AND
TRACY HICKMAN

The best-selling conclusion to the stories told in the Chronicles and Legends Trilogies. The War of the Lance is long over. The seasons come and go. The pendulum of the world swings. Now it is summer. A hot, parched summer such as no one on Krynn has ever known before.

Distraught by a grievous loss, the young mage Palin Majere seeks to enter the Abyss in search of his lost uncle, the infamous archmage Raistlin.

The Dark Queen has found new champions. Devoted followers, loyal to the death, the Knights of Takhisis follow the Vision to victory. A dark paladin, Steel Brightblade, rides to attack the High Clerist's Tower, the fortress his father died defending.

On a small island, the mysterious Irda capture an ancient artifact and use it to ensure their own safety. Usha, child of the Irda, arrives in Palanthas claiming that she is Raistlin's daughter.

The summer will be deadly. Perhaps it will be the last summer Ansalon will ever know.

Hardcover	Paperback
$23.99 US; $29.99 CAN	$7.99 US; $9.99 CAN
8369	8369P
ISBN: 0-7869-0189-6	ISBN: 0-7869-0523-9

THE CHAOS WAR

This series brings to life the background stories and events of the conflagration known as The Chaos War, as told in the *New York Times* best-selling novel *Dragons of Summer Flame*.

THE DOOM BRIGADE
MARGARET WEIS AND DON PERRIN

An intrepid group of draconian engineers must unite with the dwarves, their despised enemies, when the Chaos War erupts.

THE LAST THANE
DOUGLAS NILES

The Choas War rages across the surface of Ansalon, but what's going on deep under the mountains in the kingdom of Thorbardin? Anarchy, betrayal, and bloodshed.
AVAILABLE JUNE 1998

TEARS OF THE NIGHT SKY
LINDA P. BAKER

A quest of Paladine becomes a test of faith for Crysania, the blind cleric. She is aided by a magical tiger-companion, who is beholden to the mysterious dark elf wizard Dalamar.
AVAILABLE OCTOBER 1998

1999 DRAGONLANCE® CALENDAR

Twelve of the year's best DRAGONLANCE fantasy art covers. Artists include Larry Elmore, Todd Lockwood, Jeff Easley, Keith Parkinson, and more! This calendar will contain major Krynn holidays and birthdays of popular characters, sure to be a favorite with DRAGONLANCE fans. Available May 1998

THE ART OF THE DRAGONLANCE SAGA

The ultimate coffee table art book that set the bar for all others is reissued due to popular demand. The visual creation of the DRAGONLANCE world is depicted through artists sketches. Also included is commentary on the processes behind creating the many characters, dragons and artifacts of the DRAGONLANCE novels and game products. This book is being reprinted with a new foreword by Margaret Weis and Tracy Hickman. Available September 1998